Praise for

"Patel infuses *Tell Me How* ̤... ̤ss, humor, and warmth. . . . Mo.... ..... son share a love of guilty pleasures in a novel that asks: When you find the melody that speaks to you, why let it go?"
— *The New York Times Book Review*

"If you like stories about families coming to terms with long-held secrets, Patel's self-assured debut should be on your radar."
— *Harper's Bazaar*

"A beautiful book about a mother and son . . . I really loved this book."
— Rumaan Alam, *Today*

"If you want your heart broken open, Neel Patel's *Tell Me How to Be*, about an immigrant mother still longing for the man she left behind and her mostly closeted son still struggling with his own desires, is perfection."
— Jennifer Weiner, *USA Today*

"This is a dream of a novel—the story is, among so many things, about family and its endless forms, about loves found and lost and reimagined. It's deeply funny and full of feeling, by turns wickedly funny and emotional. I was smitten, and I'm so glad it's a part of our canon."
— Bryan Washington, *The Cut*

"This debut novel about an Indian American family has all the right ingredients: family secrets, love, sexuality, loss, identity questions, and remorse."
— *Good Morning America*

"A moving saga of identity and reconciliation."
— *People*

"Poignant . . . Fresh . . . Soulful and convincing."

—*The Guardian*

"In this soulful, moody novel, Patel shows how Akash and Renu suffer from the impossibility of emotional honesty within their Indian immigrant community in the Midwest, its norms enforced by gossip and social snubs." —*Star Tribune*

"Both irreverent and tender, this story of a recently widowed mother and grown son going through the motions of selling the family home, each trying to figure out how to best make each other happy while learning to accept their mistakes and each other, is a love story at its heart." —*Reader's Digest*

"*Tell Me How to Be* is a quietly wise novel, a love song to families, however imperfect they may be, as well as a tender and fierce celebration of queerness. It's a lot of books in one, and each one is a knockout." —*Alta Journal*

"Neel Patel's gorgeous debut novel flows so seamlessly that you hardly notice you're reading it; it feels more like you're simply existing with his characters." —*BookPage*

"On one hand, he entertains like Kevin Kwan; on the other, he queries like Ayad Akhtar. . . . *Tell Me How to Be* resides in asking rather than telling, designed to satisfy readers who prioritize questions over answers." —*Chicago Review of Books*

"Patel's well-drawn characters and richly metaphorical style carry the reader along." —*New York Journal of Books*

"A funny and moving story about forgiveness and learning to move forward." —*Book Riot*

"Readers who enjoyed Nadia Hashimi's *Sparks Like Stars* and Jonathan Franzen's *The Corrections* will enjoy similar complicated family dynamics and needing to read between the lines of what is being said to get at what is meant. Highly recommend to anyone keeping secrets from their families."

—ALA's Rainbow Round Table

"A funny yet heartbreaking story of a mother and son grappling with grief and moving on from the past together."

—*PopSugar*

"This excellent debut novel explores themes of love, betrayal, and reconciliation in a modern, funny, and tender way that is sure to make it a readers' favorite in 2022."

—*The San Diego Union-Tribune*

"[A] resplendent debut . . . Patel skillfully maneuvers through the treacherous territory of abandoned dreams, family squabbles, and cultural clashes before finding a resounding catharsis for mother and son. The result is noteworthy and memorable."

—*Publishers Weekly* (starred review)

"Once in a while there comes a book that reminds us of why we read: to feel, to question, to grow. This is that book. A love letter to R&B, youth, and the unforgettable agonies of one's first love. The emotional truth of this indelibly portrayed family and their messy lives will leave you weeping and shattered. I will read everything Neel Patel writes from here on."

—Susie Yang, *New York Times* bestselling author of *White Ivy*

"*Tell Me How to Be* is daring, hilarious, poignant, and impossible to put down. Neel Patel is a fabulous storyteller!"

—Deesha Philyaw, author of *The Secret Lives of Church Ladies*

"A soulful and seductive love song of a book, *Tell Me How to Be* is a keen and sharply hilarious celebration of the universal messiness of desire and the necessity of coming clean first with ourselves. I laughed out loud at the prickliness of Renu and ached for Akash through the book's careful unfurling of the past. Patel has crafted an unforgettable duet between mother and son." —Nancy Jooyoun Kim, *New York Times* bestselling author of *The Last Story of Mina Lee*

"I loved *Tell Me How to Be*'s story of family, first love, and figuring out your place in the world. Neel's writing is vulnerable, authentic, and entertaining. This book gives a fresh perspective to complicated family relationships . . . something everyone can relate to." —Lilly Singh, #1 *New York Times* bestselling author of *How to Be a Bawse*

"Compelling . . . Deeply moving. *Tell Me How to Be* explores the high price of secrets, deceit, and regret and the redemptive power of speaking one's truth. Patel's short chapters, immensely readable prose, and talent for continually raising the stakes for his complicated characters kept me turning the pages late into the night. A memorable debut." —Stephen McCauley, author of *My Ex-Life*

"Immersive, seductive, and elegant, this novel shimmers richly on the surface, even as its depths pulse with potent heartbreak and loss." —Mahesh Rao, author of *Polite Society*

TELL ME HOW TO BE

NEEL PATEL

FLATIRON
BOOKS
NEW YORK

For my mother

TELL ME HOW TO BE. Copyright © 2021 by Neel Patel. All rights reserved. Printed in the United States of America. For information, address Flatiron Books, 120 Broadway, New York, NY 10271.

www.flatironbooks.com

Designed by Jonathan Bennett

The Library of Congress has cataloged the hardcover edition as follows:

Names: Patel, Neel, author.
Title: Tell me how to be / Neel Patel.
Description: First Edition. | New York : Flatiron Books, 2021.
Identifiers: LCCN 2021028643 | ISBN 9781250184979 (hardcover) |
    ISBN 9781250184962 (ebook)
Classification: LCC PS3616.A86648 T45 2021 | DDC 813/.6—dc23
LC record available at https://lccn.loc.gov/2021028643

ISBN 978-1-250-18498-6 (trade paperback)

Our books may be purchased in bulk for promotional, educational, or business use. Please contact your local bookseller or the Macmillan Corporate and Premium Sales Department at 1-800-221-7945, extension 5442, or by email at MacmillanSpecialMarkets@macmillan.com.

First Flatiron Books Paperback Edition: 2022

10 9 8 7 6 5 4 3 2 1

Loving you is like a battle
and we both end up with scars.

—Lauryn Hill, "Ex-Factor"

PART I

AKASH

My mother always told me to be a good boy. I suspect she knew that I wasn't.

I'm lying next to Jacob when she calls. The last time she called this late was to tell me my father had died of a heart attack. Now, sweat licks my spine as I slide my finger across the screen: maybe my mother has found out about Jacob and me.

"Hello?"

"Akash, you're up?"

A slant of light illuminates the silky sheets on Jacob's bed. He snores by my side.

"Mom. What's wrong?"

She's silent as I pad into the bathroom, the glass shower beaded with water, jeweled soaps lining the shelves. I stare at my reflection, shadowed and puffy. I wonder how she could have found out, what clue she could have stumbled upon. Facebook. Instagram. A sighting by a mutual friend. Maybe Chaya Aunty's daughter, Neera, saw Jacob and me holding hands on Santa Monica Boulevard. Maybe my mother sent me something in the mail and was confused when it was returned—after moving in to Jacob's place, I had forgotten to forward my mail. This is the problem with lies: they always circle back to the truth. My mother breathes deeply into the phone.

"I just wanted to make sure you booked your ticket home."

"Oh." I relax. "Yeah. I fly in Saturday."

"I'm keeping Dad's puja next week. I can't believe it's been—"

"A year, Mom. I know."

She falls silent, and I get the sense there's something more, something she's holding back. I think of all the things we haven't said to each other, emotions buried beneath my mother's stiff smile. I can hear Jacob twisting in the sheets, outside. I pray he doesn't come inside. I'm still haunted by the time he approached me from behind at the grocery store and buried his face in my neck. "I wanna fuck you right here." I had been on the phone with my mother then, too, asking whether to use red onions or yellow ones to prepare the lamb keema she'd once made for me every Friday night. I'm about to lock the door behind me when my mother sighs softly into the phone.

"Akash," she says. Her voice is uncharacteristically small. "There's something else."

"What?"

She's silent, the static sizzling between us. "It's the house," she says.

"What about it?"

"It's sold."

I picture it: white brick with a slate roof, ivory pillars, trimmed hedges, and windows that reflect pinkish-gold whorls at dusk. All week long, I've prepared for my return, reimagining every glossed surface, every cozy nook. "The house? When did you—I didn't even know it was on the market."

"Well, you don't call home."

I think back to the last time I called my mother. It must have been June, or was it April? A rare wet day. Strong winds rattled the floor-to-ceiling windows in Jacob's condo.

"When do you move?"

"Next month."

"That soon? To where?"

She's silent, and I fear she's going to say she's coming to Los Angeles. Jacob has been talking about her recently, that he would like to meet her, that we could fly down for Thanksgiving, or maybe she would like to attend his cousin's wedding in

Newport Beach, wouldn't that be nice? We don't talk about the truth: that my mother has no idea who he is, that in her world people like Jacob don't exist.

When she answers, her voice is resolute.

"I'm moving back to London, Akash. I've made up my mind."

"London?"

"I'll explain everything when you come home. This will be the last time you see the house. The last time you see—everyone. All our memories are here."

The word "memories" is like the sharp nick of a blade, breaking skin.

"But what about—"

Suddenly, the door opens and Jacob's bearded face appears in the light, his hair slicked over. He puts his arm around my waist. "What's wrong, babe?" I want to shush him, press his back against the wall, but it will only make things worse, so I say nothing instead, letting his fingers glide up my shirt, pinching my nipple. I close my eyes. I know it's too late, because my mother asks, "Is someone there?"

"No, Mom," I say. "It's only me."

RENU

My husband liked me to wear makeup around the house. "Come, Renu," he'd say. "Taiyar thaija." According to women today, this would make him a bad man. I never questioned his motives. I never said, "Why? Don't I look good without it?" Instead, I powdered my face, applied lipstick the color of red wine. Sometimes I tried on an expensive gown, something I'd bought at one of the posh stores when Ashok was not around. I turned side to side, batting my eyes like Susan Lucci in *All My Children*. I liked Susan Lucci. I liked it when she slit her eyes and said something nasty like, "I know you're sleeping with my husband, Cassandra—you whore!" then turned around and slept with someone herself. Everyone was sleeping with someone on these shows—slapping people, too. Sleeping and slapping, sleeping and slapping. Until it was time to throw a drink in someone's face. Such vile disrespect—I liked it. Before I moved to this country, I had assumed all American women were whores. I was wrong. Not all American women are whores. Only the ones on TV.

I would not have chosen to live in this town with its quiet roads and its dark winters, but back then, I didn't have much of a choice. I married Ashok. He brought me to Illinois. There was no alternative. I could not have been what the whites call a "spinster," drinking martinis at three p.m. According to my parents, women like those were failures. They were dangerous. But what's so wrong with a dangerous woman? Women have choices now: what to wear, whom to marry, even whether to be a woman at all. It's all fine with me, as long as everyone shaves their legs. I didn't choose this life for myself, but now I'm choosing to leave it. The women in my book club say this is very feminist. They're all very young and very blond and very excited—about everything. I made the decision to move six months after Ashok died, contacting a Realtor and putting the house on the market, replacing the carpets and doors, fixing the leaks in the gutters, doing all the things Ashok had been meaning to get done before he passed, before God took him.

I don't wear makeup around the house now. I don't do a lot of things I used to do, like preparing a full Indian meal: vegetable, lentil, roti, rice. I don't chop mint leaves for cucumber raita. I don't set out jars of pickled mango, floating in red oil. I don't stock the refrigerator with Ashok's favorite cheeses and wine. Sometimes I don't even buy groceries at all. Instead, I eat simple things, sandwiches and soups, cereal with milk, Chinese takeout or Thai, watching the sun set behind black, skeletal trees. It's the first time in my life I've been alone.

Before marrying Ashok, I lived in a small flat in London with my brother and his wife, working in a pharmacy nearby. I can still see the red buses and perpetual silver drizzle, the small Peugeots with their mustard-colored plates. I can see the sleek shops on Oxford Street selling cashmere and silk, luxuries I couldn't afford at the time but now, with millions in my account, can buy in bundles if I like. I lie awake at night and dream of the day I will return, landing at Heathrow Airport, walking along the Thames. Maybe I'll buy a flat, one of those chic glass cubes that juts out like cut quartz in the sky. I have languished in this town with its Walmart and its Applebee's, its quiet, rural roads, where I was known only as Mrs. Amin, only as Ashok's wife, only as Bijal and Akash's mother, and where I have thought, even after all these years, only of you.

Kareem.

AKASH

It's the morning after my mother called and I still can't believe it. The house: gone. My mother: gone. I had planned only to honor my father, to preserve his memory among family and friends. But now everything's changed. I suppose I had taken it all for granted: the house, my mother, that town—even you. You're all I've thought about this morning. Your dark eyes still flicker in my mind. But then there's Jacob, lying next to me in bed. Jacob, scrambling eggs over the stove. Jacob, sipping orange juice while reading *The New Yorker* on his sun-soaked deck. Jacob, following me into every room.

"Why can't I come with you?"

"Because it's a family thing."

"Then what am I?"

Not family, I want to say. Instead, I tell him it isn't the right time.

"It's never the right time."

"That's not fair."

"To whom? You, or me?"

He follows me into the bedroom as I fold underwear and T-shirts and stack them into neat piles, then slide them into a carry-on bag. I can feel him breathing. I can see his face, the small emerald eyes, woolly beard, chestnut hair sculpted back with pomade. The tight line his lips make when he's angry or sad. This time it's both. He wants to know when I'll be back. I have no answer. I don't want to tell him about my mother; I don't know why.

"It's my father's anniversary. My mom will want us to hang around."

I had only just met Jacob when my father died. Perhaps that's what drew me to him: the loss of one man driving me into the arms of another. We met on Tinder. Later, I'd stalked him online. Jacob played the violin. He owned a beagle. He had a sister named Emily; she was in pharmacy school. I'd memorized her name. Emily. Emily. Emily. Later, when Jacob mentioned her on our first date, I'd smiled.

"Ah, Emily," I'd said, as if we were old friends. "The pharmacist."

Later, he would tell me it was this that made him fall for me: my eagerness. He was my first boyfriend. When he'd asked me to move out of my dark studio in North Hollywood and into his light-filled condo in Santa Monica, I didn't have to think very hard. It was simple: I was twenty-eight, a struggling artist. Jacob was thirty-seven and owned a successful business. He cared for me like a father would, holding me accountable for my goals. He took an interest in my career as a songwriter, listening to demos and promising to connect me with people in the industry, managers and record label executives, people I never actually met. Sometimes I wondered if he dangled these opportunities just to make me stick around.

Now, I can feel Jacob watching as I zip my bag shut, slide an extra pair of socks into the front pocket, and check to make sure the whole thing isn't too heavy.

"Don't forget dinner tonight," Jacob says. "Nathan organized it. The whole gang will be there."

"Okay."

He's silent. "So you'll come?"

"Of course I'll come. Why wouldn't I?"

I regret my tone. I can sense Jacob's injury when he says, "I just want you to be close to the people I'm close to, Akash. Even if it's not the other way around."

I don't like Jacob's friends—especially Nathan. I can already picture it: a bunch of white queens in rompers making snide remarks. Everything will be "terrible" and "horrendous." I don't know what Jacob sees in them. Once, Nathan told me it was a shame my country is so homophobic given how spiritual it is. When I reminded him that my mother is from Tanzania, not India like he had assumed, he'd swatted the air. "Don't get me started on *them*." I'd fought with Jacob that night, saying the only thing worse than a straight white man was a gay one—because gay white men conceal their racism with sequins, while straight ones wear it proudly on their sleeves. My father once said the most dangerous creatures in the jungle are the ones you don't see. Mosquitos fat with malaria. Tiny, poisonous frogs. Jacob said he was sorry—though for what, it wasn't clear.

Still, I know he tries. When I come home from work, he rubs my shoulders. When I cry out in the middle of the night, he cradles me in his arms. Once, moments after I'd vomited in an Uber on the way home from a bar, he kissed my mouth. I had recoiled, but Jacob just shrugged. *It's only puke.* That was before, when the newness of Jacob and me was like the first spritz of a perfume, fresh and sexy, before it dried down to an odor that was ultimately too intense.

"Look," I say, my back still facing him. "Once I get down there, I'll talk to my mother. I'll tell her about . . . us. I'll tell her everything. Maybe you can meet her."

I swallow hard, wondering if he can hear the hollowness in my words, but when I turn from my packing, Jacob is gone.

RENU

I've never liked American grocery stores. They're too cold. Too many products line the tables and shelves. There are fifty different cereals but only two types of green chilies, and neither one of them has any actual heat. On TV, white women tell us to remove the seeds and the ribs—otherwise it'll be *too spicy*.

"Oh, for god's sake," I want to tell them. "Just eat a bell pepper."

Sometimes a cashier will smile at the person in front of me, but when it's my turn, her face turns to stone. *What's your problem?* I want to ask. But I'm too afraid. In London, I learned to stare back, talk back, fight back. In London, there were others like me, doing the talking and fighting. But in America, where people still ask me where I'm from, and how I got here, and to what church I belong (none—I'm a Hindu), I keep my mouth shut. *Don't make waves,* Ashok liked to say. *Don't act fresh off the boat,* Bijal whined. *Don't rock the boat, Mom,* Akash once said. *Just chill.* I don't understand this American obsession with boats.

My cart squeaks against the polished tiles as I drop items into it without a thought. I remember those early years, when Ashok was in residency and we lived off a paltry sum, price tags compared, coupons clipped. Now, I don't hesitate to buy thick blocks of parmesan with perforated rinds, fresh mozzarella, Marcona almonds, the pressed coconut water Bijal likes to drink. I buy everything the boys will need. My heart swells with the thought of their footsteps on the stairs and their baritones in the kitchen, their laughter, their smells, the timbre of their rage. I miss them—even Akash.

"Excuse me," someone says.

My gaze slides toward a young woman in yoga pants and a sweatshirt, her brown hair scraped back with sweat. Her cheeks redden. She walks over to me with authority, and I prepare myself for her words. *You can't be here. Don't touch that. Are you a customer in this store?* It has happened before, women like her smiling their plastic smiles, then telling me what I can or cannot do. She holds a package in her hands.

"I was wondering," she says, nervous. "I thought I'd ask—"

"Yes?" I clutch my bag to my chest.

"This brand," she says. "Have you tried it before? Is it good? Authentic?"

She pushes a package of frozen Indian food in front of my face. I sigh with relief. Years ago, Ashok and I would have never imagined Indian food at the grocery store, but now there's a whole section, boxes upon boxes of chicken tikka masala, rounds of charred naan. The woman presents a package of malai kofta I've tried before. The kofta tasted like feet.

"Oh, it's lovely," I say, smiling.

"Really?"

"Mm! Tastes just like home."

"Oh, wow." The woman grins. "That's a relief. Thank you. My husband and I just love Indian food."

"How nice."

I start to walk away. She follows from behind.

"My roommate from college was Indian," she says. "That's how I tried it. Her name is Devi."

I turn, forcing a smile. "A wonderful name."

"It means goddess."

"Yes, I know that."

"Oh, of course." She smiles, chagrined. "I just love it. It's so feminist."

My smile disappears. Bijal's wife, Jessica, is a feminist. She thinks I've spoiled him, cooking his dinners and folding his underwear all those years. In my opinion, the most feminist women are those who don't need to call themselves one—not like these American women, who are just looking for reasons to complain. I could tell Jessica this, wipe the grin off her face, but I've only seen her three times since their wedding. Save for the girlish arcs of her cursive on holiday cards, she's a mythical creature, spoken of in hushed tones.

"Well, I think I'll be off," I say, rounding the corner. "Enjoy the food."

"Thank you!"

I can feel her eyes on me as I make my escape.

I unload the groceries in the kitchen. It'll be a shame to leave it behind: the bone-white marble, flecked with gold, the Viking stove, the pearled cabinetry, polished to a high shine. A set of windows overlooks the wooded backyard and slate-gray clouds. Evening settles in a navy cast, shading everything in relief. Twenty days. That's all I have left.

I was surprised when the Realtor told me we had an offer. When she'd first come around, six months earlier, she'd had her doubts. "A house this size, at this price. In this town. I don't know." She'd run her toes over the slick tiles, staring up at the cathedral ceiling. "Not many people can afford it." Apparently, someone could. I don't know who the family is. As soon as the offer came in and was accepted, I knew what I had to do. I phoned my brother and his wife in London and told them I was coming home.

I pour myself a glass of wine. It's a new habit: drinking alone. I wasn't like Ashok, who would come home from work and pour himself a scotch, or Bijal, who would twist open a beer after mowing the lawn—or Akash, who never needed a reason in the first place. *Drinks are for celebrations,* I'd once told him. *What do you have to celebrate?*

The wine warms my chest as I carry it through the house, making a note of what furniture will be donated to charity and what will be given to friends, the arrangement of tables and chairs for Ashok's puja next week. It will be the first time I've had guests in this house since his wake. And the last. I move between these walls like a ghost, floating up the curved stairs. The master bedroom feels cavernous without him. Sometimes I can still smell the mossy scent of his cologne. I set my wine on the nightstand, switch on a lamp. I see my reflection in the windows ahead. My shoulder-length hair has gone gray at the roots. My pale skin is shadowed. My waist is narrow, my hips slim. The lamplight falls in a vertical strip across the linen duvet, like a gold ribbon. A gift.

AKASH

When I was young, I dreamt of living in a condo just like Jacob's, with its sweeping views and rich, golden light. The living room features a distressed leather sofa and beechwood coffee table. Twin bookcases sandwich a flat-screen TV. Japanese silk paintings hang from opposite cement walls. Organic fruit spills from a basket at the center of the kitchen island, which is made of white quartz. Plums. Nectarines. Clementines. Pears.

We don't keep booze in the house—not since the time I got drunk and hurled a bottle across the room. We'd had a fight; I don't remember why. Jacob wouldn't tell me. I suppose it was his way of shutting me out. It only drove me to other doors. Often, after a booze-fueled night, I would wake up with an icy sensation that something had gone terribly wrong, that I had left my own body, and gone to a dark place, and that my life had irrevocably changed. Then I would find a text message I'd sent from my phone, something cruel or nasty I had no recollection of writing. Recriminations. Insults. Sharp, cutting words. I promised not to drink tonight. I'm going to be good.

I walk into his office and slide a pair of headphones on, connecting them to my iPhone. I play the track I recorded weeks ago. I was going for a '90s vibe, something smooth. R&B, the only music I've ever loved. Aaliyah, Brandy, Monica, TLC. I can still recall the way boys pounded the beat to Aaliyah's "One in a Million" on their desks: rat-tat-tat-tat-tata-tat-tat. Rat-tat-tat-tat. *Your love is a one in a million. It goes on, and on, and on.* We had never heard anything like it. Remember? Sometimes I joined in, freestyling over their percussion, arranging my own melodies, until someone would look at me and say, with wonder in their voice, *Damn, Osh. You got skills.* And for that brief moment I existed, I was real, a stray piece of thread woven into the fabric.

Now, I hear my voice and wince. At the time, I had been thrilled with it, blasting it from the Bose speakers on Jacob's shelf, but something is off. The first verse goes against the beat instead of gliding on top of it. The hook is predictable. The whole thing lacks melody, which is frustrating, because melody is my thing. I stop the track, yank the headphones off my ears. I walk into the kitchen and pop my face in the fridge. The blast of cold air invigorates me. I poke blindly between jars of pickles and roasted red peppers before my fingers latch onto a familiar metal cap. The flask is where I last left it, behind the energy drinks and protein shakes Jacob hates, full of artificial flavorings, the last place he would ever think to look.

RENU

I sit in Ashok's office in the lamplight, surrounded by books. I pull up Google, enter your name. It's impossible to find you among the results: Instagram pages, YouTube links, LinkedIn profiles. None of them are you. Once, on Google, I'd clicked on an article about the arrest of a man with your name, my heart ricocheting in my chest, but the picture was of someone much younger. I don't know what you look like now, Kareem. It's been thirty-five years.

Ever since I booked my ticket to London, thoughts of you have been flooding back like pieces of an interrupted dream. I need to distract myself. I move about the house, making sure everything is in order. I fluff pillows, snap sheets into place. I stand in the kitchen boiling a pot of tea.

I was sixty when Ashok passed. No one expected him to. We had the kind of bright life people dream about, full of half-truths and lies. The night before Ashok died, he devoured the pressure-cooker lamb chops with coconut masala I had prepared for his dinner, his lips glistening with fat.

"Renu, I love your food," he said. "I could die eating this."

And then he did.

At least he left this earth with good food on his tongue. This was the thought that comforted me the next day when he didn't come down for his cup of tea, and, later that morning, when the paramedic pronounced him dead, and, in the days that followed, through all the phone calls and emails and texts. He loved my food. All my boys did. They ate with abandon, licking fingers, sucking bones.

"Mom!" Bijal said whenever he walked through the door. "What can I eat?"

He would stride around like a giant, opening cabinets and drawers. Sometimes, if I happened to be cooking at the stove, he would reach around me and pinch whatever was sputtering in the pan, popping it into his mouth. Once, I was making chicken fajitas when Bijal plucked a piece of chicken and swallowed it down.

"Bijal! That was raw!"

He shrugged. "Tastes good to me."

When Bijal was nine and Akash was five, Ashok was invited to the home of a colleague named Dr. Shaw. They lived in a blue Victorian. Their dining room sparkled. Dr. Shaw's wife, a thin blonde named Georgia, made roast chicken for dinner.

"Mom." Bijal kicked me, whispering. "I can't eat this. There's no spice."

Georgia had overheard.

"I'm sorry," she said, looking not at Bijal but at me. "You must be used to eating *very* spicy food."

"Not *very* spicy," I snapped.

But Georgia only laughed. "Well, I have no taste for it. Everyone knows that. Salt and pepper do just fine."

"The chicken's delicious, Georgia," Dr. Shaw said.

They never invited us again.

"You see?" I later said, invoking them as a warning. "You see what happens when you marry a white girl? You get bland food every day."

"I don't want to marry a white girl, Mommy," Bijal said, kissing my hand. "I want to marry *you*."

I snuggled him to my breast, temporarily pacified. Twenty years later, he introduced me to Jessica.

I have an hour left before Chaya arrives to help make cocktail-sized kachoris for the puja. I turn on *Deserted Hearts*. It's a soap opera about a group of housewives who are bored with their lives. They've added a new character, a midseason twist, who intrigues me. Her name is Celeste. She's the wife of a plastic surgeon. The advertisers call her a "stone-cold bitch." I like that.

"That Renu." I imagine. "What a stone-cold bitch."

In the opening scene, Celeste is at a party when she throws a drink against the wall. It's not entirely clear why she's upset, but it doesn't have to be. Part of the fun is figuring it all out.

"I know *all* about you," Celeste now says, sidling up to a woman at the bar. Her black gown shimmers. Her frosted hair gleams. The woman, Rebecca, a redhead with powdery skin, slits her eyes.

"What? What do you know?"

"Everything."

"Liar!" Rebecca gasps, clutching her chest. "Whore!"

"I'm going to expose you," says Celeste. "At my charity function next week—it's for breast cancer, by the way."

"Oh yeah?" says Rebecca. "Well, I hope no one shows up. I hope you don't raise any money. I hope *everyone* gets breast cancer—even little babies. It'll be all your fault!"

"Bitch!"

The episode ends just as Chaya's tires crunch over the leaves on the driveway. Her headlights throw two parallel strips of light against the wall. She's standing behind the front door when I approach it to receive her, her frizzed hair shifting in the wind. I think about the secrets I've kept. All the things I've hidden from the people I love.

AKASH

I'm buzzed by the time I get to Nathan's split-level house in Silver Lake. The party is upstairs, on the second level, which overlooks the reservoir on one side and the glinting rods of downtown LA on the other. Some of Jacob's friends are here, huddled around a platter of baba ghanoush. All of them are white. All of them have striped hair manipulated into glossy architecture above their tightly clipped fades. A hush falls over the room. Jacob turns.

"Akash, you made it."

His smile is mechanical. He seems nervous. I stare at the drops of sweat on his brow. Nathan, paisley shirt, gold stud in his ear, waves from across the room, though whether it's directed at Jacob or at me is unclear. What I am clear on is what Nathan said to me weeks ago. *Don't get me started on them.* The words ping in my mind. Nathan floats over with his arms spread wide.

"Hello," he says, kissing my cheeks. Nathan never addresses me by name. He only says "Hello." I don't know what this means—whether he can't pronounce my name or he's deliberately trying to be a prick—but I don't say anything to Jacob. I don't want to add to my list of complaints. Nathan takes a step back, sweeping his hand across the spread.

"Help yourself to the food. There's homemade baba ghanoush and flatbread. Well—" He leans in, conspiratorial. "To be honest, the flatbread is store-bought naan bread. Don't tell Ina."

The words "naan bread" make me wince. *It's not naan bread,* I want to say. *It's naan. Just like it's not chai tea—it's chai.* But I don't say anything. I can't say anything. If I do, the conversation inevitably becomes about race.

"You okay?" Jacob says, placing a hand at my back.

He looks into my eyes and I wonder if he can smell it on me: the gin. A bar sits in the corner of Nathan's living room, bottles of white wine sweating in the heat. My buzz is gone. I need another.

"I'm fine."

"You seem tense."

"Why do you think that is?"

"Akash." Jacob sighs. "You're here now. Just try and have a good time, okay? For me. It's our last night together."

He slides his hand down my back and, for a moment, my desire betrays me. I lean my head on his chest.

"It can't be easy," he says, his words vibrating. "Seeing your family again."

An image flashes before my eyes: my brother's wedding. I see my mother in a peach sari with silver netting, dark hair pinned back in a bun. I hear the squeak of a microphone. I see my brother, sitting next to Jessica at the head table, glaring at me in his tuxedo. The room shimmers. A wedding song spins. My mother whispers as I struggle to get up off the floor. *Akash! What are you doing? How much did you drink?* I don't answer her. Everyone's eyes are upon us. The microphone slips from my grasp, rolls across the parquet tiles.

"Akash?"

Jacob grips my shoulder and the vision clears. His hold is steady. I used to laugh when people referred to their significant other as their "rock." But that's what Jacob is. That's what he's always been. I was tired of swimming, and there was Jacob, waiting for me to latch on.

A pair of men in trendy glasses wave at Jacob from across the room. His grip loosens. My face chills. "Go," I say to him. "Talk to them."

"Are you sure?"

"Yeah."

He plants a wet kiss on my cheek. "I'm proud of you, for tonight. For not drinking." I hold my breath. He looks at me, something shifting through his eyes. "You're not, right?"

I shake my head.

"Good. Don't disappear on me. We have to make the most of tonight."

"Okay."

As Jacob crosses the room, I look forward to the night ahead, to his warm embrace, wondering how I'll survive two weeks without it. I stare out the window at the dry, prickly hills and listen to the dance music thumping from Nathan's stereo: Kylie Minogue. A saccharine chorus loops over a metallic beat. The verses bounce like springs. Something vibrates at my back—my cell phone. A text from Jaden. *Just sold a demo!!! Drinks at our spot?* I look over at Jacob, who's engrossed in conversation with his arms folded firmly over his chest. I call an Uber, steal a drink off the table. Suck it all down. The way it sparkles in my throat is revitalizing. I take another, and another, until the world turns soft and dim. As I walk toward the door, avoiding Nathan and his friends while they titter like a flock of birds, I realize something: I hate dance music. I always have. It could never be as soulful as R&B.

RENU

One month into our marriage, Ashok came home from the hospital and informed me they had hired another Indian doctor: a pulmonologist named Bhupendra Desai.

"Dr. Price was mad," he said. "He said the hospital needs to stop hiring so many Indian doctors."

"But you're the only Indian doctor."

"Maybe that's one too many."

"That racist," I shouted, fire spreading through me. "That bloody swine! I'll go to his house and slap his wife!"

"What does his wife have to do with it?"

"Quiet, Ashok."

Ashok never liked this kind of talk; he said I had a sharp tongue. But what's the use of a tongue if it just sits in your mouth? I suppose this was the reason I was so pleased to meet Chaya. She has an even sharper one.

Now, Chaya rinses cilantro leaves and tosses them into a food processor. She adds yogurt and garlic, a knob of peeled ginger. She blitzes the mixture into a runny green paste.

"I saw Meena at Macy's," she says. "She's gained."

Chaya—who is small and trim, with fine, crushable bones—is tickled by anyone overweight. Having come from a village where the average person looks malnourished, life in America is like a trip to Sea World.

"Look, look," she once said at Sam's Club, pointing to a customer being wheeled around on a flatbed. "How big he is!"

His daughter stood behind us.

"That's my father," she said, glaring. "He has a medical condition."

I was mortified, but Chaya only smiled. She's the kind of woman who will talk loudly about someone even when they are standing right beside her. No one begrudges her this; Chaya is not the sort to elicit scorn. She's simple, with her frizzed dark hair and plain gold jewelry. According to Bijal, she hasn't assimilated. I think Bijal has assimilated too much.

"It's the medication," I say, pouring oil into a vat, flicking on the stove.

"What medication? Häagen-Dazs?"

I shake my head.

"See, Renu?" she says, sadly. "What will I do without you? Who will listen to my rubbish? You can't leave me alone in this town."

I ignore this, dropping a mound of dough into the oil, watching it sizzle to the top. I'm frying the kachoris, just like my mother taught me in Tanzania. I still remember the hot fog of the kitchen, geckos darting in and out of shelves, the briny smell of the sea. I remember you, too, Kareem. Your dark skin and thick beard. What would Chaya say if she knew that all these years, my heart belonged to someone else?

I'm dissolving tamarind into water for chutney when Chaya asks about Akash. I don't answer. She doesn't ask again. She was there when it happened. Everyone was. Sparkling crystal. Lace tablecloths. A pink, sugary cake. Akash's speech, the way his eyes had rolled back in his head. It was four years ago, but it feels like only yesterday. I can still hear the gasps that swept across the room when Akash fell over, not moving. I can feel the glare of the spotlight on my skin. Even now, I can see the pity written across everyone's faces. Or was it mirth? The pleasure we take in the misfortune of others, the ones we once thought were better off than us.

Sometimes I wonder if Akash is the reason I'm leaving America. I've yet to visit him in LA. Whenever I broach the subject, he steers me away. *Mom, I'm fine.* For as long as I can remember, when Bijal broke his arm in the seventh grade, when Akash came home with a bloodied lip, when both my boys got drunk at their cousin's wedding and vomited behind the chocolate fondue, when Ashok left us in the middle of the night, two sons without a father, a beginning without an end, the answer was the same: *Mom, I'm fine.*

"Renu." Chaya snaps her fingers in front of my face. Something is smoking. A glob of pastry. I fish it out with a slotted spoon.

"Shit."

"Are you okay?" she asks, her face softening. I don't answer. She places her brown fingers over mine. "You have to let go."

At first, I wonder if she's talking about you, but then her face brightens. Her smile spreads. "I have an idea."

"What?"

"Come." She leads me into the office where Ashok's laptop sits open on the maple desk, where, just hours earlier, I had Googled your name. "It's time."

"Time for what?"

She pulls the swivel chair out from under the desk.

"It's time you join Facebook," she says.

AKASH

I meet Jaden at a bar in Los Feliz with low-hanging ropes of Christmas bulbs. The bulbs blink on and off. The blazing sky reminds me of all those sunsets in Illinois. Fires over farmland. I don't look at my phone. I'm sure Jacob has texted me. There must be a voicemail, too. I picture him searching the closets in Nathan's house, his lips drawn tight. Perhaps Nathan is standing next to him, shaking his head. I take a sip of my drink and the buzz thickens, edges softening, lines blurred. I feel bad betraying Jacob this way, but not in the way one betrays a lover, the way a son betrays his dad.

"Maybe that's the problem," Jaden says. "Maybe you think of him as your daddy."

"He's thirty-seven."

"He seems pretty daddy-ish to me."

"I don't think you're officially a daddy until you start having colonoscopies."

At this, Jaden snorts. His nutmeg skin is glossed with sweat. The sky outside darkens. A familiar song blares from the speakers above. Ashanti, "Foolish." We look at each other and grin.

"Aye," Jaden says, knocking his glass against mine. "I haven't heard this in forever."

"One of the few samples I actually like."

"People always try to act like Ashanti didn't have jams," Jaden says. "She's the princess of R and B."

"Now you're pushing it."

Jaden moved here from Atlanta; he's a producer, and we've worked together on a couple songs—none of which have sold. For Jaden, all of that changes now. His song is going to be featured on an album alongside Grammy-nominated producers.

"What are you gonna do with the money?" I ask.

I'm always curious about what people do with their money, maybe because I don't have any of my own. My account is steadily thinning, while the bills fatten like cooked rice. I've received three phone calls from Chase Visa, threatening to put me in collections. It should be a crime to have no money while everyone around you does. Like my brother, Bijal, who just bought a brand-new Porsche. Sitting across from Jaden and his newfound success, I feel myself shrink.

"I'll probably pay some bills, maybe buy some new recording equipment. Put the rest in savings."

"Boring."

"What am I supposed to do? Walk around in Gucci track-suits like everyone else in this town?"

Jaden is gay. Like with me, his mother doesn't know it—or maybe she does. Maybe she's hoping it's a phase he'll outgrow. He doesn't talk to his parents about it, just like I never talked to mine. We bonded over this the first time we met, laughing at all the ignorant things our families have said. Jaden's family is religious, and it's one of the reasons he left Atlanta, even though there's a music scene there. When I'm with Jaden, I don't have to explain myself. He isn't like Jacob, who thinks everything can be solved with communication.

"Communication is for white people," Jaden says. "*We* get whooped."

It's easy for Jacob, with his liberal family, his deep, inscrutable voice.

"*He's* gay?" people often ask, as if it were a compliment. "You wouldn't even know."

I know. I know that Jacob is frustrated with me for still being in the closet, for leading a double life. He says I have "internalized homophobia," that it's like PTSD; unless I get help, I'll never get over things. *Things*. What a simple way of putting it.

"Slow down," Jaden says, as I gulp my drink. "Are you okay?"

"I'm stress-drinking."

"Is it Jacob?"

You blacked out, Jacob often says, the night's activities pirouetting away from me like helicopter seeds. *Do you remember what you did?* The accusations are always glossed over, phrased as questions instead.

"Yeah."

We finish our drinks and order more. Jaden tells me about a beat he's working on.

"I'm tired of all this sleepy R and B. It's uninspired. If I hear one more Jhené Aiko lullaby . . ."

"Jhené is dope—her melodies are beautiful."

"Yeah, all three of them."

I ball up my napkin and toss it in Jaden's direction. He laughs and tosses it back. The light reflects off his milky smile. The tip of his sandaled toe meets mine.

"I'm onto something new," Jaden says. "Something fresh. I just need to figure it out."

"If anyone can do it, it's you."

Jaden is otherworldly. Sometimes it scares me, the way he can fill up a track, all the textures and layers and tones. He could turn the plink of a leaky faucet into a lush waterfall of sound. I've been dying for us to sell a song, but I'm afraid, with Jaden's success, that he's slipping away from me.

"Hey," he says, dropping his beer onto the table. "I want you to help."

"Seriously?"

"I think you could do something with it."

"When?"

Jaden looks at his cell phone. "Come to the studio with me."

It's late. Ten o'clock. I think about Jacob, pacing the driveway outside Nathan's house, and quietly choke with guilt. I take another sip, flushing it down.

"Okay."

RENU

Chaya has been begging me to join Facebook for months. According to her, it's all the rage. The gossip that can be mined.

"Look at this, Anju's daughter," she says, pointing to a young woman in a plunging dress. "Showing her breasts to the world."

I remember Anju's daughter as a shy, gap-toothed girl, hiding behind her mother. Now, she wears lip gloss and eyeliner and has blond streaks in her hair. Her hips defy the fabric of her dress. She sticks out her tongue while holding a bottle of Jose Cuervo. I laugh.

"That could be us, Chaya," I say. "If there was Facebook in our day."

"Thank god there wasn't."

I move aside as she shows me how to make a profile and post pictures and write clever things on my wall. She points out all the people who have joined Facebook recently: friends of Ashok, Chaya's relatives, people I haven't spoken to in years. I choose a picture from Bijal's wedding for my profile picture. In it, I wear a peach sari with a silver blouse, earrings dipped in gold, a diamond necklace. I'd bought it at a posh store on Breach Candy. It was Ashok's idea.

"Our son is getting married," he'd said. "This is once in a lifetime."

Once in a lifetime. I remember the things I said to Akash the morning after Bijal's reception, when the whispers had reached a fever pitch. *Did you see? How shameful. How much did he have to drink?* Akash flew back to LA the next day without saying goodbye. Bijal left for his honeymoon in Greece. Ashok and I drove home in silence. It was true, what Ashok had said: the wedding was once in a lifetime. But sometimes once is all it takes, one misstep, one fall, and your life can change forever.

After Chaya leaves, I pack up the kachoris and place them in Ziploc bags to be fried the morning of Ashok's puja. I do the same with the chutneys. I clear up the kitchen, wiping the marble island with a sponge. I go to bed late, around one, still thinking about Anju's daughter, everyone, all those lost connections, suddenly found. A simple click is all it takes.

I'm still thinking about this as morning birds begin to screech in the sky, announcing the arrival of a new day, at which point my eyes flip open. I creep downstairs and pad into Ashok's office. I log in to Facebook. The images tumble down: birthdays, baby pictures, weddings, cats. I have ten notifications in the top corner of the screen. People have already found me. Old classmates, a cousin I lost touch with, a few people in the neighborhood. A woman I had met once at a party. My eyes flick past the stream of articles and videos and political rants. People are angry. People are sad. Some people want to show off their plate of food. Others share tidbits from home, something trivial their baby has done, as if their baby is the only baby to have ever been born. It's all too much. Still, my hand flies to the mouse, clicks the search bar at the top. I bite my lip, hard, and enter your name.

AKASH

At the studio, Jaden plays the track for me and opens a bottle of wine. We drink while I write to it. The wine spreads quickly, dulling my nerves. The beat is tricky, never staying in the same place. It takes a while to figure it out, to wrap my head around the oscillating claps. Soon the pieces come together, forming an image in my head. The image looks like you. A melody slips like smoke from my mouth and exhales over the beat. Dissipating.

"That's dope," Jaden says, sliding into the seat next to mine. "It has an Aaliyah vibe."

"All thanks to Static Major," I say.

The studio is dark, lit by a flickering blue glow. The effect makes it seem like we're underwater. A memory surfaces. Aaliyah. I'm in a parked car with you, listening to "Rock the Boat." My hand reaches for yours. Your eyes widen.

"Yo, Osh. You okay?"

Jaden grips my shoulders as I rise from my seat.

"I'm fine."

"You don't look fine."

He stands in front of me, and I see the concern in his eyes, which are dark and thickly lashed. His T-shirt clings like film to his chest. He grabs my hand, his brown skin the same walnut shade as mine. And then it's happening. He pushes me against the wall as his tongue swells in my mouth. I kiss him back, sliding my hand up his shirt. His chest is hard, hot, pulsing under my grip. He spits into his hand and shoves it down my pants. I stiffen inside his grip. Jaden smells like laundry detergent, deodorant, mint-flavored gum.

"Wait," I gasp. "Maybe we shouldn't—"

But it's too late. Shirts slide off. Belts unbuckle. Skin touches skin. Jaden turns me around and pushes my face against the insulated padding of the studio wall, pulling down my shorts. I feel the cold, slick head of his cock, slippery between my thighs. Soon he's inside me, grinding me to dust. Our bodies slap wetly. I groan into the wall. It's over before I know what happened. The lights come on and Jaden hands me my shirt. We don't talk about it.

We never do.

"I should go," I say, heading toward the door.

"Wait," Jaden says. His eyes cloud over, pleading with me to stop. I know he's about to say it: that we need to talk, figure this all out. I remember the drunk text I sent him two weeks ago. *Why can't we be more than friends?* I regret it now. Or maybe I'm just upset that he never replied.

"You can call me," he finally says. "Even if it's just to talk."

"I know."

He nods. My hand curls over the knob as I open the door, light streaming into the room. Jaden heads into the booth.

"And hey." I turn, waiting. "Let's finish that song."

By the time I get home, Jacob is already in bed. I climb in next to him. He doesn't move. I set my cell phone—still flashing with his missed calls—on the nightstand next to my head. I can't sleep. The alcohol makes me restless. The image of you still smolders in my mind. Jaden's music fills the spaces in between, like the soundtrack of a film. The glossy synth, plucking chords, resonant bass. I turn to face Jacob and stare at the small freckles on his back, whispering his name. He doesn't answer. He doesn't have to. It's obvious to both of us that he's still awake.

RENU

At first glance, there are only young people in places like Lahore or Cairo, names scribbled in Arabic, pictures of BMWs. There's a Kareem Abbas holding a bow and arrow, a Kareem Abbas playing with a dog, a Kareem Abbas standing in front of Machu Picchu. According to Facebook, everyone has been to Machu Picchu. Everyone loves cappuccino art and truffle oil and the Kardashians—until it's time to hate them again. I feel sorry for these people, who spend their days quibbling with one another in the comments. I log out, boil a pot of tea. I sip it in front of a window. The sun begins to rise in the distance, staining the sky a tropical pink. You had a nickname in Tanzania. If only I could remember. Maybe you have it listed under that. Maybe you're not on Facebook at all. I see your glowing face on the shoreline of Coco Beach. I push the thought from my mind. Later, I trek upstairs to shower and dry my hair, putting on makeup in front of the mirror. I skim through a novel I was supposed to have read but didn't, Googling the premise instead, in preparation for book club.

I met Taylor at the gym one morning shortly after Ashok had passed. She's young, with stripes of cinnamon in her platinum blond hair. She has a master's degree, which she likes to remind us of whenever anyone brings up her job, which is selling lotion over the internet.

"Like Avon?" I once asked.

She looked offended.

Taylor's face is always fussed over with cosmetics—even at the gym. She talks loudly and enthusiastically, regardless of who's around. I don't have the confidence these American women have, to act as if the world belongs to me.

"You should join my book club," she'd said, dabbing her face with a towel. "It would be great to get your perspective."

She had emphasized the word "perspective." By then, I knew enough to know that book clubs were only vaguely about books, and more acutely about the wine. I told her I would join. I was bored, I suppose. I needed something to do. The women are all white like Taylor and around her age: late thirties, early forties, with kids who range from five to fifteen. They're self-identifying feminists—even Taylor, who wears makeup to the gym. They love drinking sauvignon blanc. Taylor calls it "sauvi-b."

Gotta have my sauvi-b. Am I right, ladies?

The book club usually meets at someone's house. Once, I hosted it at mine. Taylor spent an uncomfortable amount of time praising the statue of Lord Ganesh in a corner of the room.

"It's so beautiful," she said.

Everything was beautiful in my house, or worthy of some larger discussion about politics or art. *It's a bowl,* I wanted to say, when Becca picked up a silver dish and moaned.

"Is this from Rajasthan?" she said. "I heard they have the most exquisite dishware."

"It's from T.J. Maxx."

"Oh."

The women had asked me to make samosas. They wanted my "authentic" food. When Taylor bit into one, her eyes rolled back in her head like she was having an orgasm.

"Mmm," she said. "What's the spice in this?"

I suppose American women only use one spice in their food, because they're always asking the question: "What's the spice?" *It's many spices,* I wanted to tell her. *More than you have in your house.*

"It's curry powder," said Becca. "I can taste it."

"Yes, I thought so," said Taylor.

I could have explained to them that curry powder has nothing to do with Indian cooking at all, that someone has been lying to them. Instead, I smiled.

"You're right."

Now, I leaf through the contents of a book I haven't yet read, thinking of something intelligent but not incendiary to say. On my way out the door, I pass a framed portrait of Ashok. It hangs on a wall opposite the kitchen. The portrait is crooked. His dark eyes penetrate. His toffee skin glows. His smile, effortless, as if there was no room for anything else on his face, slashes my heart. I place both hands on the frame and shift it back into place.

AKASH

The next morning, I rise and shower and finish packing in the dark, careful not to bump into the furniture. The city twinkles like a trail of spilled treasure. Jacob snores under the covers. My flight leaves in two hours. I toast a bagel in the kitchen, watching the sun spill over the horizon like a broken egg, a golden syrup that glazes everything in sight. Staring at the city, I remember my first night in Jacob's place, the way he'd pointed out the old apartment complex where he used to live, nestled in a strip mall, with cracked tiles and cockroaches, nothing like where we live. He'd placed a hand at my back when he spoke, reassuring me. He talked about manifestation. He said he'd manifested this condo. He'd manifested his career. He spun me around so I could see the lit bulb of his face when he told me there was one more thing he had manifested: me. Jaden thought that was weird, but I found it romantic. That someone could have everything but still nothing without me. Now, I call an Uber just as Jacob walks into the room. He stares at me, frowning.

"I can't do this."

"What?" I say.

"This. Whatever this is—with you."

My stomach knots. "I'm sorry. I had to run to the studio. I didn't want to interrupt. I tried, Jacob. You know I did."

"It's not that," he says, scratching his head.

Jacob's hair is greasy, flat like a swimmer's cap. He wears a ripped T-shirt through which I can see his wiry chest hair. For a moment, I feel like walking over to him and kissing him, hard. But the impulse vanishes.

"I found your stash."

"Huh?"

"Your stash."

"I don't—"

"Did you think I didn't know, Akash?" I don't say anything. "I know when you're lying. I know when you've been drinking, and do you know why? 'Cause it makes me nervous. You make me nervous. Every time you take a sip I wonder where the night is gonna go, what things will come out of your mouth, or what you'll even—"

"What?"

He shakes his head. "And now you're leaving."

"I told you, I'm just going home for a few days. I'll be back in no time."

"That's what you say."

"That's what I'm doing."

"And then what?" Jacob says, squinting in the light. "What happens after that? What happens to you and me? When are you going to let me in? When are you going to—Jesus." He shakes his head. "When are you going to come out?"

I know this will upset him, but I say it anyway.

"You're being unreasonable."

He looks as if he's stepped on a sharp pin. "I just want to be there for you. This can't be an easy time."

I want to tell him the truth: that he has no idea what's easy or not. He doesn't know me at all. Jacob sees only what he wants to see, nothing more. *You're such a good person, Akash,* he once said, our bodies still damp from sex. And all I could think was, *Wrong.*

"I can't keep on like this. That's all I'm trying to say."

"Are you breaking up with me?"

"Akash . . ."

"Then what?"

He sighs. The toaster clicks; the bagel is ejected. I wrap it in a napkin, taking a quick bite. My cell phone chimes. The Uber.

"Look, I have to go. I'll call when I reach home. We'll talk every day."

He looks unconvinced. "What about my cousin's wedding?"

"I'll be there."

He nods, approaching the kitchen island, where a snakeskin

wallet gleams atop a stack of old mail. Then he plucks a few bills and walks them over to me. "Here, take some cash."

The bills curl between his fingers. I shake my head. He looks at me, knowingly, and I hold out my hand. "Thanks."

The cash feels like dried leaves on my palm, in danger of disintegrating. I stuff it in my pocket. Jacob follows me to the door.

"I love you," he says, sunlight striping his skin.

I see your face when I say it back.

RENU

Taylor has on a cable-knit sweater over Lycra pants. She holds a red wineglass full of white wine. The wine sloshes precariously. She takes a big gulp. We're at her house, which has white wicker furniture and pale yellow walls. Everything looks incredibly blond. This month, we've read a novel by a handsome Latino man. There's eight of us in this week's discussion. Though I'm the oldest, Taylor never starts with me.

"So, ladies, what did we think?" she asks, grinning. She makes a display of scanning the room as if deciding whom to ask first, even though she has figured all of this out the night before.

Now, she points to a young white woman I've never seen before. The woman has short hair and ripped jeans. A backpack sits at her sandaled feet, patched over with rainbows and a peace sign. Something catches my eye, a small rectangular sticker with the word: BITCH!

"This is Shane, everyone," says Taylor. "She's new. I think she'll provide an interesting perspective."

Shane doesn't smile.

"Let's start with you, Shane," Taylor says. "What did you think?"

"I didn't like it," she says, holding up the book. "I found it to be problematic. I mean, it's practically dripping with misogyny."

"Interesting," says Taylor.

"And it's an eye-opener," Shane continues. "That it's not just white men who are the problem; it's brown and Black men, too. And their misogyny is worse, because it's cleverly disguised as 'tradition.' It's woven into their culture. I mean, just look at rap videos. The women don't help either. If anything, they enable it."

She looks at me when she says this. I don't like this woman at all. *Tradition*. What does she know about tradition? Her ancestors are thieves. Something stirs inside me.

Taylor looks at me from across the room. "Did you have something to add?"

I can feel their eyes shift toward me. Shane seems irritated, as if she wasn't expecting to share the stage. Maybe she thinks she's the authority on all things related to women, and I couldn't possibly have anything to say. I look at the sticker—BITCH!—and think about amending it: *white bitch*. I've said it before, when women like Shane cut in front of me in line at the supermarket or make me walk around them on the path. *White bitch. White bitch. White bitch.* Of course, no one can hear me. I only whisper it to myself.

"I don't really have anything to say."

Taylor nods with relief. Later, when she ends our session, she informs everyone about my departure, explaining that, because of this, our next session will meet earlier than usual. Then she tells us she has a special surprise selection just for me. When I get up to leave, I notice Shane looking at me as if she wants to say something, her eyes hard and penetrating, but I walk out before she has the chance.

Two hours later, as I'm preparing for Bijal's arrival, collecting fresh towels and bottles of soap for his room, it occurs to me: your pet name. I remember it now, the way you answered to it on the football field in Dar es Salaam, or sometimes outside the mosque. Men shouted it at the dark back of your head. Women shrieked it whenever you teased them on the streets. Ndugu. It means "brother" in Swahili. The name pops like a soapy bubble, disintegrating on my nose. I rush into Ashok's office, log in to Facebook. I type in the word: Ndugu. A list of names cascades down the screen. In the distance, I can hear the revving of an engine, the screech of tires, the familiar growl of a sports car. Bijal's Porsche. The sound gets louder and closer, until a blade of light slashes across the wall. I look out the windows to find a silver Porsche idling by the curb. The door flicks open. Bijal slips out. I face the screen, my heart pounding in my chest, when I find it: Ndugu Kareem Abbas. I can hear my son's footsteps as I click: ADD FRIEND.

AKASH

I've had a drink. Actually, I've had two. Three if you count the one at the airport. I wonder if anyone can tell. It's a delicious feeling, like a secret no one else knows. I listen to music and smile at the other passengers on my flight, even though no one is smiling because everyone is asleep. There's Wi-Fi on the plane, so I send Jacob a text—*Almost there*—before putting my phone away.

I sit back in my seat and listen to Aaliyah's "Rock the Boat." My ears fill with her silky voice, like water gliding over stone. That's how I had described her voice to you. Water over stone. We were in my car that night, blasting *The Red Album* while watching charter planes light up the sky. The wine spreads through me like warm syrup. I close my eyes. My phone vibrates, and when I slide open the screen, I see a text message from Jacob. *Text me when you land*. His words are a comfort, though little else is.

The plane shifts, and through my window I can see the slanted view of farmland, a green-and-yellow grid, loaded with painful memories. Jacob says life is all about balance.

He says you have to find your flow. When you're in flow, he tells me, everything falls into place. I don't know about flow. But I know about falling. I know what it's like to hit the floor, split your lip, feel the heel of someone's shoe at your back. I know what it's like to be called a faggot, a sand nigger. A camel jockey. Apu.

The first time I was attacked, I was in the eighth grade. I was walking home from school. Ordinarily, my mother picked me up, but Bijal had an SAT class and needed a ride. Earlier that afternoon, Mrs. Masterson had asked me to get up in front of the class and talk about Hinduism. She made me draw a picture of Lord Ganesh. I had obliged, drawing his four arms, one and a half tusks, and pink, swollen belly.

"You worship a fat elephant?" Bryce Burnham, the class bully, had said. "That's hilarious."

Everyone laughed. I didn't know what to say, but Mrs. Masterson, who was always looking at me and smiling as if to reassure me of my place in class, gave Bryce detention. It was the wrong thing to do.

"Hey, elephant boy!" Bryce said later that afternoon, running up behind me. "Thanks for getting me in trouble."

It was a bright, sunny day. The straps of my JanSport dug into my skin. I glanced casually in his direction, though my insides roiled. Bryce was not the kind of person you wanted to piss off. It was like walking past a house with a sign that read: BEWARE OF DOG. You needed to move quickly, so as not to alert him. He was bigger than all of the other kids, with wide shoulders, thick arms. His buzzed brown hair was the stiff texture of turf. Bryce caught up to me easily, with two boys—Evan Samuels and Lance Mayfield—in tow. They had matching crew cuts and red flannel shirts.

"You fucked up my afternoon plans," Bryce said.

His pink face glowed. Sometimes it helps to communicate

with your attacker, remind them that you're human. I had seen that in a movie once. "I didn't mean to," I said.

"*I didn't mean to!*" Bryce flailed his hands. "Well, you did. And now I have detention. And it's all your fault—gay wad."

I blinked away the hot sun.

"I'm not gay."

"What?"

"I'm not . . . gay."

I don't know why I said this. The particulars of my sexuality were irrelevant at the time. But it felt good to deny it, to make him think he was wrong. I would later regret this, too.

"Are you calling me stupid?"

"No?"

"Do you think I'm a retard?"

"You seem pretty smart to me."

"Shut up!"

"Yeah! You can't talk to Bryce like that," said Evan.

"Yeah!" said Lance.

"Yeah!" said Evan again, as if we hadn't heard him the first time.

People like Evan and Lance don't get very far in life. Most of them end up with mediocre jobs and terrible wives, even worse kids. I knew that then. Maybe that's why I smiled.

"What the fuck are you smiling at?"

I learned something that day: it's better to act the way people want you to act than to go around showing your nerve. Bryce moved quickly, in spite of his size. I didn't have a prayer. The first blow was like a pan of hot water scalding my face. The second felt like a knife in my gut. The third and fourth felt like nothing. The hot pavement sliced my skin.

"You'd better watch your back, OshKosh!" Bryce said. I heard their dying laughter. I wiped the blood from my knees. I walked all the way home, remembering what my mother had once told me about Lord Ganesh: he was the remover of obstacles. It was the first time in my life that she had lied.

The plane touches the ground just as my buzz wears thin. I open my eyes. A flight attendant flits by. The fasten-seatbelt sign turns off just as people begin to rise, opening the overhead compartments, sliding on coats. I look out the windows, at the flat black land stripped clean of its crops, the distant city lights. I wonder if you're there, among them, if you had watched our plane land.

RENU

I waited all day to log back in to Facebook. Bijal had come in like a storm. He brought two large suitcases to pack up all of his things: the trophies and certificates and memorabilia in his room. Boxes of baseball cards. Stacks of CDs. Collegiate sweatshirts and old athletic equipment he would never use.

"We have a big house," he'd explained. "I have space to store it."

I have seen Bijal's house only once, shortly after it was constructed, when I insisted he host a puja for everyone to bless it. It's even larger than ours, with a kidney-shaped swimming pool and an outdoor kitchen, a three-car garage. The inside is modern, with a glass staircase and something Jessica calls a "She Shed."

"What nonsense," I'd said, when I first heard of it. "Is she planning to build furniture?"

"No, Mom," Bijal had replied, exasperated. "It's a place for her to have her own space. You know—to get away."

"Get away from what?"

He didn't answer. I didn't tell him what I really thought, that Jessica doesn't need to "get away" from anything. The whole house is hers. They don't even have children. What more does she want? I was partially relieved when Bijal walked into the foyer alone, his dark face sweating. He said Jessica wasn't feeling well. She would take the train in the day of Ashok's puja and leave a few days later. It was all fine with me.

It's not that I don't like Jessica. I'm not that kind of mother-in-law. When Bijal introduced me to her, I was very polite. I asked her where she went to college and what she was planning on doing with my son. Is that so bad?

"Mom," Bijal said, the day he came home from medical school and told me about her. "I'm in love."

"Jaja haave," I said. "What love?"

But I should have known better. I do know better. It's not Jessica I despise; it's what she did to my son. Turned him into someone I no longer recognize. I used to spend all day cooking for him: lamb keema and paratha, butter chicken and naan. Now, it's "I can't eat that. Jessica has me off carbs."

Still, she tries, calling every year during Diwali.

"Happy Dee-waal-i, Mrs. Amin."

If she was any other girl, I would tell her to call me Mom. But I don't know this girl, with her straw-colored hair and her cinnamon freckles, her foundation two shades too light. Once, after Bijal called to say that he and Jessica were spending Thanksgiving with *her* family instead, I'd shouted at Ashok.

"You let him do this! You let him marry that girl! If he was going to marry a white girl, he could have found someone beautiful."

"Why?" Ashok said. "Did you expect him to find someone as beautiful as you?"

"Quiet, Ashok."

I think about all the Indian girls who were interested in my son, good girls from good families with even better degrees. Jessica has a bachelor's in art history.

"Is she going to work in a museum?" I'd said. "How much does *that* pay?"

My son is an anesthesiologist. He makes six hundred thousand dollars a year. God only knows what his "Jessica" does with it.

"You don't know this new generation," Chaya likes to say. "These nawa girls are smart. First, they trap our boys. Then, they make *them* do all the cooking. Can you believe? Amit's wife can't even boil a pot of rice. Now tell me: What does she contribute? Finding recipes on Pinterest she can't even make?"

This is why I love Chaya: she gets it.

The house is silent when I finally sit down in front of the laptop. Bijal is showering upstairs. Akash's flight arrives at the local airport any minute. A few stars blink prematurely in the sky. I log in to Facebook and land on your page. The friend request hangs in the balance, unanswered. Sala! What cheek. Who are you to ignore me? I consider canceling it. Maybe you'll assume it was a mistake. Maybe you hadn't seen it at all. I wasn't expecting you to accept my request so soon, Kareem. I was prepared to wait days, even months, for you to respond. Still, I can't help but feel slighted.

I stare at your profile. You look the same, only now your beard is marbled, your thick hair snowy. Your eyebrows are the swirled colors of a wolf's coat. I look for your location, but your profile is limited. Only one clue remains, a photograph of the London Eye, dated three years ago. There's no caption, just the stunning pink-streaked sky above a modern glass structure. You must be married. You must have a life of your own. Still, a part of me hopes that you don't, that one day we'll be standing in front of it together.

"Mom?"

I spin around, slamming the laptop shut. Bijal stands in the doorway in a white T-shirt. His wet hair drips onto his shoulders. He holds up a gold watch, thick, braided. I recognize it at once.

"I found this in Dad's closet," he says, his tone soft. "I thought I might keep it."

"Oh."

"You know, something to remember him by. Unless you want it."

My throat closes. I see the watch on Ashok's wrist. I was there when he bought it. It was at the same shop in Breach Candy, weeks before Bijal's wedding. I remember what he had said: *This is once in a lifetime.*

"You keep it, beta," I say. "Dad would have wanted you to have it."

He nods, turning. Then he stops at the door. "What about Akash?"

I notice the tension in Bijal's jaw when he mentions his name. Before I can say anything, my cell phone chimes.

"Oh," I say, reading his text message aloud. "He's here."

AKASH

My mother doesn't say much during the drive home from the airport. I don't blame her. The answers to any questions she might have—are you making progress in your career, do you have enough money, have you decided to go back to school, are you talking to your brother—are all a resounding no. I don't want to tell her I've been fired from the only job I had, which was a receptionist position at Interscope Records, greeting clients and fielding calls, attending to people with actual careers. I'd taken to drinking during lunch. At first it was negligible, just a splash here and there, a little wine with chow mein, a shot of vodka with salad, a beer with my burger. But soon that wasn't enough. I started filling up a thermos with vodka and sipping from it all day. The buzz helped the long hours slide away. It made my boss's jokes funny. Sometimes I would fall out of my chair laughing at them. Once, I couldn't get up. That was the day I was fired. I wonder if my mother can sense all of this—and more.

"Akash," she says. She assesses me with a sharp glance, and my shoulders tense. Maybe she *does* know, about Jacob, the job. Everything. Streetlamps strobe her face.

"You're not wearing your seat belt."

When we turn onto my old street, I see our house at the very end. The mailbox is made of white brick. The windows are bathed in golden light. The columns and circular driveway are a self-conscious display of wealth. Inside, the surfaces are slick and polished, the staircase sweeping up in a curve. My parents did not furnish the house out of necessity, like most Indians, but with a deliberate sense of style. Every piece of furniture, every painting or vase, is meant to elicit awe. I remember when my father had first built the house and invited all the other Indian families in town to marvel at it, to run their fingers over banisters, flick their eyes over walls, oblivious of the secrets that lay within.

As we pull up to the driveway, I'm reminded of all the times Bijal and I used to play together in the neighborhood. Ours was the first house that was built on this street. During evenings after school, Bijal and I would explore the construction sites of other homes, wandering into unfinished basements reeking of wet dirt. We chased each other between plywood slats. We ran up stairways covered in wood shavings and dust. Through windowless frames, we watched the sun set, rose gold turned liquid spilling over our skin. Then our mother would call out to us and we'd run home, anticipating her fury, our faces sweaty, our legs caked with mud.

"Nakamo chokro!" she would say, a rolling pin secured in her hand. She called it the velan. We called it the Lightsaber. Sometimes she chased us around with it and Bijal and I would laugh.

"Uh-oh," Bijal once said, when we'd been caught driving my father's car without a permit. "Mom's got the Lightsaber!"

We'd dash upstairs, my mother shouting at us from below.

"Don't you laugh!"

This was when Bijal and I were more than brothers, when we were friends, before the world turned its lens on us, splitting us apart. Soon came his growth spurt and athleticism and acceptance to Troy, the same prestigious private school you would later attend. Bijal passed the entrance exam on the first try. After three failed attempts, I finally gave up. I watched from a distance as his closet swelled with bright green blazers, gold emblems stitched to their sleeves.

It was clear Bijal got all the best bits, and maybe that's why I resented him, the way my mother waited on him hand and foot. The way she addressed him always as "Bij," an abbreviation my own name would not accommodate. The way, after I dropped out of college junior year and my parents had to pick me up from the dorms, she said, very softly, "Maybe we shouldn't have had a second child." I hated Bijal for being everything I was not, everything beyond my reach, for living effortlessly in a world designed specifically for him, but mostly, I hated him *because* I hated him. Because hate is a self-inflicted wound.

The last time I saw Bijal, after our father's funeral, he'd said it was my fault that our father was dead, that he had died worrying about me, and that maybe, if I had been a better son, none of this would have happened. I could have struck him, pummeled him to the ground. I could have told him to get lost and never speak to me again. Instead, I cried, our dead father's picture hanging on the wall behind our heads, and I asked Bijal: *How? How do I do it? Tell me.*

Tell me how to be like you.

My mother pulls up to the house and I see Bijal's silver Porsche parked on the side. The garage door rises with a whine. My father's licorice S-Class Mercedes-Benz has been sold. My mother's pearl Lexus will soon follow. Two days ago, Bijal sent my mother and me an email indicating that he had found a buyer.

He said other things, too, that we would have to meet with my father's accountant and close his accounts at the bank. My father had listed Bijal as the executor of his will; it would have been laughable for him to put his trust in me.

Within moments, we pull into the garage, and every new piece of me is plucked away, like pearls on a string: Jacob, Los Angeles, music, Jaden. I'm home. Old tricycles hang from the ceiling. Bijal's skateboards are lined up against a wall. My guitar, a gift my father had bought me on my sixteenth birthday—in spite of my mother's protests—lies on a workbench, coated in dust. My mother switches off the engine. She opens the door.

"We're here."

Inside, she watches as I slide off my shoes, place my bags in a corner, hang my winter jacket on a nearby hook. She's aged since my father's death—small lines crease her skin—but she's still beautiful. Her hair is cut in a stylish bob. She wears a cashmere shawl. The pale complexion my father once fell in love with has gone pink in certain spots, like rose syrup swirled into milk. We stare silently at each other. Then my mother says what I know she has been meaning to say ever since I arrived.

"I smell alcohol on your breath."

RENU

They say your firstborn is like your first love; you can never let them go. It's not that I don't love Akash. It's not that I don't wake up in the middle of the night worrying about him. It's not that I don't ask myself, every day (especially when something goes wrong), what I might have done differently. Maybe if I had paid more attention. Maybe if I had been more affectionate. Maybe if I hadn't compared his every movement to Bijal's. Despite what Akash might think, I don't love Bijal more than I love him. Bijal was easy to raise. It's only natural that loving him would be easy, too. These are the lies I tell myself each night.

"I smell alcohol on your breath," I tell Akash, standing in the mudroom while he hangs his coat. He looks tired; dark rings circle his eyes. His thick black hair is tousled, the way it once looked when he and Bijal used to wrestle on the floor. The drink exhales from his pores.

"You said you had stopped."

"I just had a glass of wine."

"Jaja haave. Don't lie."

The word "lie" pierces his placid expression, causing it to fold. I regret my tone. Haven't I lied before, Kareem?

Upstairs, alone in my room, I listen to his movements below, remembering all the times I've spoken to him this way, an uncontrollable rage spreading through me, cooling like molten rock. The only other person to make me feel such rage was you.

I crouch down on the floor, slip my hand beneath the bed. The safe is where I last left it. The metal dial gleams. I still remember the code, even after all these years. A date: 09/14/73. The day your hand reached for mine on the train. I can hear the liquid rush of the wind, the screech of the wheels. I feel the heel of your palm pressed tightly against mine. I open the lock and the cache of letters rises up. It's been years since I last read our letters, but each one is like a song I'll never forget. An envelope the color of a Tiffany's bag is among them. I'm not sure how it got there. I pinch it between my fingers and flip it over, discovering my name. It's written in Ashok's hand. A birthday card from years ago. I put it back. The guilt wraps around me like a stranger's hand—squeezing. I push the safe back under the bed.

AKASH

Bijal is sitting at the marble island when I enter the kitchen. He faces the black windows, sipping a beer. I drop my backpack on the floor. He turns lazily, barely registering the soft thud.

"Hey."

My father always said children are like agony and ecstasy, disappointment and pride. It was evident—to all of us—which one I was.

"Hi."

He doesn't move toward me, doesn't rise to give me a hug. He feigns interest in a crumb instead, sweeping it away. I know from the look of relief on his face that the crumb has bothered him for some time.

"Where's Mom . . ."

His tone does not carry with it the lilt of a question, but the stab of accusation, as if I have done something with her.

"She went for a shower. When did you get in?"

He doesn't answer. Instead, he turns back to the window as if there's something to see in the gathering dark. A deer. A fox. Our father's spirit. I can hear the gentle rush of water through the pipes. A pot of lamb keema rests on the stove. The kitchen smells like my childhood: ginger and cloves. I open the fridge.

"Any more beer?"

Bijal looks at me the same way he had that night, four years earlier, after I'd called him from the police station and asked him to bail me out.

I need you to come pick me up.

From where?

I was pulled over.

Where are you, Akash?

They gave me a Breathalyzer.

Jesus Christ, he'd said, and later: *It's my wedding night.*

He had arrived in his tuxedo pants and a half-buttoned shirt, his hair ruffled, eyes red. He paid the fine and ordered a taxi to take us back to the hotel. He didn't talk to me the whole way back, until we had spilled out of the cab and burst through the lobby doors and ducked behind a potted plant on our way to my room, fearful that someone would see us.

What the hell? he'd said. *What were you thinking getting behind the wheel?*

I was hungry.

You could have ordered a pizza.

I wanted Taco Bell.

A laugh burst from my lips; I was still drunk. Bijal was not amused.

You ruined the whole weekend, Akash. You embarrassed Mom and Dad. What the hell was that speech?

What speech?

His eyes grew wide.

Oh my god, Akash. You don't remember? You don't remember what you did?

Panic is an insidious thing: its bite is quick, but its venom is slow. My brother used to call me Osh, as in, "OshKosh B'gosh." I hated it up until the moment he stopped. It's funny how a thing like that can tell you everything you need to know. In the elevator, with Bijal by my side, I tried to piece together the night: the first drink and the second drink and the third drink and the fourth. I remembered the cocktail hour where I'd avoided my mother's gaze. I remembered the cubes of chili paneer coated in brown sauce. I remembered the best man announcing my speech. I remembered rising to make it, my voice slurring, eyes rolling in the back of my head. Then I stopped remembering. The next thing I knew, I was being asked to step out of my car.

I'm sorry, I said, tears leaking from my eyes. *Bijal, I'm sorry.*

The elevator chimed open. I stepped out alone. He looked at me just as the doors slid shut.

It's a little late for that.

I drop the need for a drink the way you drop a penny on the floor: the loss stings mildly, but you don't want anyone to know.

My mother comes into the kitchen, hair wet. She toasts some naan over the stove. The naan blackens on one side.

"Akash," she says. "Warm up the keema. Bijal, you can set the table."

We do as we're told, working silently while steering clear of each other. If my mother notices this, she doesn't complain. She tells us the puja has been scheduled for the following week, and that her flight has been booked. She says it's the right move to make, that all her family—her brother, Jagdish Mama, her cousin Kalpna Masi, her nieces and nephews and grandnephews, too—are in London, and besides, she reminds us, it was our father who brought her here. She never wanted to live in America. We nod in silence, not mentioning the obvious: that her family lives here, even if we don't act like it.

My mother runs down the guest list while mixing diced onions into yogurt for raita. My father's colleagues. Nurses at the hospital. Chaya Aunty and Bhupendra Uncle and Vinay Uncle and Asha Aunty. A few younger couples my parents have met in recent years, whose kids are in high school.

"What about Parth?" Bijal asks.

Your name is like a sharp pin through my chest. I look up from the table, steadying my hands.

"He won't be there."

Why? I want to ask but don't. I can't bring myself to say your name. Part of me is relieved, and yet part of me wishes you were here. That I could see you one last time. Tell you how sorry I am. That not a day goes by when I don't regret what I did.

I watch as Bijal sets out two hot plates on the breakfast table and places the sizzling pot of lamb keema on top of one. I stare at the glistening, browned meat. My stomach groans. My mother brings the naan to the table and we wait for her to drop it on the hot plate before sitting down. I stare at the empty chair at the head of the table. We all do.

"Soon, it will be one year," she says.

RENU

I wake up to a mass email from Taylor. She's selected the book for our next meeting. Her text is large and pink. She uses excessive exclamation points and all capital letters, as if she's screaming at us. The book, which she explains is inspired by me, is called *A Fine Balance*. It takes place in India. It's an Oprah's Book Club selection.

WE ALL LOVE OUR OPRAH!!! AM I RIGHT, LADIES? ☺

Our Oprah. What would a Black woman think of this? I suppose it doesn't matter, since Taylor has not bothered to include any Black women in the club. Perhaps their perspective is one Taylor is not interested in, or maybe she's simply afraid. Maybe a Black woman would balk at the assumption that a white woman could pick a book in her honor, especially when the book has nothing to do with her life. What does *A Fine Balance*—a book about poverty and corruption in India—have to do with me? I have never lived in India. I have no interest in poverty. White people, on the other hand, love it—especially when it's abroad. They love backpacking through jungles and hugging strange babies, documenting the evidence for everyone to see. I wouldn't dare touch those babies. Imagine the smell.

Taylor's email has been met with equal enthusiasm. Everyone can't wait to read the book! One woman says it's the perfect thing to prepare for her trip to Sri Lanka. Perhaps to people like them, brown is brown, no matter what part of the world you are in.

I bring my iPad into the kitchen. The cold marble gleams. It's early, pale light beginning to warm the edges of the yard. Akash and Bijal are still asleep. Their presence has created tension in the house. When they were kids, I could simply tell them, "Be nice!" and they would. Now, I don't know what to say. I compose an email to Taylor and the others, sharing my excitement in the book, even though I probably won't read it. I put down my iPad, pick it back up. I'm tempted to check Facebook to see if you have accepted my request. I don't. Instead, I take my cup of tea and sit in the breakfast nook overlooking the backyard and think about our letters, every last one of them. I think about the letter I never sent you, Kareem. The one I wish I had. Maybe if you had read it, maybe then.

AKASH

It was Bijal's idea to go out for dinner. It's our third night, and the puja is two days away. He wanted to give our mother a break. All day she's rolled dough for puris and fried corn fritters in oil, stewed red and green chutneys from tamarind and mint. I sit in the backseat of her Lexus, on thick, perforated leather, staring out the windows while Bijal drives. We don't speak. My mother is on her cell phone again. Her eyes have a distracted look to them. I wonder if it's me, if my presence in this house is too much for her. Outside, lit houses flick by like fireflies. At one point, all I can hear is the rapid ticking of the turn signal as Bijal swerves onto a road, and then, the sound of his voice.

"Look at this."

The car rolls to a stop. We glance out the window. Bijal points to a bar.

"That's new," he says.

The bar has tiny bulbs that spill puddles of blue light. I wonder if they see it, the bright rainbow flag. My mother pushes her glasses up the bridge of her nose.

"Rawhide," she says, slowly. "What a name."

Just then a pair of men emerge from the bar in a sweaty haze. One of them, a thin white man with frosted blond tips, swings his arms above his head. His companion, bearded and dark, slaps his rear. I can sense my mother watching them. I sink lower in my seat.

"Oh," Bijal says, accelerating through the light. "It's a gay bar."

I try to think of something to say, something to lighten the mood, but even this would seem like an admission. My mother peers through the window to catch a glimpse of Rawhide as it rushes by. She clicks off her phone.

"Do you know . . ." she starts vaguely. "Kavita Aunty and Vinod Uncle's daughter is gay? She has a partner."

The fabric of my sweater clings to my back.

"I think I knew that," Bijal says, turning onto an opposite road. "I mean, she looks it."

"Vinod Uncle doesn't seem to mind," my mother continues. "He goes everywhere, tells everyone, but Kavita Aunty doesn't leave the house. She stopped going to weddings. She doesn't want to be seen—not that I blame her."

Bijal nods silently.

"It's hard, you know," my mother says, softly. "What us parents have to go through."

A memory falls into my lap at dinner. It was 1993. We were in London, visiting my mother's brother, Jagdish Mama. I was eight. Bijal was twelve. We stayed in a semidetached house with narrow, damp rooms. Bijal had just discovered jungle music, and he wouldn't stop playing it. The spastic beats bounced relentlessly off the walls. He would stomp around the house and slap his chest like an ape, shouting the words, "Jungle is massive!" I don't think he even knew what that meant. He did it anyway, pushing me against a wall.

"Hey, Osh! Jungle is massive!"

When I didn't say anything back, he pinched my ear.

"Do you agree?" he said. "Do you agree that jungle is massive?"

"I agree that you're a massive douche."

"Shut up, Osh."

He was riding high because he'd just had his ear pierced with our cousin Nikesh, and my mother wasn't speaking to him, which meant that he was just as cool as the rest of our British cousins, whose mothers weren't speaking to them either. It was the only time in my life I can remember Bijal making her upset. He didn't have to try very hard on that trip. My mother was out of sorts, snapping at us for no reason, lapsing into sullen moods. Once, I'd heard her whispering with my father in the garden, asking him if we could move back to London, abandon the practice in Illinois. She said Bijal and I would get a better education here, and there was family nearby. When my father gently refused, reminding her that his practice was the reason we could enjoy such a comfortable life, that doctors in London were not the same as doctors in Illinois, she stormed back into the house and slammed the door.

Later, when my father took Bijal to play golf and Jagdish Mama was at work and his wife was in the kitchen with my mother, I wandered upstairs to my parents' room. I slipped through the door and sat on their quilted bed. I noticed my mother's makeup pouch, partially unzipped, revealing a set of cosmetics inside. I inhaled their powdery scent, admired the gleam of their casings: a compact made of black lacquer, twin lipsticks sheathed in gold. I poured the contents over the bed and swam my hands through them. Something was jutting out of the pouch, the edge of a photograph. I stared at it. It was a picture of my mother standing next to a man I did not know. At first glance, it looked like any of the other photographs displayed around the house, stone-faced Indians in black and white, all the relatives I had never met, whose names I couldn't remember. Only my mother wasn't scowling; she was smiling, her smile a beam of sun on my face. I had never seen her that way. I reached for it when the door opened. My mother walked into the room.

"What are you doing?"

I turned, my hands trembling.

She stared at the makeup scattered over her bed. "What is this? What are you doing?" She lunged forward, grabbing my wrist. The lipstick dropped to the floor. Her face blazed red. "What is wrong with you, Akash? Are you a girl? Do you think you're a girl?" She moved her fingers to my shoulders, gripping them like claws. "Look at me, Akash! Look at me."

But I couldn't look.

"Don't you ever go through my things again, do you understand?" she shouted, shaking me. "You're a boy. What would Nikesh say if he saw you playing with girl's things, huh? What would Micky say? What about Rakesh?"

I didn't answer her. My mother listed off the rest of my male cousins, then pushed me back onto the bed. It was the first time she had ever been violent with me.

"I don't want a son like this, Akash," she said, her eyes bulging. "Do you hear me? This is not how we are."

Now, I sit at a booth across from Bijal and my mother. A menu is slapped onto the table. Water is poured into my glass. A basket of warm bread is set down alongside ivory slabs of butter. My mother wraps her cashmere shawl loosely around her shoulders.

"Would you like a few moments to look over the menu?" the waitress asks.

Bijal nods. "That would be great."

I'm still thinking about that bar, about Rawhide, when a young couple sits down at the booth next to ours, their children in tow. The father leans over to wipe something off his daughter's face. My mother smiles.

"Look at that," she says. "Don't you want that, Bijal?"

"Did you see the size of that booger?" He laughs.

My mother clucks her tongue. "I don't want to be an old grandmother."

"I hate to break it to you, Mom, but a car seat doesn't exactly fit in the Porsche. When we're ready for a minivan, you'll get your grandkids."

My mother folds her arms in mock exasperation. It's an old routine. I need a drink. I slugged a bit of vodka in my room earlier tonight, rinsing my mouth out with Scope, but now the buzz has gone. The waitress returns.

"Can I interest any of you in a drink?"

Bijal orders a beer, my mother a Diet Coke. Everyone turns to me.

"I'll have a rum and Coke."

My mother glances at Bijal, her lips thinning. The waitress smiles. "Great! I'll be right back."

"Do you really think you should be drinking?" Bijal says, when the waitress places our drinks on the table. He raises his brow. I pick up my glass.

"I'm drinking for Dad," I say.

Then I gulp it all down.

RENU

According to Ashok, the TV shows I watched were a joke, but at times they were my only hope. I reimagined myself as these women, with their smoldering tongues. I suppose I'm not so different from them after all, am I? Because to be an American woman is to be full of desire. To pluck fruit from forbidden trees and scream when they bear worms. In America, love is a fire. It scorches and consumes.

"I need passion!" the white women on TV like to say. "I need fire!"

Then they cry when they get burned.

In this week's episode of *Deserted Hearts,* Celeste has taken a lover.

"I've taken a lover," she announces, smoking a cigarette. "He's my gardener."

I don't understand these American women and their obsession with gardeners. Why not a lawyer instead? If Ashok were here, I know what he would say.

"Look at these women—sleeping with gardeners. Meanwhile the garden is dying of neglect."

Did my husband die of neglect?

On TV, Celeste explains to her therapist that her plastic surgeon husband wants to give her enormous breasts. She scoffs bitterly.

"He just loves those damn things."

The operation would require a special bra, and the bra is hideous, so Celeste has taken a lover—Juan—who adores her small breasts.

"Juan just gets me—you know?"

"Really?" I say, reaching for the remote. "A gardener?"

I switch it off. Evening settles around me like a warm blanket. Outside, the sky is blue gold. Branches scrape the windows like kittens' claws. I worry about the boys, if they're getting along, and what will happen to them when I leave, when the glue that once bound them no longer sticks. I don't know what to say to Akash anymore. He's changed, no longer the boy I once held before school.

"The boys will make fun of me," he'd whimpered.

"So?" I'd snapped. "Make fun of them back. Who are *they,* anyway? To make fun of you."

Later that afternoon, he came home with a swollen lip.

"What did you say to them?" I'd asked. "Akash!" I grabbed him by the shoulders. "What did you say?"

He whispered the words. "I told them what you always say— that their mothers are whores."

"I never said that!"

I had said it once, but I didn't think he'd overheard. It had happened during an argument with Ashok. He was praising our neighbor, Heather, who was mowing the lawn while her husband sipped a beer.

"Look at this Heather," Ashok had said. "Some husbands have all the luck."

"Heather is divorced!" I'd shouted. "That's her second husband. Is that what you want? Some lawn-mowing American whore?"

Ashok said I was a hard woman; I don't think he meant it as a compliment. He said I needed to be softer, especially with Akash.

"You're too hard on him," he would say.

"Because you are too soft!"

But it wasn't that simple. I knew that then. I feel bad for shutting him out—for a lot of things. Still, what can I do? I've given up trying to figure it out. When Akash dropped out of college and told Ashok and me he wanted to work in the music industry, I'd lost my head.

"What?" I'd said, heaving the question like a sword. "You think you're Michael Jackson? You're going to be world famous? Is that why Dad goes to work every day, so you can sing songs?"

"I don't want to sing songs. I want to *write* them."

"For whom? Taro baap?"

"Just forget it."

"Oh, now you want me to forget! Hu tari ma chu, Akash. I'll never forget."

He went up to his room and didn't come out until the next evening, at which point he announced that he was moving to LA. By then I was exhausted, depleted of my will to fight. Maybe I gave up too soon.

AKASH

Over the next couple of days, I wake to an unfamiliar gray light in my room, half expecting Jacob to be lying next to me, his freckled back inches from my face. He calls twice. I don't answer. The third time, I'm with my mother in the kitchen, watching her chop onions and tomatoes for a Spanish omelet. I place the phone on mute.

"Who was that?" she asks.

"A friend."

She doesn't say anything, chopping faster, juices flinging from her knife. I could say it then: *I'm gay, Mom. I have a boyfriend. Isn't it obvious?* Sometimes the words form in my mind without warning. *I'm gay. I'm gay. I'm gay.* It makes me laugh. *Haven't you figured it out?* But then the memories surface, like insects scattering from cracks. That bedroom in London, my mother's viselike grip. *This is not how we are.* My mouth clamps shut.

Finally, Jacob sends a text.

Akash, I've been trying to reach you. I hope you're okay. Please call me.

I still can't bring myself to respond. The life I left behind—the unpaid bills, the collections notices, Jacob's calls—everything is trapped like ice on a window: visible, but unable to harm. I check my account balance and laugh: $60.58. A single expense—a monthly gym fee, an automated payment, a trip to the store—

could wipe me out. Erased with a single swipe. Nothing, I once told myself, slapping my face. You are nothing.

But here, in this place suspended in time with its open fields and milky sky, those worries fade like colors in the wash. The sounds below, of Bijal blending a smoothie with celery and kale, of my mother chatting on the phone, of Chaya Aunty ringing the doorbell to drop off a set of burners for the puja, of the freight trains that howl in the night, lull me into a comfortable rhythm. Sleep, rise, eat, pack.

The time is characterized by activity and inertia, bouts of industry followed by hours of nothing. We have two weeks to pack up our things and ship them off to charity or toss them in the trash. A fortnight is nothing and everything. Laboring but quick.

Boxes fill with things we never used: dumbbells and notebooks, cookware and tapes. We move slowly, unearthing objects filmed with dust. Gift cards, certificates, old CDs. It's under the thick cushion of a suede couch in the basement, in the sleeve of an old nylon case, that I find it: *The Blueprint*. I remember that night you and I listened to it in my car. "All I Need," and "Song Cry," and "Girls, Girls, Girls." I remember your face, Parth, the way the light had danced across it like the golden ripples on a pond. The memory is overwhelming. I drop the CD from my hands.

In the kitchen that Friday afternoon, my mother approaches Bijal and me with a box full of photographs. We've managed to stay out of each other's way, occupying different floors of the house, but my mother corners us near the stove, pushing a shoebox across the island.

"I found this downstairs."

She pulls out a photograph of Bijal and me at Disney World. We're wearing matching tank tops with shorts. Bijal's arm is draped around my neck. Our parents look stunned, as if the photographer has just delivered some very confusing news. But it's the expression on my face that catches all of our eyes: lips curled, tears streaking my face. Bijal looks at me and says nothing. My mother smiles fondly. I take the picture from her hands.

"Pretty much sums up my childhood."

"Don't say that, Akash. You had a very nice childhood."

"How do *you* know that?"

"What do you mean, *how do I know?*" my mother snaps. "I was there, wasn't I? Look how many nice places we took you."

"Thanks for taking me to Disneyland."

"Disney World," Bijal interjects.

"What?"

"You said Disneyland. They took us to Disney World. It's better."

My mother smiles wistfully. "Oh, I wish we could go back."

"Jessica and I were thinking of having our anniversary there, just for fun," Bijal says.

No one responds. My mother takes the picture from my hands and places it into the box. She closes the lid. We finish a bit of packing in silence, sorting through worn clothes. Then my mother makes lunch—green chili quesadillas—and we eat in the breakfast nook, overlooking the soft green lawn.

"I'll need you boys to go to the Indian store," my mother says, rinsing dishes in the sink. "We need ghee for the puja."

"What Indian store?" Bijal says.

"You don't know? my mother asks, taking his plate and dropping it into the sink. "Vinay Uncle and Asha Aunty have opened a store."

At the mention of your parents' names, I feel a tightness in my throat. I picture them: Vinay Uncle with his reddish-brown hair and bloodshot eyes, Asha Aunty, plump and pleasant. The kitchen fills with steam, fogging the windows. My mother twists off the tap.

"What's wrong?"

"Nothing," I say.

Bijal looks up from his phone. I avert my eyes. My mother walks over to me, dropping a list into my hands.

"Get some mango pickle, too."

RENU

For the first time in days, I have the house to myself. I count down the days till my departure: fourteen. I move about the kitchen, packing the Wedgwood china for Bijal to take home, along with a Vitamix, a cappuccino machine, red wine goblets we never used. I know it is Jessica who has requested these things. Chaya always says men are the head of the household, but women are the neck; they turn the head whichever direction they choose. I have prepared the house not only for Ashok's puja but for Jessica's arrival as well. It's what you do when you have a daughter-in-law. You buy almond milk and Greek yogurt and rosemary body scrub. You put out elegant towels, ones with silk panels. For as long as she's in your house, you never let her see you frown. Otherwise she'll think it's about her. Which it probably is. Because inevitably she'll do something to irritate you. She'll scold your son or go quiet at the dinner table, or complain, in private, about the spiciness of your food. Sometimes she'll challenge you, suggesting you spread less butter on your son's toast, because all his life he's been eating rich food.

I suppose the only good thing about Jessica's arrival is that I haven't thought about you. I don't plan to either. It feels like an achievement, that I can move through this house without you moving through me. I walk into the kitchen and pry Ashok's portrait from the wall. We'll need it for the puja, placing it behind a small altar, stringing a garland around his face. His kind eyes watch me as I set him on the floor and at an angle against the living room wall. I remember the first time we were alone, in the bright sitting room of my brother's flat in Croydon, minutes from where his parents lived. He had been born in Nakuru, Kenya, and attended medical school in Mumbai, did his training in Michigan before moving to Illinois. He knew Jagdish from university in South Bank, where they first met. He was striking in his rayon shirt, his longish dark hair split down the middle, his bright eyes and butterscotch skin. When I sat down across from him, he arched his brow.

"What?" I said. He looked around, folding his arms. "What is it?"

"This must be a mistake."

"Excuse me?"

"I don't believe you are the woman I am supposed to meet."

"Are you mad?" I said, my cheeks burning. "I am her. Idiot."

He flinched, momentarily stunned. Then he smiled. "I'm only kidding, Renu. I meant to say that you are too beautiful, more beautiful than you were described. But now I know something else, too."

"What?"

"That you are wild."

"Ey!" I said, glowering. "You dare speak to me this way? What shame!" I covered myself with my shawl. "You think because you are an American you can talk any which way?"

"I think, because I am an American, I can get my way." He grinned, flicking a piece of lint from his shirt. "But thank you for scolding me. Now I have made up my mind."

"Oh, good," I said, rising. "Then I won't be seeing you again."

"Ah-ah," Ashok said, catching the end of my shawl. He gave it a slight tug.

"What is it now?"

"You have not really seen me to be concerned about seeing

me again," he said. "You have not even looked. One day, Renu, you will see all that I am."

I scoffed.

"Don't count on it."

I adjust the portrait and get up from my seat and wander up-stairs to make sure the linens have been freshened in Bijal's room. From my perch at the top of the stairs, I glance below, at the square marble tiles, the curved lip of the stairs. The windows flood with bluish-gray light. Liquefied. Outside, rust-colored leaves fall in papery piles. At some point my cell phone chimes. Probably Chaya telling me what last-minute items she's bringing to the puja: dhokla, pakoras, a batch of gulab jamun. I told her not to bring anything at all, but as usual, she's insisted. I smile to myself as I pad down the stairs, making my way across the foyer, into the kitchen, where my cell phone rests on the floating island. A message flashes across the screen. I pick it up. The words blur, then sharpen, taking shape in my mind. I swipe my finger. The screen enlarges. The first thing I see is your name.

AKASH

We've managed to drive ten minutes in silence. Bijal keeps his eyes fixed ahead. After his wedding night, he didn't speak to me for months. It was my father who came to my room the next morning with two Advil and a bottle of water, some food from the farewell brunch. He sat at the edge of my bed. There were tears in his eyes.

"Is this about what happened?" he said, his brown face wrin-kled. "Is this about the letter? About what I told you to do?"

I shook my head.

"Akash, are you sure?"

My chest cracked. I hadn't thought about the letter in years. Not since that night. Not since you disappeared. A sob buckled.

I threw my head in my hands. My father rushed to my side, pulling me close.

"Even parents make mistakes, Akash," he said, rubbing the back of my head.

"You didn't make a mistake," I croaked.

He left shortly after. An hour later, my mother sent a text: *Why, Akash? Why would you drink so much? Why would you ruin this for us, after all we have done?* I didn't respond. I couldn't explain what had happened. She wouldn't have understood it if I could. The only person who would is you.

Five minutes later, I turn on the radio. Another song drenched in auto-tune. Ask me what R&B is and I'll tell you it's love. Sexy, soulful, gut-wrenching love. But now no one wants to make it. No one wants to hear it. So tell me, Parth: Where did the love go?

I turn off the radio. Bijal turns it back on.

"I like that song."

"You would."

"What was that?"

I don't respond. Bijal nods his head to the music, waving his middle finger and index finger in the air like he's holding a cigarette. But there's no cigarette, no smoke. I used to think Bijal was in the midst of an identity crisis: he couldn't decide if he was Will Smith or Carlton Banks. He reeked of wealth and privilege, but he didn't want anyone to know about it—unless he did. Like the time he went to college and told all his Indian friends that our father was a cardiologist who made a million dollars a year. He never told his Black friends that. It wasn't until his wedding—an extravagant affair at The Palmer House Hotel—that Bijal's Black friends knew we had any money at all.

"*Damn*, Bij," said Cameron, Bijal's roommate from college. "I didn't know you had it like that."

My mother, on the contrary, tells everyone everything. I suppose she has to, considering my current station. She's become clever, adept at steering a conversation away from uncomfortable territory. If all else fails, she just talks about Bijal's house.

"Six thousand square feet, can you believe?"

Once, a particularly vicious aunty managed to slip through the cracks.

"But Renu," she said. "What is the point of all that space, when there are no grandkids to fill it?"

My mother smiled, thwarted, but later, she breathed fire.

"That bloody bitch!" she cried, storming the house. "Look at her son. Look at Vikas. Three times he's failed the bar. Does he have a *learning disability* or what?"

We all knew to avoid her when she was in one of these moods. According to my father, my mother was a kitten in public and a dragon at home. All Indian women are. They smile and pander in the presence of others, then go home and burn the house down. I have felt my mother's fire; I have nursed the burns. After parent-teacher conferences, where there was never anything good to report, she would come home and spit flames. *Why can't you study? Why don't you pay attention? What are you doing with your life? Look at your brother—how good he is!*

Back when we were close, Bijal would come to my room and comfort me.

"Don't worry," he would say. "It's just how she is."

But even he knew this was a lie. I suppose it wasn't easy for her to raise a child like me. Sometimes even dragons give birth to runts. It's not the runt that's the problem; it's the task of shielding him from the world.

In a few moments, Bijal parks outside the store, which is plastered with posters for Bollywood films. Inside, a movie plays on the TV above our heads. A woman in a pink Punjabi outfit reads a magazine on her seat. The store is lined with shelves full of powdered spices and a glass case of jalebi, sticky coils that dissolve like sugar on your tongue. My mouth waters.

"Here," Bijal says, thrusting the list into my chest. "Find what we need. I'm gonna look around."

"Look around at what?"

He ignores me. I pick up a basket and select boxes of amchur and garam masala and methi and drop them in one by one. Bijal stares vacantly at a few boxed DVDs, Bollywood films with provocative covers, half-naked women in smiling repose. Once, when my parents and I were watching a Bollywood film at home, Bijal had laughed. It was 1996. He was sixteen.

"What the hell is this?"

"It's Salman Khan," I'd said.

"Who?" Bijal replied. "He looks like a fag."

"Bijal," my mother said. "Be nice."

But he couldn't. "Why's he dancing like that? Look at his hair. Oh my god."

I glanced back at the screen, at the sequined outfits, '70s style hair, the wild, untethered moves—one of the men appeared to be having a seizure. I had always loved Bollywood films, the romanticism and drama, but seeing it through Bijal's eyes, through the lens of America, where everything dripped with effortless cool, I realized I didn't love them anymore.

I twist a plastic bag full of green chilies and take the basket to the counter to check out. The woman at the register smiles. Her lipstick is bright pink. There's a small, hard mole on her cheek.

"You are new to this town?"

"Visiting."

"Ah." She nods. "Visiting Mom and Dad—very good."

I could tell her my father is no longer alive, my mother is leaving the country, that the family we once had will soon be no more. I smile. "Yeah."

Bijal approaches from behind with a DVD of *Khabi Khushi Kabhie Gham*—K3G. "Mom always loved this movie."

"Mom? Or you?"

He suppresses a smile, and suddenly we're kids again, laughing at something in the backseat of our parents' car. The woman slides the DVD through the scanner. I pull out my wallet. Bijal jabs me lightly in my side. I shove him back. It's the most contact we've had since I arrived. The gesture, however small, is a morsel of hope.

"That will be sixty-six dollars and seventy-two cents," the woman says.

Six dollars more than I have in my account. I can feel Bijal shifting behind me. I panic, fumbling through the folds of my wallet.

"All right," I say casually. "Okay. Yes. Sixty-six dollars. Here we are . . ."

A pair of men queue up behind us. I look back at Bijal; he rolls his eyes.

"Here," he says briskly, shoving his card into my hand. "I got it."

"Are you sure?"

"Are you serious right now?"

"Thanks."

He doesn't say anything. It's apparent, by the way he's looking at me, that the moment between us has passed. We walk outside in the direction of our parked car and Bijal throws me the keys.

"You're driving," he says.

We fold ourselves into the car and pull out of the parking lot. The drive home is silent save for the sound of Bijal texting rapidly on his phone. We pass his old school, Troy Academy, with its glass doors and bronzed sculptures, an oblong sports field for soccer and lacrosse. Bijal looks up vaguely, taking it in. I picture him in his forest-green blazer with the sleeves rolled up. I avoid the road that passes my school. I'm not ready to face it. Instead, I make a U-turn and turn onto an opposite street.

"What the hell are you doing?" Bijal says flatly. "You're going the wrong way."

"How would you know? You're never home."

"What's that supposed to mean?"

I don't answer him. I pass the temple we used to visit during Diwali. The pillars and white marble façade look at odds with the rows of identical square homes in the distance. I stare at the space near the entrance, where the graffiti once blared: DIE MUSLIMS. My eyes adjust as the sun dips beneath a cloud and pierces them. Bright spots of color pop in front of my face. I blink them away. The car swerves dangerously close to the curb.

"Watch it," Bijal says.

I jerk the wheel, pulling away from the curb. The sun returns. I press my foot down on the accelerator. In the distance, I can see it, a rectangular building two stories high. The windows shudder like a mirage, shrinking and warping. Grills of parked cars glimmer. The sign rises like a tower: SUPER 8 MOTEL. I imagine you standing there, shooting hoops in the parking lot. You turn and smile, raising your hand. You open your mouth to say something, but it's not your voice that calls out to me. It's Bijal's.

"Akash! Watch out!"

The intersection hurtles toward us just as the image fades. I slam on the brakes. The tires shriek. The seat belt cuts into my neck as I pitch forward, then back against my seat. A cloud of dust settles around us as I look over at Bijal, who's panting heavily, his eyes wild with disbelief.

RENU

The message appears at the top right corner of the screen: NDUGU KAREEM ABBAS HAS ACCEPTED YOUR FRIEND REQUEST. My heart jumps, like an animal slipping from my grasp. But now what? I have yet to learn the implicit rules of Facebook. Should I send you a message? A poke? Maybe I should "like" one of your photographs. Chaya has already liked all of mine. I don't understand this business of "liking." Earlier, I saw a post in which a young woman had shared some tragic news: her mother had died in a car accident. Eight people liked it. One person laughed—though I think this was a mistake. I could message you, Kareem, but I wouldn't know what to say. Not after so many years.

Is it foolish of me, to expect something more? I don't know where you are or to whom you belong, or if you have really thought about me at all. Before he died, Ashok had reconnected with many lost friends from college and beyond. It was nothing new. Is this new to you? The garage whines open as Bijal and Akash return home. Within moments, I hear their footsteps rain across the hall. Bijal pushes past Akash, his lips curled.

"What is it? What happened?"

"Nothing new," Bijal says, ascending the stairs. "Same old bullshit."

"Please don't swear, Bijal."

Akash emerges from the shadows with a sweaty sheen on his face.

"What's wrong, Akash?"

"Nothing."

Bijal tromps up the stairs just as a cell phone rings. I turn to Akash. He struggles to place it on mute.

"Who is that?"

"No one."

"What do you mean, no one?" I snap. "All the time it is no one. Is it a ghost calling you?"

He winces as if I have struck him, and my anger subsides. I see him as a child, inky black eyes, a thick, dark fringe, his frail body shaking in my grip. *What are you doing, Akash?* I can't remember where we were, or what I had said. I only remember the rage.

"Akash, I—"

He darts into the hall before I can finish what I was going to say to him, which is probably for the best; the words had evaporated just as soon as they were formed. I walk back into Ashok's office and open the laptop. Before I can even think, my fingers fly over the keys.

Kareem! It's you! How are you?

I don't know what else to say. I've never done this before. Though I probably shouldn't, I grab the mouse anyway, close my eyes, and click send.

AKASH

I wake to the sound of voices. My mother and Bijal are in the kitchen, talking about the guest list for the puja. Bijal is complaining that we've invited too many uncles he doesn't like. Corny uncle and drunk uncle and the uncle who spits when he talks. My mother is speaking to him in a pacifying tone—as she always does.

I get up and splash cold water on my face, dabbing the swollen skin under my eyes. My cell phone chimes. A FaceTime call from Jaden. I smile and slide my finger across the screen, enlarging his face. He stands in front of a wall of blue light, his thick lips spreading, revealing perfectly square teeth.

"Whoa," he says. "You look like shit."

"I just woke up."

"I haven't even slept."

"Then why do *you* look like that and *I* look like this?"

He grins. "You're still cute though." He walks back toward an API console, full of switches and dials, blinking lights, and drops onto a swivel chair. "Listen to this."

He plays the track he had played for me that night at the

studio, only this time there's a layer of synth I had never heard before, and the bass is stronger, more booming, pounding like a heart. "Well?"

"I love it."

"Yeah?"

"Yeah, but only if I can write on it."

"I've been telling you to do it. What else you got going on over there?"

"You don't wanna know."

"It's missing something though," Jaden says, worrying his brow. "I don't know what yet."

"Send me the track when it's done."

"You got it." He sinks back in his seat, smiling at me.

"What?"

He shrugs. "Nothing."

Sometimes I wonder if Jaden and I were meant to be together. It's not just about music. We both know what it's like to be part of a world and simultaneously on the outside of it, looking in. We've had intense conversations that last until the pink traces of dawn. I've confided in Jaden about my parents' circle of Indian friends, even people my own age, the comments I've heard, the things people have said, the idea that being Black in America was something to fear. *Sala karia,* an uncle once said, when a Black person happened to cut him off in traffic. Had the person been white, he would have just honked his horn. Jaden understands all of it, even though he doesn't have to.

Once, during a break at the studio, we watched a video of three Black people fighting in the street on WorldStarHipHop .com. Jaden shook his head.

"We need to do better," he said, and in the same breath, "They shouldn't even be posting this shit."

I know what that meant. I know what it's like to be labeled. Once, I was in line at the grocery store when the customer in front of me, an Indian immigrant, was arguing with the cashier; he thought he was being cheated. The sight of him angered me, but I didn't know why. His jacket stunk of garlic. His hair was windblown. His accent was incomprehensible. His clothes—dark slacks, a horrible cardigan, bright gym shoes—had been put together without thought or style. It was the outfit of someone who was trying to survive. In America, there are two kinds of Indians: the ones who survive and the ones who thrive.

"Excuse me," the cashier had said, looking helplessly in my direction. "Do you know what he's saying?"

I shrank under her gaze, forcing my chin up.

"No," I said, briskly. "I don't know him at all."

Now, Jaden turns the music down and stares intently.

"There's a new artist coming up; her name is Kaya. She's kind of nineties R and B with a contemporary twist. Not exactly a balladeer, but she sounds great over mids. She just signed with RCA. She put out a mixtape last year and—"

"I heard it."

"What did you think?"

"It was decent," I say, sitting back on my bed. "But kind of all over the place. The last three songs sounded like they were from different projects, and it wasn't mixed very well."

"Okay, *Rolling Stone*."

"Shut up."

"Anyway," Jaden says, pausing to unscrew the cap off a bottle of water, sucking it all down. "They just extended submissions for her album. It's called *The Train*? Or *The Rain*? I don't know. They're looking for something different. She wants a new sound."

"What kind of sound?"

"They said they'll know it when they hear it."

"Oh, lord."

"Akash, be serious," Jaden says. "Do you want this or not?"

"I want it."

"Good." Jaden gets up from his seat and I see the dim lights and the speakers and the condenser mic through the wall of glass behind him, and for the first time I miss LA, miss the studio, the listening parties, the piece of me I left behind. "We gotta get to work then," Jaden says. "Look out for my email. I'll send you the track when it's done. They're looking for new voices, Akash." His eyes harden. "This could be something."

He salutes me in the way he always does, and then he's gone.

Downstairs in the kitchen, my mother stands at the stove.

"I'm making cheese toast."

She slathers butter onto bread. I take a seat at the nook. I haven't had my mother's cheese toast—a riff on an American grilled cheese with onions and green chilies and cilantro—in years. I look out the windows at the dull gray sky.

"Where's Bijal?"

"He went for a run."

"Since when does Bijal run?"

"He does a lot of things differently now."

She looks tired, the color leached from her face. She twists a napkin in her hands. I tell myself it's just the puja. She always gets this way before a party, as if she's anticipating all the things that could go wrong, the comments people will make if anything does. *The rice is overcooked. The potatoes are bland. No chutney for the samosas? Is she mad?* It's nothing my mother hasn't done a hundred times herself. They say people in glass houses shouldn't throw stones. My mother lived in a house made of cement. Everything was perfect. Nothing was amiss. Until my father died.

I finish my cheese toast and place my dish in the sink and wonder what to do. I'm desperate for a drink.

"Is there anything you need from the store?" I ask, hoping for an excuse to get out.

"The store?"

"For the party. Beer? Wine? I'm assuming people will want a drink at some point."

My mother nods, then shakes her head. "We don't need anything."

"What about dessert? Cookies? A cake?"

"I've made barfi."

"God, Mom. BARF-ee?"

"Don't say that, Akash." She frowns. "It's our food."

"It's disgusting."

"I don't like that. Don't say food is disgusting. There are people in this world who don't—"

"Yeah, yeah. Won't there be kids at this thing? C'mon, Mom. Don't make them eat barf-ee."

"Fine." She folds her arms. "Pick up some ice cream, and get some plastic cups, too. I don't want them breaking my glasses."

I give her a thumbs-up, grabbing the car keys from the counter. I can feel her eyes on me when I walk off.

The bar is surprisingly busy for a weekday afternoon. A pair of older women drink white wine at a booth. Two men in workman's clothes drink beers down the bar. A cluster of college-aged girls eat nachos and laugh hysterically over something on someone's phone. I like bars, the sense of community they evoke. I like it when time spreads freely like spilled water on the floor, when faces get redder, and eyes turn to pools. The bartender pours me my second glass of wine. I'm counting. *Two drinks,* my father had once said gently. *Just limit yourself to two, Akash. Why do you need more?*

My blood warming, my ears buzzing, I check my phone to see if Jacob has texted. It's been four days now. I open Grindr and scroll through the profiles. Most of the men are younger, nineteen or so, with smooth pale torsos and cheaply dyed hair. Some are older. One is a nerdy-looking Asian guy, a graduate student. A few of the profiles are blank, a single green dot, bright as a jewel, indicating their presence. A message flashes across my screen. *Hey.* The user is named "R." That's it. No corresponding picture. No witty introduction. One simple letter, as if he couldn't be bothered to finish. I click off. I don't know why I ever joined in the first place. It's merely part of a rotation, a cycle with no end, something I check in with every few hours: Facebook, Instagram, Twitter, Grindr. Something happens on the TV screen above my head, a touchdown or a winning goal, I'm not bothered to know which, and the room erupts in cheers. I down the wine in a single gulp, ask the bartender for one more. Three drinks. I'll cap it at three. I can already feel the comforting glaze as I take a sip. A memory lands as light as a feather, brushing my eyes. I hear the sounds. The laughter. The screams. The music. I feel the warm air on my skin, see the stars blinking above. I see you, too, Parth, my face reflected in your eyes.

RENU

It's the morning of the puja. I stand in a pink sari Ashok had picked out for me. The clerk had spun yard after yard of fabric, throwing it at my feet. A wash of embroidery. A storm of silk. I had gained weight recently, and the candy pink assaulted my eyes.

"I look like a gumball."

"Nonsense," Ashok said. "You look wonderful."

"I feel like Pepto Bismol."

"You cure all my stomachaches."

"Must you be this way, Ashok? I'm being serious."

I sucked in the slab of my gut, frowning. The store clerk approached.

"Oh, no. This is not for you."

"Arre hat jao!" Ashok said, raising his hand. "Who asked you?"

The store clerk retreated. Ashok dropped his hand. I looked at him and smiled.

Downstairs, I arrange napkins and cutlery and candles, spray fragrance in each of the rooms. It's a gray, overcast day, with clumps of steel clouds. The wooded backyard rustles in the wind. I can hear Bijal's movements upstairs. I look at my watch. Jessica's train should arrive any moment. I've prepared my script, all the compliments I'll lavish her with.

"Oh, I love your hair," I'd once said when she last visited, pointing to her pixie cut. "You look like Ellen DeGeneres."

"Mom," Bijal whispered harshly.

"What? People love Ellen."

"Actually, I was going for Charlize Theron," Jessica said, smoothing her hair with the palm of her hand. She cut her eyes at Bijal.

"Your hair looks great, babe," he said, planting a kiss.

She looked like a boy. Later that night, I'd overheard Jessica's admonishments through the floorboards above, the pleading tone of her voice. I couldn't make out what they were saying, but I knew it was about me. The next morning, Jessica suddenly remembered some last-minute computer work she had to do for her job. They would have to skip lunch and drive back. I'd spent all morning grinding peanuts and desiccated coconut for chutney to be served alongside paper-thin dosas. I threw everything in the trash.

Now, I imagine what will happen when she arrives, the way

she'll fill up this space with her sullen looks, her quiet demands, the way Bijal will bend to her, like a reed in the wind. I'm ashamed to admit that in my darkest hours I've imagined him snapping— floating back to me. It's because of Jessica that I declined Bijal's offer to move in with them. I have presided over this house, sinking my teeth into it like a shark. Everything is by my design. Jars of spices are sorted and labeled in clean script. Containers brimming with lentils sit tightly in rows. Items in the freezer are dated with a tiny hand, legible only to me: chicken curry, lamb biryani, kadhi, urad, or dal. If anyone needs something—a butter knife, a lint roller, a spoon—it's me they ask. Sometimes they don't have to ask at all. I have become a seer, arriving in advance with the jar of pickles or peanut butter they were looking for. The thought of living in Bijal's home, asking Jessica for a knife, is laughable. Maybe if they had children, if there was someone on my side. But according to Bijal, he has his whole life to be a father. He's earning good money; Jessica loves to travel. They've yet to see Iceland. They want to wait.

"When I was Jessica's age," I once told Bijal, "I already had two boys."

"And look what that brought you."

"What?"

"You're not happier than anyone else," Bijal had said. "You're not really happy at all."

I could have slapped him right then, brought a rolling pin to his head, but I've never done that to Bijal. Something always got in the way.

I check Facebook three more times before giving up hope you'll respond. Maybe your internet isn't working. Maybe you haven't seen it. But that's worse, isn't it? Because that means you aren't looking. You aren't like me, checking obsessively, imagining all the things I will say in response. *Kareem! It's you!* The words make me cringe. Of course it's you. You don't need me to remind you. I think about taking a selfie, something to put on Facebook, angling the phone in front of my face.

"Mom?"

I jump, putting my phone away. "Bijal, you scared me."

"What are you doing?"

"Nothing. I was just admiring the yard."

I wonder if he believes me. From a young age, Bijal idolized Ashok, accompanying him to the hospital on weekends, greeting patients with a smile. In the first grade, he told all his classmates that Ashok was the "number-one" doctor in town. I don't know how he gathered this. It wasn't a competition. But Bijal was consumed by rankings. The few times I raised my voice at Ashok in front of the kids, Bijal's eyes turned to stones. Once, when he was home from college, I'd shouted at Ashok for leaving food out on the counter overnight, causing it to spoil. It was Bijal who intervened.

"Why do you care?" he'd said flatly. "It's Dad's money."

The comment stung. Ashok was the blueprint by which Bijal designed his entire life: medical school, private practice, golf. The only difference was Jessica. What would he say about us, Kareem?

Now, he looks tired, his face swollen, his eyes puffed. The dark hair on his head is mussed, as if it's been licked by a dog. He wears a white T-shirt and red basketball shorts. His legs are matted with hair.

"I'll miss this place," he says.

He takes in the length of the room: the cream sofas, triangular cocktail table, picture frames glinting from shelves. Seeing the sheen of his eyes, I feel a sliver of a crack somewhere deep inside. "I will, too."

He nods. "You can still come to my house—our house, I

mean. There's plenty of space. You don't have to move away, Mom. London is so far."

I turn and face the backyard, the freshly shorn lawn. "I know."

"It wouldn't be a burden. For me—for anyone. If that's what you think . . ."

"I don't think that."

He nods with relief. I hear the rush of water through the pipes above. Instinctively, Bijal casts his gaze toward the ceiling. My cell phone chimes, and I immediately reach for it, my heart skipping, hoping it's you. It's Chaya. I look at the time and gasp.

"Bijal," I say. "You're late. Jessica's train . . ."

He doesn't move.

"What?" I say, staring.

"She's not coming."

"Why not?"

He doesn't answer. His expression dims. I know, without him saying it, that it's because of me.

AKASH

My father used to tell me there was no such thing as bad people, only good people who do bad things.

"What makes them do bad things?"

"The world, Akash," he said, sitting on my bed. "The world is a difficult place to live—so being bad is their way out."

I was six. I started crying.

"I don't want to be like that."

My father smiled and stroked my head. "Then don't."

Ten years later, he came to my room again, a wrinkled paper in his hands. I knew what it was. I remembered typing it on his computer, printing it out, folding it so that I could tuck it into the windshield wiper of your car. A letter.

"I found this, Akash," he said, slowly. "In the trash." His eyes were red, not from crying, but from the exhaustion only a father can feel when his family is falling apart. "Is this true?" he asked. "What you said . . . in the letter . . . is it true?"

I could have denied it, the way I had been denying it my entire life, when my mother shook me that day in London, when Bryce chased after me after I drew a picture of Lord Ganesh, when you climbed out of your father's Toyota and into my life. I cried instead, hot tears of admission that blurred my father's face. I still don't know what he looked like when he came and sat next to me and pulled me into an embrace and told me he loved me and whispered the words, "Don't tell Mom."

I only know what I felt.

I wake to the sound of my cell phone: a text from Jaden. I sit up and read it.

This beat has me stumped.

LA, with its blue skies and ginger-colored hills, feels like a past life. Jacob says success is a drug, and everyone in LA is an addict. I must be in withdrawal. I haven't written a song in months. The inspiration has left my body like a high in fast retreat. I still haven't returned Jacob's calls, or responded to his text message. It's been five days. I know he's giving me my space, worrying about me in silence. It's what he does. Once, I got drunk and fought with him over something trivial, a comment he'd made about a music video he didn't like. The video featured Black women twerking in a desert, sequins of sweat shimmering against their skin. I loved it. Jacob did not. He said it was objectifying, offensive to women. I told him it was culture—the dancing was part of a history of people that had nothing to do with him—and as a white man, it wasn't his place to comment. He said I was taking it personally. "Don't take it personally," he said. I threw the remote control at the TV. The screen shattered. The next morning, after getting it repaired, he came over and stroked my head. "Let's move on." But sometimes you don't want to move on. Sometimes you can't. Sometimes "moving on" means you didn't have anything to be upset about in the first place—when you did.

I get out of bed and text Jaden back.

Let's quit.

His response is swift. *Stop.*

I smile in spite of myself and stare at my reflection in the mirror—eyes bloodshot, face greased—when I hear a knock at the door. Bijal.

"Open up."

The knob jiggles. I open the door. He doesn't smile. He seems bigger somehow, his shoulders spreading, closing the gap between himself and the doorway.

"Mom needs you downstairs."

"Okay."

He looks around the room, his eyes pink at the edges. I heard him late last night whispering over the phone.

"What were you doing?" he says.

"Getting ready."

"We needed you."

"For what?"

His eyes widen. "What do you *think*, Akash?" He hasn't shaved; white hairs poke through the inky smear of a beard. "You know," he says, blowing a puff of hot hair. "You could be a little less selfish on a day like today."

"What's your problem?"

He doesn't answer. "We need to get wine for the party," he says. "Hurry up."

"Fine."

Just as I watch him walk off, I feel the crippling urge for a drink. I rush to my dresser, where I've hidden a stash of airplane-sized bottles. Vodka. White rum. Gin. I twist off the cap of one and suck it down. I run my fingers through a pile of loose change collected at the bottom of my dresser drawer when something catches my eye: an oxidized gold coin. I pinch it between my fingers. The coin is embossed with the image of a genie's lamp. I see the inscription: Aladdin's Palace. I flip it over, remembering that first night, my birthday party, how you had flicked it in my direction. I think about all that I have lost in my life—my cell phone, my wallet, my car keys, my father—everything I should have paid attention to but didn't. Yet here you are.

"How can I do it?" I had asked my father, sitting on his lap. "How can I be good?"

"By asking God every day. *God, please make me a good boy.*"

"God," I repeated. "Please make me a good boy."

"See?" he said, pinching my cheek. "It's already working."

RENU

My husband was a good man. I'm reminded of this every day. *He was a good man,* people like to tell me. It's what you say when someone has passed. I don't disagree. My husband *was* a good man, though I didn't see it at first. At first, he was the man I was arranged to marry, the man who took me away from you, bringing me to this country where no one could pronounce my name. Ray-nu. I remember the first time a telemarketer had called and asked to speak to "Reno."

"Reno!" he'd said. "Like Nevada! You must be *real* lucky!"

I'd imagined a sweating man with cheese dust on his fingers. I'd hung up the phone.

"Look where you've brought me! Look where we are! What kind of place is this?"

"Calm down, Renu. It will get better."

So I waited for it to get better: in line at the bank, at the grocery store, in the shower, rinsing my hair. I waited while people looked at me with suspicion, speaking loudly and slowly, as if

I were deaf. I waited for something to happen, some moment that would make me fall in love with America, with Ashok, too. I took my anger out on him instead. Whenever I had a particularly bad day, when the cooking was ruined or when someone had been rude to me at the store, it was to Ashok I complained.

"I'm not going to die in this place, Ashok!" I cried. "You can if you want, but not me."

My warning had the opposite effect.

"Who is dying? Are you planning to kill me so soon?"

His attempt at humor would assuage me, but then something else would happen: there were no chilies at the store, the spices had no heat, the American women stared at me like I had two heads. My rage simmered like the oily sheen of a curry, splattering the stovetop and walls. Morning. Afternoon. Evening. Night. It was there when my stomach roiled because Ashok was working late. (It was inappropriate to eat before him.) It was there when, after serving him a bowl of dal, he'd seasoned it with salt. It was there when a resident at the hospital wanted a home-cooked meal and Ashok had invited him over without asking. Just like that.

"Am I a barmaid?" I'd said. "Is that what you think?"

It was there when Ashok insisted on things I didn't like: a walk in the park, a road trip to Memphis, Western movies on Friday nights. My rage lived inside me, a fiery thing, glowing like hot embers, brighter each day. This was his life. His dream. Not mine.

Now, as I wait for guests to arrive, I imagine him moving between these walls, his rich, boisterous laugh, the resonance of his voice. Soon, the house will swell with guests and coats will pile up and perfumes will thicken the air. Food will be warmed over six burners. Diyas will dance. I hear the tread of Bijal's and Akash's footsteps as they slip out the front, then the low growl of Bijal's Porsche. The car drives off. I fix my dupatta. My heart pulls as it dawns on me: this is the last party in this house.

———

AKASH

Bijal sails down a country road flanked by wheat fields. The lead sky presses down on us. The drink has settled, calming my nerves, but I'm ready for the next one. I can feel the edges starting to lift, peeling back like a sticker. I need a drink to fix them in place. Back home, my mother is probably pacing the house, adjusting vases and dimming lights, dusting the furniture, all the heavy pieces that will be packed up and shipped off next week, leaving nothing but imprints in their wake.

I glance out the window as we pass your motel. I try to think of what I would say to you, Parth, if we ever met. I've tried for years, but the words are caged in some dark recess of my mind, like an animal, pacing. I hear the music again. See your face. I feel the cool night air on my skin. My phone chimes, yanking me back. A message on Grindr. Bijal looks at me through the corner of his eye.

"What was that?"

"A text," I lie. He shakes his head. "What?"

"They keep making the tones weirder and weirder."

While Bijal is stopped at a light, fiddling with the navigation on his phone, I open the app. It's "R" again. His profile is still blank, but this time he's sent me a picture. An image of his bare torso. His abdomen glitters with sweat.

I ignore it.

"So, what's your deal now?"

When we were young, Bijal would put his arm around me and ask me how everything was going—now, it's "What's your deal?" When kids picked on me because I was small, Bijal would rush to my defense, knocking them down like pins. *Leave my brother alone!* Then he got older and I got weirder, and the whole thing became harder to reason.

Your brother's kind of girly, a friend of Bijal's once said, when he'd come over to our house. Bijal didn't say anything back. Later, when the friend left, he came to my room.

"You shouldn't walk around like that when we have people over."

"Like what?"

"Like you have snakes in your pants."

I had laughed, thinking this was a joke, but Bijal wasn't smiling. When I was a freshman in college, Bijal picked me up from the dorms for Christmas break. On the drive home, he asked me if I had fucked a girl.

"No."

"Why not?"

"Because I'm studying."

"Studying for what? You're a freshman."

I didn't answer him.

"You're not . . ." He paused, shaking his head slowly. "Never mind."

"Not what?"

"Nothing."

We didn't talk the rest of the way. That night, I bought a fifth of vodka using my roommate's fake ID and drank it in my room. I had taken to drinking whenever the subject of my sexuality came up, when the whispers flew like darts that pricked my ears. *Is he? Do you think? Does he seem a little, I don't know?* I spent the rest of Christmas break avoiding Bijal while drinking alone. I wasn't alone in a car with him for another five years, until the night of his wedding. The night I got my DUI.

Now, Bijal's question hangs between us, unanswered.

So, what's your deal now?

"What do you mean?"

"Like what are you doing?"

"I'm writing."

"Songs?"

"No, Hallmark cards."

Bijal speeds through a light.

"Are you getting paid for these songs?"

I grip the seat belt until it cuts into my skin. "Not at the moment."

We pull into a parking space outside a wine shop that sells flowers and olives and specialty cheese. I unfold the wine list our mother gave us. Bijal puts the car in park. He rips the list from my hand.

"I'll be right back."

It's clear to both of us he doesn't want me to come inside. Perhaps Bijal and my mother have already discussed it—that I'm to remain in the car. I've lost my buzz by the time he returns with a crate full of wine. He slides it into the backseat and folds himself behind the wheel. We take off without a word. Bijal stops along the way to fill up the tank and wipe the windows and windshield. By the time we reach home, a string of cars is already parked outside, their wheels glinting in the afternoon sun. I see a familiar car: your parents' Camry. A string of prayer beads swings from the mirror above the dash.

"We're late," Bijal says. "We should have left sooner."

It's clear what he means: it's all my fault. Bijal parks his car on the street and we carry the wine into the garage, lining the refrigerator with bottles of white. A case of IPAs catches my eye.

"Come on," Bijal says. "We have to change."

"Into what?"

"Into kurtas. Mom wants us to wear them."

"But they make my balls itch."

"You barely even have balls," he says. His lips betray him, spreading into a brief smile. It quickly fades. "Do this for Mom, okay? It's an important day."

"Fine."

He walks toward the door, then turns.

"I'm gonna hang out here for a second," I say. He looks me over, his eyes searching for an explanation. "All those uncles and aunties."

I find my old guitar on the workbench, covered in a tarp, and pick it up in my hands. I make a display of strumming a few chords. Bijal abandons his resolve.

"Okay. Don't be long."

As soon as the door shuts behind him, I return the guitar to the workbench and cover it back up with the tarp. I walk over to the fridge. The cold blast is restorative. So is the IPA, fizzing down my throat.

RENU

The notification flashes across my phone just as the last few guests arrive. I haven't read it. I can't read it. I need to be alone. I see only the words: NDUGU KAREEM ABBAS HAS SENT YOU A MESSAGE. I could jump out of my own skin. I slip the phone back into the waistband of my petticoat and drape my dupatta over it, smiling at a guest who passes by.

"Do you see Timi?" Chaya whispers to me. "That's her third helping of bhel. No wonder she wears a size twelve."

The world sharpens around me. A swirl of sequins. Chaya's toothy grin.

"How do you know what size she wears?"

"I saw her trying on a dress at JCPenney. I looked at the tag." Chaya grabs my arm. "Look, look! How much yogurt she took."

The doorbell rings and Bijal runs to answer it; a cloud of guests sweep into the room. I stand in my pink sari, the beads clacking as I shift my weight. *What does it say? What does it say? What does it say?* I imagine all the possibilities. *I love you. Run away with me. Don't ever message me again—cheap woman.* My eyes follow Chaya's to the central dining table where I have arranged a generous buffet. Fried samosas and kachori are arranged in pyramids on a plate. Slit chilies drip with oil. Timi, the wife of an engineer Ashok had been friendly with, is among them, piling her plate. She looks up and smiles. I smile back. I don't dare look at Chaya, who is preparing her next jab. But her expression darkens.

"What am I going to do without you? Who will I joke with?"

"There are plenty of people here."

"These people are all uneducated."

"Chaya!"

"It's true," she says. "Look at Sarita, she's been in America thirty-one years. She still can't pronounce the word 'Arizona.' She calls it 'Ar-jona.' Her son lives there. She still can't say it? Now I ask you—what can I talk to *her* about?"

"You can teach her English."

"She gets an F."

"Be nice, Chaya."

"I don't want to be nice," she says. "But now you're leaving and I'm afraid I'll have to."

Briefly, I consider telling her about you. Chaya has never judged me, not like the other women in this town. She didn't question my decision to move back to London instead of moving in with Bijal or Akash. She knows me too well. The morning after Bijal's wedding, outside the marquee where the brunch was being held, she adjusted my shalwar kameez and gripped my jeweled arm.

"You just go in there with your head held high, Renu. Don't worry about anything else."

"How can I do that? You saw what happened. It's all they can talk about."

"Not true."

"Then what?" I said. "What is everyone whispering about?"

Chaya stood before me in a lilac kurti, silver globes swishing from her ears. A pair of girls rushed by in a hush of whispers. A woman turned and stared. The marquee sparkled beyond us, twinkling with gold. "They're saying what a beautiful ceremony it was," she said. Her plum-toned lips spread into a smile. But I had already seen it: how difficult it had been for her to lie.

Throughout the years, when the subject of Akash came up, Chaya knew how to circumnavigate it. She didn't ask pointed questions. She wasn't like the others. She didn't feign ignorance just to hear the words come out of my mouth: Akash didn't finish school. Chaya knows all of it, so she doesn't ask. Just like I don't ask her why her husband never accompanies her to parties, or why they've never taken a vacation together, or why her son, Amit, got fired from his job. We are like sisters, expressing our solidarity in silence. If we were witches, we would cast spells. Once, shortly after Ashok had passed, a woman from a neighboring town had approached me at a party.

"Renu," she'd said, sneering. "At a party so soon? I can't believe it. How long ago did Ashok pass?"

"What business is it of yours?" Chaya had said, leaping in like a cat. "When *you* die, your husband will dance!"

The woman had drawn a hand to her mouth.

"Bloody bitch," Chaya had muttered, watching her retreat.

She hasn't judged me, but she doesn't know everything. If I told her about you, about the life I had before Ashok, about the secrets I buried long ago, what would she say? This woman who has so many things to say about everyone else. The crowd thickens around us, and I gaze at the blur of faces I may never see again, in this town I have never loved. I realize that once I'm gone, away from this place with its cornfields and strip malls and Chinese restaurants named after feelings I have rarely felt— Happy, Lucky, Joy—I will never look back. I reach for her hand.

"Chaya," I say.

She turns, confused. "What?"

But I can't do it. Not yet.

AKASH

I'm not wearing the kurta. I can tell by the way my mother glares at me from across the room that she's not happy. I suppose it's deliberate, this act of defiance, but the way she's fawning over Bijal, introducing him to this person and that, I feel a small pearl of satisfaction. Instead, I wear a ribbed sweater over jeans. My hair is tousled. A toe pokes through the hole in my sock. Bijal is unusually at ease in his outfit, a dark green tunic with an embroidered Nehru collar, white silk pants. He's changed—he would have never worn it before. The house is warm with laughter, awash with smiles. Women gather in shimmering clusters. Men stand staggered with their arms crossed. I wonder if anyone notices me, if these hushed whispers are directed at me.

"We live in a society, Akash," my mother once said. "There are rules."

The moment I see your parents standing near the windows, I know I need another drink. It's one in the afternoon, but I'm already feeling the onset of a hangover. I see only the back of your mother's head, a flash of gold brocade, but it's enough to make my insides twist. She's talking to an older woman in a white sari. Your father stands next to her, politely nodding his head. I catch snippets of their conversation, but all I manage to glean is that your parents are leaving for India in two days, for a six-month stay. What about Parth? I want to ask. Your mother turns and notices me. Her smile is like vinegar on broken skin.

I dash out to the garage. Open another bottle. Suck it all down. The drink flushes my nerves. A sense of calm washes over me as my stomach settles and the lightness returns, like I'm trapped in a bubble, floating up toward the sky. I open the fridge and take out a second bottle, twisting off the cap with my free hand, the beer misting my face, when the door swings open.

"What are you doing?"

Bijal stands at the other end of the garage. His eyes shift from the bottle on the floor to the one in my grip.

"Are you serious right now? You're drinking? During Dad's puja?"

"I'm not," I say. "I just—the puja hasn't started yet."

"What the hell, Akash?"

A vein at his temple thickens with blood. I put the bottle down.

"Maybe you don't give a shit about us," he says. "Maybe you don't give a shit about anyone inside. That's on you. But at least give a shit about Dad."

"I do care about Dad."

"You're not acting like it. You never did."

The words sting. I wonder if he remembers what he said last year, after our father's funeral, that it was all my fault. It was in the living room after everyone had left. We were arguing about who was going to keep the framed photograph of our father, the one that sits near the altar now. I was the one who had taken it, the day before Bijal's wedding, intending it to be a wedding gift. Photography was a hobby of mine, a pointless activity according to my mother, a distraction that would lead to nothing. Just like writing songs. I took the photograph on the balcony of my parents' hotel suite, the morning sun illuminating my father's skin. He wore a simple sherwani with elegant stitching. His thick salt-and-pepper hair was swept back with gel. His smile was directed not at the camera, but at me, as if he knew what I was thinking.

When I presented Bijal with the photograph the morning after his wedding, after he'd picked me up from the police station the night before, he turned his head.

I don't want it.

But it's your gift.

For what? All that planning—for what?

He sat facing the wall. Jessica was downstairs with her parents. Her dress hung like a shed skin from the bathroom door.

I said I was sorry.

Do you know how embarrassing this is for Mom and Dad? It wasn't just our people out there, Akash. What must Jessica's family think? Lucky for you she likes you.

Or what?

He didn't say anything, scowling at the floor. *You should leave.*

But Bijal, I—

He looked at me, his eyes rimmed red. *Get out.*

Now, he stands at the other end of the garage wearing the same expression. "Do what you want. I don't care. Just don't ruin this day for Mom."

The door closes behind him. I stare at the bottle by my feet.

RENU

Ashok liked to call me "Queen Renu." I always hated it. A queen is someone lazy who sits on her rear. I hated when he came home and asked me what I did that day, as if I had done nothing at all.

"What did you do today, Renu?" Or once, after a fight, *What do you do all day?*

"What do you mean, *what do I do?*" I'd shouted. "I cook your food and clean your underwear. What do *you* do? Chitchatting with nurses all day."

"I don't chitchat with nurses."

"I have seen you."

"When?"

"In my dreams."

"Oh, Renu."

He used to try hard to make me laugh. He would make silly faces, and prance around the house like an elf. Once, I woke up to find him wearing my sari. A slash of red silk flowed like wine from his waist.

"Ashok! What on earth are you doing?"

He swung his hips from side to side. "Who is this in my husband's bed?"

"Stop this now."

"What cheek! You dare talk to Madam this way?"

"Ashok, please. You're being ridiculous."

"Be sharam!"

"ASHOK!"

He dropped the dupatta, exposing his smooth chest, his nipples like small hard stones. "I'm only trying to make you laugh, Renu. You need to laugh more."

"I laugh plenty."

"When?"

"In my dreams."

"Oh, Renu."

Now, he stares back at me from a black-and-white portrait, his smile a muted gray. Marigolds burst like fireworks from the garland around his face. A plume of incense curls between us.

"Take this prasad," the priest says, offering me a single almond. I swallow it down with force. "Jai Sri Krishna."

"Jai Sri Krishna," I say.

"JSK," Akash says. I glare at him; he reddens. "Jai Sri Krishna."

My boys are on either side of me, bowing their heads. The room is hushed. The aroma of boiled rice fills the space, along with the powdery scent of perfume. I remember it. Chanel No. 5. It was the first expensive perfume I had ever owned. You bought it for me, Kareem, shortly before I left. We were walking through a department store, lights swirling like ribbons above our heads, our feet squeaking against the tiles. My hand was fixed tightly in yours. It was a winter day, and I remember how the cold shone in the wet gloss of your eyes. You had only been in London a year; you were still used to the heat of Dar es Salaam. I hadn't told you yet. I hadn't told you about Ashok, that I had met him days earlier at my brother's flat, and that he had grabbed my shawl, telling me one day I would see all that he is. I hadn't told you that my parents would be arriving the next day—to fix the date.

"This one," you said, spritzing the perfume on the inside of my wrist. The sensation was like the kiss of a breeze.

"Why this one? It's too expensive."

Your bearded face turned grim. "Is that what the queen says?" you said, your eyes pulsing. "No, she just takes what she wants. So why can't you?"

"Because I am not a queen."

You smiled. "Are you sure? The way you order me around, I would not know the difference, my queen."

You bowed gallantly. I pinched your arm.

"Jaja haave! Queen waro!"

Years later, on my fiftieth birthday, Ashok presented me with the same bottle of perfume. Instead of thanking him, I'd pushed the bottle aside. "No one wears this anymore," I snapped. "Are you living under a rock?"

He had frowned, momentarily shamed, before his face slowly melted into a conciliatory smile.

"I'm living under you, Queen Renu. You're as soft as a cloud."

"Just stop it, Ashok."

But the word tore through me: queen.

AKASH

There's nothing like being drunk during the day. The brightness surrounds me, sparkles like the lemony vodka in my cup. Outside, the clouds have cleared and the lawn is dappled with sunlight. I've lost track of how many I've had; I've set up a filling station in my bedroom, bounding back and forth. The sun throbs as powerfully as the blood in my veins.

The ceremony is brief. All that fanfare for a chant over a fire, a red smear on my head, almonds in the palm of my hand.

"I don't like almonds," I whisper.

"Just eat it, Akash."

I was always "just eating" things for my mother. When we went to the temple one Sunday and a priest dropped a mound of jaggery into my hands, I'd recoiled.

"What's this?"

"It's gur."

"It looks like boogers."

"Just eat it, Akash!"

I ate it. Such faith we place in mothers and gods.

The room is full of my parents' friends and their children and grandchildren, all the people they have connected with over thirty-five years. The furniture has been pushed back— twin sofas, a coffee table, a moveable bar—and for the first time I begin to imagine what this house will look like without it. A shell. My father's portrait sits behind an altar decorated with marigold flowers. His thick black brows provide a canopy for kind eyes. I stare at it, forcing the lump back down my throat.

After the puja, I stand at the back of the room so no one will notice me.

It doesn't work.

"Akash." I turn my head to find an uncle and aunty I vaguely recognize. "How are you?"

The aunty wears a fuchsia outfit. The uncle is in a wool sweater. His eyes look shrunken behind thick plastic frames. I wonder if they can tell that I'm drunk, if little bubbles are rising from my head.

"Hi, Uncle," I say, rearranging my face. "Hi, Aunty."

"How is Los Angeles?" the aunty asks. "You know my daughter Sheena is also there. She's finished her education. She's a pharmacist."

"Maybe you two can meet," says the uncle. "You know, just so there is some familiarity."

Familiarity. At this, my mother arrives with a stiff smile. "Ushaben, Maheshbhai, how are you? So good of you to come."

"It was nothing," the uncle replies. "I have known Ashok-bhai since we were ten. It's a shame we couldn't come to Bijal's wedding. We were just telling Akash about Sheena. She is also in LA. Maybe Akash can call her."

"Of course," my mother says brightly.

Her eyes land on me. She knows I've had a drink.

"We don't want to be forward," the uncle starts up again. "But if both of you are single, then what's the harm in meeting?"

I avert my gaze.

"So, Akash," the aunty says. "I heard you're studying music now. Which college?"

I pause, giving my mother an exasperated look. The smile on her face falters.

"I'm not in school," I say firmly. "I'm a songwriter."

I take an ounce of pleasure in the way her expression cracks, the effort she takes to hold it together. Something lifts inside me, not caring.

"I work as a receptionist," I continue, the words spilling

freely. "You know, filing, answering phones, making coffee. That sort of thing. Well, before I was fired. I guess I don't really have a job now. No real source of income, anyway."

A hush falls between us as the uncle and aunty trade looks. My mother laughs.

"Oh, Akash," she says. "Stop it. He's being silly. You know how boys are."

"Yes, well, our daughter is thirty-two," the uncle continues. "No harm in meeting. I'll give your mom her number before we leave."

"And I'll be sure Akash gives her a call," my mother says as they turn to walk away.

I catch a glimpse of my mother shaking me in the bedroom, her eyes wide with fear. *What are you doing, Akash? This is not how we are!* Suddenly, I want to tell her the truth, that I'll never be interested in a woman. I never was. But the words dissolve on my tongue.

Instead, I say, "You told them I was studying music?"

My mother waits for the couple to be out of earshot before holding my gaze.

"Just control yourself, Akash. Please."

Then she slips back into the crowd.

Just as a memory of you catches up to me—the lights, the music—my phone pings. A text from Jacob. *I've been trying to get a hold of you. We need to talk.* I feel a slight pull, a flicker of desire. I think about sending him a message. *I miss you. I'm sorry. I wish you were inside me.* But I can't. I open Grindr instead. A stream of messages awaits. The first one is from "R." He's sent three photos. I look at them one by one, the blood leaving my face, descending far below.

"R" is cute in a small-town way, with his reddish, buzz-cut hair the color of dried leaves, the faint whisper of a beard. His eyes, an Icelandic blue, are penetrating. His lips are thin and colorless, but the rest of him—cheeks, arms, wooly chest—glows bright like embers, as if lit from within. He doesn't smile in his pictures. No one ever does. To smile on Grindr is to reveal too much—that you have emotions and are sometimes beholden to them.

R's pictures are all variations of the same pose, a deadpan expression that never shifts. Sometimes he wears a backwards hat. Other times you can't see his crown at all, only his face looking down at you, as if you're on your knees looking up. Those are the pictures I like best, the ones that intimidate. His stats are all there: height, weight, race, age. Under "tribe," he's listed "discreet." His message is brief: *Wanna hang*. It's a neutral greeting, without punctuation, as if it would be perfectly all right if I never replied.

I don't.

I put my phone away and look around the room. The vodka has done its work. All the warm, familiar faces take on a dreamy edge. My mother has disappeared somewhere. Bijal is locked in conversation in the kitchen. A cluster of uncles whisper urgently about another uncle's finances. I glance across the room and notice your parents. They're all alone now, their backs pressed to the window, arms folded over their chests. I wonder if they know what happened between us. If they know the truth. I've had nightmares about you telling them. I can't sleep at night when I think about it. Suddenly your mother catches my eye and smiles at me, waving me over, and I take a long sip of my drink before making my way.

RENU

Now that the puja has ended, the party begins. Bijal pours drinks for the men at the bar, splashing scotch into tumblers, beer into mugs. The food is served in the dining room. Guests eat standing up or on the chairs borrowed from Vinay and Asha's motel. I'm too distracted to look at your message. Every few moments, I cast my gaze around the room for Akash. I don't see him. God only knows where he is. I don't understand him, why he behaves this way. I know he's been drinking. I can see it in the laziness of his smile. I wonder who else can see it, too. I've tried teaching him how to be in the world. *Smile, Akash. Say hello, Akash.* Tell them what they want to hear. It's easier this way. Am I wrong, Kareem? Have I not seen what the world does to people who don't belong?

When Ashok first brought me to this neighborhood, the women didn't know what to make of me. They arrived with baked goods and stiff smiles. They had strange names: Deborah and Lou Anne. They were always laughing and waving, as if that was their primary function: to laugh and to wave. Deborah took it upon herself to introduce me to the other women. Her husband was an accountant, and she had three teenage boys. The way she spoke of them, of her life in America, was what struck me most. It was like she was talking about a movie she had seen or a roller coaster she had ridden and survived. She knew how things would turn out; she had seen it a million times.

"Soon, they'll be raising hell and you'll be thanking your stars the cops weren't involved!" she once said, when Bijal had turned three.

Later, at home, I'd shouted at Ashok. "This is where you want to live, where mothers joke about cops?"

When Deborah introduced me to her colleague Margery at her weekly bridge night, she made sure to tell her my English was very good.

"She speaks so *well*."

"Do they speak English where you lived?" Margery wanted to know.

"Do they speak English in *England?*" I said, testing the seriousness of her question. "Yes. They do."

"I'm sorry," Deborah said, her face coloring. "We thought you were from India."

"Actually, I'm from Tanzania, and English is spoken all over the world."

They never invited me again. People get uncomfortable when you're not what you seemed. After that, Ashok found a circle of Indians and it was to their homes we went every Saturday night. I had hoped things would be different there, but they were not.

"You're very *modern,*" a woman once told me, at her husband's birthday party.

In England, being "modern" was a good thing, but in this cocoon of Indians, clinging to an old way of life, it was not. I saw the way they eyed me, the clothes I wore, the length of my hair, the glass of red wine I accepted from the woman's husband at the bar. I had assumed other women would be drinking. They were not.

"Renu, you drink?" said another woman, a dark mole quivering at her lip. "I suppose East Africans *are* different."

Different. I learned to hate that word. The first drink I had was with you, Kareem, at a pub in Oxford. *Try it,* you'd said, pushing the glass in front of me. *How else will you know if you like it, if there are things in this world you never imagined you would enjoy?*

Like you? I'd said.

Now, your message burns a hole in the lining of my petticoat. I'm tempted to leave the party, lock myself in my room to read it. But every few seconds someone is pulling me in a different direction. Everyone wants to talk about Ashok, how kind and caring he was, how he always had wisdom to share. They ask me how I will leave it, this town, this community, this house and all its space, and I tell them what I know they would want to hear.

"Because there is no one left to fill it."

They moan with appreciation and I smile in return, and finally, when there's a break in the conversation, I rush into Ashok's office and shut the door. I pluck my phone from my petticoat and pull up your message. My heart stills as the words take shape on the screen. Through thin walls I can hear an eruption of laughter, followed by another, a wave that travels across the room. I begin to read.

> Dear Renu,
> I couldn't believe it when I saw your name. I still can't believe it. How far have we come, that your words can find me so easily? Remember when we used to wait weeks for our letters? How are you? Where are you? I hope, wherever it is, you are happy and well. Please write back soon.
> With love,
> Kareem

My fingers quake, but part of me is disappointed. *With love?* "With love" is not the same thing as "love." Just like "love you" is not the same thing as "I love you." It's a passive statement, too flimsy to stand on. Still, I'm buoyed by your request: that you would like me to write back soon. I think of what I might say, all the details of my life without you. I flip through your pictures and envision where you live—a semidetached house with a glossy red door, chocolate-brown brick. I see a back garden with rosebushes and vine-laced walls. A vision clicks into place. Rosé poured into two glasses, your top button undone. A small iron table at the center of the yard, enrobed in white linen.

I scan your page once more, pausing at one of your posts,

before I hear someone call my name from outside. I push the phone back into my petticoat and walk out the door. I admire the way the rooms drip with light—candles, jewelry, the sun dipping behind the trees—when I absorb what I had just seen. I take out my phone, pull up Facebook. I click on your page. The post was from two days ago, a check-in. The location is listed in blue letters above a map. I click on the map, waiting for the page to load. Chaya calls my name from across the room, where she's standing next to a couple I recognize from a neighboring town. I make my way over, the phone still clutched in my hand. Bijal is always complaining about the speed of our internet, the time it takes to load a page, and for the first time, while I wait for the pixels to sharpen, I agree. The wait is agonizing. Then, just as I'm about to give up, click off my phone, I see it. I read it three times. A restaurant I've heard of. A location I know. Evanston, Illinois. How can it be, Kareem? You're only two hours away. I slam into someone walking in the opposite direction. Then I take a step back.

"Akash," I say, my pulse racing. "What are you—"

His cheeks swell. The color drains from his face. A roomful of eyes is upon us when he bends at the waist, retching, and vomits all over the floor.

AKASH

The thing about apologies is you have to know what you're apologizing for. It doesn't help if you were drunk and have no recollection. No one will listen to me, anyway, no matter how hard I try to explain.

"It wasn't the alcohol," I say lamely. "It must have been something I ate."

"Oh, so now it's someone else's fault," Bijal says. "You've been drinking since noon. This is my wedding all over again."

"It's not the same."

The party is over, the vomit contained. A veil of fog clouds my thoughts. A sour taste coats my tongue. My mother has washed the makeup off her face, a ghost in her nightgown, her hair pinned back. She wipes down the kitchen island and drops the rag into the sink.

"I don't want to talk about this anymore. My whole life I have been talking about the same thing."

The words sting. I had expected her to shout at me, to scream even, but her resignation is worse. "I'm tired, Akash," she says softly. She packs up some containers and places them into the fridge. The house has been restored, Vinay Uncle and Asha Aunty's chairs put away in the basement, furniture returned to its rightful place. Tomorrow, it will be one week before we leave.

"I don't know what to do anymore," she says, her eyes red. "I don't know how to help you. I won't be here. No one . . ." She pauses to glance across the room at Bijal. "We all have to move on with our lives."

"I wasn't drunk. I just got sick."

"That's not the point," Bijal snaps. "It's always something with you. If it's not the drinking, or school, it's money issues." He looks at me knowingly. "You think we don't know? The way you slink off to answer your phone. Mom got a call from a debt collector. You owe money to Chase Bank."

"Shit."

"Where are you gonna get it from?"

I don't answer. My heart pounds as I watch my mother fill a mug with hot water.

"You know Mom wants to open a separate account for you?" Bijal continues, crossing his arms. "She's scared one day you're *really* gonna fuck up, so she's setting money aside in case I need to bail you out. She doesn't want you to go and do something stupid. Steal it or something."

"Bijal," my mother says softly.

"No, he needs to hear this." His eyes smolder. "This isn't what she should be thinking about. This isn't what Dad wanted. You know why Dad never yelled at you? Huh? You know why he always defended you all those years?"

The mention of our father pulls tears from my eyes. Bijal's shape shudders, blurs.

"It's because he was scared of you, Akash. He was scared of what you might do, that maybe if he told you what he really thought, what he *really* wanted to say, you would go and . . ." His voice breaks. "You would do something stupid—something you couldn't take back."

My mother takes her mug and slides onto a barstool, watching me. I wait for her to jump to my defense. She doesn't.

"He cried once," Bijal says. "Did you know that?"

I shake my head.

"The night of my wedding, after you made that speech, after you got your DUI. I went to Mom and Dad's room to tell them what happened. It was my wedding night; I should have been with my wife—but no." He grimaces, as if the memory has left a bitter taste in his mouth. "He cried on his bed. He said it was his fault, that he should have been there for you. Can you believe that?" Bijal shakes his head. "You go and fuck up your life, and Dad is blaming himself."

I remember the morning after Bijal's wedding, when my father came to my room. The questions he had asked. *Is this about what happened? Is this about what I told you to do?* I remember the letter, my father's grim words. *Don't tell Mom.* It was the secret that binds us, even in death. My father said he loved me. He never told me he was afraid. I think about explaining this, telling Bijal and my mother everything there is to know, about the letter and the truth and even about you. But I can't. There's no room for my burdens, my problems. They take space in my throat instead.

"I'm sorry," I cry. "I don't want this. I don't want anyone to feel those things."

My mother looks up from her mug, cutting her eyes at Bijal. He stands his ground.

"You've said this before. We've heard it a thousand times."

A small white dash, the size of a fingernail clipping, clings to Bijal's forehead: a grain of rice from the puja. Had we been young, I would have flicked it off. Bijal would have chased me around the house. But we're not young anymore. Our father is dead. Bijal stopped chasing me years ago, and I never looked back.

PART II

AKASH

The first time we met was at my thirteenth birthday. I didn't want you there. It was my mother who convinced me to invite you. Your family had just moved to town and purchased the Super 8 motel. It was isolated among plots of soybean and corn. Because you were Indian, our parents were friends. There were only six Indian families in town. We would have been foolish not to unite. Because an Indian in America with no friends is like a spider with no legs. Just a thing to be stared at, ultimately dismissed.

"I don't know him," I'd told my mother. "He doesn't know my friends."

"What do you mean, you don't know him?" my mother had yelled. "Vinay Uncle and Asha Aunty are our friends, therefore Parth is *your* friend!"

I knew better than to argue. I invited you. The party was at a miniature golf course with an attached arcade. The arcade was called Aladdin's Palace. It didn't look like a palace. It looked like an old office building that had been converted into an arcade. I had no real friends at school, so my parents invited some boys in the neighborhood with whom I had been friendly. It was assumed that parents would drop their kids off and pick them up later. My father dropped me off in his Mercedes-Benz, handing me a hundred-dollar bill. *Make sure you buy everyone's food.* At Eric Hoffman's birthday the week before, his mother had told us we were responsible for our own meals. I waited with my father's money in my pocket until, one by one, everyone arrived, exiting their parents' cars. Before long, a Toyota Camry pulled into the parking lot and parked in a corner spot. The engine died; the doors flicked open. You stepped outside. I was surprised by the sight of you. You wore a polo shirt and indigo jeans. Your hair was slicked up. A shell necklace encircled your throat. Maybe I had expected you to look different, like the other Indians in town who so obviously did not belong. I was relieved.

We had never met in person, but it was clear to you who I was. Out of six teenage boys, only one of us looked like you.

"What's up?" you said.

I had never known how to respond to this. Is it an actual question, or merely a greeting? Do I list off all the things that are currently on my mind, or do I simply say the same thing in return? I chose to say, "Nothing."

I used my father's money to purchase tickets and rent clubs, and we gathered at the entrance, swinging them around. I was struck by how easily you fit in with my friends, how smooth your transition was into my life. Until your father approached.

"*Hullo*, boys."

He looked like he had gotten dressed in the middle of a disaster, grabbing whatever he could find: windbreaker, dress shirt, sneakers, slacks. He was nothing like you, with your honey-eyed skin, your feline eyes. Your thick brows had little space between them, lending you a severe expression. People often asked if you were sure you were Indian—if you weren't Persian or Italian instead. I envied you this access to other selves. Because it meant something to be Italian. It meant something to be Persian. It meant something to be Mexican or Spanish or Greek. It meant nothing to be Indian.

Your father had pockmarked skin and reddish hair. His teeth were stained brown. My father, with his Brooks Brothers shirts, was nothing like yours. Still, they were friends, drinking Heineken in square kitchens, trading tips about stocks. In India, my parents would have looked down on yours, but in America, there was nowhere to look but up.

No one else's father had remained at the golf course, but yours showed no sign of leaving. I could tell you didn't like this. Some of the other boys looked at your father and smirked. I could tell you saw this, too. I'm ashamed to admit this now, Parth, but that day, I was embarrassed by your father. I didn't want anyone to think we were related, that I was more like *you* than them.

"Okay, Parth." Your father pointed to a collection of tables. "I will be just there. *Have a fun.*"

My cheeks burned with indignation. One of the kids in my neighborhood, Brad, snorted. You marched over to your father, shouting.

"Go home, Dad! No one else's dad is here."

I held my breath as your father's eyes slowly widened, absorbing your rage. Then he folded his arms. He reprimanded you in Gujarati, a language only you and I understood. When you lowered your gaze, I saw my chance.

"My dad is picking me up," I said quickly, walking over to you both. "We can drop him off at home."

Your father turned, the offer taking shape in his mind. Then he stood up.

"Okay," he said, nodding. "Okay, thanks, beta." And later, as he walked away, "Tell Daddy I said hello."

Brad snickered. "Daddy."

"I will," I quickly said.

Had we been at your parents' home, or at the temple, I would have addressed your father in the polite form, as "Vinay Uncle." But I only said thanks.

At lunch, I secretly hoped you would sit next to me. I was sandwiched between Kevin and Brad. You were at the other end of the table, eating nachos with Brett Fine, a Jewish kid from my neighborhood who was your classmate at Troy. I wished I hadn't invited him. I wanted to talk to you instead. There was something intriguing about you, the way you laughed and made jokes, the confidence in your voice, the wide spread of your shoulders. It might as well have been your party. At one point, you told a joke that everyone found incredibly funny. Your face went bright red, creases forming at your brow, but when I asked you to repeat it you only shrugged, saying it wasn't that great. My insides flipped.

Later, I watched you through the corner of my eye while playing *Street Fighter* at the arcade.

"Dude." Brad elbowed me. "Why do you always have to be the girl?"

"Because Chun-Li is fast."

"She's a chick."

"So?"

"You're a dude," Brad said.

Across the room, you threw a basketball and raised your fist as it swished perfectly through the net. You wiped the sweat from your chin with the hem of your shirt, adjusting yourself through your pants, and I realized, then, that you would have picked Ryu.

The rest of the afternoon was spent playing Skee-Ball and air hockey and eating pizzas by the slice. I willed you to turn and notice me. You didn't. A song played over the speakers. Tamia, "So Into You." *I. Think. You're. Truuuly something special.* The melody had staccato, but it flowed like silk. I rocked my head to the sound. At one point, I bought a stack of gold tokens and pretended I didn't need them anymore just so I could offer them to you instead.

You shook your head.

"Brett gave me his."

I silently fumed. *I . . . really like . . . what you've . . . done to me . . . I can't . . . really explain it.* The words spun inside me. My feet left the ground every time you looked at me, then came crashing down when you turned your head.

Soon, it was time to leave, and everyone's parents whisked them away in their SUVs. Brett was still waiting for his ride, so the two of you huddled by the popcorn machine, talking about school. I migrated over and pretended to understand what you were saying. That Kevin Kim didn't deserve to win the science fair because his dad is a physics professor and obviously helped.

"Plus, the teacher is his uncle," you said.

"That's total nepotism."

I had no idea what "nepotism" meant. I thought it was something funny—so I laughed. Brett looked at me with an arched brow. You shook your head and grinned. Soon, Brett's father arrived in a black Escalade and we waved goodbye to him from the entrance. Finally, we were alone.

"Thanks for inviting me," you said, as we made our way outside. "I had a great time."

"Sure."

We stood in silence for a while, staring up at the metallic sky. I didn't know what to say. I tried to find something clever or funny, but I didn't trust myself to speak. It was you who finally broke the ice, asking me about school. Slowly, our tongues loosened. We talked about the subjects we took, the teachers we hated, the activities we had signed up for that fall. I liked the way you fixed your gaze on me when I spoke, as if you didn't want to miss a single word. It started to rain, and I watched goose bumps rise like braille on your skin. Your white shirt turned gossamer. Your nipples shone blue. We stood close to each other, your wet hair giving off the rich aroma of your shampoo. We could have moved inside, sought shelter under a tree, but it didn't occur to either one of us to move.

"Your friend's pretty cool," you said. "He goes to Troy."

The mention of Brett, of Troy, made my heart sting. I feigned ignorance.

"Which friend?"

"Brett."

We were silent, watching the rain come down even harder, streetlamps blurring in the distance. The roads turned slick and iridescent. I couldn't help myself.

"Brett's kind of weird."

"Really?" You seemed surprised. "I thought you two were friends."

"Well, we aren't."

"Why not?"

"Because we aren't," I said angrily. "I didn't even want him here." And then, because I couldn't help it, "My mom made me invite him."

As soon as the words flew out of my mouth, I regretted them. You looked at me, knowingly, and turned your head.

"Got it."

We didn't talk after that. My father arrived in his Mercedes, and the low whine of the windshield wipers was the only sound on the way to your parents' motel. Lightning flashed. You opened the door. You thanked my father and looked back at me with blank eyes, your wet hair dripping, diamonds clinging to your face. "Here." You tossed a gold token in my direction. "I don't need it anymore." The coin flashed in my palm. You closed the door. I thought that would be the last time I would see you, Parth, the end of you and me. But it was only the beginning.

RENU

I was living in Tanzania when we first met, in Dar es Salaam. It was 1972. My parents had left India in the '40s to do what was expected of them: follow the British. My father was an accountant; my mother stayed at home. My brother, Jagdish, was studying to become a dentist. I was in school, dreaming of attending university in London.

I had just gone to a movie with a friend. It was late, the sky turning sapphire. Street vendors hawked spicy fried snacks. Gulls circled over our heads. We were discussing the actress, how beautiful she had looked in the film, when you walked by.

"Not as beautiful as you, eh, bibi," you said.

"Excuse me?" I'd snapped, offended. "You can't speak to me that way."

"Sorry, hah? I take it back. You're not beautiful."

"Now you insult me!"

"Which is it, bibi? Beautiful or not beautiful?"

"Neither," I said. "You should have said I was smart."

You laughed. You had dark brown skin the color of dates. Your beard was finely trimmed. You wore the kind of shirt my father would have called "stylish," in the way that was not meant to be a compliment.

"I can only speak on what I see," you said. "I see a beautiful woman. If you want me to see a smart woman, you must let me pick your brain."

"Jaja haave!" I said. "Brain picker. Go pick your underwear from your ass."

Your eyes shone like marbles when I pushed past you with my friend.

The next time I saw you was outside the mosque when the same friend and I went to Bambuli Beach. We were drinking coconut water and eating fried yucca. You wore a white tunic that fell past your knees. The sun illuminated the slick of sweat on your face when you called out to me, "Habari!"

I turned my head.

I ignored you again two weeks later when I saw you outside my parents' flat on your motorcycle, waiting for me in a sleeveless vest.

"Eh, chamcha!" I called out from the balcony. "Go from here!"

"Only if you go with me."

"When my father comes, he will thrash you," I said. "Or don't you know he's not fond of Mussulmans?"

You grinned. "Then I'll tell him, Jai Sri Krishna."

Your muscles gleamed. I shut the curtains. I ignored you three more times after that, in the market, on the beach, outside the cinema, all the places you had seen me before. Two years later I was in London, crying because I was alone and had lost my way on the tube, when you reached for my hand.

"Bibi," you said. "In this strange city, you and I are the same. Now tell me: What is your name?"

I couldn't ignore you again.

I had always dreamt of living in London. Its perfect rows of narrow homes, its tidy streets, the green hedges and vine-laced walls, the pink-cheeked children in school uniforms with accents as bright as the chime of a bell. I could reinvent myself there, enter as one person and leave as another. Maybe I would become like those women on British sitcoms, with bellies full of red wine. But London was for my brother, Jagdish. I was meant to stay home. When my papa sent him to study at South Bank University, I begged him to send me as well.

"London is no place for a girl your age."

"But I'm not a girl; I'm a woman."

"Eh, jabri!" my mother cried. "Don't talk so freely in front of your father."

"Should I have said I'm a boy?"

"Watch your tongue," my mother snapped. "Which man will marry you, hah, with a mouth like that?"

"A smart one."

I was sent to my room. The next day, I pleaded with my father again, reminding him that the schools in London were far better than in Tanzania, and that it was only a matter of time before we could all live there together.

"Bas, Renu, I have made up my mind."

For weeks I watched dolefully while Jagdish prepared for his move abroad. I helped my mother grind lentils for khichuri, and roll rotis from scratch, and sort through trays of long-grain rice, removing fibers and stones. Jagdish went for drinks with his friends and bragged about the flat he had found and the girls he would date at university. I sat on my bed and watched him pack.

"It's not fair."

He looked at me with his dark, shadowed eyes—like a raccoon's, I had once teased—and sighed. Later that evening, he knocked on my door.

"Let me talk to Papa," he said. "I'll make sure he agrees. You can stay with me in London. Don't worry." He smiled. "I'll handle it."

The next morning, like Jagdish had promised, Papa changed his mind. I didn't ask my brother what he had said to make this happen. I only thanked him profusely. Two months later, I was boarding a plane at Julius Nyerere International Airport and thinking about all the things my life in London would bring me. I had no idea it would bring you.

AKASH

After my birthday party, I didn't see you for a while. We went to different schools. I had camp over the summer. During the holidays, my parents always took Bijal and me abroad. It wasn't until two years later, when we were both fifteen, that I saw you at a garba. It was a Saturday in October. The garba was at my high school gym. I remember being embarrassed by this, the idea that, at any moment, a classmate or teacher might walk in. I wondered what they would think of it: a hundred Indians gathered around an altar, a multiarmed goddess flashing her tongue. I imagined what Bryce would say, how he would point and laugh. I slunk in the shadows.

You arrived shortly after I did. You wore a puffed black jacket, a FUBU sweatshirt. Your cheeks blazed from the cold. The shoelaces in your Air Jordans were untied. We were the only two boys not wearing Indian clothes. The raw silk made my balls itch. I had told my mother this the night before.

"I don't like that, Akash," she'd said. "Don't talk about your balls."

I watched as you noticed someone across the room and nodded, grinning shyly before approaching, as if you were pleased to see them.

A girl. Her name was Monika. She had wide, moon-shaped eyes. She was your classmate at Troy. I had heard she was brilliant, but also a bit of a slut. I chose to believe the latter. It was obvious, from the way the light danced across her liquid gaze, that she wanted you. Maybe this is why I walked up to you that night instead of ignoring you like I had planned.

"Akash." You looked up at me, surprised. "Hi."

If you were still bruised from that afternoon at the arcade, you didn't show it. It had been two years since we'd last spoken. I wasn't sure what to expect. Fortunately, you seemed just as pleased as I was.

The three of us—you, me, and Monika—went to the parking lot. It had been my idea. I had thought we could listen to music in my father's car. I didn't think you would ask Monika to join us. By the time I retrieved the keys from my father and met you at the entrance to the gym, she was lacing up her shoes.

"It's freezing out," she said, blowing into cupped hands.

You offered her your coat. We slid through the maze of parked cars before finding my father's jet-black Mercedes-Benz, glazed with moonlight.

"Nice car," you said.

Monika shifted her feet from side to side, looking bored. It was obvious, by the way she folded her arms, that she wanted you and her to be alone.

"*Why* are we here again?"

She twisted a lock of hair around her finger, and it was this, her bold display of disinterest, that made me hate her.

"Because it beats being in there," I said.

"Whatever."

We climbed into my father's car. You sat next to me; Monika was alone in the back. I was struck by your presence, the proximity of our limbs. I turned on the stereo and slid down the windows, letting the night air seep in. We listened to Jay-Z's "99 Problems."

I got ninety-nine problems, but a bitch ain't one.

"This song is so offensive to women," Monika said.

"No, it's not," I said, twisting around to stare at her. "He's talking about a police dog, not a woman. If you actually listened to the words, you would know that."

She scoffed, turning her head. You looked at me and smiled.

"Akash knows his shit."

For a moment, our eyes locked. I noticed the faint fuzz already darkening your upper lip. The song faded and Monika grew chatty, gossiping about some of the other Indian girls inside.

"Did you hear about Shweta? I heard she gave a blow job to some guy on a field trip to the Mall of America. Who does that?"

"Damn," you said. "Wish I went to *her* school."

She slapped the back of your head. You rubbed it gingerly and grinned. I knew, then, what I had suspected all along: she was your girlfriend.

"Well," I said, flashing Monika a knowing look. "I hear a lot of things about a lot of people—I hope none of them are true."

Her eyes slowly widened. She turned her head.

"Whatever. I'm bored. C'mon, Parth. Let's go."

The way she said this, with a proprietary lilt, made my skin burn. I wanted you to stay. I wanted us to be alone. Before that moment, I had never known real desire: the sick-sweet feeling of wanting something beyond your reach. You looked at me, then, your eyes bright with longing, and if you hadn't followed her inside, I would have thought you wanted it, too.

After that night at the garba, I saw you in flashes, clips. There you were at Chaya Aunty and Bhupendra Uncle's anniversary party, in an Abercrombie shirt, your hair freshly faded. At Radhika's sixteenth birthday party, at a rec center her parents had rented and filled with catered Indian food, you charmed my parents at their table, your smile wide. I was too nervous to approach. I wanted *you* to come to *me*. You didn't. The night your parents invited mine for dinner at your apartment, to thank my father for the free medicine he had given them, I spent all afternoon planning what I would wear. I decided on a white polo and khaki trousers, a brown, braided belt. I was nervous when we walked around the motel to your front door. I had worn Bijal's cologne.

"What's that smell?" my mother had asked, in the car on the way over. "It smells like rotten fruit."

I wiped my neck until it turned raw. During the few moments before your mother answered, I went over in my head how I would act, the things I would take interest in—sports, automobiles, girls—and the things I would not—Mariah Carey's new hair color. I re-created your face, the honeyed skin and thick black brows and fuzzy down above your lip. When your mother answered, her expression gave everything away.

"Akash," she said. "If I had known you were coming, I would have made Parth stay home. He went out with his friends."

I was humiliated, certain you would think less of me knowing I had no plans of my own. It was weeks before I saw you again. The people at my school made fun of the people at yours. They called you Troy Boys, or Troy Fags, or simply: nerds. Your test scores were higher, your student lounge fancier, the success rate of your graduates superior to ours. I had heard my mother asking my father once how your parents could afford it; Troy was a private school. She had posed the question delicately, as if the difference between our finances was an unspeakable thing. I suppose this was her way of remaining "humble." *The more you have,* my father once said, *the more you should pretend not to have it.* It wasn't until someone cornered your parents at a dinner party and asked them about it—as Indians often do—that we found out the truth: you were brilliant. You had a full scholarship. Just when I thought you couldn't be more special, there you were.

And then came your cousin's wedding. It was a Saturday in March. There was a light dusting of snow on the ground. The sky was the same washed-out shade as the earth. Dark sludge lined the pathways and roads. My parents complained: *Who plans a wedding in March?* All the Indians in our town bemoaned the inconvenience of your cousin's wedding, only to show up in their finest gold.

The wedding was at a hall reserved for graduation parties and birthdays. My parents decided to skip the ceremony—they were busy planning our family trip to Vail—so we showed up to the reception instead.

"They've catered food from Raj Palace," my mother warned us, on the car ride over. "Stay away from the meat."

"Ew," said Bijal, who was home from college, his long, suited legs folded up in the back. "Raj Palace tastes like shit."

I stared out the windows at the shadows floating by, fidgeting in my suit. When we walked into the venue, Bijal shook his head.

"This is it?"

He swept his gaze across the sparsely decorated room.

"The flowers are fake," said an aunty in passing. "I touched them."

With each comment, each brow arched in your family's direction, I felt more and more protective of you. You wore a black suit with a black shirt and a glinting gold tie. You were swarmed by cousins, whose side you refused to leave. Halfway through the cocktail hour, my mother approached Bijal and me in her wine-colored sari. She whispered in Bijal's ear. They looked around the room and smiled. I knew what they were looking at: the wild gestures, the cheap jewelry, the waggling, oil-slicked heads. I knew what my mother was thinking before she even said the words aloud.

"These people—they are not like *us*."

My mother's words were like a rope of fire that cordoned us off from the rest of the room. "We are not *those* Indians," she seemed to say. The freshies. The FOBs. The Bud-Bud Ding-Ding 2.99s. The cabdrivers. The store clerks. The waiters at Raj Palace. The people who have lived in America for thirty years but still look like they leapt off a boat. According to Bijal, Indians look like models or refugees; there's no middle ground.

"Look at that," he once said, pointing to a man in a grease-stained coat, splattering the sidewalk with orange-colored spit. "Makes me fucking sick."

We were on Devon Street, the Indian neighborhood in Chicago. The man was eating paan.

"But it's the Indian neighborhood," I'd said. "Let him do what he wants."

"It's America," Bijal said. "If they wanna act like hooligans, they should've stayed home."

Now, whenever someone asks me where I'm from, my answer is always the same. "I'm Indian, but I was born here." *Born here. Born here. Born here.* We are not those Indians. They are not like us.

I spent the majority of your cousin's wedding reception avoiding my family. Bijal was posturing in front of a group of kids his age, showing off his Nokia phone. My mother was gossiping with an aunty. My father approached me with a hunk of lamb wiggling from his fork.

"Food is not bad, Akash. Eat up."

"Okay, Dad."

He gripped my shoulder, concerned. "All right, beta? Having fun?"

I shrugged him off.

Soon the cocktail hour was over, and Radha's father made a speech. Bijal laughed, not at a particularly funny joke, but at the way Radha's father pronounced the word "special"—like "spatial."

My daughter is very spatial.

"Oh, man," Bijal said.

My mother shot him a warning look. Soon the music started and the dance floor flooded; bodies gelled together to form a quivering mass. Your mother approached.

"Akash, come join us. Parth is also there."

She pointed to the dance floor. You were dancing with your

cousins, your face shining under the lights. The DJ was playing a Nelly song, "Ride Wit Me."

If you wanna go and take a ride with me,
We three-wheeling in the fo' with the gold D's . . .

"Go," my mother encouraged, not wanting us to seem rude. "Dance, Akash."

Dance, Akash. I remembered when she found me dancing in my room one night. *Don't dance, Akash! You're not Michael Jackson.* I made my way toward you. You didn't notice me at first. You were too busy bouncing up and down with your cousins, throwing your hands in the air. The floor shook beneath us. The walls vibrated. Flashing bulbs spilled puddles of pink light across the tiles. Suddenly you saw me, waving your arm.

"Akash!"

I might have thought you were drunk by the way you pulled me into a humid embrace. But it was the music, humming from within. The sweat from your chest left a patch on my shirt.

"Sorry, man," you told me. "I'm sweating bullets."

If I could have, Parth, I would have licked it right off.

That night, I taught you how to crip walk. The DJ played "Let's Get Married" by Jagged Edge—the remix, not the original— and I skipped across the floor. Right-left-right-right-left-right-left-right-right-left. You did a windmill. The crowd formed a ring around us. Blue lasers penetrated the gaps. At one point, mesmerized by my moves, you walked away in feigned defeat, bowing as you left. Then you came right back, moonwalking around me. The crowd roared. I watched you, the way your face lit up whenever I did something new, the way your lips curled in a mock grimace, as if my talent was a pungent smell. It was apparent by the way you couldn't peel your eyes off me: you were seeing me for the first time.

"I didn't know you could dance," you said later, at the water fountain. The reception had ended; guests were clearing the hall. Your tie had come loose. Sweat rolled off the slick ends of your hair.

"I'm okay."

"You're more than okay. Where'd you learn to do that?"

"Around."

We stood like that for a while, ignoring the urgent press around us. My head spun. I was afraid that someone would come and pull you away from me, that this moment, however tenuous, would unceremoniously end. I didn't want it to. I tried to find the right words, my brain cramping instead. Then Bijal slung his arm around my neck.

"Yo, Osh-y. Time to go home."

"Don't call me that."

"Osh-y Kosh-y B'gosh-y, let's go. You can dance like a fairy later."

I pulled away from him, burning with shame. But you looked unfazed.

"We should hang out sometime," you said.

"Yeah," I replied. "I mean sure, if you're free. If I'm free, too, I guess. You know, if we both have time."

"Right." You smiled. "I think that's how it works."

Bijal looked at both of us, his eyebrows arched.

"Whatever, weirdos. I'll be in the car."

He shoved me as he walked off; you followed him with your eyes. Then you turned back around.

"So . . ." you said, smiling. "Are you on AIM?"

RENU

After you saw me on the tube, you led me to a small café so we could talk. You said your name was Kareem.

"It rhymes with dream. What is your dream?"

"That you'll never write poetry."

When you laughed, the sound struck my chest like the palm of a hand. You were studying at King's College. You had arrived from Tanzania three months before. We both missed the red chili-dusted yucca sold for shillings on the street. We missed freshly cracked coconuts and their treacly milk. We missed the markets and hawkers and the lazy froth of the sea. But most of all, we missed that solid feeling of being rooted to the earth. Here, in London, we were adrift.

I did not expect to be so taken by you. I did not expect to re-create, over and over, your likeness in my head. Your broad shoulders and barrel chest, the brown sheen of your face. Your impressive height, six foot two. Tall for an Indian, taller than anyone I had met.

"I could carry you on my back," you once told me.

"Then why didn't you offer? All this time I have been walking like a fool."

Because my parents were still in Tanzania, and Jagdish was in school, we were able to meet privately. I still did not know what Jagdish had said to my father to convince him to let me move. I didn't need to know. Once you found me, Kareem, I knew it was fate. We marveled at the coincidence that we should both be in London at the same time.

"It's destiny," you said.

I was twenty-four. My parents had begun sending me letters about prospective grooms. I tore each letter into a million shreds.

In London, my ego shrank like meat on a skewer, onions in a pan. Once, on a walk in the neighborhood, I stopped to admire a woman walking her dog. The woman was very pale. The dog was like a cloud. I had smiled at both of them, but the woman only glared.

"Oi!" she'd said. "What's your problem?"

"I was admiring your dog."

"Mind your business, Paki."

I am a formidable woman, Kareem. I speak my mind. Had this been Tanzania, I would have silenced her for good.

"Shut up!" I would have said. "You corpse."

Instead, I said nothing. I had heard the story of my cousin, Praful, who, after walking home from a pub, had been attacked by a group of English men in an alley while their white girl-friends laughed. They called him a Paki. They called him a wog. They told him to go back. *Go back. Go back.*

"The British invaded India with gunpowder," Jagdish often said. "Now *we* are invading *them* with curry powder."

"It's not the same thing."

Of course, there were good people, like Vivienne, who worked with me at the pharmacy. She was always telling me stories about the men she dated and the things they bought her and asking me to share stories of my own. I didn't tell her about you. I didn't tell anyone. Not my parents, not Jagdish, not even his new wife, Smita, who, after my parents had scouted her for him, managed to capture his heart. You were a secret, a small jewel pressed tightly in my hand. You sparkled in darkness. Your presence was a pulse.

We saw each other most weekends, eating kababs in greasy restaurants or falafels on the street, planning picnics in Rich-mond Park, its meandering gold pastures reminding us so much of Serengeti National Park. But there was no wildlife here, only white people with dogs. It was under the shade of a tree, a lemon square crumbling from your lips, that you first kissed me, Kareem.

Do you remember the night you took me to the theatre in the West End? It was raining; a fat, syrupy drizzle pounded the streets. I had no umbrella, so you sheltered me underneath the canopy of your coat. I kept my head down and stared at the swirls of bright light reflected in the puddles at my feet. We were going to see *Jesus Christ Superstar*. A rock opera. I had never heard of such a thing.

"Bibi," you said. "This is why we're in London: to experience a world beyond our wildest dreams."

"That sounds very melodramatic."

"I'm practicing, bibi. We're going to the theatre. It will be full of drama."

The concept of "the theatre" was foreign to me. We didn't have "the theatre" in Tanzania, and before that, in Gujarat, India, where my parents lived, "the theatre" would have been scoffed at. I dressed up for the occasion. I wore a spangled top and bell-bottom jeans. My hair was ironed flat. You guided me down the streets, pointing out restaurants and people and hotels.

"Look, look," you said, gesturing toward a juggler on the street. "There are all sorts here."

Perhaps we were "all sorts," too. I liked it: the danger of it. We were like Romeo and Juliet. Sometimes, Kareem, you were Juliet.

When we reached the entrance to the theatre, you felt around your pockets and panicked.

"What is it?"

"The tickets."

You looked like a child who had just lost a toy. I handed you your jacket and you searched frantically in every pocket. "It's not here," you said. "Goddamn it."

You kicked a lamppost in frustration. Soon, the doors opened, and a crowd of people disgorged from the theatre, all very trim and very white and very neat.

"Now what?" I said, the rain stabbing one side of my face.

You handed me the jacket; I held it above my head. I could

see disappointment cloud your face—you had planned this for weeks—then you looked down the road and pointed toward the juggler.

"Come with me."

We walked down the street where the juggler, in a white-and-black suit, stood idly by.

"Sir," you said. "Excuse me, sir."

The juggler looked confused. "Me?"

"Yes, you, sir." You quickly motioned for me to sit on an iron bench a few paces away. Then you plucked a few sterling notes from your wallet. "Can you please perform for my wife?"

Your wife. The words warmed my face. Until then, I had never tried them on, had never stretched them over my skin, but they fit like the soft leather of a glove. The juggler looked at the money fluttering between your fingers and beamed.

"Of course," he said, gazing at me. "Good evening, my lady."

"Good evening!"

"What's the special occasion?"

I looked at you, confused. You came to sit by my side. "No special occasion," you clarified, dropping your arm around me. "But you see, sir, I like to call this lovely woman my wife, even though we're not married. I was thinking, maybe, if you charm her, she'll decide to say yes."

The juggler looked at us and laughed. "A beautiful lady like this? I'd have to be very charming."

The balls orbited like tiny planets in the air. You kissed me on the mouth.

AKASH

The first time we hung out was at your motel. My father dropped me off. There was a mild spring breeze; a fresh rain had soaked the earth. Everything was green and glimmering. Your father was manning the front desk because the manager had called in sick, and your mother was visiting her sister in Florida. You greeted me at the door to your parents' apartment, wearing a sleeveless T-shirt.

"Do you want anything to eat?"

The few times I had hung out with white boys in my neighborhood, food was never involved. They either assumed I'd eaten or didn't seem to care. I knew it was your mother's doing: this impulse to push food in front of someone the minute they walk through the door. Already, there was little we needed to explain to each other.

"No thanks."

You shrugged and led the way to your bedroom, where we played video games for a while, me on a beanbag, you on your bed. Your room was no bigger than the others, a small rectangle with a full-sized bed pushed up against the wall. A stack of *Star Wars* books curled on your shelf. Your closet was open, revealing the tight press of your clothes. You were more relaxed than I was. Being in your home made me aware of every little thing: the way I had dressed, the way I smelled, the things I said, all the little things I could possibly do wrong, humiliating myself in front of you. You were at ease in a way I could never be.

"Relax," you said, looking at me.

"Huh?"

"I mean you can sit back. You're all hunched up over there."

"I like to be hunched."

You laughed. "Choksi."

"What does that mean?"

"You don't know?"

I shook my head. You sat up and placed your controller on the nightstand next to your bed. Then you swung your feet around to the floor. "It means nerd."

"Oh."

"Do you even know what kem cho means?"

"Of course I know what that means. I'm Gujarati."

"Just making sure."

Another person might have taken offense to this, but I was quietly pleased. You were comfortable enough to insult me; it was a sign that we were friends. Girls expressed their approval with compliments; boys did it with jabs. You picked up an apple from your desk and casually bit into it, looking around the room. Then you tossed it in the air. I saw the way your bronzed arms flexed when you caught it.

"Let's go for a bike ride."

I was never very good at riding bikes; not like Bijal, who rode with one hand or no hands at all.

"Are you going to be okay?" you asked, when I ran into a parked car. "When was the last time you rode a bike?"

We were practicing in the parking lot behind your parents' motel. You gave me your cousin Radha's old bike. It was white with pink accents and frills. I wobbled and braked too hard and nearly fell off. I hopped back on and wobbled some more. At one point I had to get off altogether and walk alongside it for a few feet. It was pathetic.

"I don't know. Maybe when I was eight?"

"I think we might have some training wheels in the storage closet."

"Shut up."

You grinned, kicking off. "Come on, Evel Knievel."

I followed you down a path littered with paper cups and broken glass. A car swooshed by us, kicking up a spray. The roads were still sleek and mirrored, and the sky presaged rain.

"Having fun?" you said, turning to check on me.

"Yeah."

"You look like you're in pain."

"That's how I always look."

You laughed so hard you nearly fell off your bike. I cut in front of you, zipping ahead. "Well, look at that!" you said, whistling. "Speed Racer!"

We rode past the last few commercial buildings before hitting an expanse of farmland. A county road stretched open before us. My mother had always complained about how flat Illinois was, how there was nothing to see, nowhere to go, but it was this nothingness that arrested me. A place with no beginning and no end.

You rode ahead of me and let go of the handlebars, winging your arms. I stared at the back of your head, the way the top was ruffled by the wind. Your T-shirt ballooned. You looked like you were flying.

"All right, Akash," you said, turning around with a smile. "Your turn. Let go!"

"No way."

"You can do it!"

"I think I'm good."

You shook your head. Then you took a sharp turn and pedaled back to me, hitting the brakes. A cloud of dust smoked between us.

"What are you afraid of?"

"Breaking my neck? Dying? Not to mention the humiliation."

"All reasonable things—if you're bungee jumping. This is a bike ride, idiot. The worst you can get is a scrape." You reached out and mussed my hair, your hand lingering. "But I guess to a little raja like you, it's the same thing."

"I thought I was a choksi."

"You're both."

You set off ahead of me. I pedaled fast. When I finally caught up to you, you grabbed my arm.

"Ready?"

"No!"

"Great!" You let go and stretched out your arms. "Come on. Just keep pedaling fast!"

I looked at you then, the gleam in your eyes, the bright stretch of your smile, the soft pink flesh of your lips, and the feeling I got was the same feeling I had when I finally let go, like anything could happen, but nothing bad ever would.

"I'm doing it!" I cried, the wind rushing under my arms. "I'm doing it!"

"Yeah you are!"

"I'm flying!"

We soared like twin birds to the edge of the earth.

"You're a fighter jet, Akash!" you said, howling into the empty space. "Who can stop you now?"

RENU

The girls in Tanzania used to say the first night with a man was like a hot knife between your legs. But you were gentle, stroking my hair. You slid your fingers into me.

"You've done this before," I said.

"Not with you."

I slapped your shoulder. We were in your shared flat, with its dripping pipes and low-hanging ceiling, no window in your room; like being in a small cave. The pressure was unbearable, but the warmth of your body, the firm grip of your hands released me. The next morning, when I slid down my underwear in your loo, I was surprised to find that it was not spotted with blood.

Little things endeared me to you: the way your ears went pink in the cold, the way you laughed at all my jokes, the way your brow sprung beads of sweat after drinking too much beer. Your deep voice hummed like strings beneath my skin. Though you were quiet at times, disappearing into some small, private space, every now and then you said something profound.

"Being in London is like being a child in a strict school," you once said. "No matter how fast you learn, it is never fast enough."

You wanted to finish your degree and move to America. You said we would be treated better there.

"What is this we?" I said. "Are you planning to marry me?"

"Are you asking me to ask?"

"Jaja haave! Ask waro!"

I secretly hoped that you would, though it was foolish of me. Hindus didn't marry Muslims—this went without saying. I remembered all the conversations in my parents' kitchen in Tanzania, when uncles from all over came to discuss the riots of 1969. Six hundred people dead; my cousin Himesh was among them. Houses burned. Temples defaced. Hindus and Muslims. Renu and Kareem. But on the streets of London, where we were both equally brown, equally isolated and alone, the oceans between us dried. No one cared what we were. I could imagine a future. I saw a house with a fence and a son with your eyes.

I remember the first time I told you I loved you. We were lying in your bed watching the seconds tick by on your clock. It was morning, just moments before I would have to bathe and dress and take the tube back to Croydon to slip unnoticed into my brother's flat. I was already dreading the cold. You were gripping me under the blanket. Your hair was slick, your eyes thick with sleep. Your mouth, the bitten color of fruit, was searching mine. I pulled away.

"I haven't brushed."

"Neither have I."

"I'm aware."

You pinched me. "If not now, then when, Renu? One day

your breath won't matter. Your figure won't matter. Even that beautiful face of yours, arresting as it is, won't matter."

"What *will* matter?"

You pushed the palm of your hand onto my forehead. "This," you said. "And when that goes—" You brought your hand to my heart. "This."

"Who said my mind will go before yours? Once that happens you won't even know who I am."

"I will always know," you said. "Just like the sun has always known the earth."

"Which one of us is the sun and which one of us is the earth?"

You smiled, kicking me. "You are my sun, Renu. Is that better?"

"Fine," I said, and later, "I love you, too."

I was happy to leave that morning knowing I would return, that there were still new places to see, new restaurants to try, new pleasures to discover in your bed, new memories to be created and stored. I smiled on the tube and the bus and during the short walk to my brother's flat. I smiled at the bitter old woman who lived across the street. I smiled at the stray cat that nipped at my heels. I smiled at the rude schoolchildren who stared at me on their walk to class. That afternoon, at work, I even smiled at ornery Mr. Hamilton, who always accused me of getting his prescription wrong. Later, when I walked into my brother's flat and saw the shoes lined up by the door and the strange coat hanging on the wall, my smile disappeared.

"You're home," Jagdish said, standing in the hall. "Go quickly. Change. He's here."

"Who is here?"

"Ashok."

"But who is Ashok?"

"What do you mean, *who is Ashok*?" Jagdish said angrily. "He's my friend from university—the doctor from America. He's visiting his parents. They're keen to get him married."

"And who said I was keen to get married?"

It is this that I will always remember: the grave look on Jagdish's face.

"Renu," he said, softly. "Why else would Papa send you here?"

AKASH

The next time I saw you was at Best Buy. You worked there on weekends, in the computers department. My father needed a new TV. I saw you from across the room, in your royal blue shirt. You were laughing with a coworker. A girl walked by and you smiled. There was a glow about you, your skin golden, a wash of pink blooming across your face. The stubble around your jaw was dark. All day I had prepared for this moment, but now I didn't know what to do. Would you be pleased to see me? Would you pretend I didn't exist? I didn't want it to seem like I was stalking you—that I had invented some pretense to show up at your work—so I stuck by my father's side instead, feigning interest in a plasma TV.

"What do you think, Akash?"

I shrugged, annoyed by his presence. Had I been alone, I could have strolled obliviously until you happened to notice me, at which point I would pretend to be shocked. *Oh right,* I might have said. *I forgot you work here.*

But it was my father who noticed you, pointing across the room.

"There's Parth. He will help us."

"He looks busy, Dad."

"Nonsense. He can help."

"Dad, let's just ask someone else."

"Beta, he's right there. He's Vinay Uncle's son. Why can't he help?" He called out your name. "Parth!"

When your eyes landed on us, you strode over and smiled.

"Hi, Ashok Uncle." You looked at me. "What's up, Akash?"

"Hi."

If you were excited to see me, you didn't show it. You stood with your back facing me while my father showed you the TV, nodding your head. You folded your arms. I was disappointed, flattened by your professional manner, the way you explained to us the merits and drawbacks of the TV, assuring us that it was an excellent buy. You didn't even look at me when my father shook your hand.

"See this, Akash?" my father said. "I told you Parth would help."

You seemed confused. "Did he need convincing?"

"Akash didn't want to disturb you. I think he was embarrassed."

Your eyes met mine. I was certain this was both the end of our friendship and the end of my life, but you smiled. "He should know better, Uncle. I'm Employee of the Month."

"Employee of the Month!" My father clasped your shoulder. "That's excellent, Parth."

You offered to walk us to the checkout counter and help us load the TV into the car. You let my father walk ahead, hanging back to walk alongside me. You nudged my arm.

"Evel Knievel. Break any bones?"

"No."

"Well, we'll have to do something about that, won't we?" You stopped short of the checkout counter, pushing your fist into my chest. "Come over tomorrow. We'll hang."

After that day, we were inseparable, chatting for hours on AIM, meeting on weekends and after school, playing video games at my house or yours. We rode bikes down sunlit roads flanked by wheat fields and corn. Every now and then, our parents met for dinners and you and I sat on opposite ends of the table, flinging water with our straws. We exchanged secret kicks, knowing looks, escaped into the bathroom to avoid our parents' talk. You came into my life and rimmed it with gold. Everything was more bearable with you by my side.

Shortly after 9/11, my teacher, Mr. Einhorn, wheeled a television set into our homeroom so that we could watch the coverage over the news. I sat still while looped footage of the attack aired on-screen. The glinting silver planes and thick black smoke was an image I'll never forget, a stamp that refuses to fade. Mr. Einhorn explained that guidance counselors were available in case anyone wanted to talk, in case we were afraid. I was afraid. But I didn't want to tell him why. I looked around the classroom, at all the stunned white faces, sinking lower in my seat. That afternoon, I heard my mother telling Bijal to shave his beard. *It's not safe,* she said. *It's not safe for us anymore.* I wanted to laugh. We were never safe to begin with.

The next morning, Bryce and his friends approached me in the locker room after PE. I still remembered that afternoon, the picture of Lord Ganesh on the board. I was changing, my body turned toward a wall so as not to expose my frail torso, an act of modesty none of the other boys seemed to require. No one else was like me, wanting to disappear.

"Well, look at this," said Bryce, slipping between his friends, standing inches from my face. "Elephant fag is causing trouble again." His breath was damp. The locker room was ripe with the smell of soaked towels and steaming shit. I gagged.

"Why do you always change like that?" said Bryce, digging his finger into my chest. The pressure made me wince. "What do you have to hide?"

"Nothing."

"Maybe he's a hermaphrodite," said Evan.

"Yeah, a tranny," said Lance.

Bryce flicked his cold gaze down the length of my body.

"Let's find out."

He grabbed at my shorts, his fingers fumbling with the knot. Lance and Evan pinned me against the locker. The rest of the boys ignored my cries, flooding out of the room. I thrashed like a fish in their grip. The knot slipped loose. The waistband slackened.

"Hey!"

The janitor, a Black man named Mr. Washington, whose bloodshot eyes had seen more trauma than mine, pointed at Bryce. "You leave him be," he said. "Go on! Get out of here!" They withdrew. The only sound I could hear when I tightened my shorts was their laughter echoing through the hall. It was ten in the morning; Mr. Washington only cleaned the locker room in the afternoons. I knew what it was that had saved me, what caused Bryce and his friends to ignore me the rest of the week. You.

Sometimes we hung around the front desk of the motel with nothing to do. Your father would leave you in charge, and I would watch as you entered guests into the computer, handing them their keys. I stared at the garlanded silk picture of Lakshmi fixed to the wall behind the desk, her nose ring twinkling. Next to it was a family portrait. You wore a tennis shirt, and your hair was center-parted. Your parents smiled proudly behind you—as if presenting you to the world. You, their only American-born son. It was you who taught them how to pronounce certain words, expressing frustration when it confused their tongues. Salmon. You hated it when your father pronounced it "sall-mon." You were their interpreter, their guide to the outside world. You taught them everything there was to know. When there was a miscommunication, when a waiter had trouble with your father's accent, and your father had trouble with your waiter's tone, it was to you they both turned, awaiting your answer. You didn't ask for this. None of us did. Still, you obliged, a dutiful son. Perhaps this is your greatest achievement, Parth: that when your parents gave you life, you taught them how to live it.

Though my parents were vigilant when Bijal hung out with his white friends, enforcing strict curfews, they allowed you and me to roam free. I think my mother liked that we were friends. Your brilliance, your aptitude for math and science, the fact that you already knew you wanted to become a doctor, was a good influence on me. I suppose she hoped in time I could be more like you, reinvented in your image, the type of child you paraded instead of explained.

She also liked that you brought me to the temple. Though my parents wrote checks for donations and showed their faces during Shivaratri, they were not religious like yours. My mother ate meat and drank cocktails. She didn't light diyas at the temple. She was pleased one morning when I told her you had invited me to participate in the cleanup efforts the youth program had organized after a recent vandalism—someone had spray-painted the words DIE MUSLIMS across the temple façade. Bijal was home from college that weekend.

"Osh, you hang out with the temple freaks now?"

"They're not freaks."

"Have you seen them? I can't tell who has more facial hair, the boys or the girls."

I'd gaped at my mother. "Do you hear this?"

"He's only kidding, Akash."

She walked over to Bijal and made as if to slap him, but only gently pinched his arm.

I rolled my eyes. "Good lord."

"Lord Krishna or Lord Shiva? You'd better practice, Osh. They'll quiz you."

They didn't. When I arrived at the temple that afternoon, you were standing with a group of boys and girls our age, your pant legs rolled up. The half sleeves of your V-neck revealed the lean muscles in your arms. A sponge, fat with soapy water, dripped from your hand.

"Akash," you said, waving me over. "You came."

You introduced me to the others, one of whom, Snehal, was also your classmate at Troy. My eyes flew to Monika. I remembered her from that night at the garba. She'd just scored a 1550 on her SAT. I don't know why I knew that, but I did, and whenever I saw her, at the cinema, the mall, someone's dance recital, the number floated above her head like a conversation bubble. I'd scored a 1210. According to my school counselor it was a perfectly reasonable score, enough to secure my admission to a number of state schools, but when I brought the score home to my parents, my mother immediately asked when I could retake it, and my father said, "That's okay, Akash, it happens," as if I had urinated in my pants.

I looked for signs in Monika's behavior that might explain her 1550-ness. What made her so special? Monika played tennis and loved *Buffy the Vampire Slayer*; she wouldn't shut up about it. She kept pulling your arm and telling you about the most recent episode. Though you had denied she was your girlfriend, it was evident she liked you. I could see it in the way she hung on your every word and laughed at your jokes. The pink gloss on her lips that was for your benefit, the way she kept interrupting me to talk to you—it was a thorn in my heel. Because if Monika liked you then other girls would, too, and how could they not? They say 16,000 women fell in love with Lord Krishna in Vraj. Is it so hard to believe that one of them could be a man? Because that's what it felt like, Parth. It felt like falling, like the world was rushing toward me and there was nothing I could do to stop it.

That afternoon, I stood next to you and scrubbed hate graffiti off a temple, but all I could feel inside me was the sick-sweet pang of a word I rarely used. I watched the way you bit your lip in concentration, the care you took in rinsing your sponge. I saw the beads of sweat run down your neck and swivel down your chest. Halfway through, you mopped your brow, squinting in the sun.

"Everyone is saying we should put up a sign: Hindus, not Muslims."

"Oh."

"But that's not right either," you said, your nostrils flaring. "It shouldn't matter if we *were* Muslims. It shouldn't matter what we are. No one should be targeted this way."

The passion snapped like sparks off your tongue. I could feel your voice in my chest. Had it not been for you, I would not have been there, wiping the gray smear off a temple I rarely visited, while dozens of cars whooshed by on the main road. I could have told you this. I could have thanked you for opening my eyes. Instead, I asked, "Who did it?"

"Who knows," said Monika, sidling up behind us. "It's happening everywhere."

She wiped her hands on her shirt. Her black hair was cinched with a band and exploded in a puff down her back. She had a beauty mark, like a stray drop of ink, near her left eye. I was aware of the way she inched closer to you.

"Fortunately, we have cameras," you said. "We're gonna take a look at the footage."

You directed this not at her, but at me, your eyes focused on mine.

"I can help."

"Okay, Kojak."

"Who's that?"

You laughed. "Never mind."

Later, when Monika got tired of being ignored and walked off, you flicked your soapy sponge at me. "Choksi," you said. "When are we hanging out?"

The day I got my driver's license, I picked you up in Bijal's old car—a pearl-white Audi with leather bucket seats. You were waiting in the back lot of your parents' motel, shooting hoops. The sun gleamed off your ball as it arced across the sky. You missed, the ball bouncing with a thwack. You smiled and shrugged. Then you picked up the ball and tried again. This time it sailed victoriously through the net. You were so comfortable in this, your boyishness, the way you dribbled the ball and pivoted and shot, and the satisfaction on your face as it swished through the net. I envied you this, the ease you had of living inside your own skin, the relaxed way you spread your legs or spat on the road, adjusting yourself through your pants, the depth of your voice. *A real boy,* people would have said. Once, I'd heard a cousin of mine describing her five-year-old son the same way.

"He's a real boy," she'd said. "He loves trucks and trains and wrestling in the mud."

She'd said this with pride, as if the opposite, a boy who loved Barbie dolls and his mother's lipstick, was a fate she had narrowly missed.

"Choksi," you called, bouncing the ball off the blacktop and tossing it over a fence. You jogged to my car. You wore a hooded sweatshirt, athletic shorts. Your hair was slicked up.

"Nice ride. I hope I don't die in it."

I flashed my license. "They don't give these to just anybody."

You grabbed it from my hand and brought it close to your

face. "Let me see this," you said, peering. "If your driving is anything like your bike riding, I'll lose faith in the state."

"I drive just fine."

You examined the license while walking around to the passenger-side seat and folding yourself in. Then you tossed it back.

"Cute picture."

"Shut up."

"No," you said, shutting the door, reclining in your seat. "You look good."

You held my gaze, the words landing between us. I put the car in drive.

We had nowhere specific to go, so we drove around aimlessly. These were the best moments, Parth, when there was nothing holding us back. You told me where to go and I listened, hugging the curves of the road. Sometimes you pointed out a mistake I had made, that I had missed a turn, that I was driving below the speed limit, that I was going the wrong direction on a one-way road. At one point, I grazed a mailbox. You jerked the wheel.

"Holy shit, Akash!" you said, righting us. You looked at me very seriously. "You're a bad driver."

"No, I'm not. That mailbox came out of nowhere."

"Did the house come out of nowhere, too?"

"Whatever."

You laughed, whistling. "Oh, man."

"Shut up."

"Who gave you a license? Did your daddy buy it for you?"

The comment stung, not because it was particularly cruel, but because it pointed out the obvious: that I lived in a world where things could be bought. And you did not.

"Hey," you said, when I didn't respond. "You okay?"

"I'm fine."

"Pull over there."

You guided me to an open clearing overlooking a park. It was the same park my father had taken us to when Bijal and I were small. I remember one day in particular, when a group of boys were harassing me on the bridge, forming a barrier on either side. They called me all sorts of names—only one of them stuck.

"What's a fag?" I'd asked Bijal.

"It's a freak who fucks boys. You better not be one."

Daylight faded over the park; green pastures turned gold. You waved a hand in front of my face.

"Yo, Akash. Where'd you just go?"

"Nowhere."

I turned off the car and we sat watching a few birds peck their way around a park bench. You talked about the temple, about how you'd seen the footage from the camera and identified a car and a license plate. You even saw a clear shot of the person's face.

"I guess this is what it'll be like from now on, huh?" you said. "This is what we'll have to deal with. Everything changed after it happened."

There was no need to discuss what "it" was. We both knew. The way everyone seemed to look at us differently now, with a hostile reserve, as if daring us to speak. A month ago, Bijal had gotten into a fight at a bar with a bouncer who referred to him as "Osama." Bijal told him to get a real job. The bouncer punched him in the face.

"I don't get it," he'd said later, icing his bruise. "I'm not even Middle Eastern."

"It doesn't matter. It would be wrong even if you *were* Middle Eastern."

"Yeah, but I'm not. When you think about it, I'm barely anything."

"Are you saying you're white?"

"Shut up, Osh."

After the incident, Bijal went to Lowe's and bought an American flag to hang outside our garage and a bumper sticker supporting American troops to glue to his car, just in case anyone questioned his allegiance.

I told you this story and you shook your head, not with judgment, but with concern. You said it was normal for Bijal to feel this way, that everyone was frustrated and confused.

"I can't wait to get out of this town," you said.

"Where will you go?"

"I don't know. Maybe the East Coast—anywhere but here."

I hadn't even thought about college; the future was a shapeless thing. I was more concerned with what was happening now, the gossip at school and the drama at home and you, Parth, sitting next to me in a parked car. You spoke of your plans to apply to medical school. You said you had known you wanted to be a doctor ever since you were a child, but you didn't say why. I didn't ask. I could tell, by the tension in your voice when you spoke of your parents—the mistakes they'd made in business, their fear of spending money, the cloistered life they led in that motel—that it had something to do with them. Perhaps you wanted to be more like my parents than yours. I was ashamed to think this way, but I couldn't help remembering what my mother had said to me at your cousin's wedding: *they are not like us*.

The light outside dimmed and the sky turned blood orange. I could see the color reflected in your eyes. You opened my dash and pulled out a vinyl CD case, full of reflective discs.

"Where's *The Blueprint*?" you asked.

"In the trash where it belongs."

"Get out of here."

"I don't get the hype. I prefer his earlier stuff. *In My Lifetime, Volume One* was full of jams."

"It was too pop."

"It was fun."

"Rap isn't supposed to be fun." Your eyes lighted on something; you pulled out a CD. "Found it."

Without asking, you popped it into the CD player and turned up the volume. The windows shook. We listened to three songs before you nudged me with your fist. "Evel Knievel," you said, "how about letting me drive?"

"You don't have a license."

"I have a permit."

"Is that legal?"

"I don't know. Move out of the way." I tumbled out of the car so we could switch places. You lowered the steering wheel. You adjusted my seat. "You sit like a grandma," you said.

You pushed back a few inches and sat low with your elbow resting against the interior of the door. Then you pulled out of the space and sped down a wooded road. We flew under a canopy of trees.

"Listen to these lyrics," you said, adjusting the volume. The song was called "Girls, Girls, Girls." You sang along with it. "I got this Indian squaw, the day that I met her, asked her what tribe she with, red dot or feather?" You grinned, playing it over. "Do you hear that? He's talking about *us*."

"What?"

"Listen again."

You played it back; I listened to the words, the lyrics connecting. "That's awesome."

"See? You see?"

You kept jamming the rewind button, your smile never fading. I opened the moonroof. We sang the lyrics out loud.

I got this Indian squaw, the day that I met her,
Asked her what tribe she with, red dot or feather?
Red dot or feather.

"We're famous, Akash!" you said, as we hurtled ahead, the wind loosening your hair, lifting it from your face. "They know who we are!"

I closed my eyes, letting the music hold me together.

It's sad, isn't it? We can listen to a song a million times until one day we decide to never listen to it again.

––––

RENU

Sometimes, when my rage refused to dim, Ashok would tell me to smile.

"Smile, Renu. Don't look so mad."

According to the nawa girls, this is very bad. Men have no business telling women to smile. They shouldn't be telling us anything at all. "See, Renu," Ashok would say, before lapsing into a detailed explanation of something. This is also bad. It's called mansplaining, and the nawa girls hate it. They hate everything now. Sometimes I want to ask them: *What do you actually like?*

Grain bowls.

When I left you, Kareem, I thought I would never smile again. Your touch, the bristle of your beard, your smooth ribbons of muscle, all of these sensations left me until nothing remained, only a vague recollection, like the tenderness of an old wound.

I didn't smile during my wedding to Ashok. Fortunately, I wasn't expected to; it was not custom to express joy on what was to be the happiest day of one's life—mostly because it wasn't. When Bijal married Jessica, she stood up in front of the reception hall and announced, "This is the happiest day of my life!"

"Of course it is," I whispered. "We paid for the whole thing."

At our weddings, we lowered our eyes and nodded our

heads, took the dust from our parents' feet, wondering if we would ever see them again. It was all highly dramatic. After the ceremony, we sat on four-poster beds while our husbands fumbled with our bras. Fortunately, I was spared; Ashok was nervous. Earlier that morning, he had cried.

"What's your problem?" I'd whispered in the mandap. "What's wrong?"

"You're so beautiful, Renu. I have never seen a more beautiful bride."

"Oh, for god's sake."

But later, when Ashok and I were alone in the hotel suite, dried rose petals curling at my feet, I cried, too. I cried because I realized I had made a mistake. I should have been brave. I should have fought for us.

You should have, too.

On my last night in London, weeks after Ashok and I had married, my green card filed, my suitcases packed, you had asked to meet me. You'd said we should run away.

"Where?"

"To Ireland."

"And do what? With whom? What about my family?"

"We can be our own family."

I told you I needed more. A promise. A plan. You gave me nothing but blind hope. I walked away. But not before you led me into your bedroom one last time. Sometimes I wonder if this was all you had wanted, Kareem: a parting gift. A final taste of what lived between my legs. I went home and washed myself three times. Still, I could feel you, dripping down my thighs.

You don't know this, but the next morning, at Heathrow Airport, I waited for you. I waited until my family left before telling the agent at security that I had left something behind. A scarf? A purse? I can't remember. I walked through the terminal and toward a set of sliding glass doors. I was sure you would come. I had given you the details of my flight hoping you would. I don't know what I was expecting. Maybe that you would kidnap me and take me against my will, fighting off anyone who dared to stand in our way. Maybe I had seen too many films. You didn't show up. I was paged to the gate. I boarded the flight and buckled my seat belt, staring at the lavender sky beyond my window, and never saw you again.

AKASH

I realize now that I was in love with you. You were the most beautiful thing I had ever seen, Parth, with your eyes like black pools slashed by the moon. Your skin like cane sugar, a light brown shade that reddened when you laughed. *Choksi,* you would say. *Duffer.* I wore these words like a crown. The more you teased me, the more you questioned my intelligence, the more you poked and prodded and ridiculed, the closer we became. You did not do this to anyone else. I saw how you spoke to Snehal and Monika, with the stiff formality reserved for classmates, not friends. It was not their necks you slapped. It was not their wrists you pinched. It was not their backs you pushed whenever they walked too slowly.

"You're dragging, Akash," you would say, whenever we roamed through the mall. "Pick up the pace."

You slipped into my world; I slipped into yours. It was not unusual to have you at our dinner table, eating pizza or fajitas, or rotli, dar, baath, and shaak. RDBS, you called it, a mnemonic Bijal laughed at but I soon adopted, complaining to my mother whenever she made it on weeknights. *Mom, I don't want RDBS.* Sometimes I would sneak you the food off my plate. You were happy to devour whatever it was I couldn't: peas and potato shaak, sour kadhi, tindora—sliced bitter melon that, to me, looked like centipedes.

"Tindora's good," you said, smacking your lips. "You're so white, Akash."

Soon, when my mother complained about the noise I made playing *Mortal Kombat* in my room, she included your name.

"Akash, Parth! Stop this now."

Akash, Parth. We went to movies every Saturday afternoon, ate ice cream in the park; sometimes, after your parents had gone to sleep, we snuck into one of the available rooms at your motel to watch HBO. There, locked inside a small, dank space, our eyes reflecting the blue glow of the screen, I studied you. The way your brows knitted when you were lost in thought. The way your mouth hung open when something didn't make sense. The flick of your lips when a naked body flashed across the screen. You looked at me when this happened, grinning.

"Did you see that?"

I pretended I didn't, that I was inspecting a loose thread on the duvet. We never shared the same bed; it would have been inappropriate to do so. I knew that even then. What I didn't know was how to name the emotions that roiled inside me.

Of the many things we shared—a taste for mystery novels and irreverent comedies and obscenely spicy foods—it was music, Parth, that bound us like a rope. We agreed on many things: That there would never be a producer as innovative as Timbaland. The Neptunes were a close second. That Aaliyah's "We Need a Resolution" was ahead of its time. When I got my driver's license that month, we blasted *The Red Album* in my car, parked outside the local airport. "Rock the Boat," with its sultry vocals and soft, clicking beat, became one of the songs I will always associate with you. We were listening to it while watching the planes through my moonroof. It was the night you told me I was your best friend. You said it casually, dropping it into conversation like spices into a pan.

"Other than a couple people in my debate class," you said,

"I'm kind of over everyone at school." You stretched back against your seat, looking at me. "I mean you're pretty much my best friend."

You closed your eyes and nodded your head to the beat as the light from a half-moon spilled generously onto your face. Your fingers, long and slender, tapped a rhythm on your lap. I stared at this, my mind racing, while a plane dazzled in the sky. I couldn't help myself. I traced your finger with my thumb. The feathery sensation made my stomach drop. The act was liquefying, dissolving every part of me. Your fingers withdrew.

"Sorry," I said, pretending to adjust the volume instead.

You said nothing, turning your head. That night, when I slid off my underwear, I noticed a dried, milky crust down its center. I rinsed it under the tap.

It was like that for a while. We were edging toward something—what, exactly, I wasn't sure. You were my best friend. It was enough for the time. I think you liked it when I said I wished *you* were my brother instead of Bijal. The night I told you this we were in my parents' basement. Your parents had come over for dinner; everyone's voices thundered above. I said that it was a shame we weren't related, that we didn't live in the same house.

"I don't know," you said. "Bijal seems all right."

"Bijal's a tool."

"Well, at least you have someone. It sucks being an only child. It's just me and my parents for the rest of my life."

"What about Monika?"

I regretted my tone; I hadn't meant to sound shrill. You shrugged, casually.

"She's just a friend."

"I think she wants to be more than that."

"Well, I don't. Besides, there's another girl I like."

"Oh, yeah? Who?"

You smiled. "Your mom."

You laughed when I threw a cushion at your head. You ducked and threw one back. Then you leapt toward me, knocking me to the ground. We rolled over the carpet. I could feel every part of you, every tendon, every bone. You sank into me, refusing to let go.

"Come on," you said, hitting me with my own hand. "Fight back."

"I don't want to."

"Why not?"

I shrugged. The heat from your chest warmed me. Your breath kissed my lips.

"Choksi," you said. "Remind me never to get stranded with you on an island."

Then you released me from your grip, and the simple act of this, the separation of our limbs, was like being dunked in cold water. Later that night, you caught me staring at you while you skimmed a puddle of chicken curry with the funnel of your naan, brown sauce dripping onto your plate.

"What?"

"Nothing."

For every boy I ever loved, there was a corresponding song. Mateo's was "Angel of Mine" by Monica. I hummed along to it on the radio when my mother drove me to school. Then he stopped talking to me and I listened to Brandy instead: "Almost Doesn't Count." When I first saw Kyle in gym class, mopping his face with the end of his T-shirt, flashing his bare stomach, it was Mariah Carey's "Heartbreaker." After he made out with Elise, he was a "Case of the Ex." For Dakota it was simple: 702, "Where My Girls At?" There was no specific reason; I just really liked the song. For you, Parth, there were many, every beat ever pounded, every melody ever hummed, all the songs ever written, including the ones we never heard.

There we were, flying down the road, the breeze sliding over our arms, *Full Moon* belting from the speakers. We had never heard anything like it, all the layers and textures, harmonies and riffs. The quickness of Brandy's runs, the way they spiraled like twisters and disintegrated like breath. I let you drive, closing my eyes, paying attention to every detail, every tone.

"Earth to Akash," you said, pulled over in a parking lot. We were outside the temple. The sky was black velvet; the stars, crushed gems. "Where'd you go?"

"What do you mean?"

"Just now. You clocked out."

"I'm listening to the music." You looked at me, confused. "What?" I said.

"The song is over."

"Oh."

"Choksi." You jabbed my arm. "You must be listening to the music in your head."

A fresh snow was melting on the ground. It was March, exactly one year since your cousin's wedding. I didn't want to tell you this. I didn't want you to think I was weird. But it was all I could think about, your face lit from pulsing pink lights, our bodies moving in sync. We got out of the car and cut a path to the temple, which glowed ivory in the night. The façade had been rinsed clean, the words, DIE MUSLIMS, visible only if you stared hard enough, only if you remembered. You shook your head.

"We still need to paint over it."

We arrived just in time to help serve food in a buffet line for the procession of worshippers. It was an auspicious day, something I had heard explained in the car but later forgot. I didn't tell you the truth: that I didn't believe in God. The looks on those deities' faces, with their sly, languid smiles, angered me, as if they could see all the pain inside me, and considered it a joke. I stood next to you spooning dal into Styrofoam bowls. At times you nudged me, flicking rice grains at my head. We smiled to the aunties who passed our table, kicking each other underneath. I could have stayed in that moment forever. Our elbows touching. Your skin grazing mine.

"Monika," you said, when she happened to approach, spooning a mound of spiced potatoes onto her plate. "What's up?"

She tucked a piece of hair behind her ear and said something in return. But I was no longer listening. I saw the light in your face when you spoke to her, the way you dropped what you were doing, stepping away from me. My body went cold. Later, when you followed me to my car, I didn't hand you the keys. I let you sit in the passenger seat. I slammed my door shut.

"Is everything okay?"

I burned with shame, turning the key in the ignition, switching the stereo on. "I'm fine."

"You don't look fine."

"Well, I am."

"Hey." You stared at me, and I wondered if you would touch me, stroke my face. "Akash."

I blinked back tears. I remembered what my mother had once said to me. *Don't cry, Akash. You're not a girl. There are people in this world who have more to cry about than you.* So, I raised my chin, swallowing it down. I told you the only thing I could think of at the time.

"Some kids are bothering me at school."

I pulled out of the parking space and turned onto an empty road. The dark farmland stretched around us. You were silent for a while, gazing out the window, your hand curling over my wrist.

"I won't let anyone hurt you."

RENU

I first heard from you in March, three months after I had moved to America. I was pregnant. Ashok was at work. I had given you my address before leaving London, so it should not have come as a surprise that you would write. Still, I was struck by the scrawl of your penmanship across an airmail envelope, checkered with stamps.

Dear Renu,
Forgive me for writing. I trust you are well. If this is a good way to communicate, please let me know.
—Kareem

It was hardly the love letter I had imagined, but I knew right away that you had chosen to remain vague—had Ashok checked the mail and read the letter himself, it would have meant the end of you and me.
I wrote back immediately.

Kareem,
How my heart sang when I saw your name! Yes, this is a good way to communicate. I am home most days alone. Ashok works late. How are you? Please tell me everything. I feel very alone here in America. Everything is different. Do you know what Spam is? It's revolting. Anyway, please write back soon.
Love,
Renu

I regretted it as soon as I had sealed the envelope and dropped it off in the post. *My heart sang?* What rubbish was that? I didn't receive your reply for several months. Ashok was sitting for his exams; he was finishing his first year of fellowship. I was busy preparing his meals: pigeon peas and moong dal and Balti chicken karahi.

"Do you ever stop eating?" I'd once asked.

He'd looked up from his plate, lips smattered with oil. "I love your food, Renu. It reminds me of my Ma." Then he started to cry.

"Oh, good god."

By then, I had started checking the mail religiously, sometimes two to three times a day. It was all I looked forward to. I raced to the mail room in our apartment building whenever I heard the familiar growl of the truck. Nothing interesting ever came, only bills and catalogues and letters from the hospital where Ashok worked, the occasional invitation to a party, a perfumed fashion magazine. Each day your letter didn't arrive, I fell into a darker and darker abyss, banging drawers, slamming doors. I was rude to Ashok.

"What's that noise?" I once snapped, when Ashok and I were sitting in the living room watching TV.

"What noise?"

"That soft, whimpering sound. Is that you?"

"It's my breathing."

I'd gaped at him. "You mean to tell me that's how you breathe? That's how it sounds? This is what I'll have to listen to my entire life? Mari aki jingi?"

To my surprise, Ashok had laughed.

"Not your whole life, Renu. Don't you know? One day I'll be gone, and then you will miss the sound of my breathing."

He was wrong. I still hear it.

Your letter came on a Tuesday. It was sealed in a pink envelope; the stamps had pictures of sunflowers and cats. I tore it open and read it over the stove.

Dear Bibi,

I was so happy to receive your response. I didn't know if you would write to me. I am sorry it took me so long to write back. My father passed away in Dar es Salaam. I went back for many weeks. It made me realize something, bibi: I have made many mistakes in my life. The biggest mistake was not marrying you. I don't know where we can go from here—you're married now—but I do know that I want to know about your life. I want to see it through your eyes, hear it through your words. I want to know all the little things, too, like what you eat in the mornings and what the view looks like from your room. Is that crazy? Am I mad? I don't know. What I do know is that every day without you is like ten. I am back in London now, getting a master's in business administration. I live in a shared flat with a Bangladeshi man named Chintan. He sings very loudly in the bath. I think he's having an affair with the Russian woman on the second floor. Once, I came home just as she was leaving our flat, buttoning her blouse. It worries me a little, because her husband is our landlord. I asked Chintan about it, but he said they are only friends; she is teaching him Russian. Is he moving to Moscow? Is she teaching him with her breasts?! I have so many questions. I will let you know what happens. Please let me know what is happening in your world.

Love,

Kareem

I wrote you back that night, telling you about the Corn Flakes I made do with in the mornings—there was no Weetabix at the store—and the blank stretch of farmland beyond our windows. I told you about the American women who stared at me everywhere I went, as if I had invaded their space. I told you about the bland food at the restaurant Ashok took me to, Cracker Barrel, where the waitress had recommended something called chicken fried steak.

"It's good," she'd said. "Tastes just like chicken."

"But isn't it steak?"

"I don't know." She shrugged. "Tastes like chicken to me."

I told you that, in America, everyone thinks everything tastes "just like chicken": frog legs and rattlesnakes and apparently steak. I complained about the meat at the grocery store, how fat and artificial it looked, pumped full of god only knows what. I told you about the cicadas at dusk and the bird cries at dawn, and the complete silence in between. I didn't tell you I was pregnant. It made it too real, this revelation, my marriage to Ashok, my move to the States, this baby inside me, plunging its roots into soil. It was a betrayal.

"Arre," Chaya said, slapping my arm after I had vomited into the bushes during our morning walk. "The newlywed is not so new!"

Soon, there were two things I lived for—your letters and my child—two things that reminded me, even on the worst days, that I was not alone. I looked forward to all the updates on your life. The classes you took and the exams you had passed and the latest foods you had tried. Tapas. Vietnamese. Malaysian. Thai. You finally splurged on tickets to see *Jesus Christ Superstar,* and the way you described it, with such vivid, gushing details, brought it to life in my mind. You transformed my living room; you changed its oatmeal carpeting and thin pale walls. It was like I was right there, Kareem, sitting beside you.

I was worried when you told me that Chintan had been caught in bed with the Russian, and the landlord had kicked you out, and I was relieved, three weeks later, when you had found a new home. You were living in Wembley with a Pakistani family, eating all their delicious food: mutton biryani, Lahori kababs, sajji, nihari, and haleem. My mouth watered at the descriptions. I could taste their spices on my tongue. The simplest details—the rinsed-out color of the sky, a yellow raincoat, a kitten you had seen with the palest pink nose—sharpened the world around me, bringing it into focus. *Love, Kareem.* I cherished those words. Sometimes I said them out loud, standing naked in the mirror, my breasts growing tender, my waist thickening like cream. *Love, Kareem. Love, Kareem. Love, Kareem.* Once, I had forgotten that Ashok was in the next room. He flew to the doorway.

"Did you say something?"

"Huh?"

"It sounded like you said, *Love, Kareem.*"

"Oh, no." I smiled. "I said, *love sunscreen.* I love it! You know I don't like to get dark."

"Ah." He smiled. "I'll get more tomorrow."

It was a disaster narrowly missed. But I no longer cared. As weeks passed and my stomach swelled to the size of a drum, during doctors' appointments and prenatal class, through long afternoons propped up in bed, sweat beading my face, I knew I had your letters, your words. I knew that there was always you. I knew I had you in other ways, Kareem.

That this baby was not Ashok's. It was yours.

AKASH

People are like pencils; they shade us in. Sometimes they smudge us. Other times they define. I had no definition before I met you, Parth. I learned very quickly how dangerous this was.

Where are you from?

America?

What does your name mean?

The sky?

What's that on your wrist?

A rakhi?

My mother always told me to be assertive. *Speak up! Don't let these kids talk over you.* But it was through questions that I found my true voice. *Can I? May I? Am I allowed?* Because that's what it was like to be us, Parth. We were seeking the same thing. We both wanted something the world would never give us: permission.

Do I belong?

No.

Soon, the school year wound down. I spent most of the summer at your place. We went for bike rides and drives, listening to burned CDs, songs Bijal had downloaded off LimeWire. "Turn Me On" by Kevin Lyttle. *Let me hold you, come caress my body.* Dancehall was sweeping the nation, metallic beats that made hips click and pop, choruses that got stuck in your head. Patois over percussion. I closed my eyes and saw the shimmering sea. *Hug me, hug me, kiss me, kiss me.* Now, we no longer called ahead before showing up at each other's doorsteps, CDs in hand. You got your driver's license and drove often to our house, parking in front of white pillars, discarding your shoes on pearlescent floors. Sometimes I visited you at work, picking you up outside of Best Buy. You bounded through the doors with a grin on your face, the collar of your polo flipped up, crescents of sweat beneath your arms. We sat in the back of Arby's and Burger King, picking at fries.

I had hoped we would grow even closer, that the heat of summer would form a binding slick, fusing us together, but there was always something in the way. Did you not see through it, Parth? The way I drank you in. The way your smile glanced off my eyes like shards of light. That's what you were. You were a light so rich and golden you gleamed from within. You didn't protest when I leaned my head against your shoulder one night, after watching a movie in your room. You let it rest there, like a butterfly that had landed on your wrist. When you wrestled me in my parents' basement, you didn't care that I let you overpower me. I think you liked me this way: easily won. You straddled me on the ground, pinning my wrists to the floor, panting on top of me, flushed and humming. Lingering touches were not rare. Neither were hugs. But there was a limit. I suppose you weren't prepared to give in completely, to let the tide sweep us beyond safety, to a place from which there was no return.

Then one night, a Friday, we were watching *Armageddon* at your parents' motel when you asked if I wanted to go swimming.

"I don't have a bathing suit."

"You can borrow mine."

"Okay," I said. "Let me go to the bathroom first."

I examined my belly under the harsh yellow lights. You knocked on the door.

"Ready?"

"Yeah, one second!"

You tossed me a pair of shorts.

"These should fit."

When I returned to your room, you were undressed.

"Oh, shit," I said, backing away. "Sorry."

Your chest was bare; you were wrapped in a towel. Aside from a sprinkling of dark hair between your nipples, your body was smooth. I tried not to look at it. I tried not to notice the swell of your chest, the ropey muscles in your arms, the soft, fuzzy pelt at your navel. You didn't seem to mind.

"I have a towel on. It's not like my dick is out."

"Right."

"Unless you want it to be." You wiggled your hips. "Like that?"

"Shut up."

Heat spread through my face as you bent down to slide a pair of swim shorts on underneath your towel, then pried the towel from your waist. You tossed it at me.

"Smell this."

I pretended to be disgusted, but I could have buried my face in it. You led the way through your parents' apartment and into the lobby and down a narrow hallway toward a pair of sliding glass doors. The smell of chlorine sliced through the air. Inside, the pool was large but empty. The walls rippled with emerald light. You immediately dove in, splashing me.

"The water's great." You flicked some at my feet. "Come in."

Your voice echoed above our heads. You watched as I peeled off my shirt. I was sure you would point out the fat at my sides, which was soft and springy like two hemispheres of dough. You didn't.

"Come on." Your tone turned pleading. "I'm all alone."

I dove headfirst, icy water flooding my shorts.

"Ack!" I cried. "It's freezing."

"I know."

"You asshole!"

You laughed, tipping your head back. "You should have seen your face."

"Jesus Christ."

I splashed you. You splashed back. Then you dove underwater and surfaced inches from my nose. Water streamed down your face like rain from a gutter. Your puckered fingers gripped my neck.

"What are you doing?"

"You need to learn how to fight."

"And who are you, Evander Holyfield?"

You let go, splashing. "Sala."

"That's what my mom calls me."

"Oh, yeah? You must be a naughty boy."

You pushed off me and swam the length of the pool, sending a ripple of foamy waves in my direction.

"She also calls me nakamo."

"Do you even know what that means?" you said, reaching the other side.

"Of course I know what it means. Why wouldn't I?"

"I don't know." You shrugged. "I wasn't sure if you did."

"I'm not a coconut," I said. "That's Bijal."

You laughed. "Yeah."

Then you told me how your English teacher had asked you, in front of the entire class, if you were going to have an arranged marriage.

"She never asks any of the other kids that kind of shit. I don't know why she has to ask *me*."

You gripped the edge of the pool and lifted yourself up, water sluicing down your back. Then you twisted yourself to face me. Your hair was limp. You lifted your arm to scratch the back of your neck and I saw the moist dark hair underneath.

"You need to trim your pits."

"I'm becoming a man."

"Yeah, right."

You shrugged. Then you stood up and walked over to the plastic chairs where we'd left our towels and flip-flops and shirts. Your feet squelched against the tiles. You wrapped a towel around your waist.

"Come on," you said. "Let's hang out in my room."

Every disaster has a point of origin. They say a breeze in one country becomes a hurricane in another. Drop a penny from a skyscraper and watch it crush someone to death. Take a sip of pinot noir and drive your car through a tree. Show a person who you are, the aching, craving belly of your soul, and watch them run away.

We listened to *The Miseducation of Lauryn Hill* in your room while taking turns showering in the adjoining bathroom. Clean and soap-scented, we debated which song was best.

"'Ex-Factor.' Lyrically, melodically, and everything in between," I said.

"Wrong."

"How can I be wrong? Art is subjective."

"Not always. There was a *Scream 3*—unanimously, a terrible film."

"All right," I said. "What's your choice?"

You leaned against your headboard, the front of your T-shirt damp. I was sitting at the edge of the bed near your feet even though you had said there was room for both of us. I didn't want to sit next to you; I was afraid of what might happen if I did. I made a bet with myself that if you mentioned the song I was thinking of, it would mean you felt the same way I did.

"'To Zion.'"

I grinned, my heart lifting.

"What?" you asked.

"Nothing. It's a good song."

"I told you."

"'Ex-Factor' is still the best."

"Yeah, yeah. Are you some kind of music producer?"

"One day I might be."

"Really?" You seemed surprised by this. "That's so cool."

"Why is that cool?"

You kicked me. "Why are you sitting all the way over there, choksi?" You shifted over to make room, patting the area next to you. "Come sit by me."

I stretched out onto the bed beside you, our arms touching. You picked up the remote control and switched the track to "Lost Ones." You closed your eyes, and I fixed my gaze on your mouth. You smiled, eyes still shut, as if you knew I was watching.

"What are you doing?"

"Nothing," I said.

You opened your eyes and turned your head toward me. I could see my face reflected in your gaze, could feel the damp of your breath. Your chest rose and fell in rhythm with mine. The music slowly faded, and when your lips parted, revealing a chunk of white, glossy teeth, I gently kissed you.

"Whoa . . ."

I had never known a single syllable could hold so much weight. That a word so small could have so much power. Our lips disconnected. You shoved me aside. I don't remember what you said to me, Parth, only the panic in your eyes. I remember a car throwing parallel strips of light against the wall opposite your bed. I recall how the room felt, the temperature, the texture, the greasy slip of the carpet underfoot, the tug of the scratchy comforter on the underside of my legs, the cold damp coming from the window behind our heads. But I don't know what you said.

You weren't angry, only afraid, which somehow made all of it worse. You withdrew, scrambling out of bed and standing on the carpet in front of me, backing away. I tried to explain.

"I'm sorry, I don't . . . I've never . . . I'm sorry."

But it was too late. There was nothing I could say to mask my naked desire. I was humiliated, ashamed that this thing inside me had clawed its way to the light, irrevocable now that you had seen it, impossible to be unseen. You didn't say anything when I got up from your bed and grabbed my things and packed them in my bag. Your back was pressed against the wall. You didn't stop me when I walked to your door. You didn't say a word. Only when I stepped into the hall did you whisper it. *I won't tell anyone.* I turned one last time, and it wasn't your face I saw, Parth, it was the back of your head, the way you pedaled down that open road with the wind ripping through your hair, the sky deepening, the clouds shading us, protecting us from everything we were never meant to see.

Do you know what it's like to have so much love inside you and no one to give it to? To be the vessel of unwanted light? My father said even the sweetest things turn sour if there's no one to consume them. Jewels tarnish. Flowers die. Fruit goes rotten. Love turns to bitterness and hatred and rage. That night, when I left your parents' motel, I went home and locked myself in my bedroom, dropping to my knees. I looked at the statue of Lord Ganesh my mother had stuck to the middle of my bookshelf, closing my eyes. *The remover of obstacles.* I had never prayed for anything in my life, had never felt the presence of God in my soul, but that night, the heat from your gaze still warming my face, I whispered the words.

Change me.

———

RENU

Lies are like children: the second you conceive them, you must protect them at all costs. You certainly can't abandon them. What kind of mother does that? This was my justification during those first few months. I simply allowed Ashok to assume the baby was his. It's not as if he questioned me. He never once asked, "Are you sure this baby is mine?" Maybe then I would have told him. Maybe then I would have left. But I was never given the chance. When the doctor told me how far along I was, Ashok wasn't even in the room; he was on call. I remembered my last night in London with you, when you led me into your room. I knew. But Ashok didn't have to. So, I accepted the soft, caramel-filled chocolates he brought home from the hospital, and let him rub my feet, and thanked him when he propped my pillows or drew a steamy bath. I told myself it was all for him, that this was what he wanted. It wasn't just my lie anymore; it was his, too.

Seven months into my pregnancy, I decided to write you and tell you the truth. *You have a baby, Kareem. We have a child.* I wondered what you would have said. Maybe you would take it as a sign, that you should come to America and whisk me away. It wasn't too late. There was a child involved. I wrote down every moment, every shudder, every kick, all the names I had come up with in my head, the visions I'd had, too. We were having a girl. You were a father to a daughter. Ashok and I spent weeks decorating the small second bedroom in our apartment, pasting decals and painting walls. We bought satin shoes, velvet dresses, tiny pink bows. Ashok found a jeweler to design a small ruby ring. I picked a name in my head, a name I didn't share with Ashok: Bijal. It means "lightning." That's what you were, Kareem. That's what this baby was. I could feel her shifting inside me, our hearts beating as one. Your blood still flowed through me. I felt it at every turn. Then one day, I awoke to a bright shaft of light streaming in from the windows, the smell of chai warming on the stove. I sat up and touched my belly. I felt nothing at all.

"Mrs. Amin," the doctor said, her eyes still. "I don't hear a heartbeat."

God doesn't make mistakes, Kareem. People do. That morning, when the doctor explained to me that there was no explanation, the baby had stopped living, I realized what I had done. My sins had caught up to me. The doctor assured me that these things happen—it was no fault of my own—but I knew the truth.

When Ashok picked me up from the hospital that morning and took me home and wiped my tears and boiled my tea and promised that we would try again, that there would be another child; when I found him whimpering in the bathroom hours later, holding the sonogram to his chest, I knew what I had to do. I had to let go of you. I had to learn to be good. If not for my sake, then for his. I never sent that letter, Kareem. I never wrote to you again. Instead, I vowed to be better, tucking the letter inside the front pocket of an old suitcase we never used, in a storage closet we rarely entered, in case I changed my mind. At some point the suitcase went missing, like most forgotten things do. This, too, was a sign.

Ashok was right; there was another child, a boy. He looked just like you. At first, I couldn't believe it. His dark coloring, his wide eyes, the thick smear of his brows. It was like I was staring into your face. But it couldn't be, Kareem. He was born a year later. He was Ashok's son. Still, I think of him as yours. "What would you like to name him?" Ashok had asked, holding him in his arms. I remembered the name.

"Bijal," I said.

"Isn't that a girl's name?"

"It's both," I said truthfully.

That baby we lost, maybe she returned. My mother told me we take many forms, but there is only one soul. Think of your soul as water, she said. Pour the water into a cube, and the water becomes a cube. Pour the water into a sphere, and the water becomes a sphere. Pour the water into a blue cup, and the water appears blue. Pour a soul into your body, and the soul becomes you.

AKASH

To say that I never saw you again would be a lie. I did see you, Parth, more than I would have hoped, because to see someone you can't have is to wade through wine you can't drink. Still, I endured. I saw you at Priyanka's birthday party, and Sonali's wedding, and the retirement dinner for your uncle after he sold off his motels. You were there each time in your plated armor; I was always unarmed. You laughed and ran and leapt with other boys, and I watched you from afar. Do you know what it's like to lose a part of yourself, only to find that part in everyone else? This is what it must be like to lose one's legs; one day, you realize the whole world is a race.

After your uncle's retirement party in April, I didn't see you for a while. Your parents went to India because your grandfather had died. Your uncle came to help with the motel. My parents had offered yours the favor of keeping you at our house, but you declined. Every now and then, my mother would call to make sure you were okay and offer to bring you food, but you always said no.

"You don't see him anymore," she once said. "Did something happen?"

I gave her the typical excuse: we were both busy, it being senior year. Before, I'd breezed through classes knowing I would see you after school, but now, the seconds crawled by at an agonizing pace. I looked around my classroom and felt even more alone; I would not see your face after the bell. I would not spend every hour with you over the weekend. Somewhere you were in another classroom, not feeling the same. Once, I drove by your parents' motel and slowed down just to catch a glimpse of you inside. I don't know what I was expecting to see; maybe you were sitting in front of the television, feeling my absence like a fading pain. A car honked and I almost crashed into a lamppost. It wasn't the fear that made me cry, Parth, but the realization that you were not there to laugh at me, to slap the back of my head.

I thought I could write you a letter. Maybe, if I was able to show you on paper just how much I cared, you would understand. I typed it out on my father's computer and proofread it three times. The words were like lyrics in a song, each syllable striking a note. I told you everything, from the first day I saw you, to the last. But when I printed it out, saw the ink drying on the page, the words lost their luster. I dropped it in the trash. I figured I would never see you again. The school year was coming to a close, and, according to my mother, your mother was taking you to London for the summer to visit her sister and niece.

You were applying early for college so that you could graduate the first half of your senior year. You planned to attend BU. We had talked about this one night several weeks before, planning my visit during spring break, a trip to New York. There was a whole world out there we had yet to see. I decided to leave those memories in the trash, along with my letter, until my father's computer crashed.

"This damn thing," he said, pounding the keys.

"See if you can fix it. You are better at these things."

I wasn't. You were. I looked at my father, an idea forming in my mind.

"I'll take it to Best Buy," I said.

I was nervous walking through the sliding glass doors of Best Buy that day, my father's computer weighing down my arms. TV screens pulsed and flashed. I knew where you would be. I scanned the royal blue shirts that blazed by me, looking for your face.

"Can I help you?"

A plump employee stood before me. His small dark eyes looked even smaller in comparison to the rest of him—round face, fleshy arms, a wide stance. I didn't want to ask for you by name. What if they made an announcement over the speakers and called you over? But I needed to see you. My hands shook.

"I was just taking this over to repairs. I'll be fine."

"Let me help you with that."

"No, it's okay."

"No, please. I insist."

"I can do it myself."

"It's my job." He scrunched his face. "Look, see that guy behind me?" I leaned to the left. A stern-looking man was staring at us, a clipboard in hand. "That's my supervisor. He caught me looking at porn on one of the computers. It wasn't even—never mind. Anyway, now he's on my ass. So please just let me help you. Okay?"

"Okay."

"Great! Follow me!"

He took the computer from my hands and made a display of leading me toward a station at the center of the room. I surveyed the room but didn't see you.

"I'm Daniel, by the way."

"Hi."

Daniel asked me to describe in detail what had happened and to fill out some paperwork and to schedule a time to pick up the computer. I did all three, glancing up every now and then. The matter was taken care of in moments. Daniel led me toward the entrance.

"Thanks for shopping at Best Buy!"

"Sure."

He beamed, his eyes leaving mine a moment to focus on something behind my head. I turned. A pair of children skipped ahead of their father. Two teenage girls giggled into their hands. An elderly couple pushed a TV in a cart. You walked through the front door, smiling and nodding, but it wasn't *me* you were looking at. You made that clear.

"Parth, my man," Daniel said. "Now I can go home."

I watched you bump your fist against Daniel's. When you turned and noticed me, your eyes went dim.

"Akash."

It wasn't that you ignored me that afternoon. It wasn't that you pushed me away. You were friendly, asking about school and my plans for the summer. You told me yours. You said we should hang out, that maybe I could come to your place or you could come to mine. Had our parents been there, they would have thought nothing was amiss, but I knew. I heard it in your tone.

"I bought a new bike," I said, hoping this might jog your memory. "A ten-speeder."

But all you managed to say was, "Cool."

When we separated, Daniel asked if you knew me, if we were friends, and though I wish I hadn't, Parth, I heard your reply.

"We used to be."

I walked back to my car and shut the door, the hot air suffocating. I turned the radio on. The melody came rushing back to me. "So Into You." I remembered the way you had looked at the arcade that afternoon, raising your fists as the ball swished through the net, when the world was full of possibility, and our story had yet to begin.

The next morning, I kept my head down while changing in the locker room after gym, a knot in my throat. I didn't want to be noticed. I didn't want to be seen. But this is the problem with being you and me, Parth. We don't get to choose.

"Hey, elephant fag."

I felt their presence like a cloud passing over the sun. I turned my head. They formed a human wall, all three of them: Bryce, Evan, and Lance. This time, Mr. Washington was nowhere to be found. The locker room sat empty. Water dripped from a leaky pipe. Steam spread like a veil, blocking us from view.

Their hands shot toward me.

"What do you have to hide?" Bryce said.

"Yeah," said Lance. "What's under there?"

I could smell their breath, the barbecue chips they'd had at lunch. Their fingers fluttered at my waist like a school of fish. If I hadn't been crying, I might have laughed.

"This is dumb," Bryce said, unable to untie the knot at my waist. Then he looked at the others, a smile on his face.

"I have a better idea."

The better idea was to drag me to the back of the school where no one would find us, after which they took turns punching me in my gut. Their fists felt like bricks warmed under the hot sun. The world around me—the school banner, the football field, the parking lot, the rows of tight square homes on the periphery— grew weak in the waning light. I could hear the peals of their laughter, followed by a calm, restorative silence. But silence is often the beginning of worse things.

"I found a new place for you to change," Bryce said, pointing to the dumpster behind our heads. Then he lifted me by my arms. I screamed and pleaded while their fingers dug into my skin, tossing me inside. Something sharp jabbed my spine. I looked up at the bright square of sky above, their faces hovering over me like sinister moons.

"He can't change in there. Someone could see him," said Lance.

"Yeah," said Evan.

"You know what?" Bryce said, his teeth flashing. "You're right."

The lid dropped over my head. The world turned black. I felt the white-hot pain of a piece of glass slicing my palm. Warm blood pooled from it, spilling down my wrist. Only after hours of screaming did someone happen to walk by.

"Who did this to you?" said Mr. Washington, lifting the lid over his head. "Who did this to you, son?"

I didn't answer him. I couldn't. They weren't the cause of the pain that cracked inside me, splitting me in two. You were.

You betrayed me, Parth, and I suppose this is why I betrayed you.

PART III

PART II

RENU

Celeste is not having a very good time; her husband has caught wind of her affair. Rebecca, Celeste's nemesis, saw Juan exiting Celeste's home in the middle of the night, telling him about it. Now, she seeks counsel from her therapist.

"I think I have to do it," she says, gravely. "I think I have to get the breasts."

"Are you sure?"

"It's the only way." She cries into a tissue. "That damn Rebecca! I should have poisoned her when I had the chance."

"Maybe you still can."

"No," says Celeste, a wry smile. "No, I have other plans."

Her plan is to get even bigger breasts than her husband had demanded, then suffocate him with them.

"Once I get the life insurance money, I'll get a breast reduction. Then I'll move to Mexico with Juan. It's perfect!"

I switch off the TV. If Ashok were here, I know what he would say.

"What's the use of big breasts if the heart is so small?"

I enter the kitchen and set a mug of tea into the sink. The Vitamix whirs as Bijal blends celery and apples and kale for his smoothie. Akash is still in his room. The puddle of sick has been wiped clean. The windows are open, allowing fresh air to seep in. I sit down in Ashok's office and stare at the diplomas on the wall, Bijal's certificates, the golden trophies that line the shelves. In three days, the movers will arrive to pack it all up. I lean back against Ashok's leather chair, still creased with the imprint of his back, and log in to Facebook.

I'm still reeling from your message, Kareem, the night's

activities. Akash. Everything. Evanston, Illinois. How long have you been there? What if our paths have crossed before? You haven't read my message yet. The words hang in the balance. I had chosen to remain vague, mysterious, saying everything and nothing. I didn't ask you about Evanston. I didn't tell you I live two hours away. I didn't want you to know that I had studied your page. Instead, I talked about my life in America and my decision to move, referring to Ashok only in the past tense as "my late husband." I remember the night you asked me about him. The night you asked me to run away. We were at a small, dark pub in Leicester. You held my hand.

"What's his name?" you asked.

"It doesn't matter."

But you wouldn't let up. You wanted to know everything about him: his name, his occupation, the place of his birth. I could see you chew each piece over, spitting it out.

"You'll never love him the way you love me."

It was a cruel thing to say.

Now, I wonder if you had been right. I wonder if I ever loved Ashok. Our love was something different, I suppose, a comfort born of habit, a warm bed at the end of the day. Ashok was always there. There was a time when it was this very thing, his refusal to leave, that annoyed me. Sometimes I would walk quickly ahead of him in a department store or on a crowded street, just to see if I could lose him, but he always found me.

"Oh, there you are, Renu," he would say, his eyes bright like a dog's.

If I sent Ashok a text, he would respond immediately. Sometimes I couldn't get him to stop. He would keep thinking of things to tell me on his way home from work or while waiting to get the oil changed in his car. He would ask a million questions at the end of the day, pointless things like what I ate for lunch and was it good and how many slices of cheese did I use?

"I just like to hear you talk," he said.

"About cheese?"

"About anything."

"Why?" I said. "What's so special about the way I talk?"

"Because," he replied. "It gives me a chance to rest my eyes. Otherwise, Renu, they would always be on you."

"Oh, for god's sake."

Now, I stare at the empty space beneath my message, waiting for your reply. Is this what it's like to be on Facebook, Kareem? A held inhalation? I log out of Facebook and walk back into the kitchen. Bijal is gone. The Vitamix contains the ruby dregs of his smoothie. Cracked windows usher in pine-scented air. My cell phone bleats at the same moment that my hand flies to answer it. A number I don't recognize. I wonder if it could be you.

"Hello?" I say.

"Mrs. Amin?"

The voice on the other end is bright, lilting.

"Yes?" I say. "Who is it?"

She sighs softly. Before she can say anything further, I know.

"Jessica?"

AKASH

I wake up with a hangover, bright light jabbing into my eyes. My entire body feels wrung out, too weak to move. I vaguely remember the night before. The puja. The party afterward. I see the disappointment in my mother's face, the resolution in Bijal's. I remember drinking more in my room, draining the miniature bottles of vodka into a thermos while listening to music. Lil' Kim. Foxy Brown. SWV. Lauryn Hill. The glass clink of ice cubes blended seamlessly with each song. My body hummed from inside. I blasted the music through the Bose headphones Jacob bought me last Christmas, collapsing in a sweaty heap. Jacob. Something feels off. Did we talk? I hear his voice, but I'm not sure.

My fingers grip the case of my iPhone as I bring it to my face, scrolling through my call log. Nothing. I put the phone aside. Close my eyes. A wave of nausea rises and subsides. The room is unbearably hot. I can hear Bijal blending his smoothie below and my mother frying onions on the stove. She's asked us to make a list of all the dishes we want to eat before she closes up the kitchen. I only have five days left, five mornings and nights. Just as I consider this, something wells up inside me. My stomach churns. I rush to the bathroom and kneel down over the porcelain rim, retching. Water splashes. A sour taste coats my tongue. A pain, more acute than ever, drills into my head. I spit feebly into the bowl and stand up and flush the toilet, scraped out from within. The room spins as I make my way back into bed. For a moment, I feel better, sweat cooling my face, my stomach settling. Until a piece of memory clicks into place. I grab my phone again and scroll through my texts. The words find me before I find them, before I've had the chance to recite them in my mind. A text message to Jacob at three in the morning.

Get out of my life.

RENU

At first, Jessica doesn't say why she's calling. She only talks about the weather and the holidays and how lovely it is this time of year.

"Have you had those pumpkin spice lattes? They taste just like pumpkin pie."

I don't like pumpkin pie, which looks like something that has been scooped out of an ear. I don't understand this American need to make certain things taste like other things. Pumpkin spice lattes. Birthday cake–flavored gum. I've never reached for a stick of gum after a meal and thought, "Oh, I hope it tastes like cake!" I suppose this is what it is to be an American, to reject reality, accept substitutions instead.

"Mrs. Amin," Jessica starts.

"Yes?"

She's silent. I'm standing in the foyer with my hand pressed to the glass, feeling the chill against my palm. The trees have begun to shed more leaves. Golden piles line the street like treasure. I hear a sniffle from somewhere in the house. I look up to see if Akash is standing at the top of the stairs, like he often did as a child, awaiting his punishment. But I only hear the flush of the toilet, the soft pad of his feet. The stairway is clear. It isn't until Jessica continues that I realize it's her.

She's crying.

"I'm sorry."

"Oh . . ."

"About—" She stops herself. "Everything. I should have come for the party. The puja, I mean. Sorry."

"Oh," I repeat, stunned. "It's all right, Jessica. You had your reasons."

She doesn't confirm or deny this. Instead, she begins to sob into the receiver. She doesn't cry delicately like I had imagined. Jessica's cries are liquid, sopping.

"Jessica," I say, though I'm not sure how to follow this. "Are you all right?"

"I just wanted to say I'm sorry about everything. About Ashok. About the way I've been . . . I guess." She blows her nose. "I want to say goodbye."

"I see."

"I wish I could have done it in person. If I had known Ashok's funeral was going to be the last time I would see you . . . I would have . . ."

At this, I laugh. "Jessica, don't be silly. I'm not dying. I'm just moving. You and Bijal love London. You'll visit. It will be fine, okay?" She doesn't answer. "Listen, don't be upset, yeah? There will be other times."

Jessica grows quiet, and for the first time I imagine what it's like to have a daughter. I wonder if it's possible for Jessica to be that person, to fill that void. I feel an odd plucking of guilt. Maybe I've been too hard on her, expected too much of her. Maybe it's not her fault Bijal changed. He has never done anything he hadn't wanted to do. Everything in his life—his job, his house, even his wife—was a choice.

"Mrs. Amin . . ." Jessica suddenly says, her voice quavering.

"Yes?" She goes silent. "Jessica? What is it?"

I picture her on the other end, her pale face glimmering. A thick sweater. Freckles the color of the leaves. Her hair, a murky blond, piled into a bun on top of her head. She squeaks into the phone.

"I hope you have a lovely time in London." And then, just as she rings off, "I think it's very brave."

I'm still puzzling through her call when Bijal returns from his run, half-moons of sweat under his arms. He mops his brow with a rag. He peels off his earbuds and flings them onto the island.

"We have to see the accountant today," he says, his ears glowing pink.

I think about telling him she called, but something stops me. It feels like a betrayal. Perhaps it's the first time I've felt connected to my daughter-in-law in years, the first time we've shared anything private, even if it was her tears. Besides, Bijal would only ask questions. *Were you nice to her? Did you ask her about herself? Did you tell her you liked the holiday card she sent?*

"I just have to shower," I say. "And then we can go."

"Okay," Bijal says absently. He leans over the island looking at a stack of old greeting cards and letters when something catches his eye. He holds up a small square postcard with a picture of Durga. Her pink tongue flares. "There's a garba tomorrow? Are we going?"

I turn my head. "No."

"Why not?"

I remember the night before, the looks on everyone's faces when Akash was sick on the floor. Bijal must sense this, because he says, "We don't need to bring him."

I turn to shush him but something in his eyes stops me.

"Mom," he says. "You can't make excuses for him, and you can't not live your life because of him." I nod slowly. He tosses the postcard aside. "Besides, it's the last garba. That means something, right? You have to go."

He smiles at me, and I suddenly remember all those evenings when we had to force him to come, when he balked at the cotton outfits I left folded on his bed.

"And what is this new interest you have, Bijal? Who is pulling your arm to go?"

He cocks his brow. "I always liked garba."

"Oh, is it?"

"Yeah," he says, grinning. "I was just faking it. Sometimes, in life, you have to pretend you don't wanna do something, that way, when you finally do it, everyone appreciates it."

"And who taught you this nonsense?"

He looks at me, his eyes shining. "Dad."

AKASH

This afternoon, while Bijal and my mother are meeting with my father's accountant, I dial Jacob's number. He hasn't responded to the text. A time stamp indicates that he read it this morning. I feel the world slip away from me. *Get out of my life.*

The phone rings twice before connecting to his voicemail.

He's declined the call. He's usually the type to answer, eager to resolve whatever problem we might have had. He hates letting things fester. I'm the one to ice him out, prone to long bouts of silence, unanswered texts, until Jacob cracks a joke or wraps his arms around me, shattering my will. I try again. This time it only rings once. The sound of his outgoing message—*It's Jacob, you know what to do*—makes me sink even further. I dial the number again. And again. The final time it doesn't ring at all. He's turned it off.

I try to pull myself together in the kitchen, drinking a liter of water, jamming bread into my mouth. I box some old plates for the Salvation Army. Now that the puja is over, the real work begins. Furniture will be collected and shipped off for donation. Clothes will disappear. Closets stripped. Dressers unpacked and dismantled. My father's things will be divided up among Bijal, my mother, and me, and the rest will be given to charity. The text message still follows me like a dark cloud. I call Jaden.

"Yo."

The sun warms my face in the breakfast nook. I look out the window at the yard, neat and square, a barbecue pit covered in a tarp, the tight wall of trees.

"I fucked up with Jacob."

Jaden laughs. "Again?"

"You think that's funny?"

"Sorry."

I hear the swish of air funneling through a window, the hum of traffic. "Where are you?"

"The 405. Why did we move to LA again?" He slams his hand down on the horn. "Move, *damn!*"

A smile spreads over my face. I close my eyes, sinking back against the booth, envisioning five wide lanes, an endless blue sky. "I miss the 405."

"No, you do not."

"Are you going to the studio?"

"Yeah, I'm still working on the track, by the way," Jaden says. "Sorry I haven't been on it."

"It's not like I'm bursting with ideas."

"So, what happened then? Is it because of me?"

We both fall silent. The memory of that night at the studio, and all the other nights before it, swirls between us. "Sorry," he says.

"It's okay. It's complicated."

"More complicated than us?"

It's the first time he's mentioned anything about us. I don't know what to say. Part of me wants to tell him to run, that I'm not what he's looking for, that the image he has of me, just like the image Jacob has of me, is a façade, bright and waxy, with a rotten core. I want to tell him the truth: that I don't know how to be good. I never knew. But how can I do that, Parth, without telling him about you?

"Listen, Osh," Jaden says. I hear the click of his keys and the soft tick of his engine as he parks his car. "I was thinking about some things, about that text you sent."

My mind flicks back to a month ago. It was the night I'd argued with Jacob about the music video, flinging the remote control at the TV. I'd texted Jaden. *Why can't we be more than friends?* There was no response. I was humiliated the next morning when I discovered it on my phone. Now, my cheeks burn as I cut him off.

"It was nothing," I say. "Really, don't feel like you have to say anything. I was drunk, and Jacob and I had just had a fight. I shouldn't have—it was stupid."

"Oh."

"Can we pretend it didn't happen?"

He's silent for a beat. Then he sighs into the phone. "Okay. I mean, I was hoping we could—"

Just then my mother's tires crunch against the driveway. I hear the whine of the garage. Within moments, the back door opens and Bijal's and my mother's voices pierce the silence in the hall. Their shoes clatter on the floor. The sun shifts behind a cloud, turning the light a dishwater shade of gray.

"I have to go, J. We'll talk later."

"Okay," he says dimly. "It's cool."

We click off. My mother enters the kitchen with a look of accusation. Bijal follows. They unload a small bag of groceries—fruit, a gallon of milk, some coffee—onto the kitchen island. It's silent.

"What were you doing?" she asks.

I remember the way she had looked at me when I rose from the puddle of my own sick on the floor, and later that night, in the kitchen, like she was drifting away. She peels off her wool coat and drapes it over a stool. "Just taking a break from packing."

My mother nods slowly, as if assessing whether this is true. Bijal doesn't address me at all. He loads the milk into the refrigerator and pulls out a loaf of bread. He pops a slice into the toaster. My mother looks at him, then at me.

"There's a garba tomorrow. It's the last one for Navratri. Bijal and I are thinking of going."

"Since when does Bijal go to these things?"

He glares at me from across the kitchen.

"If you don't want to go," my mother starts, cautiously, "it will be fine. Maybe it's better that way—since you're not feeling well."

I can tell by the way she looks at Bijal that they have rehearsed this conversation. I think about all the times my mother forced me to attend things: dinner parties, garbas, special events at the temple. *These are our friends,* she would say. *You can't stay home.*

I realize she's afraid of what I might do, what I've become. I swallow the tight ball that forms in my throat.

"Fine," I tell her, looking Bijal square in the eye. "Whatever."

RENU

The landline rings. We hardly use it anymore. Bijal is always telling me I should get rid of it, that everyone uses cell phones now, but at one point in my life it was the only link I had to my home, to London, possibly to you. I can't just cut it off. I fly to the receiver, and for a split second I have the irrational feeling that it is you, that you've found our number.

"Hello," I say.

The woman on the other end has a voice like a bird. "Renew?"

"Excuse me?"

"Re . . . renew?"

"I don't want to renew anything," I say, anger flaring. "Stop calling my house!" I hear a soft gasp before it dawns on me. "Taylor?"

It's a rare occasion that Taylor actually addresses me by name. The first time she did, she pronounced it "renew." I never corrected her. Perhaps that was my mistake. I was embarrassed *for* her. I figured it wasn't my place to correct Taylor—it wasn't *her* fault I had a name she couldn't pronounce. Sometimes I imagine the awkwardness that would ensue if I was to correct her now. How would Taylor feel? Offended? Betrayed?

"I was just calling to see how you're enjoying the book."

"Oh."

I had forgotten all about *A Fine Balance*. It's sitting on my dresser next to a stack of sweaters I'm going to donate. I tried reading the first chapter, but everything felt so bleak and dreary. Why couldn't she have chosen *The Girl on the Train* instead?

"I just love it," I say.

"Really?" Taylor exhales with relief. "Oh, I'm so glad. I was hoping you would! What do you love about it? Tell me everything."

Good god. I hurry up the sweeping staircase and into my room, panting. I find the book and flip it over to the back cover. "Oh, it's just so . . ." A word catches my eye. "Poignant."

"Mm," Taylor says. "Go on . . ."

"It really makes you think, you know?"

"Yes."

"About life—and everything in it."

"Life is hard."

"Oh, yes," I say, gaining traction. "Especially for . . ." I drop my voice to a whisper. "Third-world people."

Taylor makes a strange, squirrely sound that reminds me of a child at a playground. "Exactly!"

"It makes me feel so grateful to be living in America," I add. "Where we have food. And water."

"I can't imagine what life must have been like for you."

"Terrible. *Terrible.*"

I take the phone back downstairs and into the kitchen. Taylor tells me how much she's going to miss my insight when I'm gone.

Really?

"I was wondering," she says. "Would you happen to know someone who could take your place? You know, someone with your *perspective.*"

I don't know why Taylor can't just be forthright: she wants someone Indian. I think about all the connections I've made in this town, the forced smiles, the small talk, the people with whom I've shared nothing but time, and the people with whom I've shared more.

"As a matter of fact, I do."

"Oh, great!" Taylor says. "You can bring her with you to book club. And I can't wait to hear all your thoughts on the book when you're done, Renew! Bye!"

She rings off.

Later, when Bijal is running errands and Akash is brooding in his room, the thump of his stereo sounding through the walls, I swipe my finger across the screen, open Facebook, and read your message.

Dear Bibi,

I was pleased to hear from you, and even more pleased to hear that you are moving to London. What are the odds that our paths should cross again, and in such a coincidental way? I'm in Evanston at my daughter's house. She's just had a baby boy. After Farrah and I divorced, my daughter decided we should take turns visiting her home, so now I alternate between Evanston and London, two very different places. Is it strange to share all of this with you? I don't know what's appropriate anymore. What I do know is that I'm pleased to hear from you, and, if I may be so bold, I hope we can chat further. Please do give me your phone number, if you would rather text instead. I have only recently gotten the hang of emojis. So I will share one now. ☺

Love,
Kareem

Not "sincerely." Not "with love." Just "love." A simple word can hold so much weight; you can stand on it or let it crush you. I had not expected to feel this way. Now that you're real, Kareem. Now that you've asked for my number. Now that you're not the silver memory from my past but a person very much in the present, full of hope and expectation, I don't know what to do. What if you've changed? What if you're no longer the person I remember? I have seen it; people grow angry or bitter or sullen with regret. I want you to be exactly as I last saw you, exactly as you have lived in my heart.

Later that night, I send you my number.

Dear Kareem,
There's so much I have to tell you. I look forward to hearing more.

Love,
Renu

AKASH

A melody comes to mind, something soft and lilting. I take out my phone, record a few lines. Just as I lay them down, they evaporate. It's always like this. The seed never becomes a flower. I think about texting Jaden. *Where's that track?* But then I picture him in the studio with better writers than me, mixing a demo. I change my mind. I'm about to put my cell phone away when a message flashes across my screen. Grindr. Another text from "R." His message is curt: a drop pin followed by an invitation. A single word. *Now?* Longing flares through me, but I'm quick with my reply. *Maybe some other time.*

I put my phone down and sweep my gaze across the room. My bedroom is half-stripped, clothes pulled from hangers, posters torn off walls, strips of soiled adhesives visible in their wake. Books I've never read are fanned out on the floor, their spines creased. I can hear Bijal mumbling over the phone in the next room. I can tell, by the tension in his voice, that he's talking to Jessica. He's been withdrawn all day, staring at his cell phone, disappearing into other rooms. If we were closer, I would ask him what's wrong. I used to imagine we were the kind of brothers who did that, told each other everything.

I still haven't heard from Jacob. I wonder if I ever will. I think about calling him again but I'm too scared, unwilling to confront my text from two nights before. *Get out of my life*. My hangover has since subsided, but the anxiety remains, the fear that something has happened that can never be undone. I think about having another drink, something to settle my nerves. I open my dresser drawer and stare at the pile of airplane-sized bottles inside. I slam it shut. There's only one other solution, one thing that can clear my mind. I find the CD in the bottom drawer of my dresser along with some old photographs I plan to take back to LA. *The Miseducation of Lauryn Hill*. I load it into my old boom box, skip to the third song. I wait for the instruments to kick in. The room slips away from me as I close my eyes.

My cell phone rings, and I imagine your name flashing across the caller ID. How many times have I dreamt of this moment? How many times have I willed you to return? I've lost count. Being back here, in this house and this town, I feel you inside me all over again.

I don't recognize the number on the caller ID. I consider sending it to voicemail. When I answer, I practice saying your name, just to hear it roll off my tongue.

"What?"

The room blurs and sharpens. I blink at the wall. "Huh?"

"Who's Parth?"

"Who's this?" I say, sitting up on my bed.

"Akash." Jacob's voice is soft and distant. "It's me."

I had forgotten about his office line, had never saved it in my phone. I picture him at work, his tie loosened. I imagine the wrap-around windows and concrete walls. I see the potted Japanese plants. I've only been there once, a few months back, when he asked me to meet him for lunch. The office is on the third floor of a modern glass structure. Everyone wears casual clothes: hoodies over jeans, T-shirts and shorts, leather sandals, sneakers made of mesh. Only Jacob dresses up. His uniform is standard: monochromatic shirt, Italian wool pants, a glossy black belt. He says it's important for him to look professional, to remind everyone he's a figure of authority and not a friend. Sometimes I think he can't switch it off. Still, I was proud of him, leaving my name at the reception desk and waiting in one of the leather armchairs. I felt important when he addressed me in a tone that was notably different from the one he had used with his employees—softer, more intimate. I basked under the glow of his smile, the way everyone's attention seemed to shift toward us, immediately recognizing me for what I was: the boss's boyfriend.

"I'm sorry," I say now, for what must be the fifth time in a row. "I don't know what happened."

I can hear the low murmur of voices behind him. I sit back on my bed.

"Hello?"

"I'm here."

"You're not saying anything."

He sighs audibly, and I realize I may not want to know what he has to say.

"Akash . . ." His voice trails off. I can hear his will breaking, just like it always does. Suddenly, I want him right beside me, for him to wrap his arms around me.

"I miss you," I say, thinking back to the last time we made love. "I can't wait to see you again." And I mean it, a swell of emotion suddenly rising inside me. Tears spring from my eyes. "You're so good," I say. "You know that? I'm not. I know I'm not. But you are. I just—"

"This isn't working." His voice is hard. Firm.

"But it can . . . if I just . . ."

"What you just said," Jacob interrupts. "About being good. That's the problem."

"What?"

He breathes into the phone. "You don't see your own worth."

The honesty in his voice rings in my ears. I almost hang up the phone. Jacob tells me that he's packed up my things. There wasn't much: clothes and shoes and some recording equipment that fit snugly into a box. I picture him doing this hours before, maybe even days. I remember his text: *We need to talk*. Maybe he had decided it by then. I imagine the hours he's spent packing up every last trace of me—of us—leaving it like trash by the door. Though I have no right to be, I'm suddenly angry.

"So that's it?" I say, bitterly. "You're just gonna give up? Kick me out? Did you ever think about how this will affect me— with everything I'm dealing with now?"

He doesn't say anything for a while. "Hello?"

"There's more."

"What?"

"Nathan saw you on Grindr."

"What are—when?"

"It was a long time ago. I just never said anything about it."

"I don't understand. He's in California . . ."

"He starred your profile—so he could check up on you from time to time."

"Of course he did."

"He said you've been pretty active this week, which, to be honest, kind of hurts. If he hadn't told me, I guess I would have never known."

"I didn't do anything."

"It doesn't matter."

"Nathan's a fag," I say, stinging from the violation.

"Don't use that word," Jacob says, in his reasonable tone. "You know I don't like it."

"Which is funny, since no one ever used it on you."

"What?"

"No one ever called you a fag," I say. "No one thought you were gay. Even if they did, what would they say to a six-foot-tall white guy? Nothing. You didn't have to endure what I did. Everything I experienced—you didn't. And now look at you: the fag police."

"What did you experience?" Jacob says. "I wouldn't even know. You've never told me. You never talk about anything. You just ask me how much my stereo cost or have I been to Spain or do I think your eyes are too close together. This isn't real. It never was."

His voice strikes a solemn tone. I hear him sigh. This time, it's a quick, fleeting sound. A sharp punctuation. The end.

"Look, I have to go," he says. "You can pick up your stuff when you're back." He's silent a moment, as if he's already hung up the phone, and then he does. "Goodbye, Akash."

A sob belts from my lips. I can't contain it. I throw my phone across the room and watch, through blurred eyes, as it bounces off the wall.

RENU

The dim light from a lamp throws shadows across the living room. In two days, I've learned so much about you. You've chosen to tell me everything: that you never forgot me, that you still think about me, that sometimes I visit you in your dreams. You've retired from your position as CFO of a communications company in London, where you worked for thirty years. Now, you plan to divide your time equally between London and Illinois, where your daughter lives. We both marvel at the coincidence, that your daughter should live only two hours away from me, and that I should be moving to London next month. We haven't spoken of what all of this means, a future for you and me. I don't want to be the one to do it. I can't.

You tell me that, once, during a visit from your ex-wife's family, you saw a woman who looked like me walking down a street. You were in Covent Garden. You left your family behind. They stood underneath a restaurant awning wondering where you had gone. You followed this woman for five blocks before she finally turned on her heels, shouting.

"Oye! What's the matter with you?"

By the time you returned, thirty minutes later, your wife, Farrah, was talking to an officer who had been patrolling on foot, tears streaking her face. You told her you had lost your way. She didn't ask anything further.

Though I've opened up as well, telling you about my life in Illinois, about my marriage to Ashok, my friends, my hobbies, the boys, I've yet to tell you the one thing I've been wanting to tell you all along. I can't bring myself to mention her name. I can't describe to you the smell of the hospital room or the canary-colored walls, or the feeling, after it was over, of being gutted. Cored.

"Some women find it helpful to hold the baby," a nurse had said. "You know, for closure."

Closure. What a reductive word. Some doors can never be closed, Kareem, no matter how hard you slam them. They always find a way of opening back up.

Outside, the sky strobes with lightning. Thunder cracks. Under the din of the storm, I hear someone on the stairs. I hear him walk into the room behind me, noticing his reflection in the TV screen ahead. "Mom?"

I turn around. He wears a thin white T-shirt, the color drained from his face. For a moment, my heart softens, wanting to pull him close, but then a familiar edge creeps in. What is it that makes me feel this way? It's not what happened at the puja. I can forgive him for that. By now, I've grown accustomed to the whispers and stares. In less than a week, I'll be gone from this place. Still, the sight of him awakens some dormant part inside me, like a dragon in a lair.

"Yes, Akash? What is it?"

He doesn't move, doesn't open his mouth. It looks as if he might cry, and I, too, feel a familiar knot in my throat.

"Akash, I'm busy," I say. "Just say it."

His lips tremble, and it's this, this weakness within him, the softness I once tried to make firm, that breaks me.

"What is it, Akash?" I snarl. "Tell me: what is it *now*?"

He flinches, as if I've struck him in the face. His features slowly drop. Melting. Then he turns and slinks off. Part of me wants to chase after him, pull him close to my breast. I pick up my cell phone instead.

You've sent a new text.

Look outside, you say.

At what?

The moon.

I send an eye-rolling emoji. *Is that what you have to show me? Something I have seen a thousand times before?*

You express your pleasure with three simple letters: *Lol.* Then you start typing, and the subsequent ellipses are like the slow ticking of a bomb, causing my pulse to race. I squirm in my seat. Your response illuminates the screen.

Bibi, it's not what you behold that matters. It's the eyes with which you behold it.

Just like that, I put the phone down and rush to the windows, opening the blinds. The backyard shimmers like a moonstruck lake. The evergreens loom like specters. The smooth pebbles in the landscaping shine like pearls. I look toward the sky and see it. Full, opalescent, more beautiful than I had imagined.

Do you see it? you write.

Yes.

And?

I'm careful with my reply, feeling the weight of each word.

My eyes are open.

AKASH

It's late when I take Bijal's ten-speed bike out of the garage. Aside from my guitar and my mother's car, it's the only thing that remains. The rest—skateboards and roller skates and old tools—have been tossed out or sold. I glide through the neighborhood, my T-shirt puffed like a sail. A backpack is strapped to my shoulders. I hear the chink of glass inside, feel the slosh of liquid within. You should see me now, Parth. I'm as fast as the wind. I'm listening to music from an old Discman I found in the basement. Monica, "Don't Take It Personal." I wonder what else we'll discover when everything is packed up and sent away. Maybe we'll find the images I had once printed off a website called ShirtlessMaleCelebs.com. *Don't tell Mom.* Maybe then I will be spared the awkwardness of betraying my father, telling my mother the truth. Shouldn't she know? Maybe she already does, the way mothers often do. When Sam, a friend of Jacob's who now identifies as nonbinary, had come out to *his* parents, his mother had laughed.

"Oh, honey," she'd said. "I've known since you were five."

I don't think my mother knew when I was that young. I don't think she suspected anything at all.

"Indians are not like that," she'd once said, when Bijal rented the movie *Philadelphia* for a school project and made us all watch it. I had squirmed in my seat, afraid that someone would draw the connection, that they would look at me and say, "Are you this way?"

When a commercial aired for a new hit show, *Will & Grace,* my mother shook her head. "I'm glad *I* don't have a son like that."

Like that. Always circumventing, never addressing it by name. This is what it takes to survive in the world.

The sky flashes, threatening more rain. I hope it does. I want to feel the hard spike of it on my scalp, the heavy slap on my back. I want it to rinse out every part of me, everything that isn't good. This town is full of land mines, Parth. A road map of you and me. There's the patch of farmland, now bald and black, where we once rode our bikes between towers of corn. There's the ghostly glow of your motel in the distance, steaming in the night. There's the arcade where we first met. The windows are dark. Music thumps from inside. A few people loiter in the parking lot, cigarettes flickering between their lips. I pass Troy Academy, the gold emblem still visible behind the walls of glass and steel. Before long, I'm outside my old school.

In the pitch black of night, the building looks ominous, like an insane asylum. The parking lot is empty. A banner still hangs from the front entrance announcing homecoming. I pedal my way across the parking lot, toward the back where the football field stretches beyond high bleachers. I stop just in front of them. Look to my left. The dumpster is still there. I wonder if they've even bothered to change it. For a moment, I feel a flash of something. Sadness. Rage. I'm not sure. I can hear their voices, feel the slick of their skin. I see you, too, Parth. But I push the image away. I come to a stop just outside the dumpster and dismount. I lean Bijal's bike against it, drop my backpack to the ground. It's littered with sparkling pieces of chipped glass. I stand up and, with all my might, flip open the lid, releasing its rotten fumes. I'm not sure what I'm expecting to see when I pop my head over the rim—a pool of blood, the face of a child. Bryce. Evan. Lance. You. I crouch down and unzip my bag and there they are, every last one of them, every bottle, enough alcohol to last a week. I hoist the bag over the lip of the dumpster and give it a shake, my heart pounding, watching them clatter to the floor.

RENU

I stand in my bathroom, wrapped in a sari, pinning a dupatta to my blouse. Chaya sits at the edge of my tub, painting her nails. She wears a rust-colored outfit with gold brocade. We've opened a bottle of wine. It was her idea to commemorate this, our last garba together, with a drink. My phone has not stopped pinging since I sent you my number. I read your last message.

> *I don't know if I can wait until I return to London. I need to look in your eyes, hear your voice, hold your hand. Maybe it's too much to ask, but I would like to see you in person. Can you meet?*
>
> *Love, Kareem*

I haven't replied. Before that, my texts were as faithful as the tick of a metronome, but now my fingers have stilled, my thumb hovering uselessly over the keys.

"Who is that?" Chaya says.

"No one."

"Jaja haave. My Amit used to tell me the same thing when the phone rang for him in school. *It's no one, Mom.* Then I would find out it was some dori girl."

I smile in spite of myself. "It's my WhatsApp group in London. They're preparing for my return."

I feel bad lying to her, but Chaya and I have our limits. There are things I haven't told her, things I'd rather she didn't know. Like the time Ashok, early on in our marriage, had made a bad investment that nearly cost us our home. Or that Jessica's mother is twice divorced. Or that Bijal doesn't speak to Akash. Or that, in my early years in London, I used to eat beef. It was you who introduced me to it. Steak. Burgers. Sometimes I still crave the bloody juice of a fillet. Chaya is a strict vegetarian; she prohibits Bhupendra from even bringing meat into the house. I've kept these things from her for the same reason a curtain falls at the end of a performance: at some point, the show is over. We choose what we want people to know.

"Did you hear about Jaya's daughter?" Chaya says now.

"What?"

"She's separating from her husband. She cheated on him with someone from work."

"Oh."

I blanch, turning in front of the mirror so as not to show my reaction. Light bounces off the tiny crystals embroidered on my blouse. Chaya screws the cap back on her nail polish and sets it onto the ledge of the tub. She stands, folding her arms.

"The cheating is fine," Chaya says. "Cheating, it happens. But what gets me is how smug Jaya used to be, remember? Always criticizing our kids for not going to the temple, for eating meat. Now look!" She laughs. "Her daughter is sleeping with janitors."

"She slept with the janitor?"

"No, I'm only saying."

She comes to my side, adjusting the folds of her lengha. Her gold bangles clink at her wrist. I have done her makeup, applying a sheer gloss to her lips.

"You look pretty."

"Thanks to you. Now who will do these things for me when you're gone? I can barely get Bhupendra to fasten my blouse."

"He just wants to unfasten it."

"Dear god." Chaya feigns nausea. "If he wants to see breasts, he should look down in the shower."

"Chaya!"

"I wasn't lucky to have had a husband like yours."

I turn away from her.

"I'm sorry," she says, touching my arm. "I shouldn't have said that."

"No, it's fine." I face her, the words spilling from my lips. "Chaya, I have something to tell you."

"Yes?"

"I—"

She wrinkles her face, concerned. "What is it?"

But I still can't do it.

"It's this book club I'm in. I was wondering if you wanted to take my place when I'm gone. We have a meeting coming up," I say, my breath quickening. "I can take you."

Chaya's expression straightens, her lips thinning. "What is this?" she says, in mock offense. "You never told me you were in a book club. Now I want to know, Renu: What other secrets are you keeping from me?"

Chaya smiles. The word "secrets" lingers. I make one last adjustment to my blouse, smoothing the sleek, iridescent fabric into place. "Chal," I tell her. "Let's go."

Downstairs, Bijal faces the kitchen windows in a teal kurta. He turns.

"You look nice, Mom."

I stare at the sheen of his top, the gleaming buttons. I remember when he was a child and refused to wear them. Now, he looks more at home in it than Ashok ever did, his rich black hair swept back in waves, spackled with gray. He folds his arms, and, for a brief moment, I see you.

"You look handsome, Bijal."

"Of course he does," says Chaya, approaching. "And what about me? Don't I look like I can find someone younger?"

She turns, her blouse reflecting pockets of light. Bijal grins.

"Aunty, if I was Uncle, I wouldn't let you out of the house. I'd be afraid of all the attention you'd get."

"Be afraid for the men," I say.

Chaya wrinkles her nose and raises her hand as if to slap me, gripping my wrist instead.

"Now that your mother is leaving, Bijal, don't forget me, hah? You still have family in this town."

"I could never forget you, Aunty."

She nods with approval. I'm reminded of how easy he was, the facility he had for talking to people, knowing exactly what to say. Just as we're about to leave, a set of footsteps sounds through the floorboards above. Chaya turns.

"Isn't Akash coming?"

The mention of his name wipes the smile from Bijal's face.

"Well," I say, blinking. "I'm not—"

"Aunty," Bijal says, regaining his composure. "You know Akash. He thinks he's too cool for us now."

Just like that, the moment has passed.

Later, in Chaya's car, we pull into the parking lot outside the temple. Already I can hear the drums inside, the guttural chants, voices penetrating the cool autumn night. I see the shadows of men and women in glinting attire, making their way toward the doors. Chaya finds a space near the entrance; she parks the car. We open our doors. She grabs my wrist.

"This will be the last time we do this," she says.

We follow her inside, sliding off our shoes in the front vestibule, draping our coats over hooks, smiling at guests as they cross our path, our hands folded in prayer, when someone approaches. Slim, handsome. Slanted brows. Penetrative eyes. A patchy beard swirls like iron filings over his cheeks. He smiles at us, his skin turning red. I've seen him before, but I can't place him. It's Chaya who claps both hands to her face.

"Now this I cannot believe," she says, turning to address us, a spark in her eyes. "Look. Look who it is. Do you know who this is?" Before we can answer her, she does so herself.

"Parth."

AKASH

I've been instructed to stay home, so, for once, I do what my mother has asked. Ordinarily, I would drink to pass the time, but I push the thought from my mind. I'm proud of myself—for making a change, adhering to it—but now all I want is a glass of white wine. I imagine the crisp snap of it on my tongue. I get up and turn the radio on. A DJ informs us that he's taking it back, way back, and playing an "old-school jam." The song is "I Wanna Be Down."

I was nine years old when it came out. I used to sing it around the house, emulating her riffs. *I wanna be down, with what you're going through*. Bijal and my mother would plead with me to stop, to give them a moment's peace. But music is not about peace, Parth. Music lights a match. Outside, the sun has set, the sky a blue jewel. It's late October, and people have strung Halloween decorations outside their homes. A white sheet ripples in the distance, two holes poked into it to make eyes. I open my closet and stare at the press of clothes: sweatshirts and button-downs and the designer suit I wore four years ago for Bijal's wedding, then again last year for my father's funeral. One jacket, two very different occasions. Isn't that the nature of clothes, to shield us through some moments while making us vulnerable in others?

I run my hand over the silky sheen, remembering the morning of my father's funeral—the chilled surface of the chairs, morning light spiking off the tiles, my mother unadorned in a white sari, no jewelry—and that's when I see it: the kurta my mother had wanted me to wear for the puja. Cream silk with silver threading, long pants that hang loose from the hanger, a rust-colored dupatta to match, in danger of slipping to the floor.

I stand in front of my bedroom mirror and smooth it over my chest, fastening the pearl buttons. The fabric isn't itchy like I had imagined. Perhaps they've changed since I was a child. The top is soft, a balm against my skin. I walk downstairs and glance at my reflection in the polished surfaces of picture frames and glass, the cream swish of silk like the spirits that flicker outside. Darkness gathers as I pass through the hall and into the garage. I gather the excess fabric of the kurta into my hands and swing one leg over the seat of Bijal's bicycle, dropping my foot onto the ground. I kick off slowly. I wrap the dupatta around my neck. I loop it twice to keep it from catching in the wheels. Then I set off into the night. A breeze makes the fabric billow and the ends of the dupatta lift up in a dance. If you could see me, Parth, you would think I was a ghost.

RENU

Parth wears an Oxford shirt tucked into pressed pants. The earring that once shone in his ear, a diamond stud his mother had fainted over, is now gone. His eyes look wiser, like the broken surface of a lake, but his face retains its youthful glow. He tells us he's taking time off before starting his fellowship in gastroenterology. He's in town until Christmas; now that his parents are in India, he's watching over their motel. I'm about to tell him that Akash is also in town when I stop myself. An instinct takes over—for what, I'm not sure. I still don't know what happened between them. I stopped asking questions long ago. Standing in front of him, watching him nod and smile, I'm reminded of the times, shamefully, when I wished Parth were my son instead. His ease of being inside his own skin, the knowledge of his place in the world—I wanted that for Akash. Chaya asks him when he's getting married and he laughs, saying something charming in return—not like Akash, who would turn blistering red.

After talking briefly with Bijal about medicine and his plans, Parth tells us he has to check in with the staff at the motel.

"I'll be back soon," he says, and then, smiling at Chaya, "You'd better save me a dance."

Chaya beams. He looks at me and nods. We watch him disappear. Later, Chaya doesn't leave my side all night, leading me to a small circle of women dancing in front of a framed picture of Durga. They smile at me the way everyone does, with a trace of sadness. I want to shake these sad smiles off their lips. I want to scream at them. *Stop looking at me that way! I'm all right!* But pity is only an act of kindness, no matter how cruel it may seem.

"Look at Hema," Chaya whispers, pointing across the room. "She's getting ready for her performance."

We've come to a rest near the water fountains, fanning ourselves with our dupattas. The sweat cools on my skin. Through the flurry of silk-covered arms and legs, I can see Hema walking toward the picture of Durga. The "performance" Chaya is talking about is a well-executed act of possession. Onlookers will crowd around her and say, "Jo, look! Mata awi!" and Hema will collapse into a fit of convulsions, frothing at the mouth. Ashok said it's a bunch of crock, that she does this for attention, the glory of God's favor, but I don't know. Maybe God chooses some of us over others—like mothers with their sons. The first time Akash saw this, he'd pointed and laughed.

"Look, Mom!" he'd said. "She's having an orgasm!"

"Akash, chup!" I'd snapped, pinching his ear. "Stop talking nonsense! And how do you know that word?"

Now, Hema is thinner, grayer, the skin sagging from her arms. Her movements are measured.

"I think if she fell down," I say, "she wouldn't get up again."

Chaya laughs. "Like the commercials."

I'm thankful for the opportunity to laugh, to feel that familiar lift as a portion of the weight inside me is released, and maybe this is why I do it, Kareem, the words taking shape in my mind, spilling like rice from my lips. "Chaya." She turns, her eyes searching mine. "There's something you should know." She tilts her head curiously. "It's something I've kept from you for too long. I should have told you earlier. I didn't want to . . . it's about . . ."

My voice trails off. Chaya reaches for my hand.

"I know," she says, squeezing it.

AKASH

I'm sweating by the time I reach the temple. I face the pearly white façade. For a moment, I can see it, the ghost of graffiti. DIE MUSLIMS. I blink it away. The night is clear, the moon high and bright. I park the bicycle outside the front entrance. A door opens and music spills forth, along with a parallelogram of light. The door closes. A woman walks past. Her outfit has beadwork like a glittering spider's web. She doesn't look at me as she walks toward the parking lot and disappears between the cars. I approach the entrance, feel the resonance of drums. I've stopped wondering what my mother will say. I no longer care. This is where I belong.

Inside, everything reminds me of you: the stuttering drums, the plinking bells, the tinkle of jhanjar, anklets worn by young girls who dash across the floor. The sweet, chant-like melodies that get stuck in your head. Candelabras illuminate every corner of the hall. Streamers flap from the ceiling like kites. Guests dance at the center of the room in outfits the colors of a sunset. It's like a wedding reception. I think of Bijal's. The hot lights melting my face. The screech of the microphone. All those faces staring. The slow, babbling words. *Everyone loves my brother. I can't imagine why.*

I look around the room and don't see anyone I recognize. The town has grown since we were young. What was once five Indian families became ten, then twenty, then thirty. People from neighboring towns, towns smaller than this one, have arrived with children in tow. They mingle in clusters before joining the circle of dancers at the center, swaying in rhythm with the beat. A band of musicians performs on a raised platform across the hall. I see someone who reminds me of you. A young man in a hooded sweatshirt and jeans. He's talking shyly to a girl. She shows him something on her cell phone and he laughs. The altar at the center of the room, lit by small diyas and strung with garlands, catches my eye. I walk toward it, staring at the portrait of Durga, her tongue flaring, weapons glinting, eyes wild like a caged animal's, when I bump into someone from behind. His back is damp. He spins around.

"Oh," he says, our eyes locking. "Akash."

Rivulets of sweat have already begun to swivel down the sides of Bijal's face. His teal kurta is dark in spots. He wears a gold ring on his finger. The center stone is an opal, smooth and small, like a manicured nail. I've never seen it before. The way he's looking at me now, with curiosity rather than contempt, is also a surprise.

"You're here."

"Is that a problem?"

He shrugs. "I guess if you were planning to come you could've just ridden with us."

"I decided at the last minute."

He nods, staring. "Are you . . ."

"Am I what?" I say.

Bijal raises his palms in mock surrender. "I'm just making sure you're cool."

"I'm cool."

"We just don't want any problems, okay?"

I could get angry, but the soft, pleading tone of his voice is something new. Maybe this is it: the point where penance ends, forgiveness begins. Still, a heaviness forms in the center of my chest, plunging. "Don't worry," I say, turning to walk away. "I won't embarrass you."

My mother is across the hall talking to Chaya Aunty. She looks distressed. I wonder if she's seen me, if I'm the reason her face has gone pale. Their bodies flicker behind the lace of linked arms. At one point, Chaya leads my mother toward the back door behind the buffet table and they disappear from sight. A song catches my ear. I turn in the direction of the musicians. The singer's voice is as clear and high as a bell. The notes are intoxicating, a melody that could lull you to sleep. But I'm wide awake, my brain finally finding its grip.

This, I think, slowly, over a stuttering beat. This, with a vibrating bass. A melody layered on top, dripping like honey, luring you to the pre-chorus, the chorus, the hook. A beat change in the bridge. A smooth, slinky voice like Aaliyah's. Stacked harmonies like only Brandy could do. Lyrics like Lauryn Hill's "To Zion." The second verse is an interpolation of the first. You have to manipulate it, twist it a little; it can't be the same. You have to keep the listener on his toes. I hear the hook. It's distant at first, like someone calling your name in a dream. The words are muffled, drowned out by the melody. I have to pull them to the surface. I turn them over like coins: *Tell me. Tell me. Tell me how to be.*

I take my phone out and angle it toward the musicians. I hit record. I play it back in my ear. *Tell me. Tell me. Tell me how to be.* A minute later, I'm texting Jaden.

J—listen to this.

RENU

"I loved a Muslim man once. His name was Imran."

Chaya stretches her legs against the cool marble tiles. We sit with our backs against the wall. I can feel the vibration of the adjoining hall, shuddering against my spine.

"You're kidding."

"It's the truth," Chaya says. We're in the prayer room, which is tiled with white marble. Blue light spills from a window. The combined effect has an arctic feel, as if we're trapped in a block of ice. Chaya flexes her toes, which are dark and clash starkly with the chipped polish on her nails. "He was my brother's friend. Imran Hassan Chaudhary."

I'm still reeling from the news: Chaya knows. She's known for years. How could it be? Moments earlier, she told me what happened, that Bhupendra had needed an extra suitcase to take with him to India, and that Ashok had loaned him ours. There was a letter tucked inside the front pocket. Chaya was the one who found it. It comes back to me: the missing suitcase. The letter I never sent. I had forgotten about it by then. It was years ago. Akash had just entered high school and Bijal was in college. Chaya discovered it when she was packing extra sets of notebooks and pens to gift to her nieces in Ahmedabad. The letter, our letter, was still there.

"Of course I read it," she admitted, ashamed. "For weeks it was all I could think about. I didn't expect you to tell me, Renu.

It wasn't my business. But I suppose a part of me was sad that you couldn't—that we can't tell each other these things."

She told me she had hidden the letter from Bhupendra. It's in a small jewelry box in her closet. She wanted to return it, but she didn't know what to say. In the end, Ashok was the one to tell Bhupendra to keep the suitcase; we had no use for it by then. I absorbed this information quietly.

"I didn't want you to think I had read it. I didn't want you to know that I knew. All these years, Renu." She clasped my hand. "I was lying to you. When I saw on Facebook that you had become friends with someone named Kareem Abbas, the name sounded so familiar. I remembered everything then. I knew."

"What must you think of me, Chaya?" I said, crying, but she only put a finger to my lips. Now, my mind races as she tells me her own story.

"My father never liked Imran," she says. "So of course I loved him. He went to school with my brother, Suresh. They were best friends. They played cricket in the sandlot behind our house. He wore a blue collared shirt every day after school, and sometimes, if I was lucky, he would strip down to his vest."

"*Oh, la.*"

"When it was his turn to bat, he would smile at me and say, *Eh, bibi! This is for you!* Then he would whack at the ball and watch it soar. Once, it broke my father's window."

"Arre," I say. "Who is this Chaya, causing men to swing their bats?"

I can hear the music next door, the dull thump of a drum. Someone is laughing wildly. I wonder how long it will be before anyone notices we're gone. I hope no one does.

"I haven't told anyone this, but we used to meet in private," Chaya says. "On weekends when my parents took Suresh for his tutoring, Imran would come over and we would sit on the porch, eating jackfruit. I hated jackfruit." She smiles, wistfully. "But I didn't want him to know. I was afraid he would stop coming over. He was funny; he could always make me laugh. Not like Bhupendra, with his constant scowl. I'll never forget Imran's smile. It made you feel like you were there."

"Did you . . ."

"God, no," Chaya says. "I was fifteen. Imran was three years older. Anyway, it never got that far. One day, the tutoring was canceled, and my parents and Suresh came home early. My father caught us holding hands."

She extends her leg, pulling back the jade silk fabric of her salwar, revealing a thin, braided scar.

"You know how it was back then," Chaya says. "It was okay for Suresh to be friends with a Muslim, but heaven forbid I, their only daughter, touch one."

She shakes her head. "You know what the worst thing was?"

"What?"

She looks at me sadly. "Suresh never talked to Imran again. He was angry with him, as if I were a possession, something Imran had stolen, tainted with his hands. He started believing all the bakwaas things my father said about Muslims: that they were infidels, thieves. Sometimes I wonder where he is, if he's happy. I hope so."

She's silent, tracing the floor with her toe.

"Kareem wants to meet," I say.

"Where?"

"He didn't say."

"When?"

"I don't know. Before I leave."

Her face darkens, her brows narrowed to a point. "And what do *you* want?"

"I don't know," I say. "What would people think? A woman my age . . . a widow . . ."

"Screw what they think."

"It looks bad."

"To whom?" Chaya sits up, indignant. "To those poputs next door?"

I laugh.

"Ashok is gone," Chaya says. "You loved him. You were a good wife. You did what you had to do. Now you are moving. Who cares what anyone thinks?" Some color has risen to her cheeks. Her eyes smolder. "Listen, Renu. You are free. Don't you know that?"

The word flicks the space between my brows: free. I look at Chaya and understand, for the first time in years, why God has placed me in this town—to be with her.

I pull out my phone and open your message and text you one simple word: *Yes.*

———

AKASH

I wait impatiently for Jaden to respond. He doesn't. I put my phone away just as the song comes to an end. The dancers at the center of the room take a break, dispersing. The doors open. A sharp chill enters the room. I can smell the fresh scent of pine and the acrid smoke of burning leaves. Fall. The musicians drink from water bottles, mop their brows of sweat. I walk over to the singer, a bindi blinking between her brows.

"That was great."

She tips her head back and swallows a mouthful of water, then screws the cap back on. "Thank you."

"Do you have a card?"

"You want to hire us?"

"I want to use your performance in a song."

She grins. "Oh, is it? Big-time music producer you are." But her smile is kind. She reaches into the handbag at the edge of the stage, pulling out a small square of stationery. She presses it into my palm.

"You will give us royalty for this song?"

"Of course," I say. "You're gonna hear it on the radio one day."

"Arre wah!" She flicks her hand in a gesture of awe. "Do you hear this?" she says, turning to address the musicians behind her. "You hear what this nawab is saying? We're going to be famous."

The musicians flash their teeth. I give them a nod. I remember what my mother had said so many years ago. *They are not like us.* Those Indians. This one. We have different rhythms, but we're part of the same song. I take the card from her hand and wave to the musicians, and, when I turn around, I see my mother standing in front of me, a puzzled look on her face.

"Akash?"

The strawberry cream complexion has returned to my mother's face. Damp hair clings to her cheeks. Her jewelry—chandelier earrings and a matching necklace—almost drips with light. She seems lighter, freer than before. I see a smile teasing the edges of her lips. I had expected her fury, her fire. She seems almost pleased.

"You wore it," she says, pointing to my attire.

I look down at my chest. "Yeah."

"It looks good on you."

"Thanks."

"You could've worn it earlier, you know—at Dad's puja. I told you it would look good. You never listen, Akash."

I roll my eyes. "Mom . . ."

"Fine, fine."

She wraps herself with her arms as if we're meeting on a cold, deserted street. The music starts up as one of the musicians announces the raas, and a pair of men carry a large cardboard box to the center of the room. The box is brimming with sticks—dandiya—wrapped in silver and gold ribbon, some with tassels or beads. A cluster of children rush toward it to make their selections, practicing with measured clicks. They jump and spin and toss their sticks into the air. Soon, even the adults are retrieving pairs of dandiya and practicing in corners. They partner up, clapping the sticks together twice before connecting with their partner's sticks. Hit, hit, connect. Hit, hit, connect. Some of the women twirl in dramatic fashion, their dresses fanning out like umbrellas. Hit, hit, connect. I catch the rhythm in my chest, holding it there.

"Raas is your favorite," my mother says, eyeing the commotion at the center of the room.

"I probably forgot how to do it. I haven't done it in a while."

My mother shrugs. "It's like riding a bike."

The image comes to mind: your back facing me as you sail across the road, your hair rippling, your arms spread wide. I look at my mother. "You're probably right."

We stand in a row: me, Bijal, my mother, Chaya Aunty. A few familiar faces have joined, and we form two parallel rows. Everyone else has taken their positions across the gym. The musicians strum a few chords over the percussion of a drum. We practice first, hitting the sticks against one another's to establish the beat. The object of raas is simple: your stick connects with the stick held by the person opposite you, then you shift down to the next person in line. Sometimes it gets confusing; a person drops out suddenly and the whole thing is off. A few people get overzealous and lose their sticks. Every now and then someone accidentally whacks their partner in the head. In the fifth grade, I had explained to my classmates that raas was the Indian version of musical chairs—it isn't. Like many things from my youth, there was never an American equivalent.

"All right, everyone," Chaya commands. "Let's start. One. Two. Three!"

The steady drumming of a dhol sets the pace; we move in sync. Hit, hit, connect. Hit, hit, connect. Soon, I've shifted down the line and I'm facing an aunty in a crushed silk outfit. She beams. Hit, hit, connect. I move further down. Hit, hit, connect. Sweat gathers between my toes. The room is awash with color. Rust, lavender, pistachio, rose. The colors of macarons. Everyone is smiling now—even Bijal—swept up by the music, riding its waves. Hit, hit, connect. The music gradually intensifies, the beat accelerating, quickening our pace. Dust coats the underside of my feet. The hall revolves around me in a blur. Hit, hit, connect. Each thwack sends a shock that vibrates in my hands and spreads through my chest. The muscles in my legs begin to burn. Through the corner of my eye, I see someone enter the end of the line, taking the place of an uncle who's just left. He looks at Bijal and me. I move further down. Hit, hit, connect. Bijal is next to me, twirling his stick like a baton. It clatters to the floor. He laughs and picks it up, and when I nudge him, he nudges me back. My mother and Chaya Aunty switch places, spinning and laughing. In that moment, everything is forgotten. We're not alone anymore; we're part of something larger than ourselves. The room moves collectively like migrating birds.

Soon, Bijal is standing opposite me, his smile unwavering. Here, in this room, among the people from our past, the music is all that matters, the sweat sliding down our backs, the sticks pulsing in our hands, the drums mimicking our hearts, reminding us we're alive. Bijal grins when I wobble my head like the uncles do. Hit, hit, connect. I turn with an extra flourish, making him laugh, and it feels good to do that, to have my brother back. He does a karate chop that makes my mother, watching from the end of the line, roll her eyes, and just like that, we're kids again. I picture him chasing me through unfinished homes, wrestling with me on the dirt floor. I see him running to my rescue at the park. *Leave my brother alone*. I take a wide turn, ready to swing around, and that's when I realize it. That person at the end of the line.

It's you.

Hit, hit, conne—

Just as I see your face, a loud crack reverberates through the gym. Bijal falls to the ground. He covers his left eye. The line stops.

"What the fuck?"

The dandiya slips from my grasp and clatters onto the floor. Bijal is on his knees now, rolling.

"Bijal! Are you all right?" our mother says, rushing to his side.

A walnut-sized knot bulges at his brow. Dark beads of blood break the surface, pearling. My mother glares at me.

"Akash! What did you do?"

Finally, Bijal sits up and presses a hand against the cut. My mother kneels down next to him. The line looks on with sympathy. I glance around the room for any sign of you. But you're gone. Maybe it wasn't you at all, Parth. Maybe I'm delirious.

"I didn't . . ." I start to say, looking down at Bijal. "I'm sorry. It was an accident."

"What the fuck is your problem?" he snaps, my mother helping him to his feet. I remember how he had looked at me just moments ago, as if I were something he had lost and suddenly found. The crowd soon forgets us and returns to their stations. My mother narrows her eyes.

"Have you been drinking?"

"No. I'm not . . . I'm done with all of that."

But before I can say anything further, she shakes her head.

"You see," she says, the fondness from earlier missing from her voice. "This is why I told you not to come."

Before anyone can corner me, I make my escape, slipping out through the back door. The night air wraps its icy fingers around me. My bicycle is where I last left it. My mother and Bijal are gone. My thoughts begin to spin out of focus, like a merry-go-round. I pull out my cell phone from the lining of my kurta and swipe my finger across the screen. Another message on Grindr. It's "R." He's sent a drop pin followed by a question mark, a picture of his unsmiling face. I stare at it, the cold, menacing gaze, and send my reply.

I'm on my way.

RENU

I place fresh ice cubes into a plastic bag and bring them to Bijal on the couch. He lies on his back with a towel over his face.

"Are you okay?"

He grunts his response. I stare out the front windows of the house, waiting for Akash to return. I think about texting him, but I don't know what to say. Sometimes I think I'm the one who pushed him away, twisted him into something I no longer recognize. Children are like wet clay; one wrong move, and they're misshapen for life. Did I ruin Akash's chance for happiness, simply because I had lost mine?

While Bijal rests on the sofa, a damp cloth covering his eyes, I watch *Deserted Hearts*.

Things are getting worse for Celeste. Juan doesn't want her to have the augmentation. They fight at a charity event for testicular cancer. The event is at a bowling alley and is called "Balls for Balls." Juan props two bowling balls against his chest.

"This is what you'll look like. You know that, right?"

"Oh, stop it, Juan!"

But Juan doesn't stop. He tells Celeste that if she goes through with the augmentation, he'll never speak to her again. Celeste is outraged.

"It's my body!" she says. "I can do what I want. Maybe I'll get three breasts! Like that woman in *Total Recall*."

"I'd rather you have no breasts at all," Juan cries. "They'll just get in the way!"

"Of *what*?"

He pulls her close. "Your heart."

"Oh, Juan!"

They kiss passionately. The episode ends.

Bijal removes his towel. He looks at me with his swollen eye.

"Seriously?"

"What?"

"What kind of trash are you watching?"

"It's *Deserted Hearts*."

"What kind of name is that for a show?" Bijal says, sitting up. "And look at that woman."

"Which woman?"

"Celeste," Bijal says. "What a ridiculous person. Chasing after her gardener like some kind of . . ." He doesn't say the word. "I feel sorry for her husband."

I feel my lips stiffen. "It's more complicated than that."

Bijal places the towel onto his lap and folds his arms, frowning. He looks like a spoiled child. He is a spoiled child. *Look at your wife,* I want to say. *She's not any better.* Then I remember my conversation with Jessica the other day, feeling a stab of guilt.

"Celeste is a troubled person. You can't judge her based on ten minutes."

"Ten minutes was too much." He turns defiantly toward the window. "I don't know, Mom," he says. "You've regressed."

The word snaps in my mind. "What do you mean?"

"Nothing."

"Just say it then."

He turns stoic. "I just think you've lost yourself. I don't understand what you're doing, selling the house, moving to London. Watching this crap. Whatever else . . ."

Does he know? Bijal shakes his head at me as if he is my father and I am the delinquent child. "I think you're lost without Dad. You don't know what to do anymore."

"What bakwaas," I say. "I'm lost without Dad? It was Dad who was lost without me. Do you know? I'm the one who made a life for us in this town! I'm the one who . . . even though I never wanted to be here. Don't talk such rubbish."

He mutters something under his breath.

"What was that?"

He flicks a piece of lint off his shirt, as if this is all an inconvenience for him. His foot taps impatiently. He bites his nail. "I said I know that. I know you never wanted to be here, Mom. You made it pretty obvious. Especially to Dad."

The seat opens up beneath me; the flames engulf. Before I can say anything further, something chimes beneath the cushions—Bijal's phone. He pulls it out and glances briefly at the screen. Then he pushes it toward me.

"Here."

"What?"

"It's yours," he says, staring at me. "Who's Kareem?"

AKASH

I pull into R's apartment complex, a dilapidated building near the railroad tracks. The parking lot is half-empty. A dumpster overflows with trash. I park Bijal's bike near the entrance to the building and send a text.

Here.

He responds. *Front door open. Second floor. Apartment 208.*

The whole thing feels sordid. What if he's a psychopath? A serial killer? I look at his pictures, his strong, sculpted arms, and walk right in.

The building smells of cat piss and cooked garlic. I climb a set of stairs. The hallway is dim. The air feels greasy against my skin. The sound of canned laughter bounces off a television set behind one of the closed doors, reminding me I am not alone. I wish I had a drink, something to hold me over. I can almost taste the sweet fizz on my tongue. I've removed the top of my kurta and folded it up and left it on the seat of my bike, wearing only my T-shirt underneath, the tapered silk pants. I must look ridiculous, but I no longer care. You're here, Parth. I saw you. A rush of giddiness floods my brain. I clear my head, forcing myself down the hall. I find 208 and knock three times. He doesn't answer. I knock again. This time, I hear the low thud of footsteps beyond the door before it shudders open. R stands behind it. He doesn't smile.

"The bedroom is this way."

I follow him inside.

R's apartment is just as I had imagined: dark, depressing. Posters line the walls for movies like *Goodfellas* and *The Godfather*. An elaborate video game console is vined with cords. A few half-drunk glasses of water bubble on the windowsill. A television show has been placed on mute—*Prison Break*—and music thumps softly from a subwoofer: Meek Mill. He's shorter than I had expected, only a few inches taller than me. He wears athletic shorts that fall past his knees. His white T-shirt, yellowed under the arms, is snug against his chest. We don't speak.

I'm not sure if I'm supposed to make conversation; the last time I did this I was blackout drunk.

"So . . . how long have you lived here?"

It was a stupid question to ask. Still, he answers.

"Couple years."

I follow him to his room, where the interior contains more of the same: posters of rap artists and athletes, a Mac computer filmed with dust, a small desk with a dime bag and a few mossy clumps of weed. The bedsheets look unwashed. A bottle of Ralph Lauren cologne sits on the nightstand; I can smell it coming off his skin.

"You can sit down."

We sit on his bed, facing the door. His thick arm brushes up against mine. Through the corner of my eye, I can see him swallow, the bob of his Adam's apple as it rises and falls.

"You're cute," I say, boldly. "I mean, you look like your pictures. Not that I didn't think you would, but you never know . . ."

He looks at me, smiling for the first time since I arrived. "You, too."

His name is Ryan. I learn this between kisses. He didn't want anyone to discover him on the app. His friends, most of whom he met working in a steel mill at the edge of town, don't know he's gay.

"Does your family know?"

He shakes his head.

"Neither do mine."

He smiles, climbing on top of me, pushing me back. The weight of him crushing my bones is something I haven't felt in a while, the thrill of having someone on top of you who doesn't want to let you go. He strips off his shirt and I peel off mine. His body is matted with coarse dark hair that forms a corona around his navel, dripping with sweat. He slides down his shorts. I can feel him thicken against my lips.

When Ryan is inside me, and then on top of me, pinning me to the bed, I feel only the heat of his skin. The weight of his chest. Our slick bellies sliding against each other's. The room clouds over. He grips my hair and clamps his mouth to my neck. Still, I feel empty. Only when we climax, when my legs shudder and my fingers slide away from his slippery back, when the sheets cling like film to our skin, ripe with sweat, do I realize where I am. In a strange bedroom across town with dust motes swirling under a lamp. Ryan sits up, pink and dripping, and rolls over onto his back.

We don't move for a while, staring up at the ceiling while the dampness dries on our skin. I think about what we've just done, a secret between us. It's thrilling and depressing all at once. That I can't tell anyone—Jacob, Bijal, certainly not my mother. I think about her, the way she had stood silently while Bijal berated me. Ryan turns onto his side, touching my face.

"Was that okay?"

"Yeah."

I sit up as if to leave, glancing around.

"Hey," he says. "You don't have to do that. You can stay for a while. It doesn't have to be . . ." He pauses, solemn. "It doesn't have to be like that."

"Oh, okay."

I lie back down and close my eyes, trying to imagine a future with Ryan, bringing him to LA, introducing him to my friends, watching him marvel at the traffic, the large, Spanish-style homes. I listen as he tells me all about his job and his family and the dog he plans to adopt: a Labrador retriever. He asks what I do.

"I write songs."

"Really?"

"Well, not officially. I haven't sold anything yet. I'm working on that now. But, yeah, I guess."

"What kind of songs?"

"R and B."

His eyes glisten. "That's awesome."

"It'll be awesome when I get paid."

He frowns, and I realize for the first time how vulnerable he looks, ashamed of myself for having thought otherwise. "It's just money," he says. "It doesn't change anything."

"Tell that to my family."

"I think it's cool," he says. "I don't know anyone who does that."

I hitch myself onto my elbows, kiss him long and slow. "Well, now you do."

We listen to Sade while Ryan smokes a joint. I'm surprised by his taste in music—Jazmine Sullivan and SZA and a lesser-known artist, India Shawn, whom he'd discovered on Spotify. I had him pegged for commercial rap. He asks me where I'm from.

"I'm Indian," I tell him. "But I was born here."

Born here.

"No, I mean: Where do you live?"

"Oh."

Years of answering questions like Ryan's have left me confused. *Why are you different? Why are you brown? How did you end up here?*

"I live in LA," I say. "My parents live here. Well, they did. My mom . . . she's moving. So that's why I'm home."

"And what about your dad?"

I look at him, blinking. "He's dead."

"Oh, shit."

The music cuts off in the next room. Ryan leaps out of bed and runs out of the room, his milky back striated with muscle. Moments later, he returns. A Drake song plays: "Started from the Bottom." He slides into bed, rests his elbow on a pillow, props his head up with his hand.

"What's it like?"

"What?"

"LA."

"It's . . ." I don't know how to describe it, or even how it makes me feel. "Warm."

He laughs. "You're funny."

"Really?"

"Yeah."

"Most people don't think so."

"Well, I do."

I shrug. "They say the funniest people in the world are also very sad."

"Like Robin Williams," he says.

I look at him—his crystal-blue eyes, the scatter of freckles on his nose, a bright scab, pearled with blood, flaking at his chin. His innocence is beautiful.

"Yeah," I say. "Like Robin Williams."

He rolls over and folds his arms behind his head. We're silent for a while, staring up at the ceiling and listening to the soft pulse of music in the next room. I can feel his eyes search for mine.

"I hooked up with an Indian guy in town," he says.

I turn, slowly. "Who?"

"I don't know. It's not like we exchanged vows."

My heart shudders. "Well, what's his name?"

"I don't remember. I was pretty high."

"Was it here? In this apartment?"

He laughs. "You jealous or something?"

I don't say anything. A train whistles in the distance. The music softens. Murky light gathers from the streetlamps beyond the windows. In a few hours it will be dawn and Bijal will be making his smoothie in the kitchen and my mother will be doing her morning puja. Ryan leans over me and picks up his cell phone from the nightstand next to my head and starts scrolling through it, amused. "Here," he says, handing it over. "I have a picture."

My hand trembles as I grip the screen. I don't want to look. I recall the way you looked at me earlier, Parth, your eyes wide but vague, as if you were observing a disaster from a great distance, interested but unscathed. I stare at the picture, sighing. It's not you. The man in the picture is much younger. His longish dark hair is sideswept. His skin is studded with acne. I can tell by his clothes—a satin shirt and starched pants—that he's a foreigner. An FOB. Fresh off the boat. Had he been a student at my school, I would have avoided him at all costs. Proximity to FOBs only served to remind us: no matter how familiar we acted, we would always be from somewhere else.

"He was cute," Ryan says, pinching my arm as I hand him back the phone. "But not as cute as you."

My eyes burn. I roll out of his bed and reach for my clothes.

"I should go. It's late."

"Oh." Ryan stands, too, and I stare at the pink folds of his genitals, the puff of pubic hair above it. He slides his underwear on, hopping on one foot. "You sure?" he asks. "I have some beer if you wanna chill."

"I'm sure. I have to get home."

We dress ourselves in opposite corners, snapping and buck-ling. On my way to his door, I notice something on his dresser. A few pictures sit in glass frames. One of them catches my eye. It's a picture of Ryan and his family at a graduation. Ryan is dressed in a khaki suit and his mother, blond and weathered, wears a sleeveless black top. Her walnut arms are freckled. Silver jew-elry winks from her ears. His father looks like a bloated version of Ryan, with thinning brown hair. I stare, long and hard, at the person on the end.

"I'll walk you out," Ryan says, coming to stand beside me.

"Okay."

I follow him down the hallway and across the living room and out through the front door, into the fragrant hallway. Ryan leans against the doorframe. He looks at me and smiles.

"I had fun. We should do it again."

"Sure."

I head for the stairway, curling my fingers around the doorknob. Then I spin around.

"That guy," I say. "In the picture—next to your dad. Who is he?"

At first, Ryan looks confused, his brows wrinkling. Then he nods, slowly, folding his arms.

"That's my brother," he says, the name lighting up his face. "Bryce."

———

RENU

It's late when I climb the curved staircase to the second floor, switching on the lights. My bedroom is lined with boxes pushed against the wall. Tomorrow, the movers will dismantle the bed, along with the wardrobe and long, low dresser. Only the mattress will remain.

Now that I'm finally alone, Bijal resting below, I read your text. You've named a date and time. Next Tuesday. The day after Bijal leaves. Two days before Akash's flight. Before mine. Suddenly, the thought of leaving this house behind tugs at me like a weight at my feet. I sit down on the bed.

Earlier, when Bijal asked me who you were, I had blanched.

"Who?" I'd said stupidly.

"Kareem. He sent you a text."

"Oh, Kareem," I said, stalling. "Kareem. Yes, remember Kareem Uncle? Farrah Aunty's husband?"

"Who's Farrah Aunty?"

"Who's Farrah Aunty?" I mocked, sharpening my voice. "You mean to tell me you don't remember?"

He shrugged. "No."

"She's my friend from London. You have met her many times."

He stared at me blankly. "So why didn't *she* text you instead?"

The phone pulsed in my grip. The wound surrounding Bijal's eye darkened like a mood ring, turning an eggplant shade of black.

"She's in hospital," I said, the gears shifting. "Poor thing. She has a bacterial infection. You know . . ." I pointed below my waist. "Down *there*."

Bijal grimaced.

"In fact," I continued. "Maybe you could talk to them, give them some medical advice. There are some pictures I could show you. You might want to see them, just for reference. Here, let me find—"

"Okay!" Bijal leapt up from the couch and plunged his fingers into his ears, his lips curled in disgust. "I don't want to know!"

"Well, you asked! Vaido! Now you say you don't want to know."

"God, Mom," Bijal said, stalking out of the room, his feet pounding against the floor. "That's so gross."

"What's gross?" I called after him. "You're a doctor!"

Now, I drop to my knees and reach under the bed frame. I pull out my safe and enter the code, raising the lid. Our letters spill forward like a loaded spring. I see your words, *Dearest Bibi,* and my heart skips. The letters crease in my hands. I feel the sharp edge of the unopened blue envelope at the bottom. I recognize my husband's script. *To Renu.* I think about tearing it open and revealing the contents inside when my eyes land on a picture of you and me. I smooth it over with my thumb.

You wear an open, silky shirt. Dark pants. The picture is in black and white. I remember you asking the juggler to take it. I remember the sharp drizzle smacking the wet earth. I remember the disappointment on your face when you realized you had forgotten the tickets, and later, the jubilation when you found the juggler. I recall what you said. *This is my wife*. You sent this picture to me in your last letter, shortly before Bijal was born. I kept it all these years.

Remember what I told you on our last night, that we would meet again in the next life? Here's something I didn't tell you. I almost moved back to London. Bijal was three; we were trying for another child. I had miscarried three times. I thought about our first child, the one that never survived. I still clung to the belief that she was there with me. I grew tired of trying, tired of this town, tired of our small, cloistered life.

"I want to go back," I had told Ashok. "What kind of life is this? No family. No friends. At least in London we have family. In London, Bijal has cousins. He wouldn't have to grow up alone, as an only child."

Finally, after we tried and failed one more time to conceive, Ashok agreed. He called his uncle in Tooting. He asked about a job. He started looking into visas. My heart sailed during those weeks, thinking about the neighborhood we would live in and the school Bijal would attend, all the places to which I would return. I imagined looking you up, too. According to your timeline, you were still unmarried. It could have worked. I could have left Ashok for you, or we could have carried on in private. So lifted by this possibility was I, that I no longer minded when Ashok made his silly jokes, or asked me to cook his favorite meals, or smacked his lips loudly at the dinner table, or reached for me in the dark. I waited for the moment you would hold me in your arms. I suppose this was my mistake. It was the image of you opening your door, Kareem, that allowed me to open my legs. Later, before the house was put on the market and our visas secured, I ate an apple at breakfast. I vomited it back up.

"You're pregnant," the doctor exclaimed, the following week.

"With what?"

She laughed. It was Ashok who named him. He declared it a sign from God: that America was where our family belonged, and America was where we would stay.

"This baby came from the sky," he said. "So that's what we'll name him." He looked at me, smiling. "We'll name him Akash."

AKASH

I park the bicycle outside your motel. My thighs burn from pedaling. I had rushed out of Ryan's apartment building as if Bryce himself was there, waiting in the shadows. But there was only Ryan, asking if I was all right. He was nothing like he had seemed on Grindr. Part of me was disappointed. Maybe I had been hoping for something different, another kind of punishment. Everything I deserved. Instead, I was reminded of everything I've been running from. Isn't that why we go searching for strangers in the middle of the night, to forget? The sign for your parents' motel towers over me, neon lights flickering. The black farmland is an inky puddle. Cars moan on the highway beyond, their headlights a twinkling rope. I look up at the starlit sky and hear it, your voice. And theirs.

After the attack in the locker room, after I was tossed in the dumpster, Bryce disappeared. He wasn't in the hallways between classes, or in the locker room during gym, or outside on the blacktop before and after school. A rumor started that he had been suspended for something, though it wasn't clear for what. I hadn't told anyone what happened, but maybe someone had seen us. Maybe Mr. Washington had said something to the principal. I was thankful for the reprieve. Without Bryce around, Lance and Evan let me be. Even *they* had their limits of cruelty. Maybe they felt sorry for me, having gone too far. I changed in peace after that, and walked through the hallways unscathed, and raised my hand in class without hesitation. I was like a rodent released from a human grip. Even the parking lot was no longer treacherous for me. Sometimes Lance or Evan would pass my locker and nod, the kind of clipped, cool gesture reserved only for friends. Once, after noticing my new Air Jordans, Lance put his arm around my waist.

"Little man," he said. "Nice shoes."

All afternoon I waited for him to wrench them from my feet. He never did. I couldn't understand it. When Bijal picked me up from school during his spring break from college, blasting R. Kelly from my father's Mercedes, Lance and Evan gaped.

"Yo, Osh, is that your ride?"

I nodded.

"Fuck," said Evan. "Let *me* take it for a spin."

"Yeah," said Lance. "Imagine rolling up to homecoming in *that*."

I hate myself for doing this: I smiled.

It was like that for a while; each greeting they doled out, each compliment I received for a track jacket or a pair of shoes, was like a healing balm, warmed over fire, massaged into my skin. I even entertained the delusion that, having survived their hazing, I had risen in their esteem—like a fraternity pledge. I thought we could be friends.

One morning, during math, our teacher, Mr. Hendricks, informed us of a surprise test.

"It's not really a surprise," he said, laughing. "Because I'm giving you a heads-up."

The test would take place the next day and cover everything we had learned. Everyone panicked. I felt a tap on my arm.

"Yo, Osh."

I turned, noticing Lance in the seat next to mine. His face creased with worry.

"You're good at math, right?" He dropped his voice to a whisper. "I'm failing. If I flunk this class, I can say goodbye to my car."

I stared at the scatter of sun-kissed freckles over his nose, the flecks of gold in his green eyes. I wasn't good at math. You were. Still, I smiled, not wanting to disappoint him.

"Sure," I said. "I can help if you want."

All day I was nervous, worried that he had deceived me and planned to corner me in my home. But when Lance came over that afternoon, a backpack on his shoulder, a pencil behind his ear, he was docile, polite even. He looked up at my house in awe.

"Dang. Can I have a tour?"

I didn't want to say no.

"This is sick," Lance said, of the Bang & Olufsen stereo system with its sliding panels made of glass, and the swivel chair stitched from Italian leather in our living room, and the chrome cocktail bar with sleek seats. My bedroom, with its shelf full of embarrassing childhood toys and souvenirs from abroad, was equally impressive. He poked his head in the bathroom.

"You have your own bathroom?"

We studied on the floor. I became aware of Lance in a way I never had before. Here, in the confines of my room, everything was heightened: his smells, his habits, the way he breathed and spoke. When I followed Lance down the hall for a snack in the kitchen, I watched the back of his head. *This is the back of his head,* I thought. I could smash it in with a brick. He was vulnerable in a way he never had been before. He was not Lance anymore. He was a person who bit his lip in concentration and constantly rubbed his nose, who smelled like cigarette smoke camouflaged by cologne. I wondered if he'd spritzed it on for my benefit, if he was worried, like I would be, about the smell.

"You smell good," I said.

Ordinarily, a comment like this would have been my undoing, but here, between these walls, Lance only grinned.

"Thanks, man. It's the new Calvin Klein. Shit smells like summer."

We didn't say anything for a while. We dove into our books. A few moments later, Lance tossed his aside.

"Hey, Osh," he said, solemnly. "Sorry about all that shit from before. We were just messing around. Bryce can be a real dick sometimes, but I think you're pretty cool."

I could have denounced him then, rejected his apology, but sometimes, when you're the only one left standing in a room, all you want is the invitation to sit down.

"It's water under the bridge."

That afternoon, Lance and I talked about girls and school and our weekend plans. I told him the truth: my parents were going out of town. They were visiting Bijal at college. They would be gone all weekend. I saw the way he smiled, the gears shifting. Maybe part of me knew what I was doing. Maybe I wanted it to happen. The next day, my respite was over: Bryce was back at school. Everyone was whispering about it: how his father had threatened the principal outside his home. The punishment was lifted. He came up to me in the hallway and swung his arm around my neck, the stale smell of marijuana baked into his clothes.

"Yo, Osh," he said. I turned, half-expecting him to punch me for getting him in trouble, but he only grinned. "I heard your house is pretty sick, and your parents are out of town. You know what I'm thinking?" I shook my head. "I'm thinking party at yours."

The motel is only partially occupied. Black windows separate lit ones like missing teeth. I walk toward the sliding glass doors, where I see a dark shape bent over the front desk. I'm certain now that it's you. Only a few yards separate us, Parth. A five-second jog. I could be there in a flash. I take a step forward. The doors slide open. The smell of chlorine sharpens the air. You look up, your eyes searching for something, but it's not me you're looking at. Someone crosses the room. I feel a shiver near my thigh: my cell phone.

Jaden.

Wtf is this?

He must have seen the video. My ego deflates. I'm about to click off when I see that he's still typing. Three subsequent dots shudder across the screen.

Akash, this is dope. I'm looping it into the track. Look out for my email. And write a reference—fast.

It's enough to make me forget where I am. I could jump out of my own skin. I drop the phone back into my pocket and walk quickly toward Bijal's bike. By the time I kick off and sail across the empty road, the wind in my face, I'm already humming the words. *Tell me. Tell me. Tell me how to be.*

RENU

I'm bringing Chaya with me to my last book club meeting. It's a transition—phasing her in just as I am phased out. Earlier that day, the book sat untouched while movers came to haul away some of the furniture, leaving behind only a few essential things. It still sits untouched now in the backseat of the car. Fortunately for me, Chaya had agreed to read it for the both of us.

A few days earlier, Becca had sent an enthusiastic email to the thread.

This book is fantastic! I feel closer to Renu already! I can't wait to hear her thoughts!

I don't want to be close to these women. What's the point? I'm leaving, for god's sake.

Now, I pull up to Chaya's house, and she darts across the dewy lawn.

"I didn't read it," she says, slipping into my car, her breath escaping in a mist.

"You said you finished it."

"I lied."

"Oh, god," I say, as I put the car in gear. "Now what?"

"What do you mean? Didn't *you* read it?"

"No."

Chaya turns her head, gazing out into the dark. "Hai Ram."

"They're going to want us to participate," I say, as the car glides down a tree-lined road, away from the sprawling houses in Chaya's neighborhood.

"We'll improvise."

"How?"

"Just talk about how grateful you are to be in America," Chaya says. "These whites love that stuff. Talk about how you were poor and had no food but now you're in America where there's tons of food! I'm going to say I had a pet goat."

"What?" A gas station flicks by, its sign emblazoned in the night. "What do goats have to do with this?"

Chaya shrugs, shadows striping her face. "I'll say his name was Babu."

We arrive at Vinay and Asha's motel, where rows of small windows glow like cabins in a ship. Mist rises from the roof. This time, the book club is meeting in the small banquet room attached, where Asha's niece had her wedding years ago. We make our way into the lobby. The glass doors slide open; the smell of chlorine assails us. I can hear some of the women inside the banquet hall already, murmuring behind thin walls. Chaya opens the door. We walk in and settle into our seats. I wait for Taylor to address one of the other women in the circle, who are sipping wine from plastic cups, thumbing through their books. But her gaze lands on me.

"Renew?"

She holds a cup full of wine. Her sapphire eyes sparkle. The fluorescent lights give her blond hair a plastic sheen. The other women, seated around her at the center of the hall, have directed their attention toward me, too. Waiting.

"We thought it was appropriate for you to start off today's discussion," she says, "given the subject matter."

"Oh. I see." I face her and smile. "Well, I thought it was lovely. An excellent choice."

"Mm," Taylor says, nodding. "Yes. I thought so, too. You had such insightful things to say the other day. Tell us more."

Hai Bhagwan. Taylor wears a black cardigan. A solitaire diamond floats at her chest. Her makeup is overdone, slashed with contour and blush. The other women are all dressed similarly in neutral shades. At one point, Taylor reaches inside her Kate Spade purse and pulls out her eyeglasses, pushing them up the bridge of her nose.

"It was devastating," I say, my ears buzzing. The women sigh with approval, so I keep going. "Those poor people. It made me feel grateful for all that I have here, you know? I'm just so *lucky*. Also, it made me feel . . . what's the word?" I tap a finger to my lower lip. "Seen."

"*Seen.*" Taylor inhales deeply, as if she's lifted the lid off a pot of stew.

"To have the chance to read about people with my *culture,*" I continue. "People who look and sound like me. I can't tell you how it made me feel."

Taylor claps her hands. The other women follow suit.

"We knew you'd like it!" she chirps. "We knew you would. And I totally agree about feeling grateful. Gratitude, that was the one word that kept working its way through my head. I can only imagine how *you two* must feel."

She gestures toward me and Chaya. I try not to laugh.

"Yes," I say. "Well, I just loved this book. It was a real, um . . ." A phrase comes to me then, perfect, polished. "Tour de force."

"A tour de force!" two of the women echo. "Yes, we thought so too!"

"Mm," Taylor says. "A tour de force. I couldn't have said it better myself. Thank you, Renew." She takes a sip of wine and sets her cup down onto the floor beside her. Then she looks at Chaya and smiles. "Hello!"

Chaya shifts uncomfortably. "Hi."

"Everyone, this is Chaya. We're all so sad to see Renew leave, but I think Chaya will be an excellent addition. Am I right, ladies?"

"Oh, yes!" they say.

"Chaya, we'd love to hear your perspective on the book. Maybe you can go into more detail, tell us what specifically resonated with you, what didn't? It would be great to hear an authentic and honest take."

Chaya shoots me a panicked look.

"Well, um," she begins, stammering. Taylor and the rest of the women lean in. "I felt it was. Well, I thought it was—"

"I thought it was infuriating."

All heads turn in the direction of a young woman sitting at the far right of the room. Shane. I had forgotten all about her. Her short hair is styled messily like a boy's. She wears a hooded sweatshirt and Birkenstock sandals, ripped jeans. Her eyes bore into me as she speaks.

"India is a very problematic country," she says. "Not that I wasn't aware of this before, but the book really highlights the extent. Political corruption, colorism, not to mention misogyny. I spent a summer there and saw some pretty horrific things. This book just reminded me of it all. I mean, we think *we* have it bad. The people are dirt poor, and uneducated, too. It's a shame."

No one says anything. Chaya shifts in her seat, her hand curling into a fist. A flash of heat spreads through me.

"The people?" I scoff. She looks at me, startled. "What do you mean by *the people?*"

"Well, I—"

A chair squeaks as someone coughs into their hands. "So you mean everyone, is that it? You spent a summer there and now you know everything, right?"

"I'm talking about systemic failure," Shane says, regaining her composure. "It's nothing personal to you."

"I never said it was personal," I fire back. "I'm not even *from* India—you just assumed. And who are you, anyway, a pundit? After one summer in India? Tell me: What were you doing there?"

"I was volunteering."

"Volunteering for what exactly?"

She gulps. "My church."

"Your church. It's always a church."

"Okay," Taylor says brightly. "This is a great discussion, let's maybe switch gears a bit and—"

"It's not just one summer," Shane interrupts. "I have friends who went there and were stalked by men. Indian men who stared at them and catcalled and harassed. It's disgusting."

"Don't worry, no one would do that to *you,*" says Chaya.

Shane widens her eyes.

"What you're talking about," I say, "that happens all over the world. It's easy for you to sit there with your slogans and cheap shoes, talking badly about places you visited once in your life! Your church—no one needs your church. Your people have done more harm than good, trust me. Ignorant fool. If you don't like India— here's a suggestion: don't go. But you can't do that, can you? You have to go everywhere and say everything. You can't just stay put. It's a disease your kind have. You . . . you . . ." I can't help myself. I've waited far too long to say the words. *"White bitch!"*

A gasp sweeps across the room, like the stiff breeze in a storm. Shane's face turns a crustacean red. She opens her mouth to say something, then closes it. I stand up just as her composure returns.

"See that," she says, to the rest of the room. "See what I'm talking about?"

"It's true, isn't it?" I snap. "You have the word ironed onto your backpack: BITCH. You don't want to be called a bitch? Then don't act like one. Come on, Chaya. Let's go!"

She follows me to the door. I turn and stare at the room. Taylor's smile is frozen. I feel sorry for her. She's been nothing but nice to me.

I open the door.

"And by the way," I announce to no one in particular. "It's not chai tea. It's chai. You've been saying it wrong."

I walk out with Chaya and slam the door shut. She stares at me with wonder.

"What?" I say.

She smiles. "All this time, Renu, I didn't think you were ready to leave this place behind. Now I know you are."

AKASH

My equipment is still in the storage room where I left it. The next morning, I connect the condenser mic and pop filter to a stand and plug it into my laptop. The basement is hardly a recording studio. I can hear my mother's and Bijal's footsteps above. But it will have to do. I find Jaden's email and download the track and open it with Pro Tools. I play it a few times to catch the beat, to let the rhythm find me, sync my body to its pulse.

Tell me, tell me, tell me how to be. T-t-tell me, tell me, tell me how to be.

I lay down the hook, adding a couple effects. The reverb is like a polish that glosses every word. I record another line and stack the two on top of each other, adjusting the EQ. Another stack. The hook thickens. It gains depth. I record the same line a few more times before adding a harmony in a higher register. I stack. I stack. I stack.

The verse reveals itself like a story.

> *Love ain't a mirror, it's a window*
> *If only you could see through it, to my soul*
> *Boy, don't act like you don't know it's open*
> *You can climb inside*
> *I won't leave you heartbroken*
> *But you don't wanna see it, what's inside of me*
> *My mind's telling me to leave, that's the pride in me*

I hear a pre-hook, write it down with a pen, sing it out loud, note for note.

> *So where is she?*
> *I wanna meet her*
> *That girl you're with*
> *I wanna be her*
> *Is she blind to your love?*
> *I wanna see her*
> *Is she coming or going?*
> *Or did you leave her?*

Tell me, tell me, tell me how to be
Tell me, tell me, tell me how to be
The one you need
T-t-tell me how to be
The one you need
The one you need

I listen to the playback, already thinking of backgrounds, all the little notes that gleam and pop. That's what I love most, Parth, how you can listen to something a hundred times and still find things you hadn't heard before: a harmony, a run, a falsetto or growl. A song is like a great love; it never stops surprising. You can fall for it over and over again.

I record the second verse and the bridge and some backgrounds before I take my headphones off. I send a text to Jaden. *I think I got this.*

He responds immediately.

Send me the song.

Now?

Yes, now. I have a meeting with Kaya's R and B. They're closing submissions for the album.

It's not ready.

Doesn't matter.

He sends a gif of a woman folding her arms in exasperation. I hesitate, staring at the dips and peaks that streak across the audio file. I export it and attach it to an email. After a few calming breaths, I fire it off. Then I connect my laptop to Bijal's old hi-fi speakers, the ones he brought home from college. The phone rings upstairs. I hear footsteps stomp toward it. I play the track and turn up the volume. The walls quake with Jaden's signature beat, a stuttering, skipping 808. I can feel his presence in the room. I can see his squared teeth. I can almost hear him behind me, encouraging me. The verse begins, and I know instantly that this is it. This is what's been inside me all this time. I take a seat on one of the chairs from your parents' motel and close my eyes. I'm about to hit replay when the music cuts off. I turn my head.

"You're gonna blow the speakers."

Bijal stands in front of me, a sour look on his face. The bruise above his eye is startling, a thick, greenish bulb.

"The speakers are fine."

"Someone's coming to buy them tomorrow."

"Really? These old things?"

"Keep it down. I can barely hear myself think."

"Don't worry, you're not depriving the world of any great revelation."

Bijal's lips harden into a thin line. He unplugs my laptop, throws the cord at my face. It misses and lands lamely on the floor.

"Be careful with that!"

"We need help packing," he says, glowering. "Mom didn't ask you to come here so you could fuck around."

"I'm not fucking around—I'm writing."

He scoffs. "It isn't doing you much good."

The words scald. His eyes soften. For a moment, he's the Bijal I remember, the one who gripped my hand in crowded rooms and pulled back the covers when I'd had a bad dream. *It's okay, Akash. I'm here.* He's the Bijal who spun records for me in his bedroom and showed up at the police station after my DUI. *He's my brother. He's with me.*

Now, he slides his hands in his pockets, looks down at the floor.

"Listen, Akash, I didn't mean—"

I push my chin up, glaring. "Don't you have to help Mom?"

Before I can say anything further, he turns on his heels and punches up the stairs. Love is also like a door, Parth. It swings open and shut.

The movers arrive to collect more furniture and load it into a truck to be donated to the Salvation Army. We've kept the mattresses and some bedding and a few pots and pans, so that my mother can cook us one last meal before she leaves, three days from now. Otherwise the house empties, disgorges, relieves itself of its burdens, revealing clean white walls. The veined marble sparkles. The windows overlooking the backyard gleam. The living room feels like an arena, light bouncing off its walls.

After the movers leave, my mother makes paninis in the press with onions and chilies and cilantro, and we eat them on the floor near the windows, on a clean white sheet. We don't say much. Bijal keeps staring at his phone, clicking it on and off.

"How is Jessica?" my mother asks.

He shrugs. "Fine."

My mother nods. A cardinal alights on the lamppost in our backyard, a red flame.

After lunch, we toss out our paper plates and plastic cups, and my mother wipes down the kitchen with a rag. I go to my room, to sort through all the belongings I'd emptied from my dresser before it was hoisted onto the truck. Underwear. Frayed T-shirts. A pile of mismatched socks. The CD insert from a Lil' Kim album, *Hard Core*. I remember the time I accidentally left it in my mother's car, cued up in her CD player, so that one morning, on our way to school, it blasted through the speakers as soon as the car turned on.

I used to be scared of the dick. Now I throw lips to the shit, handle it like a real bitch.

"Akash!" she'd yelled. "What is this filth?"

I was the one who had insisted Bijal play it one night when we went for ice cream at Baskin-Robbins. But Bijal took the fall. "It's mine," he explained. "I didn't realize I left it in here." My mother didn't say anything, only pursed her lips. I pick up the CD insert and toss it into a pile to be thrown out, when I see the gold coin from Aladdin's Palace. I hold it up to the light. Feel its weight in the palm of my hand. I pinch it between my fingers and toss it in the air, making a bet: If it lands on heads, I'll see you again. I'll have my chance. I'll tell you everything you meant to me, and you'll listen to every word.

RENU

I walk into the kitchen to prepare the final meal. The boys wanted lamb keema. It's the dish I lined their freezers with during college, the one they ask for by name: Mom's keema. Bijal's last night is tomorrow. I'm making it ahead of time. The morning after he leaves, Chaya will pick me up from here and drive me to the location where you and I will meet: a coffee shop in a small shopping center. A quiet location. Two days after that, she'll pick me up again, only this time it will be to walk out of this house forever.

I arrange the ingredients on the kitchen counter: ground lamb, red onions, ginger, garlic, tomatoes. The spices—cumin, coriander, cardamom, cloves, a thin stick of cinnamon, a dry bay leaf—roast gently over a flame. In order to make a proper curry, you must grind whole spices from scratch. Wait till wisps of smoke curl delicately from the pan, then take them off the heat. Pound them in a mortar. Reserve them for later use. Chop onions finely and fry them in hot oil. I'll tell you a trick: fry them till they *almost* burn. The darker the onions, the deeper the flavor. The richer the curry. The better the dish. Cook your tomatoes until they blister and split, until the oil separates, glistening over top. A curry is like a hard-earned life; the longer you cook it, the wiser it becomes. Listen carefully, or you'll miss the best bits.

The first dish we cooked together was lamb keema. It was raining. You invited me to your flat. The sky smoked and flashed, slanted pins striking the small window in your kitchen, fogged over with steam. You had said you wanted to taste my food, that you wanted my fingers to grace your lips. You had all the ingredients lined up like a chef. A bowl of minced lamb. A tray of dried spices. Chopped onions and chilies. A bundle of fresh coriander.

"What is this?" I said. "Am I Julia Child?"

"Julia could be *your* child," you said. "I bet you could teach her."

"Teach waro! How do you know that? You have not even tried my food."

You grinned. A blue apron was tied around your waist. The mist from an open window shone on your face.

"Remember Dar es Salaam, how I followed you around like a dog?" you said. "I had only just met you. You could have been anyone. Sometimes, Renu, you just know."

That night, when you slipped a spoonful of grayish-looking meat into your mouth, I cried.

"It's not good. I know it."

"Why do you say that?"

But I was too distraught to answer. You took me by the hand, kissing it gently, and led me back into the kitchen.

The keema simmers in a pool of red oil as I cover it with a lid. The rice soaks in water. The fresh ginger and chilies I plan to sprinkle on top are julienned and keeping cool in a damp cloth. Outside, the sun is already beginning to set between the gaps in the evergreens, like the roving eye of a cat. I pull out my cell phone. I send you a text.

I'm making lamb keema. ☺

Which lamb keema is this? Some are not good.

Sala! This one is the best. My boys love it. Even my daughter-in-law, picky as she is, can't resist.

Oh, is it? Tell me, Renu. Why is that so?

I remove the lid from the pot. The steam dampens my face. I can tell by the way the oil shimmers that it's done. I turn off the flame and set the pot aside and sprinkle chopped coriander and fenugreek on top. The garage screeches open. Bijal is home.

Because, I say to you, dropping the lid over the pot. *You taught me how to make it.*

AKASH

It's Bijal's last day and he's in a foul mood. Everything—the flimsy boxes I brought home from the grocery store, the packing tape that refuses to break off, the pace at which we're moving—seems to annoy him. Chaya Aunty has dropped off her van for us to borrow, and we are loading things into the trunk outside. Sweat drips from Bijal's brows and darkens his gray T-shirt. He crouches down in front of a box, slipping his fingers underneath.

"All right, pick up the other end."

We're standing in front of the house on the driveway. I stare up at the white columns, the arched windows, the SOLD sign jutting out from the clipped yard, my heart pulling.

It's been twenty-six hours since I last heard from Jaden. He hasn't responded to my email about the song. He hates it. Jacob said I shouldn't have expectations.

"If you don't have expectations, you won't be disappointed."

I don't think he understood the power of the word. Because to live life without expectations is to fall asleep without dreams.

Everything my parents did was based on expectation. They came to this country expecting a better life. My father opened a practice expecting to succeed. He built us a house with the expectation that it would be beautiful. He bought a brand-new Mercedes-Benz, an S-class sedan, expecting it to perform. Jacob didn't understand these things. His parents had children for the sake of having kids. My parents had children for the sake of planting seeds. You don't plant seeds expecting to grow dandelions. You want flowers, big and beautiful, the kind you display in a vase.

I take out my phone. Check my email one last time. No word from Jaden. I compose a text: *Listen to that song yet?* My pulse pounds as I hover over the send button, not wanting to seem pushy, feeling desperate all the same. I press the button, emitting a loud chime. Bijal looks up from the box, glaring.

"Are you really on your phone?"

"I had to text someone."

"Stop fucking around, Akash. There's still so much to do."

Together we lift the box and shuffle over to the lip of the trunk, then pivot around to push it over the stiff carpet, until it hits the back of the front seats. Bijal stands back, mopping his face with the end of his shirt. The slab of his belly, stippled with dark hair, hangs over his jeans. I'm tempted to prod it, to comment on all the weight he's gained, in spite of his smoothies, the way I would have done when we were young.

"Come on," he says, leading the way inside. "Let's get the rest of the things."

Three hours later, I check my phone again. No response. I'm in my father's office, tossing out old markers and pens, receipts from years ago, the report cards and certificates Bijal and I no longer require, old exam booklets for the SAT, when I find a folded-up paper underneath a stack of expired passports secured with a rubber band. A note. A letter. Boldfaced type. The hairs prickle at my nape. I recognize it at once. It's the letter, the one I had written you years ago. My father kept it all this time. I remember the way he had stood outside my bedroom, the paper in his hands. *Is it true?* he had asked. *What you said . . . in the letter. Is it true?* Upstairs, Bijal is showering off the stink and sweat of the day. The clock reads 4 p.m. He'll want to leave by five. I unfurl the paper and stare briefly at the opening words.

Dear Parth.

It all comes flooding back. Everything that happened that night. Everything I did. I can't stave it off any longer. There's nothing to hide behind, no shadows to conceal me, no booze to make me forget. I don't need to read anymore. I'm already there.

The party was planned for Saturday, after the football game. Bryce would take care of the booze. All I had to do was answer the door.

"It's going to be insane," he said, approaching me in the hallway the Friday before.

"How insane are we talking?"

"Don't be gay, Osh."

According to Bryce, everyone would come over at nine. I was pacing the house at seven thirty. I had already showered and shaved the neat strip of brown fuzz on my upper lip. The house was still. I worried my parents would come home early and catch us in the act, but I had just spoken to them over the phone.

By nine thirty, no one had arrived. I had left every light on in the house in anticipation of everyone's arrival. One by one, I switched them off. I went into my father's office and turned on the computer. I logged in to AIM. I scrolled through the sidebar. My breath caught in my chest. You had put up an away message.

PNASTY03: Out with the crew.

I imagined you in a car full of your friends, your hair shifting in the wind. I thought about messaging you. I logged out instead. I walked out of my father's office and pressed my face to a window, staring at the black velvet night. A wind shook the trees. A squirrel darted across the lawn. Something broke the darkness, a pair of headlights. I waited for them to disappear around the bend. They didn't. Another pair soon followed. And another. By the time the doorbell rang, there were ten.

The party unfolded the way all parties do: music gets louder, faces get redder, spaces get tighter, reason leaves the room. Bryce propped a McDonald's cooler, sloshing with spiked Kool-Aid, next to my parents' sink.

"What's that?"

"My magic potion."

"What's in it?"

"Beats me."

Someone had started playing *The Miseducation* album. Three girls with hair like silk sheets lined up for a drink. They wore variations of the same outfit: dark jeans and flowy tops; gold, strappy shoes. Their brow bones shimmered. They held out their cups.

"You ladies ready for the most delicious thing you'll ever put in your mouths?" said Bryce. He spilled as he poured. The girls laughed. Then Bryce turned and stared at me, slitting his eyes. "Where's the elephant?"

"What?"

"The elephant." He moved closer to me, blocking my path. "I loved that thing."

That thing. I remembered the way he had chased me after school—*Hey, elephant boy!*—and kicked me in my ribs. Now, he smiled fondly, as if we were old friends. My palms went slick.

"Ganesh," I said.

"Yeah, that's the one!"

"We got rid of it," I lied.

His expression changed, his face folding into a scowl. I took a step back. "Now why'd you go and do a thing like that?"

The girls floated away from us as the music roared. Bryce bridged the gap between us, pinning me against the sink. I could feel his breath on the tip of my nose.

"It was haunted."

"Haunted?"

He stared at me for a long time, his eyes barely moving. Then he laughed. "You weirdo. You're a funny little fuck, you know that?" He gripped my shoulder, squeezing hard. The pain sent an electric jolt down my back. He filled a plastic cup with juice from the cooler and pushed it under my nose. "Drink up."

"Oh, I don't drink," I said.

"Like never?"

"No."

The drink sloshed between us. Bryce grabbed the back of my neck. Then he looked at me, smiling, his eyes turning cold.

"Well, now you do."

The night of my party, I learned why people drink. I felt its comfort, surrendered to its grip. With each sip, a piece of me loosened and floated up like dandelion seeds. Then the pieces floated faster, until I was stripped clean. The clean me glided around the house without touching the floor. I was flying.

"Akash, do the accent again!" Bryce said.

"Do it! Do it!" cried everyone else.

"Okay, okay."

I was holding court in the kitchen, a cranberry stain spreading on my shirt. Everyone crowded around the island. Lance squeezed in between Bryce and Evan, and, when he saw me, he raised his cup. "That's my boy right there," he said.

"Okay," I said, lapsing into character. "Here I go." I cleared my throat, waggling my head. I looked around the room and smiled. "Welcome to Kwik-E-Mart. How may I help you?"

The room dissolved in fits of laughter.

"Shit's fucking hilarious," said Bryce.

"It's funny 'cause it's true," said Lance.

I did "the accent" three more times before Evan, his face dewy, his skin flushed, handed me his phone.

"You gotta call my brother at college—he'll flip."

A hush fell over the room. He placed the call on speaker. I was ready with my script. Winning people over is easy, Parth. All it takes is the betrayal of everything you are.

The party continued as if it had been thrown in my honor. Every few minutes, the doorbell rang, and the hallway choked. The tiles shook beneath my feet. I went downstairs. A thick fog, illumined from the reflection of the TV, traveled over my head. A crowd of students danced at the center of the room, bouncing to the music rumbling from Bijal's old speakers. "Lost Ones" by Lauryn Hill.

You might win some, but you just lost one.

Everyone's hands went up, sweeping left and right like windshield wipers. I thought about all the Diwali parties in this very space, fifty Indians jumping in midair. I thought of you, Parth, dancing among them. Then I looked at all the white and Black faces and realized I was drunk.

Consequence is no coincidence.

I sang along, sinking deeper into the crowd.

You might win some, but you just lost one.

The damp penetrated my shirt and glued it to my skin. Someone grabbed my hand. A girl. She had flame-red hair. We moved in sync, grinding and sliding, dipping and turning, laughing and collapsing.

You might win some, but you just lost one.

The song faded, and I knew what came next. I remembered it the way I remember that night in your bedroom, the light from your lamp glossing your face. "Ex-Factor."

Loving you is like a battle, and we both end up with scars.

The girl slipped away. I hardly noticed. I never thought to wonder who it was playing Lauryn Hill at a house party, with its bittersweet core, but then I turned around and saw the flash of a smile. A backwards hat. A hunter-green blazer with a gold emblem on the chest. You emerged from the crowd like a ship coming ashore.

"Akash." The way you said my name made my breath quicken. You pointed to the hi-fi system. I buckled under your gaze. "That song is for you."

In that moment, I felt something spill from inside me. I had nothing left to give.

See, no one loves you more than me. And no one ever will.

Sometimes a song is so perfect I want to cry. It's not just the lyrics, Parth; it's the melody. The arrangement of notes. The harmonies, the riffs, the singer's tone. A song can sound more like love than the word "love" itself. It can make you feel things you never thought you'd feel again. In that moment, I felt it all. You were there, Parth. You had returned. Somewhere in my heart, I had known that you would.

The energy of the room shifted. The music turned softer. People stopped dancing. Some people left altogether, seeking adventures upstairs. Our bodies moved to the rhythm as if there were no one else around. We were like a harmony, one note strengthening the other. And that's when I saw her. She sank her hand into yours.

Sometimes things happen, and I can't help but hear a song. It seems wildly inappropriate that at my father's funeral I should hear the lyrics to "Killing Me Softly," but they kept looping in my head. Bijal stood in front of the room, reciting a speech, and all I could do was rock back and forth. *Strumming my pain with his fingers.*

When I drew a picture of Lord Ganesh on the chalkboard, it was "The Boy Is Mine." *I'm sorry that you, seem to be confused.* The afternoon when Bryce and the others dropped me into the dumpster and shut the lid over my head, when the world turned black and fetid, it was Ace of Base, "I Saw the Sign." *Life is demanding, without understanding.*

Standing in front of you at my party, with *her* at your side, it was a new song altogether, something no one had ever heard. I was writing, Parth, and I didn't even know it.

"You remember Monika," you said, when she sidled up beside you and dropped her hand into yours.

My eyes flew to it. She wore a North Face vest. Her dark hair was pressed. Her lips shone beneath a candied gloss. I noticed all of these things, but it was your hand that caught my eye. The way it squeezed firmly, as if to convince me of it. The song in my head refused to fade, growing louder instead. It must have been a signal. The others must have heard. A boy our age got up from the sofas and approached us, sticking out his hand.

"Hi, I'm Greg."

He wore the same hunter-green blazer; the gold emblem struck my eyes.

"I hope you don't mind me bringing them," you said. "My friends from Troy."

Your friends. I looked past him, toward the small cluster of students huddled in the shadows. Greg's hand hung suggestively in the air.

"This is Akash," you said. "This is his house."

"Sick house," Greg said.

You could have introduced me as your friend. You could have told him everything. You didn't have to hold Monika's hand the way you did, as if it was the only thing keeping you there. It was apparent, in that moment, what I was to you: a beautiful house. Something to be toured. A place you would never live in, that you could never make a home.

"I'm going upstairs."

I turned to walk away, already craving another drink, when I heard you call my name.

"Akash."

I spun around immediately, forgiving you at once. If only you hadn't looked at me that way.

"Can you get us some beer?"

You moved into the foyer, leading Monika and your friends toward the adjoining sitting room with its curved suede sofas and crystal lamps. I watched you from the top of the stairs. You sipped a beer, your face bright and animated, Monika's hand still tucked into yours. The crowd of students below me bobbed and swayed as if floating on a sea. The sea parted. A figure crossed through it. I couldn't see who it was, only that they were moving toward you. I climbed down the staircase and pushed myself through the crowd, dark shapes shifting, elbows jabbing my sides, when I heard his voice.

"No Troy fags allowed."

You were a secret I carried with me in my back pocket. You knew little about what was happening to me at school. I didn't want you to know, for that world to cross into ours.

"Did you hear me?" Bryce said.

You turned, coolly, the expression shifting on your face. "What?"

Your friend, the one who had introduced himself to me earlier, stood up from his seat, walking over.

"Hi, I'm Greg."

"Hi, I'm Greg," Bryce mocked. "Get out, loser."

At this, you looked at me, as if to communicate something wordlessly. I turned my head.

"Listen up, everyone!" Bryce said, raising his beer. Lance and Evan emerged from the shadows and joined at our side. "This is our party, me and Osh here. And if we ask you fuckers to leave, you better leave."

Lance and Evan echoed the sentiment. I felt their hands at my back. A crowd of students turned to look at me, their faces bright. "The last time I checked," Bryce continued. "We didn't invite any of you Troy fags here. This party is Central only."

A group of people in the back began chanting our school name. *Cen-tral! Cen-tral! Cen-tral!* I caught your gaze, but it wasn't me you were looking at, Parth. It was Bryce. You inched closer to him, your eyes narrowed. Monika tightened her grip on your arm.

"So who's gonna be the first to leave?" Bryce said. "Or get his ass kicked? The choice is yours." He looked at Greg, taking a swift step closer. "Yo, Doogie Howser. You leaving?"

Greg raised his palms. "Hey man, we're just here to have a good time. We didn't mean any harm."

"Hey man, hey man." Bryce laughed, turning. "Who is this guy?"

He grinned at Lance and Evan. Then he turned around and swung a punch. The wet sound was like that of a hunk of meat being slapped against stone. A gasp spread through the room as Greg tipped his head backward, blood bubbling from his nose.

"Akash!" Monika said, rushing to his aid. "Do something!"

I remembered the way she had looked at me at the garba, and each time after that. I heard the accusation in her tone.

It happened the way it always does: a shove turns to a punch, a punch turns to a kick, a kick turns to a struggle, a struggle turns to screams. You maintained a safe distance from it all, holding Monika at your side. At one point, someone mentioned calling the cops, but that only led to more violence. I didn't look at you. I couldn't. Because to look at you in that moment, Parth, your arm snaked around her, was to jab a knife in my eye.

A few of your friends stepped in, pushing their way toward Bryce, throwing punches that couldn't land. But they were tossed aside. And then it happened. I should have known that it would. Maybe I had known it all along, ever since that day I took you for a drive. *We looked at the security footage.* Bryce swung a punch at someone and missed, staggering in place, and that's when you looked at him. You looked him in the eye.

"It was you."

Your eyes blazed as you took a step forward. The scene around us froze.

"You were there," you said. "On camera. I saw it. You were the one who did it."

"Did what?" Bryce barked. "What the fuck are you talking about?"

I saw the words smeared like mud across the temple wall, just in time for you to say them out loud.

"DIE MUSLIMS."

It was Bryce who took you outside. The others soon followed. I watched it all from the doorway: the way he punched you in the face. Blood burst from your nose and your lips and you staggered backward, wiping your mouth. He punched you again.

You fell on your back. I couldn't believe it, how easily you dropped. My mother once told me, when Lord Krishna died, he didn't put up a fight. He knew it was his time. I had cried when she told me this. How could someone so powerful give up so easily? What does that mean for the rest of the world? Lance and Evan hoisted you up. The hair from your head flung forward like ropes.

"Akash!" Monika screamed from the sideline. "Do something! Help him, please!"

But I was paralyzed with fear. Then Bryce swung around and noticed me, his eyes flashing in the night. "Osh. Get over here."

I looked at you, your face swelling up, your eye closing shut, a thin silver line, like a tear, running down your cheek. I didn't move.

"Osh, come on!"

"No," I whispered.

Bryce rose suddenly, and I could see that his shirt was torn. His fist was clenched. Your blood was smeared across it, like an open gash. He motioned to someone behind me, and a pair of hands gripped my shirt. They pushed me across the yard, my feet kicking in midair. Then they dropped me in front of you and pinned me in place.

"Go ahead," said Bryce. "Take a swing."

You were gasping for air, your face streaked with mud. I had never seen you this way, Parth. Broken. I remembered the way you had looked at me on the road that evening, your eyes reflecting the setting sun. *I got this Indian squaw, the day that I met her . . .* The world can create so much beauty; like children, we smear it with dirt.

"Do it, Osh," goaded Bryce. "Take a swing. Be a fucking man for once."

"Akash!" Monika cried. "Please!"

You rose slowly, tilting your chin. When your eyes met mine, your mouth parted, and my name was the only sound to escape your lips.

"Akash."

"Come on!" Bryce said. "Don't be a faggot."

The word sparked. I remembered the way their hands had felt on me, grabbing, groping, the slime of the dumpster, the slice of my palm. I saw the lid closing over my head, silencing my cries. I felt the cold fear, unbreakable like a stone.

This is where our story ends, Parth. This is where we said goodbye. The last thing I remember is the warmth of your mouth against my fist, the way your lips burst like soft fruit, the dark blood on my hand. My father said there's no such thing as bad people, only good people who do bad things. It's the world that makes them do them. Friends become enemies. Brothers become strangers. A hug turns to a shove. A kiss, Parth, can end with a punch.

PART IV

RENU

Chaya has come over to help me select an outfit.

"What do you think of this?" I say, holding a dress to my chest. The dress is slim and cinched at the center, with a jaguar print. I'm not entirely sure why I bought it.

"It looks like something a secretary would wear," she says.

"Oh, good."

"After work, at a party. If she's trying to seduce her boss."

"Oh, dear."

"Don't you have anything simple?" Chaya says. "A nice top and nice pants?"

"Nice top, nice pants. Nice top, nice pants," I say, giddily.

I don't know what's come over me. I feel like a young girl, lost in her own reverie. I find, at the back of my closet, a camel-colored sweater and indigo jeans, chunky gold jewelry. I hold the jewelry up to my ears.

"Oh, yes," says Chaya.

I arrange the outfit in the shape of a person on the mattress. I pull up Facebook on my phone. Earlier that morning, I'd shared my first post, a simple and informative message that received zero likes. *So much packing to do!* Even now, no one has liked it. Maybe I should have added context. *So much packing to do, as I'm leaving this town forever. Goodbye.* But no one else seems to require context. People share pictures of food with no captions, gifs of kittens with no words. One woman posted the words, "Oh my god!" with no clarifying reason. Eighty-seven people liked it. One person left a comment: "Ugh." Americans love expressing their dissatisfaction with three-letter words. Ugh! Oof! Meh. Wah! Like spoiled children. I'll miss it. I'll miss the singsong way people say, "Good morning!" at the grocery store, and the women who wave at me from their front lawns—not like London, where the appropriate greeting is a scowl. I'll miss Taylor and her voice like a bird's. I'll miss the explosive sunsets, so lush and vibrant it feels like something important is happening, even when it's not. That's the one thing I loved, the way the sky could change colors—faded denim, rocky slate, the bright, bloody gash from a jungle cat. I'll miss my boys, even though all they seem to do is communicate with grunts. But nothing, Kareem, is as powerful as the way I have missed you.

You send a message just as I'm selecting a pair of shoes. Chaya is sorting through the costume jewelry I've decided to leave behind. I read your words and smile.

"What is making you smile today?" Chaya says, holding a gold necklace up to her chest. She flips over the pendant, slapping it against her sternum.

"Nothing."

"Jaja haave," she says, grinning. She shakes her head, slipping the necklace into a plastic sleeve full of colored bangles in every imaginable shade. Then she sits down on the mattress and sinks her face into her hands.

"What?" I say, rushing over to her. "What is it?"

She doesn't say anything. When I come around to her side of the mattress, I see tears in her eyes. "Chaya . . ."

I drop my hand on her shoulder. She wipes her face with her sleeve. "I'm just being silly."

"No, you're not."

I sit down beside her. She lets her arms fall in her lap. "Seeing you this way, Renu, packing, leaving . . . I don't know."

"What?"

"It makes me wonder what I have done with my life." She looks out the window over the soft brushstrokes of trees. "Do you know," she whispers. "Bhupendra and I don't sleep in the same room."

I don't say anything, allowing her the space to continue.

"It's been this way for fifteen years," she continues. "Ever since Amit left for college. I suppose even then it was a façade. Now, our excuse is that Bhupendra snores and I'm a light sleeper and we have so much space . . . what's the point of sharing a bed?"

"Are you—were you having problems?"

"No." Chaya almost laughs. "You have to communicate to have problems. You have to love someone before you can hate them. Sometimes I wish he would shout at me, just once, maybe even strike me—at least then I would know he has feelings. Maybe then I would have a reason to leave. But no, it's like there's nothing there. We lead separate lives. He watches TV in the basement; I watch TV in the living room. Sometimes he'll eat whatever I have made for dinner, but even then, he takes it into a different room. He says we don't have much in common. Is that a thing to say to your wife of thirty-six years?"

I look at her. In spite of herself, she laughs.

"I would have divorced him, Renu. Remember Sharmila? Her husband raped her. Of course, we didn't say it back then, did we? We said he was 'forceful.' He used 'too much force.' But that's rape, isn't it? Why couldn't we say it? Now look at her. She's divorced, remarried. She called me three days ago and said it was the best decision she ever made in her life. But I didn't do it. Because my husband didn't rape me. My husband didn't hit me. My husband didn't insult me. Because he wouldn't even talk."

I feel the weight of her words. Chaya extracts a tissue from her pocket and blows her nose. I wonder if she had brought it with her on purpose, if she had expected to cry.

"You may not have loved your husband the way you would have hoped, Renu," she says, placing her cold, crinkled hand over mine. "But there's no doubt that he loved you. You could see it from a mile away. I guess that's all I ever wanted: for someone to look at me that way."

She smiles weakly, getting up from her seat. I follow her down the curved staircase and to the front door. Another moving truck has arrived, its engine roaring, and I can hear Bijal moving boxes into the garage. Chaya steps outside and turns, smiling.

"I'll be back on Saturday to drive you to see him. And after that . . ." Her voice breaks off. Tears pool in her eyes. I feel my heart crack as she says the word. "Gone."

AKASH

"The van is all loaded."

Bijal stands in the doorway. He's changed into fresh clothes: a pair of sweats and a clean T-shirt. He's shaved in preparation of his return home. A drop of blood dots his chin. I sit with my back pressed against the wall, not moving.

"Come on." Bijal's lips go thin. "It's five thirty, Akash. We're already thirty minutes late. I need to get on the phone with Jessica."

I don't move. I can't. The memory of that night is too heavy.

"Akash." He blows a puff of air. "I don't want to be late. I told you. We can't wait until the last minute to do everything."

I stand, slowly, feeling a dull throb in my head. I wonder if he knows. I think about my father, the way he looked at me that night when he told me he loved me, sitting down on my bed. *Don't tell Mom.* My blood chills. I can't forget it. That night, the way your head swung back when my fist cracked against it. I can't go back. The trail has disappeared, the door shut.

"I just . . . I need a minute."

"For what?"

"I don't know."

Bijal glares at me. "What the fuck?"

He stands there in disbelief. "What's your problem, Akash?" I don't answer. "You're ridiculous, you know that?" He grabs the car keys from the desk. "If you're not out in five minutes, I'm taking your guitar."

"What?"

"That overpriced guitar Dad bought you? The one you never played? I'm sure someone less fortunate will appreciate it. How spoiled could you be?"

The fog lifts; I realize where I am. "You can't do that," I say, rising. "It's mine."

"Actually, it's Dad's. He paid for it."

"It was a gift."

"One you barely used."

"Fuck you," I spit. "I used it."

"When? I never heard you."

"Because I didn't want you to hear."

"What?"

"Because I didn't want you to hear!" The blood pounds in my ears. "I didn't want any of you to hear. You would just shit over it like you do everything else!"

My voice echoes between us. He turns to walk away.

"You can't shit over something that's already shit," he says.

"What?"

"Nothing."

He shakes his head and laughs. Just like that, the flame is lit.

"Are you always like this?" I say, my pulse pounding. "Is this how you are at home, with Jessica? No wonder she's not around."

Bijal turns, slowly. "What did you say?"

"I said, where is she? Why hasn't she called? Why couldn't she have taken a day to come down?"

"She's sick—you know that."

"Seems like she's been sick for a long time."

Bijal's mouth falls open. His eyes narrow to slits.

"You're not in any position to interrogate me, Akash. Not after everything you've done."

"Is that always going to be your excuse, that I wasn't a perfect child? I wasn't like you?"

"Perfect?" The word trails off. "Do you think it even mattered what I did? The grades I got, the schools I went to? Do you think Dad really cared? Did you ever stop to wonder why I had to do that, Akash? Why I had to be perfect?"

"Because you're an asshole?"

"Because of *you*."

The air is sucked out of the room. Bijal walks toward me, bridging the distance. "All Dad cared about was you. *Akash needs our help*—that's what he used to say. But what about me? Where was my help?"

"You didn't need it."

"But what if I wanted it?" His eyes well up; no tears slip down his face. "I had to be everything, do everything. I couldn't fuck up because all you did was fuck up!"

I stare at him, shaking.

"No one asked you to be perfect, Akash. That was my job. My burden. My cross to bear. Believe me, we didn't expect much out of you. Get a job, sure. Stay out of trouble, maybe. Don't embarrass the family, yeah. Be a normal fucking human being? That's not too much to ask."

Suddenly, the words swim back to me, all the little things he's said. *You shouldn't walk around like that. It's a freak who fucks boys. What the hell is wrong with you? What are you doing, Akash?*

"There it is," I say, bitterly. "Normal."

Bijal stares at me.

"Tell me: Is it normal for a son to abandon his family?"

"Stop . . ."

"Is it normal for him to get married and disappear?"

"Akash, I'm warning you . . ."

"Is it normal not to bring his wife to his own father's death anniversary, to keep her from seeing her own mother-in-law?"

"You don't know what the fuck you're talking about."

"I think I do," I say, blazing. "I think your normal world isn't so normal after all, and you don't want anyone to know about it. What did you do, Bijal? Did you cheat on her? Slap her around?"

His eyes swell, pulsing.

"Or maybe you just aren't performing in bed. Maybe that's it . . ." I can barely see him now, only a wall of red. "Maybe she got tired of you shooting blanks."

The blood, once pounding in my ears, turns still. Bijal is silent, staring at the floor. I've never seen him this way.

"Look," I start to say. "Maybe I shouldn't—"

The smack comes faster than I can blink, knocking me to the ground. Suddenly, Bijal is on top of me, pulling my shirt. His hand grabs my neck. I gasp for air.

"Don't you ever say that shit again. Do you hear me? You don't know what the fuck you're talking about!"

Bijal's eyes hold a rage I've never seen before, not even the night of his wedding. Without warning, the memory returns. Only this time it isn't fleeting. This time I can see it clearly, like the image through a lens: the crowd gaping, my mother frowning, Bijal standing in his tuxedo, the microphone rolling across the floor. I see the hours earlier, too, practicing my speech in my hotel room, refusing a drink at the bar. I'd filled a wineglass with juice instead. I had promised myself I wasn't going to drink. I didn't need it. What I needed was a clear head, so that I could tell my brother everything I had been planning to say.

Bijal isn't just the person I've looked up to my entire life; he's my best friend.

I had practiced that speech every moment I could get, flipping through note cards in the lobby, next to an ice sculpture, anywhere I could be alone. Finally, I walked into the restroom, hoping for a moment of peace. I closed the door behind me and stepped past the urinals, and when I walked past the stalls, someone was standing in front of the sink. You.

"Parth?"

Your hair was split down the middle. You wore a black tie. It had been years since I'd seen you, since that fateful night, but you looked just as I'd remembered. You weren't supposed to be there—it was your first year of residency and you couldn't get the time off. My parents had explained all of this to me months before. Only later would I find out that you had booked a last-minute flight. It was my brother's wedding, Parth, the reception my parents had planned and paid for, but the way your eyes shifted away from mine, it could have been me who didn't belong.

"You're here," I said, waiting for you to turn around. You didn't. "Parth."

Our eyes locked in the mirror. You turned and walked out. Moments later, I crept over to the bar.

"I'll take a double whiskey on the rocks."

The bartender smiled at me, depositing my drink. "Actually," I said, slyly, "make that two."

Now, Bijal's hands close around my neck, squeezing. I struggle to break free. My eyes tear up just as my mother dashes into the room.

"Akash, what are you doing?" she says. Her mouth falls open. "Bijal? Stop it, both of you. Now!"

His grip on me loosens. I scramble to my feet.

"What's wrong? What is this?"

"Nothing." Bijal is massaging his hands. "He needs to show some respect."

"I said I was sorry."

"You shouldn't always have to say it."

"Spare me the lecture."

"Quiet, both of you!" my mother snaps. We lower our heads. She looks at us in disbelief. "You two are brothers. Your father is gone. Look around you." Tears coat her lashes. "This is all we have left."

My mother wipes her eyes with the back of her hand.

"You're going to regret this one day," she says. "If you carry on like this, one day you'll wish you hadn't, that you could take it all back. I just hope it's not too late."

She casts her gaze from Bijal to me, waiting for one of us to say something. We don't.

"Bijal is leaving tomorrow. This is our last night. Who knows when you'll see each other again? Is this how you want to leave things? Fighting like this? What are you going to do when I'm gone, huh? You're family. You need each other."

I search Bijal's face for a sign of concession, but he's turned it away from me. His arms are folded, his lips pursed. I almost laugh at him: this thirty-four-year-old doctor, behaving like a child.

"We'll be fine, Mom," I say. "Right, Bij?"

But he doesn't answer me. He walks out of the room.

RENU

Ashok used to say we were one. One heart. One family. When one of us wins, we all win. When one of us falls, we all fall.

"As long as you and the boys are happy, I'm happy. What more do I need?"

We couldn't even give him that. Or maybe it was too much to ask, that we distill our feelings and compress them into a single word: happy. Once, I ran into a woman from the neighborhood, Suzanne, at the grocery store. She has a son Bijal's age. His name is Ben. When I asked her about him, she smiled.

"Oh, Ben's doing just fine," she said, theatrically. "He works at Outback Steakhouse. Have you been there? It's delicious. He's home, you know, getting his bearings. It's hard—that age. But it's a treat for Fred and me. We love having him home, plus we get to eat all that good food! You should see Fred; he's getting a tummy! Anyway, he's happy, so we're happy. That's all that really matters."

I stood there in the dairy aisle, stunned. I would not have been happy to admit my son worked at Outback Steakhouse. I could not have derived my own happiness from his. I would have been devastated. My impulse was to laugh at Suzanne, to call Chaya and discuss it with her over the phone, how these Americans have no shame—doctor or waiter, it makes no difference to them. Now, I wonder if I had been wrong.

Bijal and Akash have left for the Salvation Army by the time I come down the stairs. The living room has been gutted. I sit down on the floor. Now that the TV is gone, I have to watch *Deserted Hearts* on my iPad. I cue up the episode and wait for it to load. The steam from a cup of chai curls at my side. The days have grown shorter, dusk settling quickly. A single lamp flicks on outside, and the light coming off it is hazy, weak. I wonder if it's always been that way. There are things in this house I have probably not bothered to notice. Cracks in the plaster. Chips in the paint. Stunning views from rooms I have not bothered to stand inside. I make a promise to do that over the next couple of days, to walk around this entire house and absorb it like a sponge. I sit up straight, the iPad balanced in my lap, as the episode begins.

Celeste is on-screen wearing a chic black dress. Thin streaks of mascara run down her face. She's at a funeral. Juan was run over by a lawn mower.

"I love you, Juan," she wails. "I'll never stop loving you!"

A priest stops his sermon to stare at her. "Who's Juan?"

"Huh?"

"This ceremony is for John."

"I beg your pardon . . ."

"John White."

He points to a placard underneath Juan's portrait, with the corresponding name.

"The gardener?"

"Oh, yes."

Celeste looks mortified. "But I thought his name was Juan. My little Chicano!"

"Chicano?" A woman laughs. "John's *white*. It even says so in his name."

"But I could've sworn he was Mexican!" The room turns to stare at her. "Oh, don't give me that—he's a gardener, for Christ's sake."

"Miss, I'm going to have to ask you to leave," says the priest.

"This is preposterous! How could he lie? That's illegal, right?"

"Miss, please leave."

"I specifically asked for a Mexican gardener. A *Mexican* one! How dare they!"

"Miss! This is all highly inappropriate. Now I've already asked you twice: please kindly leave!"

Celeste walks out in a huff. The episode cuts to a commercial. I don't think I'll be watching anymore. The writers have done what they do best: ruined a perfectly good show. I close out of the app and think about going back upstairs to continue packing. I pull up Google instead. The tea steams at my side as I search for homes in London. Most of them look old and crumbling, with curtained windows and tiny yards, but there's a condominium near London Bridge that has caught my eye. A two-bedroom with high walls of glass, a marble island, glossed cabinetry. The apartment is on the thirtieth floor. I think about the times Ashok and I drove to Chicago and fantasized about an apartment in the sky. Jagdish and Smita have a detached farm-style house in a posh neighborhood with a guest suite, where I'll be staying for a short while. They insisted I live with them—both their daughters are out of the house—but I refused. I have spent far too much time beholden to other people. It's time I step out on my own.

I decide, in this moment, that this condominium is where I'll live. That first apartment Ashok brought me to, with its pungent elevator and curling walls, was a far cry from this, and I'm taken by the images on-screen, of a long rooftop pool, a lobby bar, an in-house theatre, steel beams and sleek, glassy stone. When Ashok and I first married, I had only three hundred dollars to my name, the money my father had given to me on our wedding. Now, I think back to the night just months before his death, when Ashok approached me with his laptop in the kitchen.

"Look, Renu," he said. "Look how far we've come."

I stared at the balance in our portfolio, my pulse racing, all the money earned and invested and tripled over time. Millions. Prior to that evening, I'd had no idea how much we had, or even where it came from. I had no interest in these affairs. Ashok was the one who read financial magazines and watched Bloomberg Television, emailing his stockbroker at odd hours in the night. It was Ashok who decided to open a second practice in a neighboring town. I didn't coerce him. It wasn't my concern. I cared only what the money did for us: the vacations we took, the furniture we bought, the boys' tuition fees we paid. The down payment for the house Bijal and Jessica bought. It was an extended wedding gift from us. Jessica's parents bought them a blender.

"They don't have money like you and Dad," Bijal had once said, defensively. "You can't expect everyone to be as generous as you."

I was stunned. There was a time in my life when I had assumed all Americans were rich—especially ones like Jessica. I realize, now, that I was wrong. I take one final look at the real estate listing, for a building called Azure Tower, its panels of blue glass turning liquid in the light, when my mind shifts to you. I pull out my cell phone and, without thinking, send you a message.

> *I've found the perfect place, Kareem. It's right on the water. We can go for walks along the river. We can drink wine on my balcony. We can do all the things we never got to do before. By the time you return to London, I will already be there. Isn't that exciting? That our paths will cross over and over again. I can't wait to see you tomorrow, and every moment after that. I'll text you when I'm on my way.*
>
> *Love,*
> *Renu*

I fire off the message and stare longingly at the screen, waiting for you to respond.

AKASH

Bijal drives us to the Salvation Army in Chaya Aunty's van. I can feel the weight of our possessions whenever he accelerates through a light. I stare out the window, at the string of small, lamplit homes. Bijal opens the moonroof and I smell the bitter smoke of burnt leaves. It's the end of October, the end of Navratri. In three days, I'll fly home. Jacob will be out of town by then—it's his cousin's wedding in Newport Beach—and I'll pack up my things alone. I still don't know where I'll live. I can't think about that now.

"Damn it," Bijal says, pounding the steering wheel. "I missed the turn."

"Just go up and make a left."

Soon, we pull into the back alley of the Salvation Army, where a pair of workers are waiting by a set of wide doors. Bijal parks the car, pops open the trunk. I get out and meet him around the back. One by one, we unload the boxes and hand them off to one of the workers, who takes them inside. My legs wobble when I lift one of the heavier boxes, stacked with pots and pans.

"Be careful," Bijal says. "It's heavy."

He helps shoulder the weight, and together we inch our way up the ramp.

"You have to lift from your legs. You don't want to injure your back."

"That's what Dad always said."

He looks at me sadly. "I know."

The second worker approaches with a form. "Thanks, guys."

Bijal nods and takes the form, and we walk down the ramp and climb back into the car.

"Well, at least that's done," he says. He checks the clock. "See? It's only six thirty. Now we can go home and have a beer . . ." He trails off. "If you want."

"I think," I say, my voice thinning. "I think maybe I shouldn't."

"Oh."

He starts the car. The blast of heat from the vents is suffocating.

"Bijal," I say. He turns to look at me, a glaze in his eyes. "I'm sorry."

I'm surprised by how freely the word slipped from my mouth. He doesn't say anything. A song blasts from the radio. He places it on mute.

"It's fine."

"No," I say. "I was out of line. I don't . . ." I stop myself, unsure of what I'm trying to say. "I don't want us to fight."

We're silent for a while. Headlights flash behind us, and Bijal puts the car in drive and inches up a few meters before hitting the brakes. I wait for him to say something, anything, my palms damp with sweat.

"Jessica moved out."

"What?" My breath catches. "When?"

"Before I came home."

"Is that why . . ." I think about all the little clues, the whispers over the phone, the sudden shifts in mood, the excuse Bijal gave for her absence, that Jessica was sick. "Is everything okay?"

He breathes through his lips. "I don't know."

I search his eyes for a sign of emotion. He was always good at hiding them. I never understood it: how a person could stroll through a fire, stand still in a storm.

"She was pregnant," he says.

"Jessica?" My voice cracks, remembering what I had said earlier in our father's office, the way he had snapped. "You never told us."

"We didn't want to. Not until we were sure it would—it happened last year, in spring. It didn't . . . we lost it."

I look at him, my brother, and realize he's no longer the person I had imagined him to be, the person I had resented all these years, the person I had tried fruitlessly to become. We attach so many extraneous things to people when that's all they really are: people.

"I'm sorry."

"It's okay."

"But Bijal," I say, my voice quavering. "That thing I said back at the house—it's not right."

"You didn't know." He looks at me, his gaze softening. "This wasn't the first time it happened. We've been trying for a while. I just never said anything about it. I let Mom think we weren't ready, but we were. We've been ready, Akash. Everyone always asks us, *When are you having kids?* It's a fucked-up thing to do, you know? Sometimes you don't know what's going on in people's . . . anyway, we had a lot of problems after. It was pretty much our last hope. Jessica got depressed for a while. She wouldn't leave her room for days. When she did, she didn't talk. Not a word. I'd ask her how she was feeling and she'd just shrug. I got tired of walking on eggshells, canceling plans, living like the world had ended, like we were the only two people alive."

The car behind us flashes its lights again and Bijal puts the van in drive, turning onto the next street. We cruise past a pharmacy and a grocery store and a Baskin-Robbins.

"We started fighting a lot," Bijal says. "Not normal fights, like what to spend money on or where to eat, but fights about what we wanted in life, who we were. Jessica thinks I'm selfish. She says I wasn't there for her when the baby died, that I left her to grieve alone. But what was I supposed to . . ." He stops himself. "It's not my job to make her happy. I can't do that for her. That's not what a marriage is."

I look out at the illumined façades of storefronts and fast-food chains. We pass through an intersection and pick up speed, and soon the lit buildings grow fewer and farther in between. We glide through an empty stretch of farmland, black as a sea. Now I have my answer, the sudden interest in Bollywood movies, the beaded Indian clothes, the dishes he asked my mother to make, the people he went out of his way to greet. Bijal left us years ago; he never looked back. I suppose, in a way, he was coming home.

"I didn't want to tell Mom," he says. "She never liked Jessica. She would just blame her. But it's not her fault. It's no one's fault. It's just . . . it is what it is."

"Yeah," I say lamely.

"She wants to take some time for herself. A few weeks, maybe a month. Then we'll see."

"Do you think you'll work it out?"

He shakes his head. "I don't know."

I stare down at my lap as the car slows to a stop. I look out the windows and see the familiar intersection, the tall neon sign. Your parents' motel. It stands alone like a ship in the night. I wonder if you're inside. I wonder if Bijal will say something about you, your parents, everything that happened between us.

"Enough about me," he says, waiting for the light to turn. "What about you? Are you okay? Do you need anything?"

"I'm fine."

"You know you can come to me for money if you need it."

"Oh, yeah?" I grin. "Give me ten grand."

He jabs me. "You know what I mean."

"I'll be okay."

"I know you will." He looks at me. "I heard that demo you recorded."

"When?"

"I needed to use your laptop for a minute. It was on your screen. I'm not going to lie . . ." He flashes a smile. "It was pretty good."

"You think?"

He nods. The light changes. Bijal speeds through it. Within moments we're home, and Bijal parks the car in the garage. I unbuckle my seat belt and open the door when he reaches for my arm.

"Wait."

I look at him, tucking myself back in.

"Akash," he says, staring up at the roof, as if the words are written there. "You know you don't have to hide anything from me. You don't have to hide what you do. Or who you are."

I look down at my hands.

"There might be things you don't want to tell Mom, or anyone, but you can tell me. I know we haven't talked since Dad . . . I know I haven't been around. But if there's anything on your mind, you can come to me. I want you to know that. I'm not going to judge you or make you feel like you can't—"

The words drop from my mouth like fat beads of rain, nicking the soil.

"I'm gay."

It feels strange to say it. Like it didn't come from me. Like this isn't my story, my words sliding off my tongue. Bijal tilts his head, his eyes wet.

"I know."

"You do?"

Relief pools inside me.

"There were signs."

"What signs?"

"The qualities," he says. "Plus, you've never had a girlfriend. I thought: he's not *that* ugly. What's wrong with him?"

I punch his shoulder. He rubs it gingerly.

"Also," he says. "You said something to me, the night of my wedding, after you got your DUI."

"What?"

I think back to that night, the way his voice had sounded as if we were underwater. *Akash, you don't remember what you did?* Bijal kills the headlights and takes the keys out of the ignition and drops them into his coat pocket. He looks at me with damp eyes.

"It was on the ride home from the police station. You were still drunk. You were rambling. You said it didn't matter what you did, how badly you messed up, that none of us could ever love you, anyway, because of what you are. I asked you what that meant, but you wouldn't answer."

Hot tears splatter my jeans.

"Did you really think that?" Bijal says, his voice breaking. "Did you really think we wouldn't love you?"

I don't answer him. I can't. The world before me is muddled. Smeared. Bijal grips my arm and pulls me into him and I collapse into his chest, sobbing.

"I'm sorry," he says, rubbing the back of my head. "I'm sorry if we ever made you feel that way."

RENU

It's Bijal's last night with us, and I carefully stir the keema and steam the rice and roll out homemade dough for naan. The house is perfumed with cinnamon. We eat the keema on the living room floor. Something has shifted between Bijal and Akash. Their eyes are bright; their smiles spread easily. At one point, I catch them whispering to each other like they used to when they were young, playing games in their secret language on road trips in the back of Ashok's car. I don't ask them what happened. I'm careful not to insert myself, to touch the thin, delicate strands that web between them. I only watch from afar.

This is my job now.

"It's your last night in this house, Bijal," I say, the words cinching my throat, making it hard to swallow. "How do you feel?"

He serves himself a cupful of wine, then passes the bottle to Akash. Akash shakes his head. I look at him, surprised. Bijal drops the bottle into a bucket of ice.

"It feels weird," he says, looking around at the empty walls. "It doesn't feel like our house anymore."

"That is how I have felt every day this year, ever since your father passed."

"Will you come back?" Akash says, looking at me. "To visit."

"Of course. I have my boys here; wherever they are is also my home."

"I don't think you wanna stay with Akash," Bijal says. "Unless you want to use paper towels for toilet paper."

"Shut up."

Bijal grins.

"Akash," I say, smiling. "When you're a big-time music producer, you can build a wing for me in your house. Then I'll come and stay."

"Sure."

"When he's a big-time music producer, he's gonna *buy* me a house, right, Akash?" Bijal says.

"That depends," Akash says, shoveling a spoonful of keema into his mouth. "If you keep getting bigger, I might not be able to afford it. That's a lot of square footage."

Bijal balls up his napkin and tosses it at Akash's head. Akash catches it and tosses it back. It's a gesture I have long waited to see, and my heart fills with sadness and bliss in equal parts. We finish our dinner and clean up in the kitchen and gather in the living room one last time. Ashok's photograph from the puja still sits upright against a wall. The garland has dried, its shed petals curling on the floor. I pick it up. His warm eyes burrow into me, and I feel a pinprick of guilt.

"Someone should take this," I say. "I don't have room in my bag, and I have others."

Bijal and Akash exchange looks.

"Bijal can take it."

"You sure?" Bijal asks.

"Yeah," Akash says. "It's your gift. I'm moving around a lot these days, anyway. It's not like I have anywhere to keep it. You can hang it in your house."

He nods.

"That way," Akash says, "whenever I want to see it, I'll have to come visit."

"You'd better."

He claps Akash on his back. I set the picture down, relieved, though for what, I'm not sure. The three of us stand in silence, gazing at it.

"I dream about him," Bijal says.

We turn to look at him.

"Sometimes I wake up and I swear I can hear his voice, like he's still in the room. It's weird 'cause nothing ever happens in the dreams. We're just sitting around doing nothing, watching TV, eating a sandwich, but he's always telling me a story, giving me some kind of advice. *Bijal . . .*" He imitates Ashok's booming voice. "*Don't trust anyone with your money. They're all crooks. You want to know what to do with your money? You come to me. I may not be the smartest man in the room . . .*"

"*But I know a thing or two,*" I say.

"*But I know a thing or two . . .*"

We all laugh. I shake my head.

"He used to always say that. It irritated me so much."

"Me, too," says Bijal.

"Yeah," Akash whispers.

Then Bijal's shoulders drop.

"I should have listened more," he says, his voice cracking. "I never listened . . ."

He shakes his head, buckling. I pull him close, feel the heat from his chest against my face. I don't think I've ever seen Bijal cry—not even at Ashok's funeral. He was efficient, more concerned with the logistics of the day than the emotions surrounding it. Now, I can't help but cry along with him. I wrap my arms around both my boys and feel the tremor of their grief, holding it in. I learn something then: even the hardest men have centers so soft you wonder how they ever stayed whole.

That night, after staying up late with Bijal and Akash, I finally crawl into bed. Only then do I look at my phone. I open my text messages, pull up our thread. I'm too exhausted, consumed by memories of this house and the boys, to wonder why you have not replied.

AKASH

I couldn't sleep last night. Suddenly, I have two nights left. Time is a mercurial thing; it's never fast enough when you want it to be, and then, just like that, it is. I've packed most of my room up, discarding the rest. I don't know if I'll ever see you again, Parth, or what I would even say if I did. I suppose it's for the best. The previous night has left me drained. It's enough, for now, to have my brother back, feel the grip of his fingers, see the edges of his smile. Later that morning, I watch as he packs up his car and drinks coffee in the kitchen and takes one final walk around the house. Just before it's time for him to leave, he joins my mother and me in the living room, wearing a button-down and slacks. His face looks weary, stubbled and pale.

"I'm gonna miss this place," he says. "There were so many things I wanted to do here but didn't. I was going to take pictures of the house to take back. It slipped my mind."

"Well, you'd better take them now, with your mind," my mother says.

He nods, casting his gaze around the walls, the wide windows, the adjoining kitchen, and the hallway beyond. Something passes through his eyes.

"The chairs," he says suddenly. We turn to look at him. "From Vinay Uncle's motel. They're still in the basement. We forgot to return them."

I remember the pile in the back of the room, the one I had sat on to listen to my song. My mother shakes her head.

"This house is too big."

She's seemed antsy all morning, rushing in and out of rooms, busying herself in the kitchen. It's as if she's looking for something to do. A distraction. She turns her attention to me.

"Akash," she says. "Can you drop them off in Chaya's van? I'm going to be out all day."

"Where?"

She hesitates. "The big temple up north. I'm going with Chaya. I thought I should visit it one last time, you know? Just to . . ." She doesn't finish her statement. She speaks quickly, a pink stain spreading over her face. "It won't be difficult to manage. Just take them to the motel. Parth will be there. He will help you."

The mention of your name makes the blood rush to my head.

"Okay."

Bijal nods, satisfied with our plan, still set in his role as the manager of our lives. Then he casts his gaze toward the door. His eyes linger.

"I should head out," he says.

I've always hated goodbyes, the lump that forms in your throat, the shame of unwanted tears, the way your own body betrays you, revealing the messiness inside.

We follow him to the door and watch as he slips on his shoes and pushes his arms through the sleeves of his coat. He hugs my mother, who bursts into tears. Then he walks over to me.

"Remember what I told you."

"I will."

He pulls me into a hug, and I can smell the sweet musk of his cologne. He almost crushes me in his arms. Normally I would wriggle free, pivoting away, but this time I do nothing, soaking it in. Our mother folds her arms.

"Don't forget to call each other. And please, don't fight."

"We won't." Bijal releases me. "As long as Osh respects the birth order."

The name resonates, at home on his tongue.

"I respect that you're old."

He punches my arm.

"Well," he says, looking up at the cathedral ceiling, the blank walls. "So long, house."

He opens the door and the sharp air seeps in, pricking my nose.

"Call me when you reach," my mother says. "And listen." She straightens herself, folding her arms. "Tell Jessica I said hi."

Bijal shoots me a look. I hold his gaze. He nods, slowly.

"Okay, Mom."

Then he walks across the yard to his car. I stand at my mother's side and watch as Bijal slips into the driver's seat of his Porsche and revs the engine and peels out onto the open road, vanishing around a bend. We wait a while longer, the way I used to as a child when my father would drive to work, my face pressed to the window, my eyes wide and blinking, wondering if he would ever turn around.

RENU

I wear a long cashmere sweater the color of a toasted nut; that's what the woman at the department store had called it. I'd asked for the "beige one," and she'd said, "You mean the toasted nut one?" I'd nodded and smiled.

I wonder how many times I've stood before this mirror sweeping blush over my cheeks. Hundreds? Thousands? I think back to all the parties and dinners and garbas and weddings, the graduation luncheon we hosted in Bijal's honor. The Diwali party in our basement, when twenty Indian families danced to bhangra music until one a.m., the men drunk off Johnnie Walker, the kids high off sugar, the women spinning round and round until their hair sprung diamonds of sweat. No one wanted to leave. We were safe there, sealed off from the outside world. Bijal had laughed.

"It takes you guys an hour to say goodbye."

"Do you know why?" I said. "Because there was a time when we said goodbye to our families and didn't know if we would see them again. This is our family now, Bijal, so we take our time in saying goodbye."

He nodded solemnly. "I get it, Mom."

And now he's gone, the weight of his feet on the stairs, the timbre of his voice in the halls, the tang of his aftershave in the guest bath. Even his bedroom, stripped of every remaining piece of him: books, posters, sweatshirts, souvenirs. It's all gone. He is Ashok's and my son. Nothing will ever change that. Still, Kareem, there was a time when I imagined he was yours.

Chaya arrives in her black Audi at noon. Akash is out of the house. I had felt bad lying to him, but he hadn't shown a trace of doubt. In fact, he seemed relieved, packing the remaining aluminum chairs from the basement into the trunk of Chaya's van, to be returned to Vinay and Asha's motel. You've finally replied to my last message—albeit not in the way I had hoped—with a thumbs-up. You must be nervous, too. I think about what to say to you when I grab my purse and keys and a tube of lipstick and slip out the front door to Chaya's idling car.

"Wow," she says, when I slide into the passenger seat. "You look smart."

She wears a puffy winter coat. Her gloved hands grip the wheel. I'm wearing my peacoat and scarf. For a moment, I feel like a fool.

"I don't know. What if it's all a mistake?"

"Then it's a mistake," Chaya says, grinning. "Who said we're too old to make them?"

We drive off, the heat blasting my face. The plan is for Chaya to drop me at the café and occupy herself for a couple hours until I'm ready to leave. I'm thankful for her incessant chatter during the drive over. It takes my mind off the fear of seeing you. We cruise past silos and farmhouses and inexpensive motels, an outlet mall selling discounted clothes. Chaya fills me in on the details of her life: the new dishwasher she's installed, the biryani recipe she tried, her son's new job at a tech company in Portland, the woman at Sam's Club who took three hot dog samples instead of one. I realize that in a few days we will no longer have these conversations. I will no longer be privy to her world.

"Did you hear about Kavita?" Chaya suddenly says, a wry grin on her face.

I smile and shake my head, eager for the story to begin.

AKASH

The motel parking lot is nearly empty. Only a few cars remain, staggered into spaces. The sun slips past a cloud and temporarily brightens the façade. I stare up at the sign. This time, I know that you're here. I heard my mother on the phone with you earlier, informing you that I would be coming. I feel your presence all the way in my seat. I get out of the car, and the door slams behind me as I cross the parking lot and approach a set of sliding glass doors. I walk in. You're standing behind the front desk with a knot in your brow, looking over some paperwork. You don't seem to notice me. And then you do.

You don't say anything for a while. Our eyes lock, and I wonder if the memory of us is too strong for you to speak. All that separates us now is a desk. Thin, brittle, a barrier of wood. A service bell gleams. You wear a sweater that clings to your chest. You look just as I had imagined you would—your beard darker, your brows fuller, your eyes lit with new knowledge, your face hollowed, the youth stripped away like unnecessary fat from a bird—and it's this, the way you appear exactly as you had in my head, that startles me. Because you're not just Parth anymore, you're the person who has lived in my thoughts all these years.

"Akash," you say, your voice a mere whisper.

"Parth."

RENU

By the time we pull up to the café, I'm fifteen minutes late and my legs have lost the will to move. Chaya had to stop to use the restroom. We had to pull into a gas station off I-57. We did it three times.

"Sorry, hah? I have diarrhea."

"What did you eat?"

"God only knows."

She wasn't particularly worried. According to Chaya, diarrhea was the perfect way to reduce your weight.

"Why do you think I go to India every year?" she once said at a bridal shower. "Three weeks there and you'll be thin, thin, thin!"

Chaya stops the car in front of the entrance, through which I can see only the reflection of her car, the wheels caked with frost, our heads shrunken behind glass. The café is in a strip mall between a nail salon and a gym. It's called Cup of Joy. It doesn't look very joyous. I had expected something dim and romantic with tufted leather furniture, a handful of older customers like ourselves. The door opens, and out walks a young woman in a tracksuit, pushing a baby in a pram. A cup of coffee steams in her hand. Her phone rings, and she nearly drops the coffee all over her baby to answer it. My heart lurches, but the woman only laughs.

"Did you see that? She nearly burned her baby."

"This new generation, I'm telling you," Chaya says. "Amit's wife got mad at me for giving her kids Coca-Cola. She says, *Mom, they don't drink Coca-Cola. There's no nutritional value.* Then, two weeks later, she's taking them skiing. Now I'm asking you: Where is the value in that? So they can fall and break their necks?"

Her eyes spark. I stare at the storefront.

"We can turn around if you want to."

"No," I say, straining to find you among the cluster of vague shapes inside. "I'm here now."

The interior of the café is lined with booths and circular tables and a pair of soft linen sofas. The air smells of burnt beans. A few customers queue up behind the register to order. A pair of women whisper eagerly outside the restroom. I don't see you anywhere. I'm not sure what to do with myself, whether to order a drink or not. I feel silly, like a woman on a blind date, wound tightly with expectation. There's an open booth near the entrance so I slide into it, placing my handbag on the table. I look at my phone; I'm twenty minutes late. Maybe you got tired of waiting for me and left. I decide to wait a couple more minutes before sending you a message. I pull up our exchange. Everything is as we'd planned: the time, the date, the location. I'd even told you what I had planned to wear, in case there was any confusion. There wouldn't have been. As I look around the room at the pale, flushed faces, the piles of blond or brown hair, the small rosy-cheeked children with smeared chocolate on their lips, I realize that you and I are instantly recognizable here.

Kareem, I'm here. Did you leave?

I hit send and put my phone away and lean back against the booth. The door to the men's restroom opens. A pair of men walk out. Neither one of them is you.

I walk up to the register to order a coffee. I request two sugars and one cream. The coffee arrives in a cup with a brown sleeve and I carry it back to the booth. As I sit and sip from it, I think about the first night we met. I can still hear the canned noise of

Dar es Salaam: the cries of hawkers, the squawk of birds, the crackle of pastries frying in hot oil. I see your face outside the cinema. I remember what you said to me. Your voice still vibrates in my chest. I could never recall a single detail from that night—the movie I saw, the clothes I was wearing, the time I scrambled home, hoping I wouldn't be late—but I remember every detail of you.

On my last night in London, you traced the small of my back. We were tangled in your sheets.

"Tell me something."

"What?"

You looked at me. "What's your favorite song?"

I sat up in bed. "Why do you want to know that?"

"Because," you said, "I never asked you, and now you're leaving me, and I'm afraid I'll never know. I want to know, Renu, so that whenever I hear it, I can think of you."

My throat tightened.

"'Killing Me Softly'—Roberta Flack."

"A good one."

"What about you?"

You made a display of scratching your head as if you were deep in thought. Then you smiled.

"Anything Elvis sang. They say he looked like me."

I smacked your shoulder. "Jaja haave! Elvis ka chamcha!"

You held my wrist. "I'll miss that, you see."

"What?"

You kissed me, then pulled away. "Your fiery tongue."

One hour later, my coffee has grown cold. The shop has emptied. The sky turns dim. An employee begins slapping his mop against the floor. I pick up my phone. Not only have you ignored my message, not only have you let me sit here alone, but you have not bothered to answer my calls. I think about sending you another text, an angrier one, but then I look back at our messages and cringe, the urgency of my words next to the hollowness of yours. I realize what this was to you all along: an option. Something to try on.

Do you remember that morning in London, the first time I said I loved you? You had tried to kiss me. I turned away. You said one day my breath wouldn't matter, my figure wouldn't matter, my face, arresting as it was, wouldn't matter. Only my heart.

"Fine," I said. "I love you, too."

How could it be, Kareem? All this time I had never thought to consider it, that you hadn't actually said the words.

I walk up to the register and toss my cup into the trash. I send a text to Chaya telling her to pick me up. Outside, evening falls. A pinkish-gold color, blushed like plum wine, spills over the sky. A car pulls out of its parking space and crunches over the lot before merging with the traffic ahead. I look for Chaya's Audi, already preparing what I will say to her, already planning my excuse. A police siren sounds, and its pulse mirrors the pace of my heart: longing, sadness, bitterness, rage. The sound grows steadily louder, and when I turn my head, I can see the blur of swirling blue lights. I remember how I have felt all these years when a police siren sounded in the night. The guilt of knowing I'm safe in a world where others are not. The wail echoes the sound in my own heart, and I wonder, then, what it would feel like to scream, to fall to my knees, to crack my heart open and purge myself of every thought of you. A second police car follows. Its siren is even louder. I could do it, Kareem, and no one would ever hear.

AKASH

If you're angry with me, you don't show it. You open the door to your parents' office, where boxes are piled like blocks, cleaning supplies angled against walls. We make frequent trips between the office and Chaya Aunty's van. I did not expect you to be so kind. During short breaks for water, you ask questions about LA. You tell me you took the year off before your fellowship. You were burnt out from school. Then your parents left for India and you decided to move home. It's strange, you say, coming back to this town.

We've returned most of the chairs. They're stacked in your parents' office. Only one trip remains. I move slowly on purpose. You've stripped down to your T-shirt, and the front is sheer with sweat, a slash of brown skin visible beneath. I'm aware that this is my only chance, the only opportunity I'll ever have to tell you how I feel, but my lips won't form the words.

"Thanks again for letting us use these," I say, as I follow you back to the car.

"Don't worry about it. We hardly use them anymore. You could've kept them . . ." You stop, realizing your mistake. "Well, I guess you won't have anywhere to put them now."

The sun is setting just as we reach Chaya Aunty's car. You reach into the trunk, pull out a stack of four chairs. You leave the remaining two for me. Then you change your mind.

"Actually, I can take those," you say, pointing to them. "That way you don't have to make the extra trip."

My hope thins like the final traces of light. I look at your face, kissed by the setting sun. I don't want this to be the end. My words fall between us, bold in their desire.

"I thought we could hang out."

Perhaps you had expected them all along, had prepared your response, all the reasons you would have to say no. Your eyes narrow as you look out at the farmland beyond, stained violet and pink. I could die waiting for your reply.

You look at me, your eyes focused on some vague spot on my face, and then you nod your head.

"Okay."

RENU

Chaya drops me off at night. The house is dark. Akash must still be out. I don't know what to say, how to feel. I'm reminded of that morning in the hospital, the nurse looking at me with blank eyes. *Sometimes it helps to hold the baby.* I feel empty— that's what it is—just like I did then. I was too embarrassed to tell Chaya the truth, that you never showed up, so I told her I wasn't feeling well instead. A splitting headache. It gave me a reason not to talk. I don't think she believed me, though. All throughout the car ride I could see her glancing in my direction, as if she were thinking of what to say. Finally, she puts the car in park, sits back in her seat. I open the door.

"Are you sure you're okay?"

I look at her, numb. "Yes."

"Something must have happened. I don't believe you."

I look at her and she closes her mouth.

"Anyway," she says. "I'm here if you need to talk. Bhupendra will be watching his bloody cricket all night." She clucks her tongue in disgust. "I don't know, Renu. I might have to go to London with you."

I smile. "But what about Bhupendra?"

"Who cares what he wants?" Chaya says. "You have the right idea, Renu. Just do as you please. Don't think about anyone else." A hand flies to her mouth. "Sorry, I didn't mean it like that."

"Do you think I'm being selfish," I say, "for leaving all of you behind? Bijal. Akash. What about Ashok? Is this what he would have wanted? To abandon this house?"

We look up at the house together, with its white brick façade, pale blue in the moonlight. Chaya grips my hand.

"Renu," she says. "Ever since we were young, we have lived for other people. We were good daughters for our parents, good students for our teachers, good spouses for our husbands, good mothers for our kids. We have been good cooks and good cleaners and good hosts for our guests. When we came to this country, our husbands were lost. Remember? Now tell me: Who reminded them of home? Who cooked their mothers' food? Who bore them children to carry on their family name? Who was there for them every single night when they came home? We were."

Her words crackle. She releases my hand.

"You don't have to ask what your husband would have wanted," she says, pushing a lock of hair from my eye. "You were everything he could need."

The house is still when I enter. I can hear the sound of Chaya's car in the distance. In two days, she'll return to drop me to the airport. I place my purse on the kitchen counter and stare at the empty room, scraped out like the shell of a coconut. I can't help myself. I check my texts again. My unanswered message glares back at me, like the face of a woman scorned. I am that woman. I did this to myself. I held the foolish notion that you and I were meant to be. Still, I can't help but resent you. Hate you even. How could you humiliate me this way? I think about the last time we saw each other. You had asked me to stay. It was you, Kareem, who had suggested we run away. And do what? Would you have abandoned me then? Slipped out of our hotel? Ordered tea at a restaurant only to let it grow cold? I delete our text thread. I block your profile from my page. The rage is sudden. I grip the phone in my hand and feel its weight in the center of my palm. Then I smash it on the counter, over and over again. The screen chips into a million little fissures, like the cracked surface of a frozen lake.

AKASH

You need to change into a fresh shirt, so we move to your parents' apartment, accessible through a secure door in their office. It's exactly as I remembered, with its floral-print sofas, batik wall hangings, a few pictures of Hindu gods. The rooms smell of spices and grease. The only concession to current times is a flat-screen TV.

"I'm the one who made them get the TV," you say, reading my mind. "My parents live in the stone age."

You say this not with bitterness—as you would have years ago—but with the kind of fondness reserved for old friends. I realize that in the years since our adolescence you have grown to appreciate them. Their sacrifices are the war wounds you wear with pride.

I wait in the living room while you go into your bedroom to change. You've left a beer for me, and even though I no longer feel the urgent need to drink, I take a sip. The beer relaxes me. I sit back against the couch. You call out to me from your room.

"Where should we go tonight?"

The last time you and I made plans we were sixteen, limited to the cinema or the mall. I shrug; you can't see me.

"It's up to you."

A car pulls into the parking lot beyond just as you enter the room, its lights reflected on your face.

"We'll have a beer first."

You wear a flannel shirt, stiff jeans. Your hair is messy, your beard trimmed. I watch you walk into the kitchen and twist open a beer. You approach me, clinking your bottle against mine. Then you take a seat on the chair opposite.

We drink in silence, letting the buzz gain traction. Your eyes grow glassier with each sip. Halfway into the first beer, you say we need music.

"Any requests?"

"Play 'So Into You.'"

You look at me, surprised. "I haven't heard that in a while."

You load up the song on your iPhone. A clear voice, slick like resin, slides from your parents' speakers. I hear it and shake my head.

"That's the wrong one."

"What do you mean it's the wrong one?" you say. "It's the only one."

"No it's not." I grin. "That's the remix. I'm talking about the original. It's better. This is in a weird key. I don't like it."

You raise your palms in mock defense. "Well, excuse me."

You shake your head and smile, switching the song. We listen for a while, nodding our heads to the beat. I remember how I felt when I first heard it, that day at my birthday party, looking across the arcade at your face, willing you to look back. As if you can sense this, you place your beer on the coffee table and close your eyes, threading your hands in your lap. Then you open them.

"You're right," you say. "This is better."

I think about what to say to you, all the words I've rehearsed in my head. Instead, I ask about your parents.

"They're great," you say, wiping a bit of foam from your lips. "I think they're enjoying the time off. My mom keeps sending me gifs of cats."

"You can't deny the charm of a cat."

"Tell me about it."

I sip the last of my beer. You get up and open another. The room takes on a comforting glow as you slide it my way.

"I'm sorry," I start to say, my lips trembling. You look at me, confused. "That I didn't get to say goodbye to them."

"I'm sure they would have liked that."

You lean back and cross your arms behind your neck, your shirt lifting, revealing a sliver of brown skin.

"Yeah."

The song changes. I watch as you finish your beer and get up to pace the length of the room. You examine a picture frame on top of the lace covering protecting your parents' stereo system. The picture is of you and your family in India. You're standing in front of the Taj Mahal. You don't look happy to be there. I remember you telling me why: you had eaten pav bhaji from a street vendor the night before and couldn't keep anything down. You put the frame down and walk over to the window, pull the curtain back to examine something outside. You let it fall back into place.

"There's a bar we could go to," you say. "Rawhide."

The name sparks in my mind. "The gay bar?"

"Yeah."

You must have heard the surprise in my voice, because you tilt your head thoughtfully. "Akash," you say, tenderly. "I'm out. I did it two years ago. Everyone knows."

I don't know what to say. I take a slow sip of the beer. I had never expected you to be so candid. I had assumed you would live quietly with your truth. Like me.

"Who's everyone?"

"Everyone. Friends, parents. Everyone."

"Your parents know?"

I remember your father, his bowed posture, his thick accent, the confused look on his face, as if everything in America were a riddle. I feel ashamed.

"I got tired of hiding, you know? Not to mention all the girls my parents kept pestering me to call. One day I just said: fuck it. I'm telling the truth." You take a sip of your beer. "So I did."

"How did they take it?"

"It wasn't a walk in the park," you say. "But it wasn't terrible either. It could have been a lot worse. At the end of the day, my parents love me and want me to be happy. They'll never understand it, and I don't expect them to. After everything they've done for me, that would be asking too much."

I can't reconcile this new person in front of me, full of wisdom and self-assurance. I think back to that time in your bedroom— when you pushed me away. Did you know then? Were you afraid to admit it? Would things have turned out differently if you hadn't? The beer is calming, loosening all the knots inside me, and my mind begins to wander. I'm sixteen again, imagining a future for you and me. Now that you're out, Parth, now that you're not afraid, maybe it's not too late. The music ends. A car honks in the distance. You finish your beer.

"I guess I never asked about *you*."

By the time I've told you my story, neither one of us is fit to drive. You've had three beers already. I stopped at just the two. By this point, I've told you about my DUI. Your roommate in med school got one, too, and ever since then, you've been vigilant. You told me this among other things: that you almost dropped out of medical school, that you've slept with two women, that you realized you were gay at the late age of twenty-one.

"On some level," you said, "I must have known all along. I guess I was in denial."

We didn't talk about us. There were other things to fill up the space between us, which had grown smaller as the night progressed, first with you sitting on the couch next to me, then with me leaning in.

You ask about my music career.

"That's amazing. You're really going for it. Here I am, a boring doctor, but look at *you*."

I always liked that about you, Parth, the way you made anyone you were talking to feel like they were all that mattered in the world. I play you the song I recorded and you smile the entire way through.

"It's a rough demo," I say. "I'm not a singer. You have to imagine someone else."

But you wave your hand. The words glide over us: *Tell me, tell me, tell me how to be.* When it's over, you stand up and pace the room.

"I love the melody," you say. "You have an ear for it, the way it dips and soars, never stays in one place. Those harmonies on the second hook. That was key. Akash." You look at me as if you're on the verge of delivering some grave news. "You're *really* good."

Whenever I played demos for Jacob, he praised them but offered nothing more. Everything was "nice" or "wonderful." Nothing was expounded upon. To this day, I will never know why he loved me—only that he did.

"What?" you say, looking at me with a confused smile.

I realize I'm staring. If we were dating, Parth, I would choose this exact moment to tell you how I feel.

"We should go to that bar," I say.

RENU

I spend a few moments walking through each room in this house, feeling the walls, remembering the sounds and smells, the way Ashok would chase the boys around each room, the way Bijal shouted when he didn't get his way, the way Akash, soft and quiet, disappeared into corners, tuning out the world. I absorb all of this, knowing I will never feel it again.

Upstairs, I apply night cream and moisturizer. I change into a thick robe. I steep tea in the kitchen and drink it in every room. I start with the living room, floating down the hall toward Ashok's office. I make a round in the basement. Then I trace the curved staircase up to Bijal's and Akash's rooms. I take in as much as I can: the walls and windows and ghostly outlines of frames, the ceiling fans coated in dust, the smooth stone in the bathrooms, chipped porcelain in tubs. I dig my toes into carpet and brush my hands against wood. I commit every room to memory, every closet, every door, so that one day, I will close my eyes and imagine I never left.

The night thickens as I pad down the hall to my bedroom. I walk into my closet, turn on the light. The shelves are bare, the racks stripped. Only a few clear containers remain, stacked on top of one another. They contain the jewelry I plan to take with me to London. I find the safe, a metal brick in my hands. I could fling it against the wall. In a flash I'm on the floor, entering the code and opening the latch and lifting the lid, gathering your letters in my hands. I feel the weight of each word as I rip them to shreds. The strips of paper pile up like tossed confetti on the floor. My breath catches in my throat. I think about burning them, silencing you for good, but then I see the edge of something at the bottom of the safe, a small, square envelope, Tiffany blue.

I had planned to deal with it later, but what's the use in making plans? They never work out. The envelope gives way to a card, the words *Happy Birthday* rendered in gold foil. A note falls out, folded up like an accordion. I see the words, *To Renu,* and begin to read.

AKASH

It's warm enough to ride a bike, so you unearth a pair from the storage closet at the back of the motel. They're the same ones we rode that spring, when you and I became friends. I recognize the one you had forced me to ride; its pink tassels are still intact, the basket still adorned with rosebuds. I look at it and laugh.

"Who's using that one?"

"Who do you think?"

"Not me," I say.

You look at me, grinning. "Between you and me, only one of us can pull this off, and it's certainly not me."

I punch you lightly in your chest. You grab my arm, digging your fingers into my wrist. Our eyes lock. You let go.

"Fine," I say, pulling the bike toward me. "But only because it matches my outfit."

"It matches more than that."

I swing my leg around the bicycle and lower myself onto the seat. You hop on yours, a blue Schwinn. I'm unsteady at first, the wheels wobbling as I steer myself forward.

"It's not far, Rawhide. It's only a few blocks."

You kick off in front of me and glide down the parking lot and turn left at the entrance, beckoning me to follow. I pedal toward you, lifting my chin toward the sky. The clouds have cleared, and a few stars emerge like sprinklings of flaked salt. You tap my arm.

"Evel Knievel, come on."

I pump my legs to keep up with you, letting the bike sail through the night. We cut through a residential area dotted with two-story shuttered homes. You swerve left and right, zig-zagging like a pinball. At one point you stretch your arms out like you're flying. You turn and smile. I charge toward you. You slam on your brakes and let me cruise ahead. We must look like children, you and me.

Before long, we reach the town's center and its strip of dark bars. Rawhide is ahead on the left. I remember that night in the car, my mother staring at the sign. It's not like the bars in West Hollywood, with their flashing red lights. Rawhide is a square brick building with a neon sign. The windows are blacked out. It could be any bar, anywhere.

"I think that's the point," you say, as we chain up our bikes.

You lead the way inside, past a smoky, blue-lit dance floor.

A cluster of shadows bounce to a Lady Gaga song. You look at me and smile.

"Typical."

We cast our gaze around the room, which is just one large, vaulted space. There's a bar in the back, but no DJ, only a stereo system hooked up to a laptop.

"Should we do a shot?"

I look at you. "Do *you* wanna do one?"

"I wouldn't have asked otherwise."

I can feel the warm spread of vodka already, luring me, but I shake my head. We stand with our backs facing the bar looking out across the crowd. It's mostly made up of thin young white men with sideswept bangs. A few older men lurk in the shadows. Every now and then, one of the older men emerges like a dog, sniffing and poking, only to be sent back to a corner with his tail between his legs. You shake your head.

"This is sad."

"It was your choice."

"I didn't think it would be this bad."

"You've never been here?"

You shrug. "I don't really go to gay bars. They're not very inclusive. I mean, look around. It's like a Justin Bieber concert."

"So what should we do now?"

You pull out your cell phone, and I'm afraid you'll want to call it a night, that you'll suddenly remember the paperwork you left behind or some important emails to send, but then you put your phone down and smile.

"This may sound weird, but remember that arcade? The one you had your birthday at?"

"Aladdin's Palace."

"Yeah."

My heart pulls.

"Well, apparently they renovated it. It's pretty dope. The

new owner installed a full bar and hired a DJ to spin nineties hip-hop. Plus they have all our old games: *Tekken, NBA Jam, Street Fighter, Mortal Kombat II.*"

You speak quickly, as if the words are in danger of evaporating on your tongue. I look at you and laugh.

"Choksi."

"Hey, that's *my* word."

"It was your word. I took it back."

I lean in close so our elbows touch. I can feel the heat coming through the fabric of your shirt. I want you to know I was kidding, that, to me, your perceived nerdiness is the sexiest thing. I think about kissing you.

I don't.

"Okay then," I say, turning to face you, pinning you down with my gaze. "Let's do it."

The arcade is different from what I last recalled. Rotating lights throw patterns of stars against the walls. Arcade games line the walls like slot machines. You blow air into your cupped hands, the cold blazing in your eyes, nodding to the beat.

"See? I told you."

The music fades as a cluster of college students rush by, then funnels back to us like a storm. A thwacking beat, like the sound of a tennis ball bouncing off a court, lobs over our heads. Outkast: "Elevators."

Me and you
Your momma and your cousin, too
Our eyes meet.

"See?" you say, a broad smile on your face. "I. Told. You."

We make our way to the bar. I order you a beer. The song switches, and we both look at each other.

"Oh, shit," you say.

Seeing how the music brightens your face, dimming everything around you, I'm back there again. I'm on that open road next to you, singing the words. Your eyes go glassy; you raise one arm. Then you inch closer to me, the other one snaking around my waist.

We make the rounds, smashing buttons, jamming keys, sliding into thick plastic seats that shudder at our backs. Bright colors swirl around us. Pink. Orange. Purple. Blue. The music competes with the jingles and blipping lights. You challenge me to a round of *Street Fighter.* I pick Chun-Li. You're quick with your selection: Ryu.

"Typical."

"What?" you reply. "He's hot."

"He's a cartoon."

"Still hot."

Fifteen years ago, we would not have talked like this. I face the screen.

"Prepare to die . . ."

But it's Chun-Li who's thrashed up and down, screaming and wailing. Her lightning-speed kicks merely fan Ryu's face. You abandon the controls, laughing.

"My three-year-old cousin could beat you at this."

"I was just warming up."

You pull me close, your eyes gleaming.

"You seem pretty warm to me."

We play a few more rounds of *Street Fighter,* the animated characters leaping off the screens. A new song plays, "Too Close" by Next, and a group of women in hoop earrings and fur vests rush to the center, their heels clicking. We stand by a bar table and watch them. Being here with you in this moment, the urge for a drink slides away from me. I can tell, by the gradual ease of your smile, the way you turn your head slowly when I say your name, that you've had enough.

"Isn't it funny?" you say. "What this song is about?"

"It's about having an erection."

"Right." You smirk. "I thought that was the most scandalous thing in the world. I remember getting nervous anytime it came on the radio and I was in the car with my mom. I thought, dear Lord, please don't let her understand the words."

"Did she?"

You turn and smile. "No, but one day I heard her humming it in the kitchen. She was making khichuri." You shake your head. "Imagine that: your mom is humming a song about having an erection while making dinner for your dad."

I laugh. "I'm surprised you're not in therapy."

"I should be," you say.

The song ends. The women shuffle back to their friends. You finish your beer and slam it on the table. I offer you another one, but you shake your head.

"I think I'm good."

I panic again, wondering if this will be the end, the moment you remember that night, remember what I am, but then you look around the room and pull out your phone.

"It's late," you say. "You should probably crash at my place."

The streets are empty on the way back, and we ride close together. At one point you stop by a playground. I pull up by your side. You hop off the bike and look around.

"Let's chill here a moment."

I take it in, recognizing it instantly. It's the playground my father took Bijal and me to when we were small. I remember the swing set and merry-go-round and wobbly wooden bridge.

I remember my father sitting on a nearby bench with a newspaper in front of his face.

I remember standing on the bridge trapped between two clusters of boys. They shook the knotted railing, and stomped on the slats, and watched as I struggled to keep still. I can hear the words they flung at me like darts, Bijal running up the stairs. *Leave my brother alone!*

Later, my father crouched before us.

"You see?" he said. "You two are brothers. You must always look after each other. One day, Mom and I won't be here, and then what will you do?"

"We'll have each other," Bijal said.

By the time I follow you to the merry-go-round and sit down beside you, kicking out my legs, tears are dripping from my face.

"Hey, wait, what's wrong?"

"Nothing."

"Akash . . ."

I don't answer you. The tears splat solemnly onto the wood chips below. You drop your arm around me and pull me close.

"Why are you crying?"

"I used to come here, with my dad."

"Shit. I'm sorry. I shouldn't have—"

"It's okay."

"We can go if you want. We don't have to stay here. I just thought maybe—"

And then I draw my lips to yours, pressing firmly. Your eyes widen. Your arms go slack. You pull away ever so slightly, then reel yourself back in, kissing me back. Your mouth tastes like peppermint—you must have sucked on a mint earlier. You must have wanted this, too. You rope me in your arms and pull me close to your chest, squeezing hard, like I'm a lemon in a fist.

"Come on," you say, wiping the spit from your mouth. "Let's go home."

RENU

My phone is downstairs in the kitchen, smashed to pieces. If Akash needs to reach me, he'll have to call the house. I heard it chime earlier, and I'm ashamed to admit that I still hoped it was you. How desperate of me. Maybe I should audition for *Deserted Hearts*. I could be one of those women, crying in sparkling gowns. *How could you?* I'd say. *You ruined my life!*

Ashok used to laugh at those scenes.

"Look at these women," he'd say. "Their lives are ruined. But what good is a life that is so easily ruined?"

Now, I crouch down with his letter in my hands. I haven't been able to get past the first line. I broke down crying. I can feel each word as if it whispers under my skin.

> To Renu,
> I knew when I saw you that you were mine. That day at
> your brother's flat, do you remember? I know you didn't
> choose me. But I chose you. I decided that day that I
> would love you the best I could. And that one day, maybe
> you would love me, too. I know things are hard. Now
> that Akash is at college, it's just you and me! I know
> you're sad, Renu, and that you miss him very much. I
> know the house will be different without our kids. But
> they are kids. They leave. Just like you and I did. This
> morning, I saw you crying on the sofa while talking to
> Chaya on the phone. You said, "I feel so alone."
> That broke my heart. You are not alone, Renu. You will
> never be alone. I will always be here with you. Even
> when you get mad like you do, and stomp around the
> house! Even then I will be here. Because you are my

wife, and I love you very much, and I know that one day, in the future, you will turn around and look for me. I promise you this: you won't have to look very far. Until that moment, I will be here.

Love always,
Ashok

The sound that escapes my body comes from some other place. It's not me. It can't be me. These tears are not my own, drenching my shirt. The wail that leaves my lips is not my own voice. I throw the letter on the floor and draw my knees to my chest, sobbing into my clothes. The house sighs, absorbing every sound, protective as always. This was not how I wanted to leave it, Ashok. This was not who I wanted to be.

AKASH

Inside your parents' apartment, among all of their things—the dust-laden lace cloths, the flowery sofas, the silver-framed pictures of Lord Shiva and Ganesh—we kick off our shoes. You lead me by the hand to your bedroom down the hall. It looks smaller than I remembered, a box really, with a full-sized bed, a small dresser, a poster of Kobe Bryant pinned to the wall. A few pictures from your childhood are taped around your closet. The room is dimly lit from a bedside lamp. You sit down on your bed and beckon me to join you. I do as I'm told, settling in by your side. Your arm brushes mine, your breath a feather at my neck.

"Parth."

You suddenly hop to your feet and stride over to the bedroom door and slam it shut. You turn around and smile.

"Just in case."

Then you walk slowly toward me, your expression changing. I inch back against your mattress to receive you. You climb on top of me and pin me under your weight, digging into my bones.

"Parth," I say again.

But you ignore me, pressing my lower lip down with your thumb. You slide your tongue over mine. I kiss you back, twisting and writhing, holding your face in my hands. We pull away briefly. Your forehead meets mine. You start tugging on my pants, pulling them down. I turn my head.

"What?" you whisper hotly.

And then they come to me. The words. I feel them sputter on my tongue.

"That thing that happened—when we were kids."

"It's fine."

"It's not fine, Parth. None of it was fine. I didn't . . . I didn't want that to happen."

"Okay."

You smile at me, kissing my nose. Then you sit up and unbutton your shirt. I stare at the spiral of hair on your chest. You fling the shirt aside, and a gold chain, adorned with an om pendant, shimmers around your neck. When you lie back down on me, the pendant strikes my chin. You twist it so it falls down your back. Then you kiss me again. You push your hand up my shirt.

"Take this off."

I wiggle out of it and toss it on the floor. We push together. Your chest feels like a sun-warmed stone. You press down, and I can feel your heart beating through the layers of skin and hair and bone.

"I don't get it. Aren't you mad?"

"It was years ago. Why would I still be mad?"

"Why wouldn't you be?"

You look exasperated.

"Akash," you say, softly. "You were a kid. You were afraid. We all were. We all did things we wish we didn't do because we were afraid."

You look at me knowingly, and suddenly it becomes clear. I know why you pushed me away that night. I know why you stopped messaging me, and avoided my path, and turned your back to me at parties in your parents' motel. You were afraid, too. The wall breaks, and finally I can let go. I can forgive myself, Parth. I can forgive you, too. I don't say anything when you pry the pants from my feet and throw them over your head like a ball. Or when you loosen your belt buckle, and take your pants off, too. Your boxer briefs stretch over the slope of your bulge. You look at me: a challenge. I tug them down.

From that point on, each kiss, each stroke, each nibble or bite pulls me under you like a tide. I absorb every part of you. Your skin, your smell. The warm, salty taste of your spit. You flip me over and trace my back with your cock, leaving a trail of damp. Then you're inside me, pushing me into your bedding, crushing me with all your weight. The only sound I can hear is the smacking of our bodies. The slapping of our thighs. I allow myself a hopeful glimpse into the future. Maybe you'll move to LA. Maybe I'll visit you in Chicago. We could meet somewhere in the middle. It doesn't have to be hard. We've waited so long to return to each other, Parth; there are people who have crossed greater distances than ours.

When it's over, when you roll onto your back, and the room clouds with our funk, and the ceiling fan lulls us to sleep, and you grip me like a hook. When the sweat from our bodies dries on your sheets and the first light of day slips through the blinds, when your cell phone bleats and you turn to check it, and I reach for mine, plucking it from the sheets, I know that it's over. I can see it on your face. You prop your head against a pillow, smiling. And then you tell me about him.

His name is Nicco; he's a nurse at the hospital where you once worked. He's one year older than you. You've been together for three.

"He helped me come out," you say. "I would never have been able to do it without him."

I think about Jacob, all the times he wanted to be there for me, encouraging me to live my truth. I flick the thought from my mind. You say Nicco understands you in a way most people don't. He's Mexican, and his parents, like yours, came to America for a better life. When you told him about your parents' plan to go to India, he didn't question your decision to move home. He didn't beg you to reconsider. He didn't ask you why your parents couldn't lean on someone else. His sense of duty, like yours, runs thicker than blood. It wasn't easy for Nicco to come out, but he did it anyway, at the age of sixteen.

"Can you imagine?" you say, your eyes aglow. "Can you imagine what that's like? Do you think about all the shit that we've missed?"

"I think about it."

I can't describe what I feel. A hollowness, maybe, like something has been scraped out of me, surgically removed. It comes as no surprise when you tell me the truth: that Nicco wouldn't mind if he found out about us. You're open. You always have been. It's how you've stayed together so long.

"Do you love him?" I ask.

But you don't have to answer me. I should have known, all along, that you do. The clock next to your head reads 10 a.m. You start shuffling around your room. I know that this is my cue to leave, but I can't. I wish I had one more hour with you,

Parth. I still have so much to say. I will you to return to me, to pull me back into your arms.

Outside, you walk with me across the parking lot in your sweat-pants. You wear a ribbed vest. Your gold chain winks in the light. We stop at the van.

"Choksi," you say. "Where do you go from here?"

"Somewhere."

"Somewhere." You glance across the open field beyond us, squinting. "Well, make sure you send a postcard."

"I will."

"I'm serious."

"I know."

"Hey." For a moment, I wonder if you'll tell me to stay, that you love me, that maybe there's something here. "I'm glad I got to see you, Akash."

Then you pull me into a hug, pressing into my skin, and it's this that I will remember, Parth, as I drive away from you, and your frame shrinks in my rearview mirror. I will remember how you felt.

When I pull into the empty garage, I feel a sudden despair. I want to cry but I can't. I have nothing left to give. I sit staring at the blank walls for a while, mustering the strength to go in. I know what I have to do now. I've known it ever since I came home. I unbuckle my seat belt and open the door and shift my legs around to meet the floor when my cell phone rings. My hand flies to answer it.

It's not you.

I slide my finger over the screen; Jaden's smile flares across it. "Yo."

"Hey."

It's a relief to see him, and the hollowness fills.

"So, what's up?" he says casually, his smile widening. He sits down in his seat and angles the phone so I can see the dark hollows of his nostrils.

"Nothing."

"Nothing." He sighs softly. "That's too bad."

"What?" He shakes his head, grinning. "Jaden . . ."

He holds up a finger, silencing me. "You ready for that to change?"

"What do you mean?"

"I mean they loved it."

"Who loved it? Loved what?"

"The song, fool."

"The song . . ." The fog in my mind clears. "But I just sent it to you. When did you—"

"I had a meeting with Kaya's R and B yesterday. I played them the track. They went crazy, Akash. I just got the call today."

A swirl of emotions spreads through me. I try to hold myself still. "The call—so wait. You mean they want it? They want to record it?"

"Yessir."

"So it's gonna be on her album?" My heart lifts, swelling. "An actual song?"

"Akash." Jaden looks at me very seriously, his face suddenly still. "They wanna make it the single."

I never knew what it was like to float outside of my own body until now. I'd heard about it, had seen it happen to others, but I never thought it would happen to me.

"They were looking high and low for something like this," Jaden says, jumping out of his seat. "They were just about to close submissions and go with another song till they heard this one. They wanna buy it and record it ASAP. They're planning a spring release. Are you ready? Are you ready for your life to change?"

"I don't know," I say, my breath quickening.

Jaden settles into his seat again. "You need to come back to LA. You're about to be busy. What *was* that anyway?"

"What?"

"That music you sent me. The chants."

I think back to that night, and all the other nights just like it. I smile. "A little culture."

"A little culture." Jaden nods. "I like that. We need more of that. Hit me up when you head back. You know you can crash with me, right? Not that you need to now."

"I'll figure it out."

He salutes me. I hang up the phone. I get out of the car, trying to hold myself together, and walk into the house.

"Mom?"

The living room is empty. For a moment, I forgot that we're leaving, that this house is no longer ours. Sunlight brightens the kitchen and what little remains in it. I take a plastic cup from a stack my mother has set out on the counter and fill it with cold water from a jug. I sip slowly, staring out at the trees.

"Akash?"

I turn to find my mother standing in the entryway. She looks like she hasn't slept. A thin cotton nightgown stops at her knees. Her hair is tied back with a yellow band, and her eyes are creased.

"I was with Parth," I say hurriedly, worried that she was up all night because of me. "We decided to hang out."

Her only concession to hearing this is a nod.

"Okay."

She approaches the kitchen island and sorts through some mail. Then she stops. I think about telling her everything I've just heard, but I don't want to yet. It's still too raw. I look at my mother and realize, for the first time all week, that our life in this house is over. Every moment, every dream, everything we ever were. My chest cracks. The shape of my mother smudges, blurs. She calls my name and it's sucked through a tunnel. Your words still resonate in my head. I can still hear them. And I realize that I have to do it. I have to tell my mother the truth. My father's words disintegrate in my mind, like dried leaves underfoot.

"Mom," I say, my voice breaking. "I have something to tell you."

I expect her to get angry, to ask, *What is it now?* Instead, she rushes over to me, drawing a finger to my lips.

"Okay," she whispers, her eyes searching mine. "I have something to tell you, too."

RENU

Celeste is dead. I streamed the final episode of *Deserted Hearts* in the business-class lounge while watching planes make their dramatic ascents. I had told myself I wouldn't, that the show was one of the many things from my old life I would leave behind, but I couldn't resist. It was like saying goodbye to a faithful friend. In the end, Rebecca was the one who killed her. She was the one who killed Juan, too. And Celeste's husband, Richard. She killed everyone on that show. Apparently, she wasn't Rebecca at all, but a mental patient who'd escaped an asylum several years ago. The real Rebecca was someone she'd killed and hidden in a basement, before taking over her life. The episode ends with Rebecca laughing maniacally on a yacht, having stolen everyone's money, too.

"Who can stop me now?" she shouts, just before a wave throws her overboard, and she's ripped apart by sharks.

The End.

I close my iPad and sip the champagne that's been placed on the table beside me, along with a bowl of warmed nuts. This afternoon, Chaya had come to collect me, and we'd done a walk-through of the house. I'd given her the keys in case she needed them. The new owners will move in next week. I'd dropped Akash off at the airport this morning and waited until his plane climbed steadily in the sky before returning home. He'd cried into the sleeve of my shirt. I was surprised. I had assumed there were no more tears left.

Last night, when I told Akash the truth, I watched the color drain from his face. I didn't know how he would react. I was afraid of what he might say: that I was a terrible mother, a terrible wife, that I had lied to my own family for thirty-five years. But I knew I had to tell him. I had to leave behind this truth. In the end, he gave me the one thing Bijal never could: absolution. I had seen the look on Bijal's face when I asked him about Jessica, had heard the tremor in Jessica's voice over the phone. I realize now that both my boys have kept secrets from me, just like I have kept secrets from them. All Ashok wanted for us was to be happy. I suppose we've all failed.

After I told Akash, we sat in silence for a while, watching the sky change colors. Crimson. Violet. Nectarine. Blue. It wasn't until I stood up to make some tea that he reached for my hand.

"Mom."

I spun around. He looked like he did when he was a child, when I used to crouch down in front of him and squeeze his arms. *Make fun of them back.*

"Do I remind you of it?" he said. "Everything you gave up? The life you never had?"

My heart trembled.

"No, Akash," I said. "You, your father, Bijal. You are everything I got in return."

We spent the rest of the day talking. He told me about Jacob. He told me about Parth. I told him I loved him no matter whom he loved. I suppose, all along, I knew. He was always a different child.

"He's artistic," Ashok had once said.

But I knew it was something more. When Akash was in college, I'd made an appointment to get my hair done and the stylist, Fabian, was the same way. *Artistic,* I thought to myself. *See? He's not the only one.* Fabian wore a tight black shirt. His dark hair was frosted. He kept talking about his wedding in California.

"Is your wife from there?" I'd asked.

He'd laughed at this. I was appalled. How dare this man laugh at me! Then he showed me the picture. In it, Fabian wore a cream silk suit and pink tie. The ceremony was at the top of a hill. Vines snaked around pillars and flowers bloomed from pots. A man stood next to him, grinning.

"That's my husband—Mark."

I had assumed Mark was his brother. They looked exactly alike.

"How nice."

Later that day, I called Akash at his dorm. I thought I could ask him. I could ask him if he was *that way*. He didn't pick up. He had dropped out of school. I didn't know this at the time. Two months later, when Ashok and I picked Akash up from the dorms, hours after realizing the suitcase containing my letter to you was gone, I stared at him in the backseat. I could have asked him then. I could have asked if he was that way. Instead, I said something I will always regret.

"Maybe we shouldn't have had a second child."

Last night, before going to bed, Akash came to my room, and the look on his face, his eyes wide with innocence, brought everything back.

"Akash," I said, softly, motioning for him to sit beside me on the mattress. "I want to talk to you."

He nodded.

"That time we were in London," I began. "I don't know if you remember. You were a child. Maybe eight or nine. I found you in my room. You had gone through my purse. You were playing with—there was all this mess on the bed."

"I remember," he said.

I felt a sharp plucking inside me. A pull. "It wasn't because of what you were doing," I said. "I don't want you to think that. It wasn't about the lipstick, Akash, or whatever else. I didn't care about those things. It was something else. There was a picture. I don't . . . I don't know if you saw it. It was . . ."

"Him."

He looked at me, not with resentment or regret, but with a knowledge that only he and I shared. For years I have been chasing the love I never had, the life I thought I wanted, when all this time it was here, in this house. This morning, before dropping him to the airport, Akash and I walked through each room.

"It's strange," he said. "It doesn't feel like ours anymore."

"It will always be ours," I said. "You were here, Akash. Wherever you go in life, however far we are from each other. We were here."

An announcement crackles from the speaker above. Another departing plane. I check my watch. It's almost time. I pull out my cell phone—Akash took me with him to replace the screen—and open Facebook.

I compose a post. *Farewell to my family and friends.* It's simple, unsentimental, but after these last few days, I have no more sentiment to give. I hit send and return the phone to my purse. A waiter comes by and asks if I would like more champagne. I shake my head. He clears my table with a gloved hand. Within moments, another announcement is made.

"Ladies and gentlemen, we'd like to begin boarding British

Airways flight nine forty-seven service to London, Heathrow. For those of you in our business-class cabin, please make your way to the gate."

I stand up and gather my things: my handbag, a jacket for the plane, the Ziploc bag full of fried snacks Chaya had made. I'd protested, but she had insisted. It was her final act of kindness to me.

"Promise you'll visit," she'd said tearfully, clinging to me outside the departures entrance. "You still have a house here. You still have me."

"I will."

"Jaja haave." She smacked my arm. "You lie."

I laughed. "When you get tired of Bhupendra, you come to London, okay? We'll do a girls' trip."

"Where will we go? I need something to fantasize about while he clips his nails."

"Paris. Madrid. Wherever you like."

Her eyes brightened. "I'm going to go home and look at tickets."

But I know she never will.

I make my way down a backlit stairway to the gate. A perfumed woman takes my ticket. She leads the way down a ramp and into the business-class cabin, which is more like a sexy lounge, with its low, blue lighting. The seats are like capsules. A red-lipped woman takes my bag. Her British accent is thick, each phrase like a question, a polished gem. It's a hint of what's to come. Months later, I'll hear an American accent at a café and my heart will lift.

"Where are you from?" I'll ask eagerly, a question I had so often answered in Illinois, at which point, I'll tell them my whole life story. I'll tell them about Illinois. I'll tell them about Ashok and Bijal and Akash. I'll tell them about Chaya and Bhupendra and Vinay and Asha and Parth. I won't tell them about Kareem. I learned something that night, sitting on the floor in my closet, Ashok's letter still crumpled in my hand: in life, the things we most desire are not always what we need.

I fasten my seat belt just as the plane disconnects from the jet bridge and inches its way forward. A stewardess rushes by in a cloud of perfume. The captain makes an announcement. A luggage bin clicks shut. I look out the window and wait for our inevitable ascent. I'm reminded of another time I was on a plane like this, thirty-five years ago. I was younger, thinner, less confident, more afraid. I cried the whole way into the crook of my arm. Upon landing, I was overwhelmed by the rush of passengers in baggage claim. All the children and parents, boyfriends and aunts. Ashok had sent specific instructions for me to wait there for him; he would help me with my luggage. He would walk me to his car. He would drive me to the small apartment in the small town I would call my home. He would show me how to use the furnace and oven and stove. He would even give me his phone number at the hospital in case I ever wanted to talk. I never used it. I wish I had.

"Don't worry," he'd said, when he'd sat down beside me on a four-poster bed. "I will be there."

He was.

AKASH

I still don't know what love is, Parth. That's why I write songs, because I feel something deep inside me that I can't describe, something I'll never be able to.

For years, I have felt only my mother's fire. For the first time in my life, I feel only her heart. I told my mother everything that night, about Jaden, Jacob, even you. I told her things I never thought I would tell anyone. This, too, must be what love is. An unveiling. To stand before someone and show them who you are. I never thought she would show it back.

After I told her the truth, my mother told me her own. She talked about her life in Tanzania, and later, in London, all the things she had found and cherished and lost. She knew what it felt like, to want something so deeply you could hear the wailing of your own heart. I realize I'm not angry with her. I don't resent her for loving a man who was not my father, or for clinging to the memory of an unborn child. I don't hate her for not expressing her love for me with the same words she used for Kareem. I love her because of all those things, because mothers can breathe fire, but they can also nurse the burns. And now, Parth, I can finally say goodbye.

I land at LAX and slip through the press of bodies. Heat strikes my face, the sun blaring like a bulb. A string of cars is lined up at the curb, honking horns. The sky is clear blue, palm trees bowed against it. I drop my bag and my guitar on the pavement and mop the sweat from my brow, straining to see beyond the sun's glare, when a cherry-red Jeep comes into view. A window slides down. "Get in, loser, we're going shopping."

Jaden grins at me, and for the first time since moving here, I feel at home. I toss my things into his backseat and join him up front. We merge into traffic. Jaden turns on the stereo. He plays the song.

Tell me, tell me, tell me how to be.

We roll the windows down and let the warm evening air brush our skin. As soon as we merge onto the 405, Jaden cuts it off. "I added some bass."

"I noticed."

"She's at the studio."

"Who is?"

"Kaya. She has your demo. She's laying down the hook." He

switches lanes, giving me a look. "So, what do you say? You ready to make some music?"

I don't answer him. I don't have to. Jaden turns the song back on and we rattle off the words. The wind rakes through my hair as we pick up speed. I stare at the rust-colored hills, the nestled white homes, the billboards that flash by. I remember to send Bijal a text, letting him know I've arrived. I don't know where I'll go from here, or where I'll live. I don't know whom I'll love either. I don't care to know these things. For now, there's this. I turn up the volume, and sing.

ACKNOWLEDGMENTS

There was a time when I didn't think this book would be possible. I thought I had nothing left to give. I've never been so grateful to be so wrong. I wouldn't be here without my brilliant editor, teammate, champion, and friend, Caroline Bleeke. Thank you for your patience, your understanding, for the numerous phone calls and for your sharp set of eyes. Without you, this book would not be what it is today. To my dear agent, Jenni Ferrari-Adler, thank you for sticking by me when I needed it the most, and for opening up a whole new world. To the team at Flatiron Books, Sydney Jeon, Cat Kenney, Katherine Turro, Nancy Trypuc, John Morrone, Eva Diaz, Keith Hayes, Malati Chavali, Megan Lynch, Bob Miller; to Manasi Subramaniam and the team at Penguin India; and to Rachel Neely and Shyam Kumar and everyone at Trapeze Books, thank you for this opportunity and for all your hard work.

To my Hollywood team, Lauren Szurgot, Flora Hackett, Raj Raghavan, Zadoc Angell, and Adam Cooper: this is just the beginning. To all the bookstagrammers who supported my first book, thank you for amplifying voices like mine. To my family, thank you for seeing me through my darkest times, just so I could get a glimpse of the light. I will always be grateful. To my friends, thank you for your support, your humor, and your forgiveness. To Brandy, Monica, Aaliyah, Missy Elliot, Timbaland, the Neptunes, Jay-Z, Destiny's Child, SWV,

Total, Foxy Brown, Lil' Kim, Biggie, Tupac, Nas, Ms. Lauryn-Goddess-Hill, and so many more, thank you for giving me something to look forward to at the end of each day, and for reminding me that I'm not alone. To Champaign-Urbana, my forever home, you are always with me wherever I go. To all the uncles and aunties and Indian kids I introduced as my "cousins," look where we are now. Look how far we've come. To myself, because everything you went through was leading you here, every tear, every fall. Keeping going. You're almost home.

And last, to Ashok, Renu, Bijal, and Akash: you are here. I see you. Now, so does the rest of the world.

Tell Me How to Be
DISCUSSION QUESTIONS

1. The novel is narrated by both Akash and Renu. What is the effect of moving back and forth between their voices? Did you have a favorite character?

2. Akash loves his father deeply, but they have a dark secret "that binds us, even in death" (p. 104): when Ashok found Akash's letter to Parth, he made his son promise not to tell Renu that he is gay. What is the significance of that moment in Akash's life? Why do you think Ashok made him promise this, and do you sympathize? What changes over the course of the novel that convinces Akash to finally come out to Renu and Bijal?

3. Music is central to Akash's life. What does music, and in particular R&B, mean to him? Did you have a favorite song or music memory from the novel?

4. Much of Renu's relationship with Ashok was shaped by resentment: "My rage lived inside me, a fiery thing, glowing like hot embers, brighter each day. This was his life. His dream. Not mine" (p. 83). Why does she have such a hard time embracing her new life in Illinois? What dreams does she have to sacrifice?

5. The Indian American community plays an important role in the Amins' world. Akash explains, "We would have been foolish not to unite. Because an Indian in America with no friends is like a spider with no legs. Just a thing to be stared at, ultimately dismissed" (p. 109). What does he mean? What positive and negative effects does the community have in Akash's and Renu's lives?

6. Chaya is Renu's best friend, almost like a sister, but there are things Renu has kept from her over the years and vice versa. What does their relationship suggest about trust and intimacy? Why, at the end, when Renu proposes a girls' weekend in London and Chaya says she's going to look at tickets, does Renu say, "But I know she never will" (p. 318)? Do you think their friendship is genuine, or one born out of convenience and necessity? Can it be both?

7. What is Renu's relationship to her book club, and to Taylor and Shane in particular? What are the points of tension and bias between these women? What are their different motivations for being part of the book club?

8. As a boy, Akash internalizes the idea that he and his family "are not *those* Indians. . . . The people who have lived in America for thirty years but still look like they leapt off a boat" (p. 122). What are the benefits and consequences of assimilation for the Amin family? How does racism affect Renu and Akash over the course of the novel?

9. Discuss the roles that class and wealth play in the novel. How does the Amins' privilege set them apart from other Indian Americans, like Parth's family, as well as Akash's white classmates, like Lance? What are the limits of that privilege, especially in relation to racism?

10. Akash describes his parents' approach to their family: "My parents had children for the sake of planting seeds. You don't plant seeds expecting to grow dandelions. You want flowers, big and beautiful, the kind you display in a vase" (p. 246). What do you think he means? Do you agree that this reflects Renu's view of her children? If so, does that change over the course of the novel?

11. Akash has a complicated relationship with his brother, Bijal. He reflects: "I hated Bijal for being everything I was not, everything beyond my reach, for living effortlessly in a world designed specifically for him" (p. 44). Later, Bijal tells Akash, "Did you ever stop to wonder why I had to do that, Akash? Why I had to be perfect? . . . Because of *you*" (p. 266). Why is the brothers' relationship so fraught, and how does it evolve over the course of the novel?

12. In telling Akash about his marriage, Bijal says, "Jessica thinks I'm selfish. She says I wasn't there for her when the baby died, that I left her to grieve alone. But what was I supposed to . . . It's not my job to make her happy. I can't do that for her. That's not what a marriage is" (p. 276). Do you sympathize with his perspective? How does it compare to Ashok's approach to his marriage to Renu?

13. Looking back on her relationships with Kareem and Ashok, Renu reflects, "In life, the things we most desire are not always what we need" (p. 319). What does she mean? Do you agree? How does this sentiment resonate in both Renu's and Akash's stories?

14. Akash is haunted by guilt for having punched Parth at the high school party he hosted with Bryce. Why does Akash make that decision? Were you surprised at how quickly Parth forgives him when they finally discuss it? In what other ways do Akash and Parth hurt each other as teenagers?

15. Why do you think Kareem doesn't show up at the café? How does the resolution of Kareem and Renu's story line compare to Parth and Akash's? How do both Renu and Akash experience closure and disappointment?

16. Near the end of the novel, Akash and Renu are finally able to be candid with each other. Akash says, "This, too, must be what love is. An unveiling. To stand before someone and show them who you are" (pp. 319–20). How does their relationship evolve over the course of the novel? What do they unveil to each other? How does the phrase "show them who you are" contrast with the book's title, *Tell Me How to Be*?

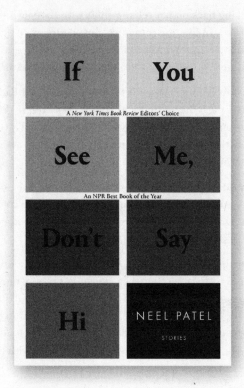